Scandalous Secrets

Scandalous Secrets:
A Royal Secret

REBECCA WINTERS

RAYE MORGAN

YVONNE LINDSAY

MILLS & BOON

First Published in Great Britain 2021
By Mills & Boon, an imprint of HarperCollins*Publishers*
1 London Bridge Street, London, SE1 9GF

SCANDALOUS SECRETS: A ROYAL SECRET
© 2021 Harlequin Books S.A.

Her Desert Prince © 2011 Rebecca Winters
Secret Prince, Instant Daddy! © 2010 Helen Conrad
Arranged Marriage, Bedroom Secrets © 2016 Dolce Vita Trust

ISBN: 978-0-263-29887-1

MIX
Paper from
responsible sources
FSC™ C007454

FSC
www.fsc.org

This book is produced from independently certified FSC™ paper to ensure responsible forest management.

For more information visit: www.harpercollins.co.uk/green

Printed and bound in Spain
by CPI, Barcelona

HER DESERT
PRINCE

REBECCA WINTERS

CHAPTER ONE

Montreux, Switzerland—The third of June

"I CAN'T MARRY YOU, Paul. Though I think you're a wonderful man, I'm not in love with you."

"Since your grandmother died, you're too sad to know your own feelings right now."

"But I do know them. A marriage between us wouldn't work."

"So you're really going on that trip?"

"Yes. I want to walk in her footsteps for a time. It's my tribute to her."

"You shouldn't go there alone, Lauren. At least let me come with you to protect you."

"Protect me? From what? No, Paul."

"How long will you be gone?"

"I don't know, but it doesn't matter. This has to be good-bye."

The Nafud Desert—The fifth of June

THEY WANDERED IN THE DESERT *in a solitary way. Thirsty, their souls fainted in them.*

The line from Psalms didn't leave Lauren Viret's mind as she drank from her water bag, surveying the indescribable vastness and loneliness of the northern Arabian desert.

Since they had left the major city of El-Joktor, bone-scorching heat had born down on their little group of twenty penetrating deeper into the desert's heart. Forty actually if you counted the camels. In a movie, the audience would consider them secondary characters. But out here where there were no movie cameras rolling, the humped female dromedary played the star role.

Lauren was less than a granule on this endless burning waste of sand where one could be swallowed alive in an instant. Before she'd set out this morning on her forty-mile journey, her guide, Mustafa, had lectured her that her camel was more valuable than any human.

She'd read enough firsthand accounts of desert survival to believe it. Besides transportation the camels provided shelter, protection, even water and food in dire circumstances.

While she was deep in thought, Mustafa urged his beast forward to ride alongside her. He talked with excitement as he pointed out the huge, awe-inspiring crescent-shaped dunes in this area of the Nafud Desert. It was true she'd never seen anything like them. No wonder her grandmother had never stopped talking about this place.

But Mustafa had no idea it was something flesh and blood, someone more awesome than these dunes that had captivated Lauren's American grandmother many years ago.

"Malik was bigger than life, Lauren," her grandmother had once told her, "the sheikh over all his people. His word was law. He was as beautiful as a god. I couldn't help myself loving him any more than I could stop breathing."

Lauren couldn't imagine a love like that.

She turned her head to glance at the camel drivers in their head scarves and cloaks, true men of the desert no doubt wondering what had possessed her to come out here alone. Lauren knew she looked out of place, a blonde American woman wearing the Arab male *guthra* and lightweight *kandura* herself, just the way her grandmother Celia Melrose Bancroft had once done.

Everyone at home had marveled over Lauren's resemblance to her grandmother. Odd how certain genetic traits skipped a generation. Lauren's mother had been a stunning brunette, as dark as Lauren was fair. Celia had given her daughter an Arabic name, Lana, meaning tender, which had added to the mystique of Lauren's beautiful mother. Both her mother and father had tragically died in a cable-car accident while skiing six months after Lauren was born, but thankfully Celia had hundreds of photographs which Lauren pored over to keep her father and mother alive in her heart.

"Jolie-laide," Paul had once murmured when he'd first seen a close up of Lana, but Lauren had heard him. In French that meant striking, in an interesting way without being beautiful. When she'd asked Paul what he'd meant by it he'd said, "I'm afraid you inherited all the *ravissante* genes, *petite*. No offense to your lovely mother."

Lauren had known that Paul had been flirting with her at the time. Of course, he didn't realize that Lauren's part-American, part-Arabic mother had the look of her father, the great Sheikh Malik Ghazi Shafeeq. Lauren had seen a copy of a picture of her grandfather from an old Arab newspaper her grandmother had once shown her. It was still with Celia's treasures.

The sheikh had been dressed in robes and head scarf, making it impossible to see much, except that he had a proud nose and wide mouth, which he'd bequeathed to his daughter. Lauren wondered if her grandfather might still be alive today? Probably not.

Now that Celia had passed away, no one else on earth knew of Lauren's relationship to her Arabic grandfather and they never would. But her curiosity where he was concerned had been one of the main reasons driving her to make this journey into the desert.

Tonight she'd camp out under the stars. Tomorrow the caravan would continue on to the Oasis Al-Shafeeq where she'd spend several weeks and hoped to find out more about the man himself.

On occasion Celia would say, "The one thing I see that reveals the Arab blood in you is your fierce passion for life. Only in that regard have I glimpsed signs of Malik. Mark my words…with the right man, that passion will be unleashed."

Paul, a newspaper journalist from Paris, could never have been that man. Lauren liked Paul, but in her heart she was waiting for the day she experienced the *grande passion* her grandmother had often talked about.

Though Lauren had turned down Paul's marriage

proposal, she feared that he hadn't given up hope of marrying her and would be waiting for her upon her return. It was this unflagging trait to his personality that had won him an interview with Celia in the first place.

For several years Paul had been wanting to do a series for his paper on the life of Richard Bancroft, Celia's deceased husband. Though Celia had been a young unwed mother at the time, Richard had married her and become a father figure to a young Lana. He had later become a favorite of Lauren's too, especially after her parents had been killed. Apparently it had never bothered Richard that Celia did not tell him the name of her lover, and Lana's father. It was simply enough that she'd loved Richard.

Richard had been a celebrated adventurer and anthropologist and had led fourteen different expeditions into some of the most inhospitable places on earth. Lauren and her grandmother had often gone along on some of his expeditions, amazed at the new sights they saw on their travels. But for some reason Richard had never traveled to the Arabian desert, and so neither Lauren nor her grandmother had ever ventured there either. Whether it was because her grandmother considered it too sacred a place to revisit with another man, or whether Richard's interests took him elsewhere, Lauren would never know.

With persistence, Paul had finally won the opportunity to interview Celia about her life with Richard and their many travels. From the beginning he'd made it his business to get to know Lauren, too, who had still lived with her grandmother in Montreux and was helping to compile Richard's many notes and diaries into a book for publication.

Celia had found Paul charming. Lauren had, too, but for her their relationship had been strictly platonic; her heart wasn't involved. Her grandmother had known that, but one day had confessed to Lauren that her greatest fear was to leave her beloved granddaughter alone without a companion to share her life.

"I won't always be alone," she had assured Celia. "Like you, I plan to travel and do something worthwhile with my life. In time someone will come along." Lauren hadn't wanted to cause her dying grandmother any unnecessary anxiety, but there'd always been honesty between them.

Once Celia was buried, Lauren had made preparations for this trip to the Oasis Al-Shafeeq. She had needed to see the place where her grandmother—romantic to the depths of her being—had experienced a soul-captivating love encountered beneath a full desert moon.

Lauren's hand instinctively went to her throat to touch the small hammered-gold medallion with its inscribed half moon on a gold chain hidden beneath her clothes. It had been her grandmother's greatest treasure, given to her by her lover during a romantic visit to the Garden of the Moon.

She'd mentioned another garden, too, the Garden of Enchantment.

The names had delighted Lauren and she knew she had to see them while she visited there. She considered the medallion a talisman she hoped would one day bring her the same kind of magic that had bonded her grandmother to her beloved sheikh, Malik, body and soul.

With her grandmother now gone, Lauren had wanted to rid herself of her intense sadness and had decided to come on this adventure. She intended to take the same trip her grandmother had taken years before, done in the exact same way.

Celia had been the only mother Lauren had ever known. Now that she was alone, Lauren's whole focus was on traveling to a spot that had resulted in a life-changing experience for Celia. To revisit the spot that had held such treasured memories for her grandmother.

Paul had begged to accompany Lauren on her trip. Earlier in the month he'd met some minor prince from the northern Arabian kingdom at one of the gaming tables at the casino in Montreux. Always looking for something newsworthy, Paul had taken the opportunity to get an interview and had snapped a few pictures of the prince and his retinue for the paper.

During their conversation, the prince, obviously flattered by Paul's attention and wanting the notoriety, had rhapsodized about the beauty of the Nafud, an area full of great photographic opportunities. He'd boasted that one day he would rule over the entire kingdom. Paul had confided to Lauren that even if it was only wishful thinking on the prince's part, it made a good story.

When he'd passed on this information to Lauren with so much eagerness, she'd hated turning him down, especially after he'd been so good to her grandmother toward the end of her life. But Lauren knew that Paul already had strong feelings for her and she'd refused to lead him on. He was an attractive man who deserved to fall in love with a woman who could love him back. Lauren wasn't that person.

Lost in thought now that she'd had hours to become accustomed to the jostling of her camel's strange gait, she hardly noticed the change in the topography to the southwest. It seemed there was a ridge of brownish mountains appearing as if out of nowhere. She frowned. Yesterday on her flight from Geneva, she'd studied a map of this area, but there'd been no indication of mountains alongside her proposed route to the oasis. She was positive of it.

Suddenly there was shouting. To her ears, the Arabic language always sounded a little like shouting, but these were guttural shouts of a different kind. They sent a thrill of alarm through her body.

"Mustafa?" she called to get his attention before realizing he must have moved further back to talk to the other men. She turned her head to find him. The caravan had stopped. "Mustafa?" she shouted so he'd hear her. "What's happening?"

His camel came up alongside hers. "A sandstorm! We must take cover at once! Pull on the reins so your camel will sit. Quickly!"

Sandstorm. The dreaded violent phenomenon of the desert. At full force more terrifying than a hurricane or a tornado. Only a few days ago she'd read about a caravan many years ago with two thousand people and eighteen hundred camels being overtaken by a storm. Enormous surges and clouds of red sand were raised and rolled forward, burying the whole tribe in its way. Only one Bedouin had survived to write about it.

The surge of wind he'd described in his account now snatched at her cloak without mercy, as if determined to remove it. A strange yellow color stained the blue sky, blotting it out as if it had never existed. It moved fast toward them like a pyroclastic flow from a volcano, but she heard no sound. Panic attacked her because she was finding it difficult to breathe.

Suddenly Mustafa pulled her off her camel with almost superhuman strength and pushed her against the camel's leeward side. "Hold on to the trappings, mademoiselle! Cover your entire head and burrow against the animal."

"But where will you be?" she cried out in fright.

"Next to you, mademoiselle. You mus— " But she wasn't destined to hear the rest. His words were muffled as he pulled the ends of his scarf around his face. One second he was there, the next second she saw... *nothing*.

There was an eerie din in her ears.

"Mustafa!" she screamed, but sand filled her nostrils and throat, gagging her. She covered up, feeling herself start to suffocate. She was drowning in sand. Her head spun like a top, gaining momentum.

We're all going to die, was her last thought before oblivion took over.

Prince Rashad Rayhan Shafeeq, acting sheikh of the northern Arabian kingdom of Al-Shafeeq whilst his father was ill, had only experienced two moments of real jubilation in his life. Both times had been in his early teens. The first was when he'd broken in the stallion his father had given him. The other time had been when his father and the pilot had survived the crash of a small plane and had been missing in the desert for three days.

This afternoon at the mining city of Raz, he was feeling a different kind of elation mixed with personal satisfaction. This moment had been a long time in coming, three years in fact. Gold had kept the royal family prosperous for centuries and would continue to do so for the next thousand years, but his gamble to do more drilling—a secret those involved had strenuously guarded—had paid off.

Rashad glanced at the heads of the various departments seated around the conference table. He'd called in the most trusted of those who worked for him.

"Gentlemen. Today I met with the chief geologist and engineer who've given me the news I've been waiting for. The recent finds of minerals are so vast, my vision of opening up whole new industries to benefit my father's kingdom has been realized. Besides thousands of new jobs over time, it will mean more education opportunities for the tribe. More hospitals and health care."

Cheers resonated off the walls of the conference room.

This land had belonged to his family for centuries. They had rights to all the minerals and metals being taken from the ground. Various tribes throughout the years had coveted this area rich in resources beyond anyone's dreams and had come against the people of

Al-Shafeeq, spilling too much blood, but they'd never prevailed. Thankfully, in these modern times, there wasn't that same kind of strife. Any problems today came from within the circle of Prince Shafeeq's own extended family, but he didn't have time to think about that now.

"Tonight when I return to the palace, I'll inform the king, who will be overjoyed." These days his father suffered from diabetes and had to be more careful in everything he did and ate. "I have no doubts he'll declare a day of celebration. Your hard work has not gone unappreciated and each of you will receive a large bonus for your excellent work *and* your loyalty to the royal family."

With spirits so high, he barely heard someone calling to him. He turned his head. "Your Highness," the gold-plant manager beckoned to him from the doorway amidst the escalating noise. Rashad saw the concerned look on his face and excused himself to go out in the hall.

"Forgive me for disturbing you, but there was a sand-storm between El-Joktor and Al-Shafeeq, catching a caravan en route unawares."

The bad news tarnished an otherwise red-letter day. "You have eye witnesses?"

"A passing horseman saw what was left of it from a distance and rode here for help. He noticed some camels wandering, but had no idea how many tribesmen survived or are dead and buried beneath the sand."

His gut clenched. "How far away?"

"Twelve miles."

"Assemble a search-and-rescue party to head out on horseback with supplies immediately. Have water loaded on to my helicopter and I'll fly over the site to assess the damage and look for survivors. If needs be, I'll airlift the worst casualties to Al-Shafeeq."

"Yes, Your Highness."

Rashad rejoined the men in the conference room and told them what had happened. The news galvanized everyone into action. They ran out the door behind Rashad to help in the rescue effort.

"Tariq? Come with me!" At a time like this, they would need all the help they could get and Tariq was a trusted colleague at the plant. His help would be invaluable.

At the waiting helicopter where water and other emergency supplies were being loaded, Rashad climbed into the pilot's seat and did a pre-flight check. One of his bodyguards sat in back, followed by Tariq, who finished loading supplies then strapped himself in the co-pilot's seat.

It was always dangerous to approach strangers in the desert, but with the knowledge that his own tribesmen might be involved, Rashad couldn't look the other way. Within seconds he had the rotors whining and they lifted off.

He wished he could fly this machine as fast as his tribe's famous streamlined falcons flew. When they went into a stoop for their prey, Rashad had clocked them doing 200 mph. Getting to the scene of the tragedy quickly was crucial if it meant lives could be saved.

This part of the desert was known for violent winds

that rose up suddenly without warning. Sandstorms weren't so common in the area, but when they did come, they could be devastating.

Before long he spotted cloaked figures and camels clustered together. Tariq handed him the binoculars for a better look. All were waving. The situation might not be as bad as first reported. He gave back the glasses and set the helicopter down a short distance off, willing to take the risk to his own safety.

"Careful, Your Highness," Tariq cautioned. "It could be bandits luring us into the open. Someone may have planned an ambush and is waiting for us to walk into it."

Rashad supposed it was possible, but then a group of men from the caravan came running toward them and Rashad recognized Mustafa Tahar before they bowed down to praise the prince for their deliverance.

"It's all right," Rashad advised his companions. Even as the blades were still rotating, whipping up sand, Tariq began lowering supplies. Rashad shut off the engine and jumped down to help carry water, that vital necessity meaning life or death under these circumstances.

Mustafa, a reputable caravan cameleer from the oasis whom Rashad had known for years, motioned him over to a spot where he saw a body laid out on the sand and covered by blankets.

"This one is still alive, but without a doctor to rehydrate her, she will not live. I tried to give her the little water I had left, but it ran out of her mouth."

"*She?*"

"Yes, Your Highness."

Rashad hunkered down and lifted the blanket off her body, surprised to see a woman lying on her side wearing a man's *kandura*. His fingers felt for a pulse at her slim wrist. It was slow, but it was there. She wore no jewelry on her delicate hands, only a gold watch around her wrist. Rashad noticed that she was already feverish.

His gaze traveled over her, stunned by the sight of hair as diaphanous as gossamer despite the sand particles. Her beauty was a revelation. It caused him to pause for a second before he reached down and picked her up; her slight weight filled his arms, sending an odd sensation through him.

Though his people believed in omens, he was more skeptical and refused to credit what he was feeling as anything more than a response to an attractive female. He hadn't been with one in several weeks. Affairs of state for his father had kept him too busy.

This woman's pallor didn't diminish her fresh-faced, porcelain complexion. A slight fruity fragrance escaped the silkiest hair ever to touch his cheek. Wisps of it, not confined, framed classic features. Her feminine scent tantalized his nostrils and further weakened him in ways his mind refused to acknowledge.

Mustafa followed him to the helicopter where Tariq assisted in strapping her into the seat behind them.

"She was traveling to Al-Shafeeq."

"Alone?" Rashad couldn't imagine why.

"Yes." Mustafa scratched the side of his cheek. "I thought it strange, too. Here is her passport."

Rashad grimaced before putting it inside his pocket.

"Is there anyone else who needs immediate treatment?"

"No, Your Highness."

"Good, then I'll fly her to the palace for medical care. Help is coming from Raz with provisions for you. They'll be here soon."

Mustafa nodded his thanks and once more Rashad started up the helicopter, this time heading for Al-Shafeeq. He reached for his satellite phone to call Nazir. His personal assistant at the palace would make certain the doctor for the royal family would be standing by ready to take over.

After a short flight, Rashad put down at the side of the palace. He let Tariq and the bodyguard lower the woman out of the helicopter. The less he had to do with this incredibly appealing female, the better. A team of medical people rushed forward and took her seemingly lifeless form inside.

Assured she'd get the best treatment possible, he told the men to climb back in the helicopter and he'd fly them back to Raz. Rashad still had business to finish up.

During the flight Tariq remained uncharacteristically quiet. Rashad cast him a side glance. "What's on your mind, Tariq? I haven't heard a word out of you."

"It's not natural for a woman to be out here alone. Especially one so young."

"I agree, but this one is foreign, which explains a lot."

"She is very, very beautiful. Some man will suffer if he learns the sand has claimed her. Let's hope the doctor can save her."

Rashad didn't respond because Tariq's words had sent an invisible wind racing over his skin, lifting the hairs on his bronzed arms and nape. That was the second time within an hour he'd felt a quickening. He didn't like it. He didn't like it at all.

Anxious to get back to work on his new plans, Rashad set them down outside the main plant, only to hear his phone ring as Tariq exited the chopper. Rashad checked the caller ID; it was the doctor back at the palace.

His body tautened. The man was probably phoning to tell Rashad he'd lost his patient. And what if he had? What could that possibly mean to Rashad, except that he would feel sorrow for anyone who'd died in those circumstances? He finally answered the call. "Dr. Tamam?"

"I'm glad you answered right away."

"Did I get the American woman to you too late?"

"No. She's slowly reviving with the IV."

Rashad released his breath, unaware he'd been holding it until he'd heard the news. "She was very fortunate. Is she coherent yet?"

"No, but that's good."

Rashad nodded to himself. "She's going to be in shock while she recovers from her ordeal." He waited for a response, but when it came, the doctor's words surprised Rashad.

"This woman needs complete privacy, away from everyone. Do you have a suggestion, Your Highness?"

This was no normal request from the doctor, and Rashad was immediately alerted. Without having to think about it he said, "The garden suite."

It was on the second floor of the palace with a roof-top view. A private passageway led to it from the main upstairs hallway. Because of its isolation from the rest of the palace, other members of the family had used it as their bridal suite at the beginning of their honeymoons.

No one would be occupying it again until his own wedding night, scheduled in six months. Lines darkened Rashad's face at the thought.

"Good. The nurse and I will transfer her there immediately."

Nothing else was forthcoming, which wasn't like the usually loquacious doctor. An unsettling feeling swept through Rashad. "I'll be with you shortly, Doctor."

"I will be waiting for you." Dr. Tamam clicked off.

The doctor who'd faithfully looked after his family for years had just ended the call before Rashad could ask any more questions. That alone told him the older man was keeping some information that would be for Rashad's ears alone.

Like everyone else on the staff, the doctor kept his ear to the ground for anything that appeared suspicious. One could never be too careful where the safety of Rashad's family was concerned.

Rashad entered the plant office, intending to work on some details needing attention, but he found he couldn't concentrate. With a grunt of dissatisfaction, he decided to fly back to Al-Shafeeq to find out what was going on. After a quick shower and a meal in his own suite, he left for the other wing of the palace in one of his silk lounging robes.

There was a cultivated garden of exotic flowers by the patio of the garden suite. His mother, along with the gardeners, often tended it because she had a special love for them. Rashad had decided on this suite for their patient partly since the American was a rather exotic species herself. He thought of Tariq's comment—*very, very beautiful* didn't begin to cover Rashad's description of the woman.

He opened the doors and nodded to the nurse who told him the doctor was still in with the American. Rashad walked on through the large sitting room to the bedroom. From a distance he saw the patient in bed with an IV drip hanging from the stand placed at the side. He drew closer. The doctor stood at the other side, checking her pulse. When he saw Rashad, he lowered the woman's arm and moved toward him.

"How is she?" Rashad asked in a quiet voice.

"Coming along. I put something in her IV to help her sleep. Tomorrow she should be in better shape to cope with what happened. I'm leaving the nurse to watch over her during the night and give her oxygen if she needs it. I wanted you here because I'd like you to take a look at what I found hanging from the chain around her neck."

Rashad's brows formed a black bar before he moved past the doctor to see what he was talking about. Closer now, he could tell the IV was doing its job. There was more color in the woman's cheeks. Her hair had been washed, and the wavy strands had a sheen like that on the sheerest wings of the butterflies hovering over the flowers in the garden. Her dark lashes and brows provided a contrast that made her even more stunningly beautiful.

The nurse had dressed her in a white cotton shift. A sheet had been pulled up to her shoulders, but he glimpsed a gold chain around her neck. He flashed the doctor a glance. "What am I supposed to be seeing?"

"*This*. I took the liberty of removing it at the clinic before I did anything else."

As he glanced at the shiny object held in the doctor's palm, Rashad drew in a ragged breath. It was a round gold medallion with a half moon inscribed—the symbol of the Shafeeq royal family.

Only when a new male member was born was another one minted. Rashad had been given his when he'd come of age at sixteen. They were all worn around the neck on a chain, but Rashad had broken with tradition and had asked for his to be fashioned into a ring he could use as his personal seal for important documents. He kept it in the desk of his office here at the palace.

For this woman from another continent to be in possession of one, let alone wearing it, simply wasn't possible! Yet the truth lay in front of him, mere inches away.

How had she come by it?

Without hesitation he pocketed the medallion before returning to the woman. With great care he found the little catch to remove the chain, aware of the softness of her creamy skin against his bronzed knuckles; such skin the women of his tribe didn't possess.

Their patient made a little sound, then moved her head to the other side, as if she'd felt the slight caress of his flesh against hers. He held his breath, half hoping she'd wake up so he could look into her eyes and see through to her soul to where she kept her secrets.

The other half of him hoped she'd stay asleep, thus prolonging the moment when she had to be told she'd almost died. There was a penalty for experiencing the terrible beauty of the desert. Sometimes the price was too great, but this foreign woman had been willing to take the risk. Why?

He stared at the medallion, fingering its smoothness until his jaw hardened. An ill wind boded no good. His mother had said it many times. Nothing about the woman or the medallion added up.

Confounded by the situation, he pocketed the chain with the medallion, then turned to the doctor whose shrewd gaze told its own story. There were few secrets between the two of them. "You were right to tell me about this, but say nothing to anyone else."

"My lips are closed tighter than the eye of the needle, Your Highness. My nurse wasn't allowed to undress and bathe the patient until I'd safely removed the medallion."

In the past the doctor had saved Rashad's life on more than one occasion, and Rashad trusted him completely. "I owe you a great deal. Thank you for taking care of her."

The doctor nodded. "I'm going home. Call if you need me. I'll look in on her later."

As soon as he left, Rashad went through the suitcases left by the maids. He did a thorough search of both, looking for a clue that would help explain this mystery, but he turned up nothing.

To his surprise the woman had packed with no frills. Unlike most females, her underwear and nightgowns were modest. Two dresses for evening, one a simple black, the other cream. A pair of high heels, some sandals and a sweater. The rest, practical clothing for the desert. A small kit with few cosmetics or makeup. She packed like a person used to traveling light.

Rashad knew better than to prolong his stay at the woman's bedside. His thoughts would wander down different paths, distracting him from his mission to unmask her. Like the fragrant white moonflower, she held her secret within her petals, only revealing it in full moonlight when no one was watching.

For the good of the family he'd sworn a holy oath to protect, he would wait until daylight to learn how she'd come by the medallion.

Once he'd said goodnight to the nurse, he strode down a long hallway to his own second-floor suite on the other side of the palace and dismissed his staff. He needed to be alone. After pouring himself a cup of hot black coffee, he wandered through to his bedroom. Reaching for the woman's passport, he sat down in a chair to study it.

Lauren Viret. Twenty-six. Few people looked good in a passport photo, but she was one woman who couldn't take a bad picture. Even lying there unconscious, her beauty had reached out to him, stirring him on some deeper level.

Address: Montreux, Switzerland.

Montreux. The town where the Shafeeq family did their banking. When he had stayed there in order to do business, he had sometimes skied at Porte du Soleil, only a half hour from the Swiss town with its exuberant night life. Rashad had no use for casinos or partying. On the other hand, his forty-year-old cousin Faisal, the ambitious son of his father's younger brother Sabeer, frequented the place on a regular basis, mostly for pleasure.

Rashad liked the snow, but he much preferred flying to Montreux in summer. The sight of Lake Geneva from the bedroom balcony of the family apartment mesmerized him. So much blue water to be seen, with steamers and sailboats, when he'd been born in a land with so little of the precious element above ground. Below the Arabian desert there was a vast amount of water, more than the uninformed person knew.

For years he'd been working to find a way to channel more of it to the surface to water flocks and irrigate crops. A fertile land for the growing population of his people. *That* was his next project in the years to come, but for the moment he was keeping his plans a secret from his uncle's family living nearby. There'd been enough jealousy from that sector to last a lifetime.

Rashad took a deep breath before studying the street address listed in the passport. It was in the wealthiest area of the town bordering the lake. Who was paying for Lauren Viret to live among the pieds-a-terre of royals in Montreux?

Where and how had she come by the medallion? There were only eight in existence.

Reaching the limit of his patience, Rashad closed the passport and tossed it on the nearest table, a beauty inlaid with mother of pearl. It was late. He had no answers to this riddle and needed sleep. Tomorrow he'd get to the bottom of it by drawing close to her. It was a task he found himself looking forward to with uncommon anticipation.

CHAPTER TWO

"MADEMOISELLE? ARE YOU AWAKE?"

The same gentle female voice Lauren thought she'd heard during the night broke through soporific waves to reach her consciousness. She felt something being removed from her nostrils.

"Can you hear me, mademoiselle?"

Lauren tried to communicate, but it was difficult because her mouth and throat felt too dry to talk. As she tried to sit up, her head reeled and she realized the back of her hand had something in it. What on earth?

"Lie back and drink," the woman urged. She spoke English, but with an accent. Lauren felt a straw being inserted between her lips and she began sucking on it. Cool water trickled down her throat.

"Heaven," she murmured and continued to drink. Suddenly every nerve ending in her body seemed to come alive, like a drooping plant whose roots took in the moisture that worked its way to the leaves.

Her eyelids fluttered open, but she had trouble focusing because she could see three women with the same dark hair and lab coat standing over her. "Are you a doctor?" she questioned.

"No. I'm Dr. Tamam's nurse. How do you feel?"

Lauren started to shake her head, but that only made her feel worse. "I—I don't know," she stammered.

While the nurse removed the IV from her hand, Lauren tried to get her bearings. The hospital room wasn't like any she'd ever seen before. It was huge with sumptuous green and aqua accoutrements, bringing the apartment of a harem to mind. As her head continued to whirl, she realized she could be dreaming all this and wished she could wake up.

A remembered feeling of suffocation took over. Panic gripped her. "Help me—I can't breathe—" she cried, unable to stem the tears gushing down her cheeks.

She heard voices in the background. Then just one. A male voice. Deep and resonant. She felt it snake right into her body and travel through her nervous system. A man's hand gripped hers. Solid, masterful.

"Don't be afraid. You're safe now." His accented English spoken in a commanding tone was so reassuring, her anxiety lessened and she slept.

When next she came awake, she discovered the same hand holding hers. This time when she opened her eyes, she saw only one figure seated at her bedside. A powerfully built male, probably mid-thirties. The nurse had disappeared.

A white shirt covered his broad shoulders and well-defined chest. A dusting of black hair showed above the opening. The color of the fabric brought out his beautiful olive skin tone. He had the blackest eyes and hair she'd ever seen at such close range. She noticed he wore it longer than some men, slicked it back from his forehead as though he'd been in a hurry.

His widow's peak suited his aquiline features. There was a magnificence about him. She'd never met a truly gorgeous man before, and he was much more than that. Her heart thundered in her chest as though she'd suddenly been given a drug to bring her to life.

Though he studied her as she imagined an eagle would do before swooping to catch its prey unaware, she glimpsed banked fires in the recesses of those eyes. He was dark and dangerous. Her body gave off a shiver of excitement she couldn't repress. Something was wrong with her to be this aware of a total stranger.

"What am I doing here?"

His eyelids lowered, exposing long black lashes that shielded part of his penetrating gaze from her. "You don't remember what happened to you?" He asked the question in a low, silky tone, almost as if he didn't trust what she'd just asked him.

Growing more nervous under his unrelenting scrutiny, she unconsciously moved her hand to her throat. Suddenly it occurred to her she couldn't feel her grandmother's medallion.

In a frantic gesture, she raised up and moved the pillow to see if it had fallen on to the mattress, but it wasn't there. Neither was the chain.

"Did the nurse remove it?" she cried. By now she was sitting straight up, staring at the man beside her bed.

"Remove what?" he asked in such a calm tone, it got under her skin.

She fought not to let her panic show. Now that the

sheet had fallen to her waist, the man's eyes were appraising her. The white shift she wore her was modest enough, but still those black orbs burned like hot coals as he looked at her. But maybe she was being too paranoid because she'd awakened feeling as though she was in a strange dream.

"My medallion is missing. I *have* to find it."

He clasped his bronzed hands beneath a chin so solid, a lesser-blessed male would sell his soul to have been created like this god in earthly form.

A god. That's what her grandmother had called her lover. Lauren had smiled at Celia's description, allowing her that flight of fantasy. But she wasn't laughing now. Maybe Lauren *had* lost her mind. Fear crept over her once more. She closed her eyes and lay back.

"Perhaps if you gave me a description, mademoiselle."

She bit her lip, discovering it was cracked and dry. Just how long had she been in this condition? Her eyes opened again. "It's a gold circle about the size and thickness of an American quarter. Maybe a little thicker."

She didn't dare give the full details. Her relationship to her grandfather was a secret and had to remain one, even down to a piece of jewelry he'd given her grandmother. "Have you ever seen a quarter?" He nodded slowly. "I kept it on a gold chain. It has little monetary value, but it's my most prized possession." More hot tears trickled out of the corners of her eyes.

"Then I'll ask my staff to look for it."

"Thank you." She dashed the moisture from her cheeks with her free hand. "How sick am I?"

His dark gaze flickered. "You've been taken off oxygen and your IV drip. That means you'll be fed juice, in fact, anything you crave, and then you'll be able to get up with help and walk around. By tomorrow you should feel much more recovered."

"But what happened to me?"

He continued to look at her with the strangest expression. She had the impression he was trying to make up his mind what to tell her. The pit in her stomach enlarged, but her natural grit came to the fore. She took a deep breath. "Whatever it is, I can handle it."

"Can you?" He'd asked the question almost seductively. Was he playing with her?

"I'm not a child."

"No. That you are not." A certain nuance in his deep voice sent a little shiver through her.

Don't let him get to you, Lauren. He was a doctor after all and had examined her. Those black eyes had seen everything, so there was nothing he didn't know. "If you won't tell me because you think I'm the fainting kind, I'll ask your nurse. I'm sure she'll oblige me."

"She's gone back to the clinic." The note of satisfaction in his voice set her off.

"I will admit you're doing a good job of frightening me."

He shrugged his shoulders with unconscious elegance. She watched his hands open, as if he were holding a bowl. She noticed inconsequently that those hands were used to hard work, yet his nails and cuticles were immaculate. "A thousand pardons, mademoiselle. My intent has been to save you from remembering too much at once."

She sucked in her breath. "You mean I have amnesia?" More silence. "But that's preposterous!"

The doctor cocked his head. "I'd prefer to call it a temporary lapse of memory. At the moment your mind is protecting you from having to deal with a traumatic experience."

"Traumatic?"

"Very," his voice grated. It seemed to underline the gravity of what he hadn't yet told her. While she contemplated his unsettling response, he got up and reached for a white cloak placed over a satin loveseat. She hadn't realized how tall he was—at least six foot three.

He moved with unconscious male grace. When he approached her again, he let the cape fall loose. "Do you recognize this?"

She tore her eyes from his striking features to look at what he was holding up to her. It was a *kandura*. Lauren had one like it. She'd purchased her desert gear after she'd arrived in El-Joktor, telling the merchant she wanted a man's cloak for herself.

He hadn't wanted to sell it to her because he said it wasn't done in his country. But she had offered him more money than it was worth and he had finally conceded to her wishes and wrapped it up for her.

"Mustafa—"

The camel driver's name came out on a sudden cry of remembrance.

The doctor's eyes flickered. "You see? Your memory is returning. Too fast unfortunately."

A kaleidoscope was filtering through her mind. Bits and pieces started falling together faster than she could keep up. "The mountains were alive. They engulfed everything—Mustafa told me it was a sandstorm. I couldn't see him—I couldn't breathe—what happened to him?"

The doctor's silence puzzled her. She pushed the sheet aside and got out of the bed. Without conscious thought she grabbed his bronzed forearms. "Tell me—did he die because of me?"

His midnight eyes seemed to bore right down into her soul. "No, mademoiselle. Death didn't come for him because it wasn't his appointed hour. In fact, he was the one who saved your life," he said in a gravelly voice. "Without his quick thinking, you would have been buried alive."

She shuddered. "What about the others in the caravan?"

"They survived."

When the words sank in, she let out a relieved cry and slumped against him. "Thank heaven no one perished. It was utterly terrifying."

He murmured something she didn't understand and pulled her into him, absorbing her sobs while he rocked her for as long as she needed. She had no idea how much time passed as they stood locked in each other's arms.

Moments went by before she became aware of his heart pounding, strong and solid against hers. When she'd cried her tears, she eased out of his arms, cognizant of not wanting to leave them. She had to be insane.

"Forgive me for breaking down like that."

"It's the shock of your ordeal, mademoiselle."

"Yes." Reeling from too many emotions, she sank down on the edge of the bed, burying her face in her hands. "If you don't mind, I'd like to be alone."

"As you wish. I'll have a tray sent to you. You need to eat."

"I don't think I could yet."

"It's the duty of the living."

Lauren's head reared back, making her dizzy. But he'd already reached the doors and then he was gone. Not a minute later, a maid came in to help her to the ornate bathroom. After a shower, she dressed in denims and a pale-blue cotton top she'd brought on the trip. The sandstorm hadn't ripped the suitcases from the camels, but it had almost taken her life.

What was it Richard had once told her? *A man who sets out on an expedition has to know he might never come back.* He'd lost men on many of his expeditions, but he'd kept on going. If Richard were still alive he'd say, *You knew the risk, Lauren, and took it.*

In his own way, the doctor had been telling her the same thing.

Lauren could never be that glib about fate, but when the maid returned with a meal of lamb kabobs and fruit salad, she didn't refuse it.

Sometime later the doctor entered the room without her being aware of it. He walked over to the table where she was finishing her food. "Feeling better now, mademoiselle?"

His presence startled her. And thrilled her, too, which

was ridiculous. She wiped her mouth with the napkin and looked up at him. He was dressed in a linen sport shirt and trousers. Whatever he wore, he took her breath. Without clothes...he would be spectacular.

"I feel stronger, thank you."

"Stronger is better, but you have a way to go before you're pronounced fit. Your body has been through a tremendous ordeal, physically and emotionally. You must stay here and give yourself time to heal."

He'd brought a tray of food in with him and sat down opposite her. She bit her lip. "Tell me something. Where is *here* exactly?"

"I assumed you knew," he murmured after biting into a fresh peach. "The Oasis of Al-Shafeeq. That was your first destination after you left El-Joktor, was it not?"

Her *only* destination.

"Yes," she whispered, shaken by the knowledge that she'd reached the place once ruled by her grandmother's lover. "How did you know I'd come from El-Joktor?"

He eyed her through veiled lashes. "It's my business to know everything that goes on here. In truth, I'm not Dr. Tamam, but I let you think it for a little while until I was certain you were on the road to a full recovery."

What? But he'd held her hand the whole time. "Then who are you?"

His lips twisted, as if amused by the question. When he did that, he was so attractive, she felt that her heart would fail her. "I'm the head of security here at the palace."

Her eyes widened in disbelief. "No wonder this room

is so exquisite," she whispered. "I couldn't imagine a hotel that could ever look like this."

"The palace is centuries old," he explained. "When I was notified of a caravan overrun by a sandstorm, I flew a helicopter to the scene. Mustafa filled me in and I brought you back here where Dr. Tamam could take care of you."

Head of security for the King?

He not only looked the part, he was the embodiment of her idea of what a king should look like. Bigger than life, the way her grandmother had described King Malik.

She swallowed hard. "So it's you I have to thank for getting me medical help so fast. I—I'm indebted to you," she stammered. It was hard to believe she was actually inside the palace instead of looking at it from the outside like any tourist.

He flashed her a white smile that trapped the air in her lungs. "Grateful enough to let me call you Lauren?"

The way he said her name in his deep voice with that beautiful accent made it sound exotic.

"Of course."

"I saw it printed in your passport, which I have in my possession." His piercing dark eyes traveled over her, missing nothing. "Lauren is a beautiful name, almost as beautiful as its bearer."

Heat spread through her body like wildfire. "What do I call you?" she asked rather breathlessly.

Something flickered in the dark recesses of his eyes as he ate his food. "Rafi. It's easier than the rest of my name which is too long and difficult for a foreigner to pronounce."

Her lips curved into a smile. "I like the shortened version. It reminds me of the spaniel I once had."

"Why is that?"

"Her name was Taffy," she rattled on before realizing he probably thought she was flirting with him. *You* are *flirting with him, Lauren.* Her escape from death had turned her into someone she didn't recognize. She tried to gather her wits, but this was all still like a dream. "Did you ever have a pet growing up?"

"Several, but they may not be the kind you imagine."

"That sounds intriguing."

His eyes glimmered in the candlelight before he asked her another question. "Where were you intending to stay after you arrived here?"

She let out a small cry. "That's right—my reservations—I don't know the name. The documents from the travel agency in Montreux are in my small suitcase. I'm afraid I'm not thinking too clearly yet."

"That's because you've been in a sandstorm and have come out of it with your life irrevocably changed."

Irrevocably. Because of this man, that was the precise word.

"I'll be happy to explain the circumstances to the concierge if you'll give me the information. The staff placed your suitcases in your bedroom. Would you like me to get it for you?"

"No, thank you. I'll do it." She stood up, but she still felt fragile. "Just a moment, please."

Lauren felt his eyes on her back as she walked through to the bedroom and knelt down to open her small case. She found the envelope that held all her travel plans on top and shut the lid, then went back to the other room.

With a wordless exchange he took it from her. Their fingers brushed, sending warmth through her nervous system before he opened the flap to peer inside. When hc found what he was looking for, he pulled out his phone and made a call. Except for a few words, she understood no Arabic. The conversation went on for several minutes before he hung up.

He eyed her with an enigmatic gaze. "Is there anyone else you need to inform about what's happened? Anyone to let know where you are?"

"No." With her grandmother gone, she was quite alone.

"Don't tell me there's no man in your life missing you, because I wouldn't believe you."

"There's no one important in my life. Only Paul, a friend, who is probably out on a new, exciting assignment for his French newspaper at the moment."

"Won't Paul want to know you are safe from harm?" His voice had fierce undertones. He talked with so much authority, she found herself opening up to him.

"Actually, I would prefer it if Paul didn't know about what happened to me. You see, he proposed to me before I came here and I turned him down. I'm not in love with him and it would seem wrong of me to ask him to come to my aid now. I think it's best if he moves on with his life and finds a woman who will love him in return."

Rafi stared at her over the rim of his coffee cup.

"After meeting you, I daresay I doubt he'll ever get over you."

"That's very flattering, but of course he will."

"I wasn't flattering you." His remark set her body trembling. "What about other friends?"

"They don't expect to hear from me this trip."

"Why not?"

"Because I came to try and get over the worst of my pain after losing my grandmother recently. They know that," she muttered, trying to keep the tremor out of her voice, but not succeeding very well.

"You were close to her?"

There was something about this man that made her want to confide in him. Maybe it was because he'd saved her life by getting her to the doctor in time. Whatever the reason, she didn't feel like holding back.

"Very. Both my parents died when I was six months old. She was the only mother I ever knew. I miss her horribly."

"I can understand your wanting to get away for a while, but why the desert, why here? This part of the Nafud is particularly harsh."

"I suppose it's because it's one place I've never visited, and it holds no past memories for me." *Only Celia's.*

"You're a world traveler?"

"Yes, from the time I was a little girl."

A definite stillness filled the room before he said, "Under the circumstances, I'll leave you alone to grieve. Silence is the medication for sorrow. If you need anything, you have only to pick up the phone by your bed.

Nazir, one of my assistants, will take care of you and send for me or the doctor should you need us."

"Thank you." She lowered her head. "I'd be very remiss if I didn't tell you how grateful I am to you for saving my life."

"I only sped up the time so your recovery could take place under Dr. Tamam's care."

"I'm *still* thankful," she insisted. "Be assured, you and your staff will be well paid for your services."

Without giving her a response, he started to leave. Being the head of security, she supposed he had too many calls on his time for her to expect his company like this again but she selfishly wished he didn't have to leave yet. "Rafi?"

He turned his dark head in her direction. "Is there something else you need?"

There were a lot of things she discovered she needed. "No, but you're obviously on intimate terms with the king. Please let him know how grateful I am for everything. The room is beautiful beyond description."

"It's part of the garden suite."

Lauren sucked in her breath. King Malik had arranged for her grandmother to stay in a private part of the palace with its own garden. Was it possible this suite was the one? The hairs lifted on the back of her neck.

He studied her for a moment. "Are you all right, Lauren?"

"Yes."

"You need a lot more rest before I'm convinced of that. When you're up to it, you're welcome to walk out and enjoy the flowers through that portico. Some are quite exotic. On occasion, the queen herself tends the garden."

She put a hand to her throat. "I don't know why I'm so lucky."

After a slight pause he said, "When word of your near-tragedy reached King Umar, he insisted you remain in this suite as his guest for as long as you want."

His guest…

Lauren's heart beat faster than a hummingbird's wings. Was King Umar a son or a grandson or even a great-nephew of King Malik? Lauren was closer to getting information about her grandfather than she knew.

"That's incredibly kind and generous of him."

His black eyes gleamed. "It's my hope that while you are recovering, the garden's beauty will lift the sadness over your grandmother's passing from your heart."

Deeply touched by his words, she whispered her thanks. Bereft after he'd gone, Lauren couldn't move any further than the nearest couch because a new weakness had attacked her, brought on by his nearness and the potent male reality of him.

She sank down and rested against one of the satin cushions. Her thoughts darted back to her grandmother who'd been a world traveler from an early age. Celia had come to Al-Shafeeq because it had been reported by a family friend highly placed in the government that this desert oasis blossomed like a rose. It had sounded so romantic to her, she'd deemed it a place she had to see.

While wandering through its palatial gardens, her waist-length blond hair had happened to catch the eye of King Malik. What had happened after that had been like a tale from the Arabian Nights tale and Celia had become enslaved by a love so powerful that Lauren's mother, Lana, had been the ultimate result.

Lauren thought about the flowers on the patio, but she was too tired to walk out there yet. Inwardly she had the presentiment that if she went out to look at them, history might repeat itself. Lauren could well imagine being so enamored of Rafi, she would never want to leave Al-Shafeeq.

His powerful image swam before her eyes until they closed and she knew no more.

Rashad stood outside the suite and rang Dr. Tamam to give him the latest update. "Our patient was well enough to shower and eat a solid meal today."

"That's good. What did you find out about the medallion?"

He pursed his lips. "Nothing yet."

"Ah?" The surprise in the older man's voice was as unmistakable as it was understandable. "Then you must have felt she still wasn't recovered enough to withstand an interrogation."

The doctor was reading Rashad's mind. Lauren had paled a little before he'd left her suite. That part was genuine. In fact everything she'd said, every reaction, had seemed genuine to him, especially her relief that Mustafa hadn't died.

He could still feel the imprint of her lovely body molded to his while word of the near-tragedy had sunk in. She'd shed convincing tears of relief.

As for her pain over her deceased grandmother, there were degrees. Upon wakening, her first thought had been for the medallion she'd lost. Rashad had noticed she'd been careful *not* to give him a full description of the gold circle.

His instincts were never wrong. She was holding a secret.

The first thing Rashad needed to do was to ascertain if the medallion was real or a fake. Quite apart from her role in all of this, he wanted the answer for himself. Of the eight male members of the family alive today, including himself, none had reported their medallions lost or stolen. It had to be a fake—some kind of joke, perhaps—but he wouldn't be able to get to the bottom of it until he'd talked to their gold expert.

In the next breath he phoned his mechanic. After being assured his helicopter had been serviced and was ready for flight, he slipped along a passage and across a private courtyard to the place where it was waiting.

Accompanied by his bodyguard, he flew to Raz. Once they'd set down, he hurried into the plant to consult the goldsmith who'd fashioned Rashad's ring. The old man was getting on in years.

"Come in, Rashad. Your face looks like thunder. Yesterday everyone was rejoicing!"

Grimacing, he sat down at the work table across from him. "That was yesterday." He pulled the medallion and chain out of his pocket and placed it in front of him.

Hasan stared at him in puzzlement. "Whose medallion is this?"

"That's what I need to know."

"You mean someone in the royal family has lost theirs?"

"Maybe. I found it…accidentally. Could it be a fake?"

"Why don't you go do something else for a little while, then come back and I'll have answers for you."

Rashad spent the next hour discussing plans with the engineers drafting designs for the new processing plant. Being an engineer himself, he gave his input before returning to Hasan's lab. The goldsmith gave him a speculative look.

"The medallion is twenty-four-carat gold, but the minting technique with respect to the dyes and style indicates it was made somewhere between 1890 and 1930, give or take fifteen years. I couldn't duplicate what was produced back then." He shook his head. "I have to believe this is not a fake, nor is the chain."

"So," Rashad murmured, "unless someone lost their medallion during that time period, the only other explanation I can come up with is that the family goldsmith at the time could have made an extra one in case of loss."

"But that practice has always been forbidden," Hasan reminded him.

"That's true." Hasan's word was as good as the gold he'd been working with for the last forty years. Rashad's mind shot back in time, making a mental list of every royal male child born within that time period who was now dead. No word of a lost medallion had ever reached his ears.

Rashad knew that no member of the family could

ever willingly part with his medallion, and they took them to their graves. Rashad's thoughts ran full circle and led him to the conclusion that the medallion must have been stolen off a dead body at the time of burial. Only family members could be in attendance at this sacred time, so that meant a member of the family had been holding on to it all this time....

For what purpose? And why had it suddenly surfaced around the throat of the stunning blonde American? Had she come specifically to attract Rashad's attention and infiltrate his inner sanctum? Certainly she'd done that!

Such an elaborate scheme for her to glean information could only have been perpetrated by his uncle's family, desperate to discover any information they could, which they could then use against Rashad's own family. Amazingly it had backfired because of catastrophic circumstances beyond anyone's control.

She'd been blown off course all right. Yet in a miraculous way she'd succeeded in penetrating his fortress in a way no enemy had ever done. Someone had coached her well, otherwise why had she held back in her description of the medallion?

Not only hadn't he learned her secret yet, it was possible she'd been equipped with a picture of Rashad from the beginning and had recognized him all along. If *that* were true, then the woman sent to spy on him was the cleverest actress alive to pretend she believed he was the head of security.

Rashad didn't like what he was thinking. Because of his strong attraction to her, it twisted his gut. He threw back his head in frustration. "You've done me an invaluable service, Hasan. I won't forget."

"It's always a pleasure to serve you, Your Highness."

With his business done, Rashad flew back to the palace. After he arrived, he heard from a trusted informant who'd done some digging for him. "What have you learned?"

"She flew into El-Joktor day before yesterday."

The entry visa stamped in her passport had verified as much. She'd only had a one-day trek into the desert. Mustafa assured him they'd met no other caravans en route, no other contacts.

"Upon arrival in El-Joktor, she stayed at the Casbah alone."

The Casbah? When there were modern hotels with amenities, why did she choose a two-star hotel in a poorer quarter of the city, once fashionable but no longer popular for close to many decades?

"Her papers are in order. She has no known occupation, but has been living in the apartment at the Montreux address belonging to an American named Celia Melrose Bancroft, seventy-five, recently deceased."

Had Lauren Viret lied about being the woman's granddaughter? Perhaps she'd been a very well-paid companion. After the woman died, had she gone looking for another kind of benefactor, this time a male? Or had a certain male found *her*? Was it possible?

"Do you wish me to probe deeper, Your Highness?"

"Not yet. You've done well."

What had Rashad's father taught him repeatedly from childhood? If the camel once gets his nose in the tent, his body will follow. With the help of the elements, Mademoiselle Viret had virtually been swept inside his tent and delivered into his hands.

Dinner with her first, away from all eyes. He needed to learn all there was to know about her. Despite everything he knew or suspected, *he needed to be alone with her.*

CHAPTER THREE

AFTER ARRANGING FOR A MEAL on the patio next to the flower garden, Rashad showered and dressed in another shirt and trousers. As he was on his way to the other wing of the palace, Nazir rang him. "Your Highness? The American has just asked me for an outside line from the palace. Should I allow it?"

"Yes." The palace's control center used a satellite tracking device. Later Rashad would check on the numbers she phoned. He bounded up the stairs and kept walking along the passageway until he reached the connecting hall to the garden suite. After knocking, he let himself in and discovered her seated at the desk in the sitting room. She spoke on the phone in French as impeccable as his own.

The minute she saw him approach, she ended her conversation and put down the receiver. "Good evening, Rafi." There was a huskiness in her voice, letting him know she was pleased to see him, even if she hadn't wanted him to know the nature of her business on the phone.

He was shaken to realize that even though elaborate preparations had been made long before she'd set out for Al-Shafeeq on a special mission, the connection between them was real…and rare.

"I'm glad to see you looking more rested."

She nodded her blond head. "I took a nap after you left."

Rashad thought she looked good enough to eat. She was still dressed in the clothes she'd worn earlier. "Are you hungry?"

"Yes."

If it was a lie, he didn't care because he sensed she wanted to spend the evening with him. During the short flight back from Raz, the thought of being with her tonight was all that had consumed him. This kind of instant attraction was different from anything he'd ever known in his life, taking him completely unaware.

"I arranged for us to eat dinner together. How do you feel about that?"

She made a betraying motion with her hands. "If you're free, I—I'd love it." The words fell from her lips with satisfying speed…unrehearsed, unguarded.

"It's waiting out on the patio."

Her beguiling features lit up in pleasure. "I haven't seen the flowers yet." As she got up from the desk, the action drew his attention to her softly rounded figure. He didn't like it that whether she was dressed in a hospital shift or western clothes, the heavenly mold of her body made it impossible for him to look elsewhere.

"Does this mean you're off duty?" Her breathing sounded a trifle shallow, alerting him to the fact that she wasn't in control of herself, either.

"More or less."

"In other words, you're like Dr. Tamam, always available if needed?"

He smiled. "That's one way of putting it."

"He came by a little while ago to check on me."

"What's the verdict?"

"I'm to relax for one more day to gain back my strength. Then I can return to being a tourist again."

"He's an excellent doctor. You won't be sorry for following his advice."

"I plan to." After a pause she said, "Are you hungry too?"

"Ravenous, as a matter of fact." All the senses of his body had come alive around her. He didn't know himself anymore.

"Does that mean you've been out saving more poor souls caught in another sandstorm?" she teased.

Her charisma charmed him to the core of his being and was so at odds with the secret she was keeping, it succeeded in tying him in knots.

"They don't happen that often, but I can tell you this much—in the last hundred years, you have the distinction of being the first foreign woman who lived through one."

He felt her shiver. "I've been blessed, thanks to you and Mustafa."

Rashad took an extra breath. "He was the one who pulled you off your camel in time."

"Yes." She turned away from him. "I need to thank him in person. That's why I was on the phone just now. I called the travel agency in Montreux and asked them to contact him for me."

"I would imagine he's out with another caravan. When your caravan takes you back to El-Joktor, you can thank him then. Now if you'll come with me, the patio is through this alcove."

He cupped her elbow. Their bodies brushed against each other, bringing certain longings alive. He ushered her out to the roof with its crenelated walls. Evening had fallen. The patio torches had been lit.

An awe-filled sigh escaped her lips as she looked out over the desert. He understood it. From this vantage point, one could see the oasis with its many lighted torches, and the sand beyond the boundary stretching in every direction. The perfumed air of the night breeze was cooling down even as they stood there. Stars had started to come out overhead. This was his favorite spot of the palace.

"I've never seen a sight like this in my life."

"Neither have I," Rashad whispered, studying her alluring profile. If he moved an inch closer to her enticing warmth, he would have to touch her. He wouldn't be able to help himself.

"It's magical and makes me want to cry."

She was so in tune with his emotions, he admitted, "Sometimes when my work closes in on me, I get the urge to slip away from my office and come out here to feel the night."

"You *can* feel it," she cried in wonder and turned to him. The glow from the nearest torch reached her eyes. When he looked into them, he was staggered by their bewitching color. They were a rare shade of green so light and iridescent, they dazzled him more than the large shimmering star rising beyond her shoulder.

How could eyes that soulful belong to a woman who'd come here to do him and his family harm? "Are you cold?" He wanted a reason to wrap his arms around her again.

"Not yet," she answered in a shaken voice.

"Then let's eat."

Rashad had instructed his staff to arrange a table for two near the lattice-covered garden so that he and Lauren could enjoy its fragrance. Flames from the candles flickered, throwing the shapes of the flowers into larger-than-life replicas against the thick palace walls.

He pulled out a chair for her. She sat down quickly, but not before his hands shaped her shoulders after helping her. By now her long dark lashes—unusual on someone so fair—half hid her gaze focused on the flowers. "How beautiful," she whispered.

"The royal family calls it the Garden of Enchantment."

Rashad heard her soft intake of breath before she said, "I can understand why. I feel only a sense of peace sitting here. It's exquisite."

"I agree it's perfection."

Goosebumps broke out on Lauren's arms. This was the garden her grandmother had talked about!

Lauren had come to the desert to walk in Celia's steps. Who would have dreamed she'd do it *literally*.

She'd always thought herself a down-to-earth, sensible person, but a force outside her sphere of understanding was at work here and it stemmed from the man seated across from her.

Feeling the full intensity of his eyes on *her* rather than garden, she was afraid to look at him directly. He was too powerfully striking. His unconscious arrogance of demeanor, his fierce male beauty, didn't need the embellishment of this glorious night to cause the blood to pound in her ears.

Something had to be seriously wrong with her to be sitting here mesmerized by this masculine force of nature whose roots had sprung from an unforgiving desert. Refusing to let him know how much his comments and nearness disturbed her, she looked down at the food placed in front of her.

There were slices of melon, fruit ice and tender portions of lamb with potatoes. She'd been so enthralled by him, she hadn't even noticed they'd been served, yet he was already eating with pleasure.

She sipped her hot sweet coffee first. "You keep late hours, Rafi. Have you no wife who's expecting you?"

"A pot needs the right cover. I've not found mine yet."

His admission made her heart leap. "In other words, you're telling me in your unique way to mind my own business." But Lauren laughed as she said it. Considering the looks of the gorgeous if not enigmatic male seated across from her, no Arabic analogy could have been more absurd.

"I'm pleased to see I've been able to bring a smile to your lips. You must do it more often."

"I couldn't help it. Your comment about a pot brought

to mind the story of Ali Baba. All those poor thieves boiling in hot oil inside the covered pots. Such a cunning servant girl," she said, enjoying each delicious morsel of food.

His sudden white smile in that burnished face robbed her of breath. "She was that," he murmured before breaking into laughter, the rich male kind she felt to her toes, deep and uninhibited.

She sent him an oblique glance. "I have a hard time believing you're a confirmed bachelor."

"I'm not," he stated matter-of-factly, "but when that day comes, it won't be the kind of marriage you imagine." He drank some coffee while he ate nuts and raisins from the bowls. "It's not written in my stars."

Lauren wiped the corner of her mouth. "If I didn't know myself better, I'd have made a wrong decision and be in a bad marriage by now. Surely you're in control of your own destiny."

"So far," he said on a cryptic note.

"Do you have family here at the oasis?"

He eyed her for a long moment. "I have parents and siblings."

"You're very fortunate. Have you lived at the oasis all your life?" She found herself wanting to know any detail he would share.

"Apart from schooling in England and France, this has been my home. Has Switzerland always been yours?"

"Yes, but we sometimes stayed in New York where Celia was born."

"Tell me about your grandmother. Had she been ill a long time before she died?"

He'd skillfully guided their conversation away from himself. "No. Celia came down with bronchitis and it turned into pneumonia. Most people in their seventies recover, but she didn't. Because she was such an intrepid adventurer, I assumed she'd live well into her nineties."

"In other words, you weren't prepared for her death."

Tears stung her eyes. "I don't think you ever are, even if you sit at someone's bedside for months or years. She was taken from me too soon."

"Every sun has to set," his deep voice raked across her skin, startling her out of her thoughts. "Your grandmother's sun set sooner than you would have liked. If you made each other happy, then there should be no guilt."

He'd picked up on her guilt with astonishing accuracy, but it had nothing to do with Celia, and everything to do with her inexplicable attraction to him. It frightened her a little. "You're mistaken if you think I have regrets."

He studied her as if he could see into her soul. "Then why do you look, shall we say...fragmented when you talk about her?"

Maybe he'd been a psychologist before going into security work. She drew in an extra breath. "That's exactly how I feel, no doubt due to her unexpected death and my close brush with it."

"No doubt," Rafi muttered, but he didn't sound convinced. On maddening cue he said, "But I'm glad to see you have an appetite. Even if you're in mourning, it's an excellent sign that you're returning to normal."

Since meeting Rafi, Lauren no longer knew what normal was. She sensed he was getting ready to say goodnight, but she didn't want the evening to end. While she was contemplating a way to detain him, he said, "Much as I would like to stare into your jewel eyes for the rest of the night, it's growing colder out here. Let's go in and enjoy a game of cards. Otherwise I'll have to explain to Dr. Tamam why his patient has suffered a relapse at my hands."

She could still feel those hands on her shoulders. Whenever he made a personal comment, she felt the blood surge to her cheeks. This time when they walked back inside, their bodies brushed. She felt like a firecracker ready to go off.

"I'll warn you now I only know how to play canasta."

One dark brow lifted. "They play that at the casino in Montreux?"

She hunched her shoulders and smiled. "I doubt it, but I can't say for sure. I only went inside it once with grandmother when I was a girl. She told me to take a good look at all the people and remember how desperate some of them looked. Then she never allowed me to enter it again. She said that gambling was one of the easiest ways to destroy people."

"And so you never went near?" he asked with a wicked smile. "Not even once as a small gesture of defiance?"

Lauren shook her head. "No. She was so wonderful, I didn't want to disappoint her."

"Disappointing people," he murmured after a noticeable silence. "The most painful of punishments." He sounded far away just then.

"Yes," she whispered.

"I happen to agree with you." Again she had the impression his thoughts were on something that brought him grief.

"Let's play over here." He gestured to the low-lying table in one corner of the sitting room. She sank down rather ungracefully into the cushions surrounding it. Rafi joined her with the ease and male agility of one who did this on a regular basis, extending his long powerful legs. Lauren tucked hers beneath her. The action brought her arm against his shoulder. Neither of them moved away.

He shot her a glance that seemed to be narrowed on her mouth. "Teach me how to play canasta."

Her body thrilled to the knowledge that he'd come with a pack of cards in order to spend more time with her. He pulled them from his trouser pocket and put them on the table. "They've already been shuffled."

"Good. I hate having to wait."

He laughed out loud, warming her clear through.

"Deal both of us fifteen cards," she instructed.

Her host took his time, smiling at her mysteriously as he did it.

Trying to ignore his dominating male aura she explained the rules of the game as clearly and concisely as she could.

He rubbed his thumb against his bottom lip in contemplation before moving the cards around in his hand. "Who taught you how to play?"

"Richard, my grandmother's husband."

They got started and she answered more questions as they went along. It didn't surprise her he had a razor-sharp brain plus a photographic memory. Once he'd caught on, they played until after midnight. The final count made her the overall winner by just a handful of points.

"I want a rematch," he growled the words, "but your eyelids are drooping so I'll say goodnight and we'll do this again tomorrow night."

She didn't know if she could live till then.

He left the cards on the table and got up in a lithe move. She clasped the hand he extended to her. "Oh—" she cried softly because the movement propelled her against him. "I'm sorry."

"I'm not." He rubbed his hands up and down her arms with growing urgency. "I've been waiting to do this all night. One little taste for a consolation prize, I think." The next thing she knew he kissed the nerve throbbing wildly at the base of her throat. Swarms of sensation filled her body, leaving her weak and trembling.

When she could lift her head, she saw fire blazing in the depths of those black eyes. "I'll come by for you at seven. If you're up to it, there's something I'd like to show you. We'll eat breakfast after that." Before she knew it, he'd slipped out of the suite.

Lauren glanced at her watch.

It was morning already.

Maybe she was in a dream. If she was, she never wanted to wake up. *Don't let me wake up. Please don't!*

Lauren prepared for bed quickly and set her watch alarm for six-thirty. She fell asleep at some point, but came awake a half hour before her alarm went off because she was so eager to see Rafi again.

After a shower and a hair wash, she dressed in tan pants and a white blouse, her uniform for the desert. At ten to seven, she heard a rap on the door before he entered the suite. He was early too, dressed like her. His piercing eyes traveled over her, causing every nerve ending to tingle.

"I like a woman who's punctual."

"That works both ways," she said, too breathlessly, as they walked along the passageway. She almost had to run to keep up with his long strides.

"Where are we going?"

"I'm anxious to show you the mews at the back of the palace where the royal falcons roost. I keep mine there. Johara loves a morning hunt. I've a feeling you'll enjoy watching her."

"You do falconry?"

"When I was young it was one of my favorite pastimes with my friends. These days I rarely have time for it." They went down a staircase and along another hall that eventually led to a shedlike room where she saw three falcons perched.

She watched as he moved over to one of the brownish birds, probably a foot and a half long from head to tail. The moment Rafi started speaking in Arabic, the bird cocked her head toward him.

He reached for a special glove on a nearby table. As soon as he put it on and held out his arm, she hopped on to it. Lauren would have given anything to have a camera to capture this splendid man interacting with a bird of prey equally noble.

She moved closer to them. "So *you're* one of Rafi's pets. You're magnificent." Just like your master. "Now I understand." The falcon tipped her head and regarded Lauren with a beady eye.

A slow smile broke the corners of Rafi's mouth. "Come with us, Lauren."

They walked outside into a world set aglow by an early-morning sun. After the cold of the night, the heat was already building. A Jeep was parked nearby. He let his falcon fly. She rose high in the sky with shocking speed.

"Her wing span is huge!"

"Three feet to be exact. We'll follow her." His excitement was contagious. Lauren got in the Jeep with him and they headed out on a road that led toward the open desert.

"Johara will circle for food. If she can't find any, she'll come back to me."

She stared at his arresting profile. "Then what happens?"

"We'll drive her back to the mews where I'll make sure she's fed. The important thing is that she gets her exercise. When I can't do it, someone else sees to it the falcons fly at least two hours every day."

Lauren shielded her eyes. "Has she ever not come back and you had to go looking for her?"

He turned his head, meeting her eyes. "She always comes back, but that's because I spent hours and hours training her in my late teens."

"Then she's old."

"Yes. I don't expect her to last much more than this season."

"Will you train a new falcon for yourself after that?"

"No. I'll never have that kind of time again," he answered in a voice that sounded so bleak, she couldn't account for it.

"Maybe if you have a child some day? A son or daughter who loves falconry as you do?"

In the next instant his countenance changed. An almost savage expression entered those incredible jet-black eyes, sending a chill that permeated her whole body. She wished she hadn't brought up something so personal.

"Forgive me if I've upset you." For no reason she could think of it hurt when it shouldn't have mattered at all.

He shot her a penetrating glance. "You've done nothing. We all have our own demons to battle from time to time. What do you say we enjoy the rest of the morning and see if Johara's old age has interfered with her ability to track down her prey? In her younger years she could spot it from a mile away."

The Jeep sped up. They'd left the road and were flying across the desert, which was flat in this part with some ground-cover vegetation. Ten minutes later they came upon a shelter which was nothing more than four poles holding up a canvas top. Beneath it she spotted chairs, and a table.

"We'll stop here for breakfast while we wait for Johara."

Lauren got out, delighted by the setup which included two thermoses of hot coffee and a supply of sandwiches and dates. Rafi appeared to have a fondness for them.

They ate with no time clock in mind. He answered her hunting questions with admirable patience. She satisfied his curiosity about her travels with her grandmother and Richard. The good times, the scary times—it didn't matter what they talked about. The sharing was what counted. The dark look she'd seen in his eyes earlier had vanished and Lauren knew instantly that she would clutch this memory to her forever.

The sun was almost overhead when she saw a speck in the sky. Rafi had seen it first because he'd started putting on his glove and walked outside to greet Johara. With great majesty his falcon circled him and then used her wings like a parachute, slowing her speed until she landed on the back of his wrist.

While he spoke in low tones to his bird, Lauren stood next to one of the poles, spellbound. "No luck today?" she eventually spoke.

Rafi shook his head, drawing her attention to his glossy black hair. "No, but there's always tomorrow. That's what I was telling her."

His tenderness with his pet reached a spot inside Lauren that gave her worlds of information about the kind of man Rafi was. She knew that there was no one in this world like him.

He walked over to the Jeep. After settling his bird on the back seat, he put a hood over her. "She feels safer like that." He satisfied Lauren's unasked question, then flicked her a probing glance. "Shall we go? One of the staff will dismantle our restaurant."

She climbed in the front seat. "I've eaten in a lot of restaurants in my life, but I'll always consider this one my favorite." She didn't care if her voice wobbled from emotion. Lauren wanted him to know what this morning meant to her.

He reached for her hand and held on to it. "Even if it isn't true, I've decided I want to believe you."

She pondered the strange remark all the way back to the mews. Of necessity he had to let go of her to carry his falcon inside, leaving her aching for his touch. After feeding the bird, they made their way back down the hallway and up the stairs.

Eventually they reached Lauren's suite. She dreaded this part because she knew he had his work to do and couldn't spend every minute of the day and night with her.

After opening the door, she turned to him. "Thank you for a wonderful outing, one I'll never forget."

He gazed at her through shuttered eyes. "Nor will I. Get some rest and I'll come by for you at six."

Joy.

Rashad left for his own suite, haunted by what was happening to him. Once he reached his own bedroom, he phoned his twin sister, Farah, and asked her to come to his suite the minute she was able. All three of his sisters were married, but it was Farah who had the most tender heart.

He didn't have to wait long before she swept into his sitting room. "Rashad?" She was wearing a rose caftan. Farah was a picture with her black hair hanging loose down her back, reminding him of the beauty of their women. Yet another image kept intruding of a female with spun-gold hair in enchanting disarray around her head and a complexion like strawberries in cream.

"Forgive me for bothering you, Farah."

"You're never a bother."

"Thank you for coming."

"You know I'd do anything for you." He knew it was true and loved her for it. She sat down on one of the chairs facing him. "Is this about our father? Is he worse?" Her dark eyes glinted with tears.

Their shape and color were different from the eyes he'd looked into out in the desert earlier. He'd had the sensation of stepping beyond the white froth of the surf where it broke into incredibly light-green water before melting into azure and then darkest blue.

"No. There's a guest here at the palace who was caught in a sandstorm two days ago. She almost didn't survive."

Farah cried out and put her hands to her mouth in horror.

"Dr. Tamam has assessed her and she's recovering well, but I think she might need a friend whilst she is here so she doesn't feel too alone. Her grandmother died recently. You're the perfect person to help her get through this difficult period. Would you be able to spend a little time with her this afternoon?"

"I'd be happy to do that. I'll do whatever I can to cheer her up. Where was she taken?"

"To the garden suite."

His sister rose to her feet. "You put her in there?" she asked incredulously. It was commonly known as the honeymoon suite for members of the royal family.

"I asked Dr. Tamam to take her there following the examination. After the horror of her experience, I thought she should be surrounded by beauty. Don't you agree?"

"Oh yes, of course! Only you would think of it. Who is she?"

"She's a young American woman, currently living in Switzerland, named Lauren Viret. She came here hoping to get over the sadness of losing the woman who raised her. Perhaps she'll tell you what it was she'd hoped to see and do while she was here at the Oasis. You're easy to talk to, Farah."

"I'll try, and you're right. She shouldn't be alone to dwell on that awful sandstorm."

"Thank you. You have my deepest gratitude for doing this personal favor for me. One more thing, I've told her I'm the head of palace security."

She smiled. "Well, I didn't think you'd tell her you were the prince."

"No. I thought the revelation might be too much for her and make her more uncomfortable about staying here. I told her to call me Rafi."

"I haven't heard you called that name in years." She winked at him before walking out to the corridor.

"Keep me updated, Farah. If she tells you anything I ought to know, come and tell me," he said as he followed her.

She kissed his cheek. "I promise."

He knew what was going through her head. In another six months Rashad would be married. Eventually the day would come when he would have to obey his father and go through with the dreaded wedding ceremony that would bring an end to his freedom.

But while he was still single, his sister suspected him of having an interest in the American beyond concern for her comfort after her ordeal. That was exactly what Rashad wanted Farah to think. If she thought she could be an instrumental part of a passing romantic intrigue, so much the better. In her innocence, Farah made the perfect spy.

In the middle of her nap, Lauren heard the maid calling to her. She sat up on the bed where she'd been resting. "Yes?"

"You have a visitor, mademoiselle."

Lauren glanced at her watch. It was only four o'clock. Her pulse raced. Had Rafi come early to see her because he couldn't stay away? She slid off the bed. "Who is it?"

"The Princess Farah."

Princess?

Lauren put up a hand to muffle her cry, unable to believe her good luck. She'd come all this way to get information about her grandfather. So far she hadn't dared ask Rafi any questions about the royal family. As head of security he might suspect her motives, but who better than the princess herself? Surely she would enjoy talking of her family and its heritage?

"Have you shown her into the sitting room?"

"Yes, mademoiselle."

"Then please tell her I'll be with her in a moment."

She slipped on her sneakers and went to the bathroom to refresh her lipstick and brush her hair. Without wasting any time, she hurried into the other room. The princess, several inches taller than Lauren, stood near the desk dressed in cream pants and a stunning blood-red blouse. With a voluptuous figure and all that black hair piled on her head, she was the most striking woman Lauren had ever seen.

"Forgive me for keeping you waiting, Your Highness."

"Don't give it a thought, mademoiselle," Farah said in beautiful English. "My name's Farah. Rafi told me your name. May I call you Lauren? It's such a lovely name."

"Please," Lauren said, warming to her at once. "You have a beautiful name, too."

Her wide smile was enchanting. "Shall we sit down at the table? I asked for mint tea to be served in here."

"Thank you. This is a real honor for me." Lauren walked over to the table and sat down opposite her.

"The family heard about what happened to you during the sandstorm. I can't tell you how horrified I was when I learned of it." Tears glinted in her eyes. Even without them, Lauren felt her sincerity and it melted her on the spot. "It must have been awful for you."

"It was, but it's over now and I'm very grateful to be alive."

"My husband, Abdul, got caught in one when he was a boy. Sometimes I think maybe it's good he and I have not been blessed with children. If anything like that were to happen to them or to my husband again…" She couldn't finish the sentence.

"You must love your husband very much. Maybe one day you will be blessed with a child, too?"

"Abdul is the sweetest and kindest man I know, but sadly I have already suffered two miscarriages. The specialists I've seen cannot promise me anything and so we only hope…one day."

"I'm so sorry."

She shook her head. "Let's not talk about sad things. Instead we'll rejoice that you are alive. According to the doctor, you were close to death. He would have had to answer to my father if he hadn't brought you back to life."

Despite Rafi insisting it wasn't her appointed time to die, Dr. Tamam had given her the medical treatment needed. "I'm very grateful to both Dr. Tamam and Rafi for everything they have done for me. If I could pay for the doctor's time perhaps or Rafi, who flew a helicopter to the accident scene and got me to the clinic in time."

"They don't want your money, Lauren. What's important is that you're all right."

"But to be the guest of the king…"

"My father welcomes all visitors if they come in peace."

If the king ever found out who Lauren really was, she would disturb his peace in ways she didn't dare think about. "Are you his only daughter?"

"No. I have two older sisters and a brother. He's my twin."

Lauren finished the sweet tea. "I would have loved brothers and sisters. Please convey my gratitude to your father and mother. I've never seen such a beautiful apartment in my life. The flowers on the patio are a miracle."

"My mother loves that garden."

"So do I."

"If you don't think it would tire you out, I'll be happy to show you around the palace grounds tomorrow. They're one big garden."

"I'd love that!" It might be her only chance to hear about Farah's family and learn something concerning her grandfather before she left the palace.

"Whatever else you would like to do while you're here at the Oasis, I'll arrange it."

Lauren's heart beat sped up. "You're very kind. Mustafa mentioned something about visiting the Garden of the Moon. Is it a place you think I should see?" Under the circumstances, she hoped the tiny white lie about Mustafa would be forgiven.

The Princess looked surprised. "I'm afraid it's not allowed."

Oh no. Quick. Think of something, Lauren.

"Between my inability to understand Arabic and his

attempt to speak recognizable English, I obviously misunderstood him. It certainly doesn't matter."

"Perhaps he was talking about one of the specialty shops in the souk. Tourists love them."

"I'm sure I shall, too."

"I'll ring you tomorrow before I come for you."

CHAPTER FOUR

LATER THAT EVENING, Lauren left the bedroom, having dressed in a pair of cream-colored denims and a light-green blouse. As she entered the sitting room she heard Rafi's knock on the door before he entered wearing a dark silk shirt and dark trousers. He was the epitome of manhood. His name came out in a whisper.

"Good evening, Lauren. How did your day go?"

She smiled. "As if you didn't know. I was paid a visit by the Princess Farah. That was your doing, so don't deny it."

"I wasn't going to." He smiled back. "The day can hang heavy while you're recuperating alone."

"It went by fast for me. She's a lovely person. We had tea and biscuits. Tomorrow she's going to take me on a tour of the grounds." All the time she was talking, his eyes roamed over her face and figure, causing a suffocating feeling in her chest.

"Speaking of tours, I'm off duty now and thought you might like to see the main rooms of the palace. We'll eat dinner here in your room afterward."

Lauren closed her eyes tightly to catch her breath

before opening them again. "I'd hoped to take a tour while I was visiting here."

He spread his hands in a way she was beginning to recognize as purely him. "Then I'm happy I can grant your wish. Perhaps your travel agency didn't know, but I've had to order the interior of the palace off limits to the public. In these modern times, there's too much danger to take risks."

She blinked. "I *didn't* know. If that sandstorm hadn't happened…"

Lines suddenly marred his handsome features. "Then we would never have met unless fate had deemed it otherwise. Shall we go?"

For the next hour Lauren wandered with him through room after room, marveling over the ancient citadel, which was a museum in and of itself. She wouldn't know where to begin describing the tiles on the floors and walls, the cutwork ceilings, the tapestries and urns, the sweeping staircases, all the trappings of a great empire.

In one of the great rooms, Rafi pointed out the lineage of the Shafeeq dynasty. Lining the walls were enormous framed oil portraits of the sheikhs. Each had a name plate, but Lauren couldn't read them. "What are their names?"

"You really want to know?"

"Yes. I think Arabic is a beautiful language. The names sound so different to my ear."

The comment seemed to please him. He turned to the portrait at the far end. With expert recall he gave her a short, stunning history of each one. In time they came to the second picture from the end.

"This one is Sheikh Malik Ghazi. The royal family calls him the great one."

Lauren's heart thudded painfully hard. It was almost impossible to believe she was standing in front of the likeness of her grandfather when he was maybe thirty years old. She'd already been given a description of him by her grandmother. The newspaper picture of him hadn't done him justice. He was everything Celia had said he was, and more.

Dark and splendid…like Rafi who had that same aura of authority, the fierce warrior look that could inspire followers and terrify their enemies. Lauren was furious with herself that she couldn't stop obsessing over this enigmatic man.

From the beginning he'd been careful to let her know he was still enjoying his bachelor status. One of these days soon she would have to leave the Oasis. For her own sake she didn't dare get in any deeper.

"Why did they call him that?"

"His father died young. King Malik had to take over the affairs of the kingdom at nineteen."

"That's too young to have such great responsibility, don't you think?" It was a miracle he'd had time for her grandmother.

"It is what it is."

Lauren had to smile at another one of those fatalistic comments she'd heard fall from his compelling lips. "I can't imagine it."

"He's the one who united many neighboring tribes

and made our nation a greater kingdom than it was before."

Her mouth had gone so dry, she didn't know if she could enunciate clearly. "Is he still alive?"

"No. He died suddenly four months ago. Dr Tamam said his heart just stopped beating."

Celia had died a mere two months ago.

The timing of their deaths shook Lauren to the core. "How old was he when he passed away?"

"Eighty-one."

"Then he had a long full life, like Johara."

Quiet reigned before he nodded. "An astute observation."

"Is that how she'll die?"

"Maybe. I could hope she'll be in flight and free when it happens. Birds weren't meant to be tamed."

"That's a surprising statement coming from you."

He flashed her a glance she couldn't decipher. "Lately I'm a mass of contradictions."

She sensed he didn't want to talk about it anymore and moved on to the last portrait. "I take it this is the king to whom I'm beholden beyond my ability to repay. King Umar Jalal Shafeeq," she said aloud. "I'm sorry for the bad pronunciation. His name and image were stamped on my entry visa."

"You said it well," he came back.

"I know he has a kind heart or I wouldn't be his guest. Is he a good king, too? You don't have to answer that if you can't, or don't want to."

A light flickered in Rafi's black eyes. "The world could learn from a leader like him."

Lauren's mother had been the king's half sister... How sad they had never had a chance to meet.

"Then he must be the best and you'll always want to work for him." Lauren took a deep breath. "Thank you for showing me this fabulous palace and giving me this much of your time." She bit her lip. "It's clear you're one of the king's right hands, but you don't have to spend any more time with me."

He angled his head toward her. "Lauren, do I detect some fear that I'll beat you at cards tonight?"

"Yes," she lied, because being with him any longer meant she might make a fool of herself and do something with this man that she might one day regret.

"Don't worry," he said with a devilish twist of his lips. "If I win, I'll only take a few more bites out of you." She could still feel his mouth against her throat and Lauren's heartbeat increased to a dangerous level.

When they reached her suite, their dinner had been put on the low round table where they could eat and play cards at the same time. Rafi had thought of everything.

They sat down and got into the game in earnest, enjoying their food in between shuffles. In the end, she beat him again, this time by a much larger margin. Lauren decided he'd allowed her to win, but she didn't care. It was enough to be together and Lauren suddenly had the oddest sensation that it could go on forever.

He put the cards in a stack and shoved it to the center of the table. "Since you've won hands-down, what prize do you want from me?" Rafi reached for her hand and kissed the tips of her fingers. "Name it and it's yours." Shock waves traveled through her body.

"Do you think before I leave the Oasis it would be possible for me to visit the place where the sandstorm overtook the caravan?"

His brows formed a black bar above his eyes, changing the tenor of the evening. She wished now she hadn't brought it up. "Tell me, Lauren, why would you want to return to the spot that could only hold a devastating memory for you?"

"The maid has never found my medallion. Dr. Tamam said they made a search of the clinic, but it wasn't there. I think when Mustafa pulled me off the camel, he must have caused my chain to break and it's buried somewhere in the sand. I would give anything to recover it."

Rashad's dark head went back while he examined her features. "Don't you realize that if the medallion is out in the desert, it's buried beneath a mound of sand?"

"I'm sure you're right," she said in a subdued voice.

"You look tired," he said, helping her to her feet. "I'm going to say goodnight and will see you tomorrow." Instead of another bite from her throat, he kissed her forehead and disappeared so fast, she didn't have a chance to call him back.

She should have kept quiet about the medallion. Here he'd done everything humanly possible to make her happy since her accident, and she'd rewarded him by asking for another favor. In making that request, she'd stepped over a line. His swift departure left her under no delusions on that score. She wouldn't blame him if he thought she was the most selfish female alive.

Resolute, she sat down at the desk and composed a letter to the king, thanking him for his generous hospitality and the services of the clinic doctor and his chief of security. After that she wrote a note to Rafi.

When she'd finished, she put them outside the suite door, then walked over to the desk and dialed number one. A male voice came on the line. "This is Nazir. How may I help you, mademoiselle?"

"Forgive me for bothering you this late, but I'd like to leave the palace in the morning and I need a driver to take me to a hotel. Could you arrange that for me?"

"Of course. I will send someone to your room after you've been served your breakfast."

"Thank you very much. One more thing. There are two letters outside my door. Would you make certain they are delivered?"

"Certainly."

She hung up the phone, wishing the travel agency she'd called in Montreux would ring her back. They'd promised to arrange for helicopter transportation for her from Al-Shafeeq to El-Joktor and would phone her with the details.

Lauren had come here with questions about her grandmother and the romance she had encountered with Malik. But now she had seen firsthand how captivating this desert kingdom was. She might not have answers to all her questions, but she knew one thing for sure. She needed to get away from the man who had captured her own heart; she needed to get away from Rafi.

* * *

Rashad had just gotten off the phone with Farah when Nazir came to his suite with two envelopes and informed him Mademoiselle Viret wished to leave the palace in the morning. That didn't surprise him.

He told Nazir he'd take care of it. After he left, Rashad stood in the middle of his sitting room and opened the envelope addressed to his father first. After reading it, he turned to the one meant for him.

Dear Rafi,
Princess Farah said neither you or Dr. Tamam wanted payment for your actions during the sand-storm. I'm left with no choice but to simply thank you for saving my life. I'll never forget you.
Lauren.

Her sentiment worked both ways. Rashad had wanted her so much tonight, he'd felt as though he was dying. He'd never known hunger like this before. It went beyond the physical to some other place, sending the same kind of shivers racing across his bronzed skin he'd felt when he'd picked her up in his arms the first time.

That same chemistry had been instantaneous for her, too. He remembered the second she'd awakened to discover him holding her hand at the bedside. She hadn't spoken for a long time. That was because a white-hot heat more blazing than the desert sun had enveloped them through no volition of their own. The harder they'd fought it, the more intense their desire had grown.

Though he believed she had an agenda, no human could simulate the chemistry between them. Tonight those heavenly green eyes had seduced him, willing him to make love to her.

Throughout his life he'd known temptation and had been able to withstand it because he was his father's son and had a sacred duty to uphold. If he hadn't been careful all these years, he would be dead by now. His father had trusted no one and neither did he, least of all this beautiful flesh-and-blood creature with flaxen hair and peridot eyes sent to weaken his defenses.

And he knew she'd been sent.

Tonight Farah had phoned and given him the proof. At first he'd thought she hadn't told him anything that could help him. By the tone of Farah's voice, Rashad thought Lauren had won his sister over completely. Just when he'd decided Farah hadn't discovered anything that could help him, she'd mentioned the Garden of the Moon.

That was the clue he'd been waiting for. Every alarm in Rashad's hard body had gone off. He'd found a link to the medallion and was getting closer to an answer.

Wasting no time, he'd phoned Mustafa who had sworn an oath he'd never said anything about the Garden of the Moon to Mademoiselle Viret. According to him, the foreigner had been unusually quiet and had appeared deep in thought throughout the entire journey.

Rashad believed him.

He finally went to bed, determined that over the next few days he would get a confession out of her, starting by giving her what she wanted first.

"Good morning, mademoiselle. I'm Nazir." The fortyish-looking man stood in the doorway wearing traditional

Arab robes. He broke into a smile. "We spoke on the phone last night, but haven't yet met. I've been instructed to accompany you to the western gate."

"Thank you for coming. Did you get the letters?"

"Yes. They've been delivered."

So fast? "Excellent. Well, I'm ready." She started to pick up her suitcases, but he said, "Leave them in here."

Lauren frowned. "Leave them? I don't understand."

He spread his hands. "All will be explained if you will accompany me."

This meant Rafi had gotten her note and knew of her plans. As head of security, nothing went on in the palace he didn't know about. "Very well."

Once out the door she followed Nazir along one corridor and down another she hadn't seen before. The palace was like a small city. Eventually they came to a portico and he led her beyond it to a glorious garden of palms and desert plants growing outside the palace.

Nazir made a gesture with his hands. "This way, please."

Several hundred yards off in the distance she spied a helicopter gleaming in the sun. She walked toward it, curious to know what was going on. Closer now she saw three men inside, one at the controls. Another one jumped down wearing tall leather boots.

There was no mistaking Rafi in a khaki shirt and trousers. She didn't like admitting it, but just seeing his burnished face and those strong hands on his hips in a totally male stance sent an explosion of excitement through her body. It wasn't fair for one man to be that endowed. She'd hoped to put distance between them, but such wasn't the case.

"How are you this morning, Lauren?"

"I'm fine, thank you."

"We'll see." He moved closer, pressing the back of his hand to her cheeks and forehead. After receiving her note, he could be excused for wondering why she'd made plans to leave the palace without telling him last night.

His touch electrified her, never mind his black eyes that reduced her insides to pulp. "I—I don't have a fever," her voice faltered.

"Let me be the judge of that," came his answer in a smoky tone. He wasn't talking about the state of her health. With a comment like that, Lauren wasn't sure if her legs would hold her up.

"Are you satisfied?"

"I guess I'll have to be," he murmured. "If you're still intent on visiting the site of the sandstorm, the king has put a pilot at your disposal."

Her debt to the king continued to grow, but of course it was Rafi who made things happen. "I shouldn't have said anything to you last night. You've all done more than enough for me."

"It won't take long. Have you flown in a helicopter before?"

"Yes. Many times, in fact."

"Then let's be off. Just remember we're flying to the sun's anvil. It'll be 122 degrees Fahrenheit, if not more, so beware."

On that note he helped her inside. His hands rested

on her hips longer than necessary before she climbed in the back and strapped herself in the seat. It was all she could do not to turn around and launch herself into his arms.

The man next to her in Arab dress smiled at her. He had to have noticed what had transpired while Rafi was assisting her.

This was madness. Shame over her desire for him drove her to keep her eyes trained on the desert. The rotors whined. When liftoff occurred, she didn't once look ahead to where she'd be able to see the back of his head.

Instead she stared out her window and watched as the palace and finally the small green settlement of the Oasis itself disappeared. It was almost frightening to see nothing but sand below, an entirely different perspective from the air than on the ground.

They flew on into a world of nothing but undulating sand dunes forming their own fantastically shaped hills and valleys, untouched except for scorching sun and air. Out in this vast expanse, you had no sense of direction but for the sun which was almost at its zenith, denoting noon.

The pilot knew where they were, with today's technology, he could pinpoint the exact spot where the sandstorm had come upon her caravan. The real marvel were the Bedouins of the desert who'd been crossing these sands for millennia and had their own ways of functioning day and night in such an inhospitable wilderness. Yet for all that it had a terrifying beauty.

No sign of brown mountains sweeping across the

horizon like a tsunami today. Maybe Rafi had been right and it hadn't been her appointed time to die. Instead fate had delivered her into his arms. She closed her eyes, trying to shut out her thoughts of him, but it did no good.

From the first moment she'd heard his deep voice and had felt his hand swallow hers—even before she saw him—she'd *felt* him to her very soul.

"Lauren? We've arrived."

At the sound of his voice, she let out a little cry of surprise and opened her eyes. She'd been so buried in her own torturous thoughts, she hadn't realized they'd landed.

"If you're feeling unwell, we'll return to the palace." What made him think there was something wrong? She didn't understand.

He opened the door and got out. When she climbed forward, he put an impersonal hand on her upper arm to assist her as she jumped into the sand, but an electric current ran through her body just the same. They'd landed in a valley with gigantic mounds of sand spreading in every direction. The pilot stayed at the controls. The other man climbed out and walked a distance off.

Stunned to be that little granule of sand again, she looked all around before flicking Rafi a glance. "Where did it happen exactly?"

"According to the pilot, beneath this mound in front of you. I flew your body from here to the palace in the hope you could be revived."

She gasped because the sand dune in front of her rose at least twenty feet. Its smooth crescent shape ran the length of the horizon. Lauren took several steps forward, but with each thrust, her foot sank and it took effort to pull it out.

How foolish of her to think she could come out here and find anything, let alone her medallion! It was buried here somewhere, forever. The knowledge seemed to bring an end to an era for Lauren.

Her grandmother, her grandfather, the medallion—all were gone. The end of the beginning or the beginning of the end? Whatever, it was written in the sand now.

Her shoulders started to shake as tears began falling. She hung her head because she was beginning to sound like Rafi. She needed to get out of here and start a new life for herself, maybe in America? Wherever, she knew she needed to be somewhere far away from everything that reminded her of the past, away from *him*.

She felt him approach her side. Her body came alive whenever he was around and the sensations were so new, so different that they upset her. She didn't know where to go with her new feelings for him. "You warned me, Rafi, but please don't say anything. I only need five more minutes."

The suffocating air was so hot that the moisture evaporated as it dripped off her chin. Though he obeyed her, he didn't go away. Instead he wrapped his arms around her neck from behind so the tears fell on his bronzed skin. He pressed his chin in her hair and drew her into him in a protective gesture where she felt the steady pounding of his heart against her back.

For the moment he was comforting her like he might a child. Unfortunately the warmth from his hard-muscled body and his great strength increased her desire for him. She'd known such desire existed after listening to her grandmother, but she'd never felt its power until now.

This physical thing between them was sublime torture for her, tapping into her deepest emotions. She couldn't hold back the tears. They burst over the dam. How long she sobbed, she didn't know. Twice now she'd fallen apart in his arms.

She couldn't fathom leaving him and this place where life and death had taken on an entirely new meaning. Her grandmother had been faced with the same decision, but somehow she'd found the will to walk away from King Malik.

How did she do that?

Lauren didn't have Celia's resolve. Never to see Rafi again…

Ashamed because she was making a spectacle of herself, she sniffed hard and moved out of his arms to walk back to the helicopter on her own. This time it was the other man who helped her inside. She thanked him and the pilot before Rafi climbed in and shut the door.

Once more they were off, winging through the sky with no trace of clouds. Nothing but hot, hot blue, the sun reflecting off the sand sculptures below and the haunting profile of a man who was larger than life to her. *Larger than her grandmother's sheikh.* For the rest of Lauren's days, that picture would remain indelibly carved on her consciousness.

The men talked back and forth. She noticed Rafi speaking into his headset. Lauren could imagine that they had much more to do with their time than ferry around the American who must appeared spoiled to them, but as she was a guest of the king, they had their orders. When she got back to the palace, she intended to stay in her room for the rest of the day.

Rafi put out a hand to help her down from the helicopter. "Enjoy your afternoon. We'll talk later," he said before walking swiftly away in another direction, taking her heart with him. Nazir stood by to escort her back to the palace.

Now that another duty was done, Rafi could get back to his job as head of security. That was as it should be, she told herself, but her pain at watching him disappear sent her on a churning, downward spiral as she followed Nazir along various corridors.

She thought they looked different from the other ones. Before she could question him, Princess Farah came out of a set of doors wearing riding clothes. She smiled at Lauren.

"I'm so glad you are back. I just returned from a horseback ride with my husband, come inside and have a swim with me. We'll eat lunch by the pool."

"That sounds lovely, but I didn't bring a suit."

"I have many I haven't even worn." She glanced at Nazir. "Thank you for finding her." He said something back in Arabic and walked away.

They entered a fabulous octagonal room with a round swimming pool and a high ceiling of fretwork and inlaid tiles. "You were looking for me?"

"Yes. I thought you might like to go riding with me, but found out you'd already left your suite."

"Your father arranged for me to fly out to the place where the sandstorm hit."

The princess looked shocked. "Why would you want to do that?"

"It sounds silly now, but I lost a piece of jewelry my grandmother gave me when the sandstorm hit, and I hoped I might see it in the sand. Rafi told me it would be buried. Of course, he was right."

Farah's liquid dark eyes were filled with compassion. "I'm so sorry, but compared to your life, something material isn't so important in the scheme of things."

"You're right, Your Highness." It belonged to the past.

The princess smiled and showed Lauren to an anteroom where she could change. When she came out again in a yellow bikini, she discovered they had company. Farah made the introductions.

Of the three black-haired sisters, Lauren found herself staring at the eldest, Samira, who had the look of Lauren's mother. Samira was forty-one with five children. She'd brought her two youngest to the pool, an eight-year-old son and a five-year-old daughter.

Of course, she was older now than Lauren's mother had ever been. Still, Samira reminded her of some of the pictures in her wallet of Lana, and it gave Lauren's heart a tug to see the resemblance.

Basmah was thirty-nine and had four children. She'd brought along her youngest twin daughters, just turning four.

Farah explained that she and her twin brother Rashad were both thirty-four. Lauren saw the longing and love in Farah's eyes whenever she looked at her nieces and nephews. They were all adorable and got in the pool with Lauren without hesitation.

After some serious playtime, she climbed out and joined the others. They lay on loungers by the side of the pool to keep their eye on the children. Lauren sipped on her iced fruit drink. Having been born princesses, all three women were the products of formal education and spoke excellent English. Lauren discovered they were well-traveled and forward-thinking about their nation's future.

Their conversation was focused fairly constantly on their brother Rashad, a chemical engineer who'd been doing great things at his lab in Raz to open up new industries. Basmah and Samira were helping their mother plan the thirty-fifth birthday party for Farah and her brother being held in another week. The lot fell to Farah to think of a birthday present they could give him. Something exceptional.

"What do you think, Lauren?"

"Well, if I had a brother, I'd find him something to enjoy when he wants to relax."

Basmah shook her head. "He doesn't know how to relax."

"She's right!" Samira echoed. "He's too busy working all the time."

"Surely he has down time."

"If he's not at work, he's off on his horse," Farah inserted.

"He likes them better than women," Basmah added. "At least that's what all his girlfriends say."

Everyone laughed, including Lauren. "In that case, why not pick out a fine saddle blanket?"

"For that matter, why not a new saddle?"

Lauren eyed Samira. "You could give him one, but he probably won't use it."

She frowned. "Why not?"

"Because it needs to fit him and his horse like a glove. No hand fits a glove the same way, neither does a man on his horse. I bet it took your brother a long time to decide on the one he uses now."

Farah nodded. "You're right. Abdul would say the same thing."

"Does he like jewelry? Maybe you could give him a ring from all of you with three stones."

"That's a lovely idea, Lauren, but he doesn't like them. He says they irritate him when he works."

"Well, he'll have to get used to one when he's married," Basmah commented.

"He's dreading that day."

Lauren looked at Farah. "In this day and age he still can't choose his own wife?"

She shook her head. "No. It's tribal law that our father chooses the spouses, I'm glad he picked Abdul for me. I love him now. But it's different for you, being an American."

"That's true. Even if my father were alive, a woman still gets to pick the man she will marry."

Lauren felt Basmah's eyes on her. "You are the most beautiful American woman I ever saw in my life. When you go back to your country, you will have many opportunities to marry and do your own choosing."

"Thank you for the compliment, but the truth is, I don't plan to marry."

"You don't want children?" Farah cried.

Lauren saw one of the little twins running along the tiles to catch up with her sister. She was so sweet. "Not without the right man."

"He exists somewhere," Farah said with her heart in her eyes. "You have to believe that."

"I do," Lauren said with a sad smile, "but it doesn't mean fate will bring us together." Rafi's image would always be sketched on her heart.

"That is true," Samira murmured. "You sound very wise."

Lauren shook her head. If she'd been wise, she wouldn't have come to the desert, but then she wouldn't have met these delightful women who were also the grandchildren of King Malik. She wouldn't have met Rafi.

"You don't know how lucky you are," Farah confided. "I worry about our brother who will have to live with a woman he doesn't love. They'll be married at the end of the year."

"Give them time," Samira counseled.

"Time won't fix anything for Rashad," Farah blurted. "I know my twin brother too well. He'll never be happy. Our mother's fears have come true, he has been too favored."

"What do you mean?" Lauren questioned her.

Farah spread her hands. "He's been given every gift a man can have. Our mother is afraid there'll be a price to pay."

"A price?"

"Yes. Heaven is jealous of him."

"Our mother worries too much," Basmah said.

Farah looked sad. "I happen to agree with her. Something will come along that Rashad will want more than anything on earth, and for all his godlike virtues, it won't be granted."

Godlike. Celia's very words. They raised goosebumps.

With nothing but the sound of the childrens' voices in the background, the women grew quiet. Their collective silence indicated they feared Farah had spoken the truth. How awful for their brother.

Before long the children grew restless and the fun ended. Everyone left the pool room except for Farah. "Perhaps later in the week you'll come to my suite and have dinner with me."

"What about your husband?"

"He's away on business and won't be back until next week."

"Then I'd like that very much."

"So would I. I'll phone you."

Lauren left the pool and headed for her suite. She'd just returned to her room where a dinner tray was waiting for her when the phone rang. It set off her pulse because she'd been hoping to hear from Rafi. She picked up and said hello, trying not to sound too eager.

"Mademoiselle Viret? This is Louis at the travel office in Montreux."

"Oh—thank you for returning my call," she said, fighting her disappointment. "Have you made new travel arrangements for me?" She was determined to leave the Oasis before…before she could no longer do so.

"*Desolé, mademoiselle.* I'm most sorry to tell you that it will be impossible for you to leave Al-Shafeeq until the date you'd originally set to return to El-Joktor."

She panicked. "But I told you I'd pay you extra."

"I'm afraid it's not a question of money. The men in charge of the caravans don't operate by the same rules as most of us. They agree on a fee and a time when they're ready to go. You can try another agency, but I can promise you won't have better luck with them."

"I believe you. Then I'll book a helicopter."

"There is no service at the Oasis except in an emergency, and it has to be cleared through the royal palace. The fee would be prohibitive."

That meant going through Rafi. She couldn't possibly ask him for another favor that would require the king's involvement. "I understand. *Merci, Louis.*"

With a growing sense of inevitability, she hung up the receiver. There was going to be no escape until Mustafa took her back to El-Joktor. Since she was a guest of the king, she couldn't go to a hotel. That would be an insult to him. But another night with Rafi, let alone another week, would melt her resolve not to get any more involved.

She ate part of her dinner, wondering if he would call or come by. Maybe she'd watch TV; she moved over to the sofa facing the cabinet holding it. With the aid of the remote, she surfed a few channels, all in Arabic. Everything reminded her of Rafi. She shut it off and rested her head on the pillow while tears slipped out beneath her eyelids.

What other man could ever cause her to burn with desire the way he did? He brought her to life in a way that frightened her because she knew no other man could ever make her feel that way again. This morning she'd been wrapped in his arms. She'd felt the essence from his soul reach out and fill hers. For a little while they'd stood in the sand dunes, one pulsating entity.

Lauren couldn't comprehend not ever seeing him again and in that moment she knew that she was falling in love with him....

Conflicted beyond bearing, Rashad returned from Raz at dinnertime, barely able to function. Taking Lauren to the desert earlier in the day hadn't shed any new light on her secret. Worse, her tears had brought out his protective instincts. He'd come close to breaking every self-imposed rule by kissing her senseless in front of the pilot and bodyguard.

He'd never believed in witches until now, but she was a temptress, a beauty who didn't seem to know it, a spy who didn't spy, a flirt who didn't flirt, a seducer who'd made no move to seduce. She was the sweet embodiment of the word *treachery* in breathtaking female form. At this point he was ready to carry her off and forget the world.

To his dismay, she'd claimed all his attention for the last three days. During that time he hadn't checked in with his father who liked daily updates on business.

Rashad needed to drop in on him now before he went to her room.

"At last, Rashad." His father was sitting in a chair with his sore foot resting on the ottoman while he drank his favorite mint tea. "I've had dinner, but I'll ask for a tray to be sent up for you."

"Thank you, but I ate earlier." Rashad sat on the seat opposite his father. "I was in Raz until a half hour ago and came as soon as I could."

"I'm glad you're here because there's something important I need to talk to you about."

An odd nuance in his father's tone made Rashad uneasy. "What is it?"

"I've had correspondence with Sheikh Majid al Din. He wants to move up your wedding date."

Rashad shot out of the seat, turning away from his father while he attempted to contain his shock and yes, *anger.* He'd been dreading this since his sixteenth birthday.

"I can see this has upset you." His father had always been kind to him. His voice was kindness itself right now, but Rashad couldn't handle it.

"By how much?" he asked through clenched jaws.

"He wants to see his daughter married in a month."

"A *month?*"

His father eyed him with love. "I've touched the only sore spot in you."

Rashad stopped pacing. "I knew this day was coming, but I thought I had more time. I need a moment to take in the realization that my world is about to change."

"I felt the same way when your grandfather confronted

me. He told me who my bride would be two years before my wedding. I decided to lessen your pain by only giving you a month to agonize about the coming ceremony."

The irony of those words would have made Rashad break out in harsh laughter if he didn't love his father so much. "Have you told anyone else?"

"No one except for Nazir who has been our go-between. I'm to let Sheikh Majid know in three days' time if this is satisfactory. This thing has to be done in absolute secrecy so as not to upset the neighbors on our other borders."

"Not even my sisters know?" Rashad persisted.

He shook his head. "Especially not Farah, who continually begs me to let you choose the woman you will marry. She wearies me with it."

"Farah believes in love," Rashad muttered.

His father grunted. "You and I know that a powerful kingdom cannot be ruled by a sheikh who is so besotted with his wife, he can't see the shadows of his enemies outside the tent."

The palace was hardly a tent, but Rashad understood the point of the metaphor well enough. It had been drummed into his head since he was a child. His father would be horrified to know that a possible enemy had already invaded the palace and, as yet, Rashad had done nothing about it!

The way his father talked, Rashad was convinced that his sister had said nothing about the American woman staying at the palace. Was it simply coincidence Sheikh Majid wanted to speed up the time? Or could it be some grand design to help Rashad fight the spell this woman had cast over him?

It *was* a spell. How else to explain the weakness he felt for her, the longing that kept him in pain throughout the night. Could she truly be like the female black widow he and his young friends had once watched in fascination while she stung her mate to death?

Tonight he would get the truth out of her. His hell had gone on long enough. Once she was exposed, his desire for her would turn to bitter gall. It had to. "If you'll forgive me, father, I need to be alone so I'll say goodnight."

"I understand that better than you do. Goodnight, my son."

Once out the door, Rashad checked the phone logs in the communications room. Nothing had turned up on their guest except for two short calls to and from the travel agency in Switzerland.

With everything taken care of for the moment, he strode down the hall swiftly to reach the other side of the palace. His wedding day had been moved forward, but tonight he didn't want to think about it. He wanted Lauren.

Right now he was the one who felt closed in. He craved a night with her where he could pretend he was a free man like any other, able to be with the woman he desired. For tonight he would forget his royal responsibilities. Until she'd been blown in to his world, he'd never felt or resented them so heavily.

At Ziyad's place he could be himself. No one would bother him or give away his identity. Tonight it was crucial he acted on the feelings roiling inside him. What made it more exciting was that despite the part she'd been playing from the beginning, he knew Lauren desired him, too. In fact, every word and gesture was putting an edge on their experience, heightening the potent tension between them.

After knocking on her door, he slipped inside and discovered her on the sofa in front of the television. When he walked around in front of her, he saw moisture on her cheeks and didn't know what to think.

"How is it that more often than not, I find you in tears?"

CHAPTER FIVE

LAUREN'S CRY FILLED THE ROOM. She lifted her head and sat up, pushing the tendrils of silky hair out of her face. *"Rafi—"* Her voice throbbed.

He knelt down next to her, all male and warm. She could smell his aroma. The scent from his shower was familiar to her now. His piercing black eyes roved over her flushed face with relentless scrutiny. "Are you still so sad?"

"I've just been thinking about my grandmother this evening. I guess it's a case of knowing that when I get home, I'll have to deal with my life on my own. As you can see, I'm a c-coward," she stammered and wiped the moisture off her face. "How was your day?"

Shadows had darkened his features. "I'd rather not talk about it." He took hold of her hand and smoothed his thumb over her wrist. "Naturally you feel closed in, so how about we go out tonight? We'll go to a local cabaret with music and dancing. I'm off duty. Here in the desert we believe music helps dispel sadness. Does that appeal to you?"

"It sounds wonderful."

"Good. While you freshen up, I'll do the same and

come by for you in ten minutes." He got to his feet. "Don't forget to bring a wrap, it will be cool out."

"What should I wear?"

"The outfit you have on is perfectly adequate, but if you wish to change, that's up to you."

She watched him leave, but she had no intention of going out with him in pants and a top. After deciding the black was too dressy, she decided on her cream-colored dress. She put it on over her head and pulled the hem down to her knees. The sleeveless cotton outfit more or less skimmed her body. An insert of cream lace formed the neckline.

She only had one pair of high heels, black. After slipping them on, she put on lipstick and brushed her hair, then reached for her black sweater. By the time she heard his voice coming from the sitting room, her excitement at going out with him was so great, it sent her heart tripping off the charts.

To her embarrassment she almost *ran* into the other room, leaving him to believe she couldn't wait to be with him. With her face hot, she stared at the tall, striking, black-haired man standing there in beige trousers and a black silk shirt.

"You look lovely." His deep voice resonated through her body.

She could hardly talk. "Thank you." There were no words to describe his masculine appeal.

Between his lashes, his black eyes gleamed. "Shall we go?"

They left the suite and walked down several long hallways to a palace entrance in companionable silence.

Though their bodies never touched, Lauren felt the electricity between them like a living thing. She stepped outside into a garden of palms where the last stages of twilight could be seen through the fronds. The perfumed air was still hot.

He took her sweater before helping her into the waiting black limo, evidently a privilege he enjoyed due to his position at the palace. Their arms brushed. The touch of silk against her bare arm left her trembling with unassuaged needs.

Lauren was so aware of him, she scarcely noticed where they were driving. Before she knew it, they slowed down and stopped in front of a restaurant with a bistrolike facade. She heard Arabic music before he escorted her through a doorway of beads to the dark, smoke-filled interior.

The place was filled with locals and a few tourists. They were seated at small square tables surrounding a dance floor with a band playing in the background. A heavyset man at the bar nodded to him and indicated an empty table beneath a balcony that ran along one side. No sooner had he seated her than a waiter came over.

Rafi flicked her a probing glance. "What is your pleasure?"

"A cola."

"Nothing stronger?"

"Not tonight."

"So be it." He said something to the other man in Arabic, then moved his chair next to her and put his arm around the back of hers. His closeness sent a wave of delight through her body. "You're about to see one of our women belly dance," he spoke next to her ear, disturbing her hair. "If she dances for me, it will be to make you jealous because you're the most beautiful woman in the room."

Lauren smiled and lifted her eyes to him. "How many times have you made *her* jealous by coming in here with one of your favorites?"

The waiter returned with two colas, followed by fanfare from the band, saving him from answering.

A woman close to forty, and built along the lines of Farah, undulated onto the dance floor. Her loose black hair swung back and forth below her waist with hypnotic rhythm while her stomach and hips did the most amazing things.

As Lauren looked around, she noticed that most of the audience was made up of men. This close to the woman, Lauren could understand their fascination. She danced with enough seductive expertise to restart a heart that had gone into cardiac arrest.

Lauren cast a covert glance at Rafi whose gaze was riveted on the desert beauty with her red lips and flashing black eyes. Her spangles and bracelets made their own brand of music. The woman worked the floor. Near the end of her routine, she approached their table.

The dancer flashed Lauren a look that could kill before her gaze settled on Rafi. While she put on a show for him alone, bending backward to give him a good long look at her, Lauren saw unfeigned desire in the woman's eyes. It was so blatant, Lauren looked down. When the music ended, the dancer didn't move away.

He said something to the woman. She backed away

slowly. But at the last moment before she disappeared, she shot Lauren a look of venom. Lauren grabbed her glass and drank all her cola at once.

The second she put her empty glass on the table, she heard the band start to play a song she could identify. Rafi stood up. "Let's dance."

In a euphoric daze, Lauren moved into his strong arms. She'd been in them before, but this time it was different. He held her so close, she could feel his hard-muscled body down to their feet. There was no place to put her arms but around his neck. As she did so, she felt his hands rove over her back and pull her up tight against him.

"It's a good thing we're surrounded by people. Otherwise I would devour you," he admitted with a frankness that caught her off guard. "Have I frightened you?" he whispered against her lips.

"No." Her voice throbbed, she needed him the way she needed air to breathe.

"That's good because I'm going to kiss you. It's something I've wanted to do since the moment you woke up after the sandstorm." So saying, his compelling mouth closed over hers.

At the first taste of him, the room, the music, the people…everything faded into nothingness. All she was aware of was this man who'd set her on fire. She didn't know where one hungry kiss ended and another one began. Filled with indescribable ecstasy, she never wanted this rapture to stop.

Her grandmother had prophesied it. With the right man, the passion in Lauren would be unleashed. She knew now her whole life had been waiting for Rafi who'd brought her to life and was making her feel immortal. *Malik's words.* Like grandfather, like granddaughter.

A groaning protest escaped her swollen lips when he suddenly relinquished her mouth and put his hands on her upper arms to separate her from him. She watched him swallowing hard. His breathing sounded shallow. "We have to leave," he said in a husky voice.

Lauren couldn't bear it, but when she saw everyone in the candlelit room looking at them, she realized she'd been so enthralled, she'd forgotten where they were. Another belly dance was about to begin. Lauren needed no more urging and hurried outside ahead of him.

She climbed into the waiting limo without his help. When he got in, he sat opposite her. The car started moving. He eyed her for a long moment. "I'm not going to apologize for what happened in there."

"Did I ask you to?" she cried. "I'm the one who practically threw myself at you. Obviously it shouldn't have happened, so please—let's not get into a dissection of my emotional lapse."

They rode back to the palace in a silence punctuated with her heart pounding out an irregular rhythm. It would never go back to normal. When they arrived at the entrance, she grabbed her sweater lying on the seat and took off, anxious to reach her suite. Halfway down the first hall, his long strides caught up to her.

She kept going and soon arrived at her destination. He followed her inside the doors. Without closing them he said, "I'll say goodnight. In the morning after breakfast,

Nazir will come for you and show you out to the limo where I'll meet you."

Her hands made a fussing movement. "Won't you have to be on duty?"

"I'm making the time for you."

His words made her body go weak. "Thank you for taking me out tonight. I loved it, even if the dancer wanted to kill me."

"I believe she did. What's interesting is that all the males in the room wanted to kill me. Goodnight."

To Rashad's chagrin, the night turned out to be an endless one. After getting up, he paced the tiles, counting the minutes until he could be with her again. When it was time, he dressed in a non-royal Bedouin robe and sunglasses.

Her eyes exploded like green fire when he slid into the back of the limo next to her a few minutes later. She wore tan pants and a white top. Her fragrance was always a feminine assault on his senses.

"Good morning." He kissed the corner of her mouth because he couldn't help himself and felt her quiver. Their desire for each other was tangible. "I thought you might like to go shopping in the souk. You'll need a translator, so I'm offering my services." He clasped the hand nearest him and heard her take a deep breath.

The Oasis, a three by five mile rectangle, contained the village where he'd taken her last night. In no time at all they reached the center. He told the driver to drop them in front of the Almond Tree Café and wait for them.

She put on a pair of sunglasses and got out after he'd

helped her. Together they started moving among the locals. A few tourists were about. They walked in front of the shops in the bazaar. With her blond hair and fair complexion, not to mention her enchanting figure, she was a target for every eye.

Enough items were displayed to please the typical tourist. Though she moved slowly and inspected everything, she didn't buy anything. "If there's something that catches your eye, I'll barter a good price for you."

"Thank you, but I just like to look." They eventually turned a corner. Halfway down she paused. "Oh good. A bookstore." After going inside, she asked in English if the owner had a book in Arabic on the Shafeeq dynasty. The old man didn't understand.

Rashad's brows met. She wanted a book on his family? That made no sense to him. "Maybe I can help. What kind of book do you mean?"

She turned to him. "Any literature on the Shafeeq family. Something I can take home as a souvenir."

There wasn't such a thing in the public domain, but she didn't know that. He asked the owner in Arabic. The old man shook his head before breaking into a long explanation.

Rashad translated for the owner. "Would you like a cigar box with a likeness of Sheikh Umar or Sheikh Malik on the top?"

A genuine look of excitement broke out on her face. "I'd love both of them! How much does he want for them?"

"I'll get the price down for you."

"No—" She put a hand on his arm. "He has to earn a living."

When Rashad told her the notated price, she signed one of her traveler's checks that paid him three times the amount. It brought a broad smile to the man's face. He put the boxes in a sack for her.

"Is this the extent of your shopping spree?" he teased.

She chuckled. "Yes."

"Then let's walk back to the Almond Tree for a juice drink."

"I could use one of those."

Rashad thanked the owner. He caught hold of her hand once more and they made their way through the village like a married couple. By the time they returned to the palace, the sense of belonging to her was so strong he could taste it, and he tightened his grip.

This would be what it was like if he could have a normal life with her. They could live and love to their hearts' content, sharing all those little things lovers did with no fear of it coming to an end.

A month.

With the sand in the hourglass steadily emptying into the bottom half, each minute meant he was drawing closer to the time when there'd be no more happiness.

He left her at the door to her suite, telling her he'd get in touch with her later because duty called. She eyed him soulfully with those gorgeous green eyes before closing the door. As it clicked, he fought to repress a curse that this thing had happened to him.

Torment didn't begin to describe his emotions.

Despite the mystery he hadn't solved, he still had the medallion in his possession so she would not be able to use it against his family. What he should do was have her flown to El-Joktor today!

Nazir could accompany her and personally escort her onto a jet headed for Geneva. If she ever tried to come back, she would discover all borders to his kingdom were permanently closed to her. Knowing she was barred from Rashad's sight, he might be able to bear going through with his nuptials.

But what if he couldn't?

Terrified of that answer, he rushed back to his suite, needing to act. He looked around the apartment as if he might find a magic solution to his turmoil. There was none. What kind of a son was he? What kind of a king would he make if a soft traitorous woman with bewitching green eyes and golden hair could reduce him to this state?

At war with himself, he fought the battle for a few more minutes before he picked up the receiver of his land line. Forcing himself to speak, he called the airport in El-Joktor and booked a one-way flight to Geneva for one passenger.

Determined as he'd never been in his life, he rang his mechanic and asked that a helicopter and pilot from his father's fleet be ready for flight within the hour. Finally he phoned Nazir and asked him to report to his suite.

Within minutes his assistant arrived at the door. Rashad invited him inside. Before he backed down from his intentions he said, "I find it necessary for you to assist me with one more matter concerning Mademoiselle

Viret. She'll be leaving Al-Shafeeq within the hour."
At least that's what he was saying while he still had a
shred of princely honor left.

His assistant looked shocked, but said nothing.
Rashad could always depend on the other man's discretion even if he'd witnessed his secret comings and
goings from the American's room.

"I want you to accompany her to El Joktor and see
that she's put on the flight to Geneva leaving at four this
afternoon. The reservation has already been made. I'll
bring her to the eastern gate and meet you there in a
half hour."

"Very good, Your Highness."

With Nazir gone, Rashad left his quarters for the
garden suite. After being out in the heat, he imagined
Lauren would be resting with an icy fruit drink. Little
did she know she was about to be scuttled away from
the palace into a helicopter and flown far away.

Once her jet was in flight, the camel would be out of
the tent.

As soon as Lauren had returned to her room, Farah
came by for her and asked if she would like to see the
new foal her husband had given her?

Lauren grabbed at the invitation. Watching Rafi walk
away just now had come close to killing her. She needed
company and enjoyed spending time with the princess.
After her hope of finding some kind of information on
the royal family had had been dashed by the bookshop
owner, she could use some cheering up.

During her travels, Lauren had been to great cities

and shrines all over the world and had always come away with souvenir books and pamphlets. But as this was her first trip to the Arabian desert, it was possible that under the laws of the Shafeeq dynasty, nothing official was put in print for the public.

She was sorry about that. If she'd been able to purchase such a book, she would have found an expert Arab translator back home to reproduce it in English for her. Naturally there was generic information in encyclopedias and periodicals on some facet of tribal warfare. But she would have treasured a tome on the royal family. After all, she shared a portion of the blood flowing through Farah's veins. Some of their DNA was the same.

While they were exclaiming over the adorable new filly, Farah was called to the phone. She was only gone a brief time. When she returned she said, "That was Nazir. He says you are to go to your suite right away."

A frown marred Lauren's brow. "Why?"

The princess shook her head. "I don't know, but it sounded important. I'll walk you back."

"That won't be necessary, Farah. I know my way now. Thank you for bringing me here. I'll talk to you later."

Maybe he had a private message from Rafi.

Nazir met her outside the door to her suite. "Thank you for coming so quickly, mademoiselle. If I might speak to you?"

"Of course."

She opened the door and went inside. He followed. "I am here to inform you that the king is aware of your distress after being caught in the sandstorm. Since he doesn't want you to have to wait any longer for a caravan, he has given his permission for you to be flown by helicopter to El-Joktor immediately. I will accompany you to your jet which will leave for Geneva at four o'clock this afternoon."

Lauren reeled, incapable of speech. With these plans having been made, it meant she would never see Rafi again. So that was why he'd taken her on a tour of the Oasis this morning. He'd known her time was up. Her heart shriveled at the realization.

"If you will be so kind as to pack, I will ask the staff to take your personal belongings to the helicopter waiting outside the gate. You have time to eat your lunch. It is waiting on the table. Do you have any questions for me? Otherwise I'll return in thirty minutes."

She was so shocked by the turn of events she couldn't think straight. "Wh-what about my passport?" her voice faltered.

"It will be given to you at the airport. Is there anything else?"

"No," she whispered in absolute agony. For once her pain was too deep for tears. "I'll be ready." She despised the tremor in her voice that revealed her emotions.

"Very good, mademoiselle."

The second Nazir left, she ran to her bedroom and packed, realizing it was all over. She would fly away, but her heart would remain here. She wondered what Rafi would say if she told him she didn't want to leave yet.

She wished there were some way she could delay her departure, if only for another day. *He'd* become the most important thing in her life. Lauren wasn't ready to be ripped away from him, but fate had decreed it.

When she carried her suitcases into the sitting room, she saw her lunch tray, but couldn't possibly eat and sank down on a chair to wait.

"Lauren?" Rafi entered the room without knocking.

She looked at him, then glanced away quickly. "Nazir told me the king has arranged for me to leave. I'm glad you came so I could say goodbye to you and thank you for everything."

He came closer. "You look ill."

"I'm sorry if you've caught me reacting to the news."

"You don't wish to leave yet?"

"I'm sure that sounds ludicrous to you."

"Not at all," he said in a benign voice. "You Americans have a saying. 'Better to take the hell you're sure of.' It's only natural to cling to what is real to you here rather than return to an uncertain future without your grandmother."

"Who made you so wise?" She smiled gently at him.

"Perhaps not that wise since I'm not satisfied you're telling me everything. I insist you unburden yourself." He hunkered down and grasped her hands. She loved it when he touched her. Lauren never wanted him to stop.

"Why do you think there's anything more?"

"Because the little nerve in your throat never stops throbbing."

She immediately pulled one of her hands away to cover the spot.

"You see?" he asked silkily. "One can try to hide, but the body will always give something away."

"You think I'm hiding something?"

He turned her hand over and made circles against her palm with his thumb. The sensation was so erotic, he had to have heard her moan. "I know you are," he whispered.

She couldn't take any more. "There is one thing, but it's an entirely selfish wish on my part. I wouldn't want the king to think I was ungrateful for everything he's made possible. I'll always be in his debt, and *yours*, even though you deny much of the part you played in my being well enough to g-go home," her voice broke.

She didn't have a sense of home anymore and Rafi knew it. Maybe she really was ill and would need to see a psychiatrist when she finally returned to Switzerland. "Nazir will be here soon. I think I have everything." She tried to remove her hand and get up, but his rock-hard body blocked any movement.

"Look at me," he said in a husky tone that sounded more like a command.

Lauren did his bidding and found herself wanting to fall into him.

His gaze fell on her lips. She had the sensation of being kissed, yet he'd done nothing! "What's the one thing you want?"

The one thing she wanted was to stay here with him, but she knew that was impossible. Still, if she could have a few more days. He couldn't help but hear the dangerous knock of her heart against her ribs.

"Mustafa mentioned a place called the Garden of the Moon. He said I would especially appreciate it." She'd already lied about their caravan driver once, but the risk of revealing the real reason she wanted to see it was too great.

"Maybe it's foolish of me, but after coming all this way, when I'll never be here again, it seems such a shame not to see it before I leave, but Princess Farah said it's not allowed."

His hands tightened almost painfully on her fingers before letting them go, but she welcomed the pain. It made her feel closer to him. "It's forbidden to tourists, but I'll make an exception for you this one time." His words came out sounding like a vow. He rose to his full, intimidating height and looked down at her with glittering black eyes.

She was thankful to be sitting because after hearing that she'd been given a reprieve, her body caved. "But the arrangements to return to El-Joktor—"

"They can be changed. A few more days will make no difference in the scheme of things. Nazir will take care of everything."

She finally stood up on legs of rubber, staring into his eyes. "You really mean it?"

He cocked his dark head. His male beauty shook her to the core. "You should have said something earlier. It's a small thing you ask."

"No, it's not." She breathed heavily. "Everything you

do for me causes an inconvenience to someone, but I appreciate this more than you can imagine."

"I believe you." There was no hint of mockery just then. "Now you have to do a favor for me."

"Anything."

She heard his sharp intake of breath, not realizing she might have sounded as if she were being provocative on purpose. "In order to get the full benefit of the garden, you have to see it after the moon comes up. Therefore, I want you to rest and I hope, get some sleep. I'll come for you tonight at seven-thirty. Eat a filling dinner."

"I will."

"Have you ever ridden a horse?"

"Many times."

Something flickered in the dark recesses of his eyes. "Wear boots and bring your cloak to keep you warm. Today it was hot in the desert, but tonight the temperature will drop."

She smoothed an errant curl off her forehead. "Don't you have to stay at the palace on duty?"

A strange gleam entered his eyes. He studied her for a moment. "Several of my staff are always available."

"But what if it's an emergency and you're needed?"

"I always keep my phone with me. If necessary, Nazir would send a helicopter for us."

He started walking toward the door. She followed him. "Then I'm relieved."

"Remember to get plenty of rest."

After his tall, powerful body disappeared out the doors, she walked through the suite to the garden unable to contain her joy. *Rafi*— Tonight they'd be alone together. She leaned over to smell the fragrance of the huge, rare yellow and white hibiscus. Just one night with him. If it was all he was willing to give her, then she'd take it and be grateful.

She folded her arms and clutched them to her waist. This man had a power over her so complete she knew she would die if she couldn't be with him tonight. Anyone hearing that thought expressed would tell her she needed some serious therapy. Anyone except her grandmother who'd made a prediction about her a long time ago.

CHAPTER SIX

RASHAD WATCHED THE GREAT ORANGE-RED BALL sink below the horizon. It wouldn't take long for there to be a drop in temperature that would continue to fall. Night descended fast in the desert. He had no concern. This had been his playground as a boy. He knew all of it. Should the unimaginable happen, such as another sandstorm, the GPS transponder he wore on his wrist would bring help.

He had no idea why Lauren wanted to visit the Garden of the Moon, but before the night was over, he would have his answer. She'd been quiet during their journey from the palace. Too quiet.

He looked back. Her white cloak flapped behind her as the wind blew here and there, tousling her blond curls. She rode as though she'd been born on a horse and allowed her mare, Zia, to follow behind his stallion. Smart woman, smart horse.

Zia was a product of the desert and had learned early to plant her hooves where Jabbar had already displaced the sand. That way she preserved her strength. Both horses had been packed with everything Rashad required for them to spend the night together.

His gorgeous tent intruder was out to seduce him in earnest. When he'd found her waiting in the sitting room, seduction had been on her mind. Unshed tears of a devil or an angel. It made little difference at this point.

Because she desired him on top of the mission she had yet to carry out, he was looking forward to the experience more than anything he'd anticipated in his life. Tonight there'd be a three-quarter moon. By the time they reached their destination and made camp, the lesser light would appear in the black canopy enveloping them.

Halfway there Rashad pulled back on the reins to allow Lauren time to come alongside him. He darted her a searching glance. Heat rising from the sand wafted before their faces. "Would you like to rest?"

"If you're worried I'm tired, I'm not. But if you want to stop for a minute, that's fine."

"I think I do." He reached for his water bag and drank his fill. She followed suit with her own.

Rashad had made camp hundreds, maybe thousands of times in his life, but never with a woman because he and his men always had to be on their guard. Having her along was an entirely new experience, and it raised the stakes.

As she lowered her bag, their eyes met. He could no longer see the color in hers, but the luminescence still shone through in the darkness. An enchantress. That's what she was.

Eager to make camp, he tucked in his water bag and rode on without saying anything to her. She caught up to him again and stayed at his side. From time to time he gave her covert glances. To his continual amazement she looked around with an air of suppressed excitement. She seemed too happy. Nothing had ever twisted his insides like this before.

"We're almost there. After we ride this long dune to the top, we will have arrived."

"I can't wait—" she cried, then raced up the slope ahead of him. She rode hard. The sight of her cloak flying behind her was like poetry in motion. Poor Zia had to be in shock.

None of his bodyguards had sounded an alarm. Clearly there were was no one out here tonight except the two of them. On a burst of exhilaration because he had another twelve hours alone with her, Rashad charged after her, bursting the bonds that had held him back.

Just once she looked behind her. When she saw him gaining on her, she laughed and urged Zia on. He overtook her before she reached the top. Feeling like a schoolboy, he leaped from the saddle.

While he waited for her to appear, he drew two parts of one of his tent poles from the camping gear and connected them. Once he'd buried the end of it in the sand, he tethered his horse's reins to it.

In another minute she came riding up the crest. He walked toward her and reached for Zia's bit to slow her down.

"That was wonderful!"

She dismounted without his help, sounding winded and carefree. If he hadn't held her sobbing body in his arms several times, he wouldn't know this laughing, happy woman was the same person. "What can I do to help?"

Rashad smiled as he led Zia to the pole to attach her reins. "We'll unload the horses and put up our tent first."

He'd purposely said *our* tent, not surprised he didn't meet with any modest protest. They worked in harmony to get it erected. She exclaimed over the beautiful rug he'd brought to put on the floor of their small tent. More sounds of excitement poured out of her as he layered the rug with silk duvets and pillows.

"Those are going to feel good. You were right. It's already getting chilly." While they were watering the horses she said, "Are we going to make a fire?"

"No. It would spoil the effect."

"What effect?"

"Moonlight. The essential ingredient to bring the garden to life. Didn't Mustafa tell you?"

"No," came her subdued response.

But someone else had.

"In the beginning, our tribe worshipped the moon god because they were a pastoral people who kept watch over their flocks at night. This garden you're going to see represents the moon god's abode. It's a sacred place and ancient as time itself. The nearby oasis is the moon god's gift to the tribe to make sure there's an abundance of water to keep it green year-round. The palace was built there for that reason."

"What a fascinating story. Thank you for enlightening me."

For a long time she'd been playing her game with the expertise of a master, but once she saw the garden, he would bring it to an end. In a lithe movement he pulled a little pouch out of his saddlebag and handed it to her. "Here. Have some *qandi*."

"What is that?"

"Candy. You Americans borrowed the word."

He felt her smile as she dipped her hand inside and withdraw some sugar-coated almonds. "Um. These are delicious." She took a few and gave him back the bag. He tossed several in his mouth before putting it inside the opening of the tent.

Rashad glanced up at the eastern sky. While they'd been busy, the moon had been making her ascent. It was time. "Walk with me up to the curl of the dune." He reached for her hand. As their fingers entwined, he felt that same quickening in his blood, but it was much stronger than on the day of the sandstorm.

With each step of their short trek, he realized he'd been tempting fate all along. It was far too late to turn back now. He didn't want to. In fact no power could make him. That was the terrifying part.

Lauren's grandmother had told her that the sheikh had taken her to the Garden of the Moon, but she'd only talked to her about Malik and what had happened with him, not about the garden itself.

When they reached the edge and Lauren looked down, she could never have conceived of the sight that met her eyes. The man at her side squeezed her hand tighter, conveying emotion she thought she understood, but still waters ran deep inside him.

A drastic change had occurred in the landscape. The dune served as an escarpment. Below she saw fantastic formations laid out so perfectly, she let out a cry of astonishment. They looked like huge, fat topiary trees, the kind you see in the parterre gardens of the Orangerie at Versailles in France. Only they were made of sand sculpted by strange wind currents favoring this particular area of the dunes.

She was so staggered, it took her a long time to take it all in. Finally she exhaled a breath. "This is the most extraordinary, beautiful, out-of-this-world sight I'll ever see in my lifetime. No wonder your tribe has always held this spot sacred. So do I," she whispered.

It explained the half moon on the medallion King Malik had given her grandmother. Everything made sense. Her hand went automatically to her throat to feel it, forgetting it was no longer there. The same wind that had torn it off her had carved this monument. There were forces here she didn't understand. Hairs lifted on her arms that had nothing to do with the chill of the night.

"Cold?" he inquired in a quiet voice, never letting go of her hand.

She was running hot and cold at the same time. "Yes."

"It's late. You go back to the tent. I'll join you in a minute."

Her pulse quickened as she started back. Already the wind, dancing about, had erased the footprints they'd made coming up. *It is written in the wind* was a phrase she'd heard many times. Now she understood what it meant.

The wind had changed her life. She wasn't the same woman who'd flown to El-Joktor on a quest to know more about her grandfather. That woman had been buried in the sand. After her body had been transported to Al-Shafeeq, a new woman had been brought back to life by forces greater than she knew, by a man greater than any other.

Taking advantage of being alone, she lifted the tent flap and tossed her cloak inside, then went around the back. When she'd refreshed herself, she moved to the front and sat down inside the doorway to pull off her boots. After she'd held them over the sand and tipped them upside down, she emptied her socks and stashed everything in a corner with her cloak.

The wind blew enough that she lowered the flap to keep out the sand. It was pitch-dark inside, but she loved it. Still in her jeans and cotton top, she picked her side and climbed under one of the puffy quilts. Tucking the nearest pillow beneath her head, she lay there and waited while he did whatever needed doing to make their camp secure.

Soon she saw a small glow and watched his shadow as he moved about. After a few minutes the flap went up. He'd lit a lantern beneath an overhang with sides that prevented the wind from coming in. He set it on a rug he'd rolled out. Next to it sat a bowl of water and a pile of hand towels. He'd already removed his cloak and boots.

Her gaze flew to his in surprise. The black fires in his eyes started her body trembling. She lay there entranced. "Are you thirsty?"

"A little."

He handed her the water bag. After she'd drunk from it, he put his mouth to the same place and drank. The gesture wasn't wasted on her. She watched the way the cords worked in his throat. His male beauty captivated her.

"Hand me your boots. I'll put them with mine." She did his bidding. "Now stretch your hands toward me."

She got to her knees and put out her hands. He knelt before her and dipped a towel in the water before washing them. The water was warm and scented with the faint fragrance of rose.

No one had ever washed her hands for her before. When he reached for another towel, she got a fluttery feeling in her chest. This time he began washing her face. With slow gentle strokes he covered her forehead and cheeks, her nose and mouth. With the tenderest of touches he wiped her neck and throat, even her ears.

Once he put the towel aside, she took a clean one. Imitating his actions, she washed his hands and forearms, wanting to bring him the same exquisite pleasure. His body was a miracle to her. She relished being able to touch him like this.

Another dip in the water and she was able to bathe his face to her heart's content, from his widow's peak to the crease in his bold chin. He'd shaved before coming. She marveled over his incredible olive skin burnished by the elements. His black eyebrows were beautifully shaped. His nose—every bold, rugged feature—was perfect to her.

Then there was his mouth. Like the mesmerizing dunes, its shape changed with his mood. Hard, soft, brooding, compelling. *Sensuous*. She put the towel aside, needing to feel it beneath hers. She ran her thumb across it, aching with need.

"Oh, Rafi," her voice shook. "If you don't kiss me again, I think I'm going to die."

"I've already died several deaths because of you," he whispered against her lips. "What a perfect mouth you have. I came close to eating you alive at the cabaret. That's why I forced us to leave. I didn't trust myself."

He cupped her face in his hands and began with a series of light kisses he pressed to all the places he'd washed, barely grazing her mouth.

She wasn't satisfied and protested with a moan. "Don't tease me. I can't take it."

"Then show me what you want," he said in a voice of velvet.

"You *know* what I want. *This*." She wrapped her arms around his neck and covered his mouth with her own, not allowing him any hiding place. A profound hunger had grown inside her. She was after his soul and his mouth was the conduit.

"*Lauren—*" he cried her name. His hands roamed her back and waist, drawing her into him as they drank both deeper and deeper. Her passion for him was so intense, her body quivered.

He lay her back down and followed her, giving her the kiss she'd been dying for. He was starving for her, too.

She knew he was, but after a few minutes she seemed to be doing most of the work.

While the cold wind blew against the tent, a fire roared inside her. Her body, her senses yearned for him. Every kiss had grown more intoxicating, yet she felt he was still holding back and couldn't understand it. Was something wrong?

"I want you, Rafi, and know you want me. I want you to love me all night," she cried from the depths of her being. "What's stopping you? Have I grown less desirable?"

"No." He sounded so distant. How could that be when only a little while ago he'd washed her hands and face in a ceremony so erotic, she would never be the same again. "You're infinitely desirable and you know it."

"Then—"

"Tell me who you are, Lauren Viret," he broke in.

"Who *am* I?" she whispered dazedly. She didn't understand. "What do you mean?"

"The Garden of the Moon is a sacred place of the royal family no one knows about, yet you admit you had knowledge of it before you came here. You claim that it was Mustafa who informed you. But if that's really true, then he will have to be punished."

"What?" Her intoxication had been so complete, she could scarcely comprehend he'd brought an end to their rapture. She sat up to clear her head.

"Mustafa knows there's a penalty for divulging that information."

"No—" she cried out, putting her hands on his arm.

"He wasn't the person who told me. I swear it! He's a good man who saved me from the storm."

Rashad raised up on one elbow. That mouth she loved had tightened to a thin line. She felt his body go rigid beneath her fingers. "Who then?"

He was deadly serious, sending her into shock. "Someone else told me about it."

"Was it Prince Faisal?"

At the mention of the name, she drew in a surprised breath.

"You *do* know him—" Suddenly Rafi sat up and became the forbidding chief of security.

"No—" she cried, shaking her head.

His hands circled her arms. "Don't lie to me, Lauren."

She could hardly swallow. "I'm not, but I did recognize the name just now. Paul, the man who wanted to marry me, told me he'd met a minor prince from the northern Arabian kingdom at the casino in Montreux. He'd said his name was Faisal."

"When was this?"

"A month ago, maybe less. He got an interview with him and some pictures."

"Go on."

Lauren moistened her lips nervously. "There isn't much to tell except that he told Paul there were photographic opportunities in the Nafud where he would rule supreme one day. When Paul came back to the apartment, he begged to come with me to the desert, but I'd already told him no. Why did you bring up his name to me?"

Lines bracketed Rafi's mouth. "He's the son of King Umar's brother, a man out to cause trouble within the Shafeeq family. It's no secret he intends to become king when King Umar dies."

"But King Umar has a son! Princess Farah said he would be king some day."

"Yes. But that won't stop Faisal from staging a coup." Rafi let go of her arms. "He's waiting for news of the king's illness and how close he is to death, but his informers can't get into the palace. Since you refuse to tell me the name of the person who told you about the Garden of the Moon, I made an assumption that there was a connection between you and Faisal. Only a handful of people know about the Garden of the Moon."

"You think I'm a *spy?*"

His eyes glittered dangerously. "Given the facts, what am I supposed to think?"

She couldn't believe this conversation was taking place. "The person who told me about the garden is dead now."

"If you're not working for Faisal, then what's the real reason you've come to Al-Shafeeq?"

"I've already told you," she said in a low voice.

"Yes, but how do I know you were telling me the truth?"

Lauren moaned. *Don't ask me any more questions.* She knew he was only doing his duty for King Umar, but it hurt her so badly she didn't want to talk anymore. He was torturing her. "Why don't you answer me?"

"With your intelligence-gathering team, it would be a simple matter to find out." She was getting in too deep and wanted to howl because it seemed her night of ecstasy wasn't going to happen.

"You lied about Mustafa. Why?"

Help. "To protect someone." *Me. My grandfather. The royal family.*

"You refuse to tell me who it is?"

"I *can't* tell you," she cried in anguish. "Have you never made a promise to someone you swore to keep to the death?"

He examined her upturned face, searching for any sign of weakness. After a tension-filled silence he said, "One."

"So have I, Rafi. One promise in the whole of my life. I can't break it, not even for you."

"Why?"

"Because it could hurt certain people." She drew in a fortifying breath before removing her hands to hug her upraised knees. "Believing that I have lied to you all along, why did you bring me here?"

"To uncover your secret." His voice sounded like the lash of a whip.

"I see." Her heart almost failed her. "Thank you for being honest with me. I thought you wanted to make love to me."

"I do."

"I wanted it, too," her voice throbbed, "more than anything you could imagine. But this thing is between us now. I can't get past it."

"You lived with it before I asked for the truth," he reminded her. That tone of mockery was back.

"I know this won't help, but I'm going to say it anyway. The person who told me about the garden didn't know this place was sacred. Now that you've explained, I'll make you a promise. No one will ever hear about it from me. When I fly away from Al-Shafeeq, the desert wind will sweep all memories from my mind."

She moved away from him and pulled the quilt over her. Beyond tears, she clutched the pillow, praying for sleep to come and bring this bittersweet night to a close.

Outside the tent she heard movement. She could have sworn he said something to the horses, then the light went out. While she lay there holding herself taut, he got in beside her, rustling her covers. He reached over and rolled her into him.

"After being outside, I need your warmth." His mouth descended once more. It was a kiss hot with desire.

Her body quivered before she tore her lips from his and buried her face against his throat. "It's too late. I'm a liar. You hate me for it."

"I would love to hate you," his voice grated, running his hands through her blond silk curls. He wrapped his arms around her. "Your body gives off heat like a furnace. Lucky is the man who warms himself next to you. I'm looking forward to holding you all night."

Being in his arms like this was divine torture. "I'm not going to ask about the women in your life because we've already had that discussion."

"You have an excellent memory." She felt his lips kiss her hair and brows. "What will you do when you're back in Geneva?"

"I'm not sure." The idea of going to America and

starting a new life sounded absurd now. In fact, the thought of leaving this tent was anathema to her.

"Have you no relatives to go to?"

"No. My parents died six months after I was born." *Ask me to stay, Rafi, and I will.* "But I have friends and plenty of money from my grandmother."

"Tell me how she came by her money."

"She was a Melrose from New York. They were in the manufacturing business and they made a fortune before they sold the company, granting my grandmother an income for life. Did I tell you she was a fabulous horsewoman?"

"She taught you well. You ride like one of my countrymen."

"I believe you just paid me a compliment." She would always cherish it. "In New York, we rode all the time and traveled everywhere together. She willed me everything including the apartment in Montreux."

"Why Switzerland?"

"Because it's so beautiful. Have you ever been there?"

"Yes."

"If I'd known you sooner, I would have invited you to the apartment. I can tell you're a horse lover. My grandmother would have loved talking horses with you."

His hands stopped roving over her back. "How do you know about my love of them?"

"I see the special way you care for them. A little while ago I heard you talking to them outside. There's a bond some people have with their horses. My mother had that same bond. She and my grandmother were very close. Now they're all buried next to each other in Montreux."

"That's where your roots are."

Some of them.

"I was born in New York, but we left for Switzerland when I was a child. I suppose that when I go back, I'll finish working on Richard Bancroft's journals. One day they'll be ready for the publisher."

"The way you refer to him, I take it Richard wasn't your grandfather."

She swallowed hard. "No."

"Then who was your mother's father?"

"That was my grandmother's secret." Like grandmother, like granddaughter. "Celia came from a time when you didn't talk about certain things." Lauren had already told him much more than she should have. "Goodnight, Rafi."

When she tried to turn away, he kept her held against him and locked his legs around hers. She was so on fire for him, she was afraid she'd stay awake the rest of the night. But she hadn't counted on how wonderful it was to lie in his arms where she could feel his heart pounding against hers. He was a bastion of safety. The sense of being protected came as a revelation. She nestled closer to him and knew nothing more until the smell of coffee brought her awake.

Lauren sat up with a start because Rafi wasn't still holding her. Outside the tent, the sky was blue. Inside was warm. She didn't need her covers. No telling how long the sun had been up.

"Rafi?" She hurriedly reached for her socks and boots

and put them on. He'd already been doing housekeeping chores. She wanted to help.

"Good morning, Lauren," he said in a voice an octave deeper than usual. His penetrating black gaze took in her complete disarray. He on the other hand looked magnificent as always. "Sleep well?"

The wind had died down. She pushed the errant curls out of her face. "What do *you* think?"

His lips twitched. When they did that, she almost had a coronary. "I think you should sleep with a man more often." But Rafi didn't mean himself. This was his goodbye speech and it hurt so terribly she wanted to cry it to the desert surrounding them. "Nine hours has done you a world of good."

"Nine? I slept that long? When did *you* wake up?"

"Half an hour ago." He handed her a mug of coffee he'd heated on a little burner.

She took a few sips. "Ambrosia. My compliments to the chef." She looked around and decided to walk up to the edge of dune, but Rafi stopped her.

"Don't."

Lauren turned to face him. "Why?"

"Let the picture of last night be the one to fill your mind when you leave for El-Joktor tomorrow morning. Without the moonlight, its impact is lost."

Tomorrow morning?

Pain caused her to take a deep breath. "I'm sure you're right."

"Try this." He handed her a roll from one of the bags. "It's sweet and will take the edge off your appetite until we return to the palace."

"Do we have to get right back?" Then she shook her head. "Wait—don't answer that. Duty calls and I've taken up too much of your time." She finished her food before returning to the tent to roll up the quilts and carry everything out to the horses for Rafi.

He was in a mood she couldn't decipher. Lauren knew that in his mind she had lied to him and continued to do so, but she felt no hostility from him. She sensed he had worries on his mind that had nothing to do with her.

Life without Rafi. *It is what it is, Lauren.*

Unlike her grandmother so many years ago, she wouldn't be going home pregnant with her lover's child. How much she suddenly longed to leave pregnant with Rafi's baby. He would never know and she could never tell him.

She worked faster to stave off her pain. Without his asking, she helped him dismantle the tent. Once the stakes and poles were packed, they were ready to leave. She threw on her cloak and headscarf before mounting Zia, but inside she was groaning from unbearable heartache.

He approached her side on his stallion and flicked her a glance. Their eyes clung for a moment. "Ready?" She nodded. They started out, making faster progress than they had last night. The horses knew where they were going. Zia was happy to have free rein.

Lauren purposely fell behind Rafi so she could feast her eyes on him in his robe and headdress for as long as possible. This episode in her life was fast coming to an end. She didn't want to miss a second of it.

Every so often they stopped to drink from their water

bags, then pushed on without talking. They'd said it all last night in the tent. Rafi wanted to hate her for lying to him. She could never get past that with him.

Before long they came in sight of the Oasis. Lauren had once read that a Bedouin burst into poetry and song when he saw the greenness after being many weeks in the sand-drenched wilderness. She'd thought it such an odd thing to do until she too had been out in it.

Ah, Rafi... I can't bear to lose you.

The palace loomed ahead. They made their way to the west entrance where Nazir and two other staff were waiting for them.

"I'll contact you later." As Rafi dismounted, she scanned his face, which had been scarfed the whole time except for his eyes. With the bearing of a prince, he walked away from her and disappeared. Naturally his first priority was to report for work, but she almost begged him not to leave her.

Needing an outlet for her emotions, she leaned forward to pat Zia, then dismounted quickly.

"Welcome back, mademoiselle. A hot bath and a meal are awaiting you."

"Thank you, Nazir." While he escorted her inside, the two other men took care of the horses.

He left her outside the door of her suite and she hurried inside. After removing her cloak and boots, she quickly discarded her clothes and stepped into the bath. Rafi had ordered it especially for her because he knew how good it would feel after riding beneath a blistering sun.

But wonderful as the scented water felt lapping

around her head and body, she'd sell her soul for another
night like last night. She closed her eyes, replaying every
second from the moment he'd started washing her hands
with the towel.

He'd created a world of beauty for her inside that
tent. They were the acts of a man who worshipped the
woman he loved. If there were no lies to have destroyed
his trust, would he have worshipped her enough to ask
her to stay here at Al-Shafeeq because he couldn't live
without her?

She knew what her answer would be, but realized the
question would never pass his lips.

After his shower, Rashad hitched a towel around his hips
and drank a cup of black coffee. He'd had his sources
checking on facts for him since early morning. So far
everything Lauren had told him was the truth.

There had indeed been a Melrose family from New
York that had made a fortune in manufacturing. Certain
other facts had also been verified. As for Mustafa, she'd
even admitted lying about him in order to protect him
because she didn't want the poor man punished. She'd
convinced him Faisal hadn't been involved, too.

He tossed the medallion and chain in his palm.
The gold he held in his hand proved she'd come to Al-
Shafeeq on a mission she still refused to talk about. But
even not knowing the reason hadn't mattered to him last
night. He'd wanted to make love to her and would have,
but for the one thing his father had engrained in him
from the time he'd come of age.

"You're a prince, destined to be king, Rashad. Enjoy

our women at your discretion, but stay away from forbidden fruit. The strongest man can be tempted to take a bite. Once he does, he will eat the whole and lose his way because of it.

"*You,* my son, don't have that luxury. For that to happen to you will bring disappointment to your mother and me, but that is nothing compared to the shame and dishonor you will bring upon yourself. You cannot reclaim your honor once it is gone, therefore you cannot be an honorable husband and father to your children, let alone serve a nation that needs its strongest son to rule."

When Rashad would have lost his head at the last moment, a picture of his wedding night to an innocent Princess Azzah in a month's time wouldn't let go of him and cooled his blood.

Tomorrow morning Nazir would accompany Lauren to El-Joktor. *As he should have done yesterday,* but for Rashad's need of her. It was so great, he'd gone off with her instead. Now his agony was at its zenith.

Today he would fly to Raz and immerse himself in work. He might even stay over in order to avoid further temptation and not return to the palace until tomorrow after she'd gone. It was a lame plan, but he was a desperate man.

Even if he pressured her enough to know the whole truth, it would change nothing. His life's path had been set from the moment he was born. She was the forbidden fruit. The ultimate test. He checked his watch. Twenty hours from now, she'd be gone. *Forever.* That word was so hideous, he couldn't dress or get away from the palace fast enough.

Once he reached Raz, he drove the Jeep to the outskirts where the foundation of the new refinery would be built. After levering himself from the seat, he walked around the perimeter, wanting to get a feel for it before the actual work began.

His plan for a new era of prosperity was about to get underway. In time they'd make enough money to build more infrastructure. The list of things to be done stretched from one end of the kingdom to the other.

He looked all around, brushing the sweat off his brows with his forearm. On the one hand, Rashad had been blessed in abundance. On the other, he was denied the one thing that brought a man true happiness.

According to his father, Rashad couldn't have that. He was a prince, and that kind of happiness was for ordinary men like Tariq. His assistant couldn't wait to go home every night to his bed where he found the woman he loved waiting for him.

Rashad's father had been right about one thing. He'd tasted Lauren last night and her fruit had been so sweet, he knew he would crave it over and over again for the rest of his life. That was his penance.

How many years was he going to be tortured by her taste? One misstep had already eaten away at his soul. His eyes smarted.

He supposed if there was one mercy, it was that Princess Azzah would have no expectations. Undoubtedly she too had a secret love she would have to say goodbye to in order to obey her own father. Rashad could conceive of no greater hell than to sleep with her when both of them would only be going through the motions in order to produce offspring.

His father had done it. So had his mother. So had his grandparents. Somehow they'd all lived through it and survived.

In the end, was that all it meant? To survive?

His thoughts were so dark and grim, Tariq had to remind him his phone was ringing. He glanced at the caller ID. Why would Farah be phoning him? If it wasn't about their father, then this had to do with Lauren. He felt a rush of adrenaline before he clicked on.

"Farah?"

"Forgive me for disturbing you. Can you talk?"

"Yes." He walked a little distance off where the others couldn't hear him. "Is this about Father?"

"No. It's about Lauren."

His body tautened. "Go on."

"I don't quite know how to say this."

He shifted his weight. "Just come to the point."

"Lauren isn't like the other women you've enjoyed over the years, Rafi. I'm afraid she has taken your attention too seriously."

His hand formed a fist. "Why do you say that?"

"Because I've been with her this afternoon. She told me she's leaving tomorrow, but she shows all the signs of a woman who doesn't want to go."

Tell me something I don't already know, Farah. The thought of Lauren never coming back was destroying him.

"You're usually so careful. I think she's really hurting."

"What would you have me do?"

"I don't know. Talk to Father. Tell him you're not ready to get married and see where this thing leads with you and Lauren. I like her very much."

"It can't lead anywhere. You know that."

"No, I *don't* know that! You'll be king one day. Prevail on father to change the rules. A good king is a better king if he's happy!"

His throat swelled because Farah was his champion. "You want me to change centuries of tradition to take what I want?"

"Yes—if it means you can live your life with the woman you love."

"I never said I loved her."

"You didn't have to. You're a different man since you flew her out of the sandstorm. There's a look in your eyes I've never seen before. Our sisters have noticed, too. If you let her go, then you have a stone for a heart. When father's gone, you won't have to worry about filling his shoes. Yours will crush his." She rang off.

The silence on the other end deafened him. He spun around and raced back to his Jeep. Tariq joined him in the front seat. "What's wrong, Your Highness?"

"You don't want to know. I have to get back to the palace immediately."

En route he phoned Nazir and told him to keep an eye on Lauren's activities. Nazir was able to tell him she was having dinner in Princess Farah's suite. Rashad gave him further instructions about the plans for her flight to El-Joktor in the morning, then he hung up.

Once he arrived at the palace, he went to his suite for a shower and change of clothes. He decided to wear a suit in a stone-gray color with a white shirt and tie. After a visit to his office to clean up some paperwork, he left for the garden suite with the half dozen newspapers he hadn't read that morning.

Normally he scanned them before leaving for Raz. He didn't trust the television to tell the truth about anything. The printed news wasn't much better, but there were a few editorials that informed to a certain extent.

He let himself inside Lauren's suite and turned on the lamp at the desk after ordering his dinner and a carafe of hot coffee. While he waited for it to arrive, he made a call to his mechanic to be sure everything would be ready for tomorrow's flight.

Once he was served his food, he sat down and began reading. By the time he'd gotten to the fourth newspaper, he heard the door open and looked up.

The blonde woman who entered the sitting room wore the sleeveless black dress from her luggage and a pair of black high heels. Between her stunning face and figure, his lungs tightened in reaction.

She stopped in her tracks when she saw him. "Rafi— I didn't realize you were in here or I would have left Farah's suite sooner."

"I only got back from Raz a little while ago." He put down the paper. "In another minute I would have come looking for you. How was your dinner with Princess Farah?"

"We had a lovely time."

"What did you do?"

She stood there, rather nervously, he thought. "Mostly she talked about her brother. Their thirty-fifth birthday is coming up and she's in charge of getting the present for him while her sisters plan the party. We discussed everything from horse blankets and saddles, to a bronze of some kind for his desk. She still hasn't made up her mind."

He nodded and got to his feet. "And what did *you* talk about?"

"This and that." She rubbed her arms. "Look— I've imposed so much on your time I feel guilty. You don't have to keep me company. I need a good night's sleep before I leave in the morning. Why don't we just say goodbye now."

"You *want* to say goodnight?"

CHAPTER SEVEN

LAUREN AVERTED HER EYES. "I think it would be best. I have to pack." She started for the bedroom, but Rafi followed her. With her heart thudding, she stepped out of her high heels and walked over to the wardrobe to get her suitcases.

After putting them on the bed, she packed her boots and high heels followed by her cloak and headscarf. Then she emptied the drawers. The pants and blouse she planned to wear on the flight home she laid out on the back of the dressing-table chair with her sandals. It didn't take her long to get the bulk of it done.

He stayed where he was with his hands at his sides. She noticed they were forming fists. Good. She was glad to see he wasn't in control any more than she was. Had he decided he wanted to make love to her after all? Maybe she'd make it easy for him.

Without glancing in his direction, she unzipped her dress and stepped out of it, putting it on top. After shutting the cases, she set them on the floor. Beneath her dress she wore a modest slip over her underwear. It covered her better than the cotton shift from the hospital had done.

When he did nothing, she looked at him half in longing, half in despair. "What is it you want, Rafi?"

He moved closer. His black eyes raked her body. "I'm going to ask this one more time. Tell me why you came to the Oasis and why you wanted to see the Garden of the Moon. Then we'll really talk."

"I'm sorry, but I told you I made a promise to someone and that's why I can't tell you." Ignoring him, she turned off the light and got into bed, pulling the covers over her. "Goodnight. I'll be ready in the morning when Nazir comes for me."

Suddenly he flung his suit jacket and tie on the end of the bed. The next thing she knew he'd pulled up a chair and sat next to her like he'd done that first day. "Don't you know there are factions that would cause harm to the king and his family?"

"I realize that," she came back. "But I'm not one of them. If you recall, I wanted to leave the palace and return to El-Joktor as soon as I was able to stand on my own two feet without fainting. You've had the authority to send me on my way at any given moment."

He nodded his dark head. "That's true, but there was a reason why I didn't, and you know what it is," his voice rasped.

"You mean because of our attraction to each other."

"What else?" Rafi reached for her hand. She tried to pull away, but he was too strong and clasped it. "You can tell me the truth. I'll keep your secret. I swear an oath on it."

Her lower lip trembled. "I swore an oath, too."

She heard him breathe heavily. "Then we're dead-locked."

"I guess we are."

"This isn't the way it has to be." He looked forbidding in the semi-darkness.

"It isn't the way I want it to be either." Whether he knew it or not, he was rubbing his thumb across her palm, sending little darts of awareness through her body. This was agony in a new dimension. "Please let go of me." If he went on touching her, she'd beg him to spend the night with her.

He released her hand as though it were a hot potato and shot to his feet. "Is there no reasoning with you?" he asked in a harsh whisper. "No way to reach you on any level?" She'd never heard him angry before.

"Not any more than there was a way for me to reach you last night, even when I threw myself at you. Your seduction of me was complete. I've been reduced to nothing. You can consider me your greatest triumph. You and I have reached the bitter end. Do what you have to do to me."

She couldn't bear it when she saw him get up and reach for his jacket and tie. It meant he was leaving, and this time he wouldn't be back. He was almost to the door.

"Rafi?" she cried out. "There's *one* confession I will make."

He wheeled around, his body alert.

"I want you to know that you made me *live* and *feel* like I've never lived and felt before. That's a distinction no other man will ever hold."

Lauren lost track of time before he left the room. It hurt so much to think he suspected her of some wrong-doing, she'd taken off her dress to provoke him to action. Never in her life had she done anything so outrageous. No one who'd known her before she'd come to the desert would recognize the person she'd become. She didn't know herself anymore.

What was really insane was that a part of her wished he would detain her here forever. That way she wouldn't be separated from him.

Of course, in her heart of hearts he wouldn't do such a thing because he wasn't that kind of man. But he *would* send her away in the morning.

Knowing she wouldn't be able to sleep for a long time, she walked out to the patio to breathe in the scent of the flowers. She marveled that they grew and thrived in one of the harshest of climates on earth.

Lauren moved around to look at each one and savor its fragrance. He'd brought her out here the first time they'd eaten together. The night had been magical.

Tonight was different. It was late and the air had grown cooler. One glance at the desert and she finally went back to the bedroom, hoping she'd be able to sleep. But her thoughts were too full of him and it was hours before oblivion took over.

When morning came, a numbness seemed to have taken over her body. Once she'd eaten breakfast, Nazir arrived for her. Before that, several maids had taken her bags on ahead. Nazir escorted her out of the palace to the waiting helicopter. Naturally there was no sign of

Rafi. It almost destroyed her, but there was nothing she could do about that now.

She climbed in the back seat next to one of the guards and strapped herself in, having to accept her fate. Nazir took the co-pilot's seat. After he'd put on his head gear they were off. Lauren couldn't bring herself to look back. Frozen with pain, she closed her eyes.

"Mademoiselle? Do you feel ill?"

Nazir always did his job. He would report everything that went on to Rafi. If nothing else, her pride couldn't bear for him to be told she'd had a meltdown in the helicopter on the way to El-Joktor, so she opened her eyes and smiled. "I'm fine. Just sleepy."

He nodded, but he clearly didn't believe her. A heavy sigh escaped her throat.

For once there were clouds in the sky. Not serious ones. They were too high and wispy. The Nafud only got a little more than an inch of rain in a whole year. There'd be no storm today.

She heard the pilot talking through his headphone, most likely to the control tower in El-Joktor. The forty miles that would have taken two days to cover by caravan would only take fifteen minutes or less. They'd already been in the air for a while.

The next time she looked out the window, she saw they were making their approach, but as they drew closer, she realized it was to a smaller city than El-Joktor with a ridge of mountains behind it. Houses, horses, trucks, cars, Jeeps.

"Nazir? What city is this?"

"Raz, mademoiselle."

"Why are we landing here? Is something wrong?"

"No, mademoiselle. Don't be concerned. You're perfectly safe."

The pilot put the helicopter down next to a sprawling one-story building at what looked like a mining site.

"If you'll follow me," Nazir said after she'd jumped to the ground. He was so polite when he knew he'd left her with no choice. He led her inside the modern, air-conditioned interior. It was a well-decorated office building with every convenience.

"This way, mademoiselle." He showed her around one corner and opened a door for her to step inside. It was a CEO's suite, to be sure. "Please be seated." She sat down on one of the leather chairs. Nazir disappeared, then came back with a bottle of cold water and handed it to her.

"Thank you."

"You're welcome. If you need a restroom, it's through that door."

Once he'd gone, she removed the bottle cap and drank while she awaited her fate. When Rafi walked in through a connecting door, the bottle slipped from her hand and fell to the floor. What little liquid was left spilled on the rug.

He retrieved it before she could, and set it on the desk. "Don't worry. It will dry soon enough." She stared up at him. "This is where I spend the majority of my time."

He'd dressed in typical Arab garb, white top and white pants. He'd tucked them into his leather boots. Rafi was all male; whatever he wore, he looked spectacular.

"Your job covers a lot of territory. It makes a woman's

head spin. Why didn't you let the helicopter fly me to El-Joktor?"

His eyes smoldered, sending another delicious shiver down her spine. "Because there's a matter of unfinished business."

"I was afraid of that." She had the pleasure of watching the muscles harden in his striking face.

"Close your eyes and lower your head, Lauren."

If this was some kind of a test, she was determined to meet it with a brave face. "They're closed."

Even before his hands encircled her neck, her heart had jumped to her throat. She felt his legs press against hers while he fastened something at her nape. After he stepped back he said, "You can open them now."

As she lifted her head, she felt something dangling against her chest. She looked down, not believing her eyes. *My medallion!* Her gaze flew to his. She discovered him lounging against his desk with a strange gleam in his eyes.

He nodded. "The second Dr. Tamam saw it, he took it off the chain and informed me. While you were still unconscious, I removed the chain from your neck and pocketed both for safekeeping."

Lauren could hardly breathe. "All this time you've had it, yet you flew me to the site of the sandstorm in my pathetic hope to find it?" She covered her mouth with her hand. "Since I was brought in, you've known everything!"

"Not quite." He folded his arms.

"Until the other night, I didn't realize the ancients of your tribe worshipped the moon. The medallion had much more significance than I'd realized." She shook her head.

"I'd hoped you'd tell me the whole story behind it so I wouldn't have to resort to these extreme measures. This is your last chance to come clean. Why didn't you give me the complete description of the medallion when I asked you?"

She unconsciously ran her thumb over the relief. "Because I needed to protect certain people from being hurt in case they saw it and made a connection."

"Certain people at the Oasis, you mean."

Lauren looked away. "Yes."

"And what connection would that be?"

"I thought you knew—" she cried out, jumping to her feet.

"I do, but I want to hear you say it."

There was no help for it. "To the royal family."

"Be more specific."

It was no use. Lauren couldn't take any more. "Oh, all right! To King Malik."

He straightened from the desk. "Why single out King Malik? The medallion is the symbol of the entire royal family who've been in power for centuries."

"Because *he* was the one who gave it to…someone I knew," she mumbled, but he heard her.

The second the words were out of her mouth, she watched in fascination the way his chest rose and fell, as if he'd sustained a shock. "But that's impossible."

She blinked, totally confused. "Why?"

"Only when a new male member of the royal household is born is one minted. He wears it for life and is buried with it."

The king's love for her grandmother must have been beyond comprehension. "Did anyone see if King Malik was buried with his?"

Rafi went so quiet, she knew he didn't have an answer for that question. It was probably the only time in his life he'd been thrown by a mystery he couldn't solve.

Dark lines etched his arresting features. "Tell me the name of the person he gave it to. According to you, they're dead. You don't have to worry since you've already broken your promise to them."

Tears pricked her eyelids. "Because you tricked me—"

"Not tricked. I only held off showing you the medallion until I could see that nothing else would work. It's my job to protect the royal family. I had to be certain you weren't working for a hostile entity sent to spy on the king or the acting sheikh."

"You mean Prince Rashad."

"That's right. You and I are both on the same side, Lauren."

Put that way, she realized they were, but she couldn't forgive him for what he'd put her through. She bit her lip. "H-he gave it to my grandmother," she said in a tremulous voice.

More silence. "When?" he eventually demanded.

"I'm sure if you went back far enough in the official documents of the kingdom, you would see that she traveled here alone, unmarried, when she was twenty years old.

"Someone told her about the Al-Shafeeq Oasis that blossomed like a rose in the desert. Being an adventurous person, she decided she wanted to see it."

Rafi stood there still as a statue. "She *met* Sheikh Malik?"

Lauren nodded. "He was twenty-six at the time. He saw her walking in the palace garden. She had hair my color, but she wore it down her back to her waist. He was so drawn to her, he had her brought to him. One thing led to another. At one point he took her to see the Garden of the Moon."

A strange sound came out of Rafi.

"It was there he told her he would love her until the day he died. But he couldn't marry her because he was betrothed to another princess."

Her voice shook as she told Rafi the rest. "H-he said she would have to leave the Oasis and they would never be able to see each other again. The only thing he could give her was the medallion. He put it around her neck and told her that every time she looked at it, he would sense it and know she was remembering their time beneath the moon when she'd made him feel immortal."

Rafi rubbed the back of his neck. A white ring encircled his lips.

"When my grandmother knew she was dying, she took the medallion off her own neck and gave it to me. She said that next to me, it was her most priceless possession. After she passed away, I had this longing to come to the oasis and see where it had all happened."

She undid the chain. "Thank you for returning this to me, but it isn't mine to keep. It belongs to the royal family. I would think King Umar would like to have something that belonged to his father. Princess Farah said that King Malik was known as the great sheikh for making the kingdom stronger.

"The more I think about it, the more I want him to have it in payment of his generosity and kindness to me while I've been recuperating at the palace." She went over to the desk and left it on top. "Now am I free to go?"

His eyes were dark slits as he looked at her. "No."

She struggled for breath. "Do you want me to stay, Rafi? If you do, tell me—"

He gave her a look so tormented, she was shaken by it. Without saying a word, he walked behind his desk and opened the drawer. She saw him take out a ring and put it on. Then he moved toward her and extended his hand, palm down.

When she saw the same medallion in the form of a ring, she got that curious din in her ears again, as she'd felt when the sandstorm had hit without warning. The same presentiment came to her now that she was about to go through another life-changing experience and nothing would ever be the same again.

One by one, every moment with him, every nuance, every warning, every word and gesture fell into place as pure revelation flowed through her. Her eyes searched his and she saw the truth written in them. She remembered him telling her that the kind of marriage she imagined wasn't written in his stars…

"*You're* Prince Rashad," she whispered.

No-o-o. Oh no—

She felt his hands cup her face and lift it. The eyes staring down at her blazed with fire. In panic, she tried to pull away from him, but he held her fast. "Don't be frightened of me, Lauren. You know I could never hurt you. Now that everything's out in the open and there are no secrets between us, all I want to do is love you."

"No—" She jerked away from him and staggered back. "We can't!—"

How could she have been so blind? He was the acting sheikh. Of course. Hadn't he talked and walked like a prince?

His hands slid to her shoulders, kneading them restlessly. "I need you and I know you need me. I have an apartment through that door. We'll start all over again and be alone for as long as we want. We'll do what we've been wanting to do from the very beginning. You're all I desire," he declared passionately, running his hands up and down her arms.

"You're all I want, too," she answered honestly. "You have no idea of the depth of my feelings, but we can't be together because—because it would be wrong!"

"Wrong?" He laughed almost angrily. "How can you say that when we know what we feel for each other is so right no power has been able to stop it?"

She agreed. There'd been something that had come over her before she'd even fully awakened after the sandstorm, bonding her to him. But she possessed a secret he didn't know anything about yet. Lauren could keep it to herself, but could she live with the guilt of it over a lifetime?

She already knew the answer to that question. No

matter how much she wanted to belong to Rafi, she realized the knowledge would eventually destroy them both. She had to tell him the truth.

"Don't look at me like that, Lauren," he implored, misunderstanding the pain in her eyes.

"I'll go to my father tonight. When I explain to him about us, he'll call off the plans for my wedding. I couldn't go through with it now." He started kissing her face, every part of it, thrilling her so completely her body throbbed with need.

"Farah said it would take place at the end of the year."

He smothered a moan before clasping her hands and kissing her fingertips. "The timeline has changed to a month away. I have to go to him before another day passes."

Jealousy drove a shaft through Lauren. "Who is she?"

"It doesn't matter."

"Of course it matters. Already she's planning to be your wife. You can't undo what's been done."

"You think not?" he came back in a voice of command. "Princess Azzah will rejoice when she learns it's been called off."

No, she won't, Lauren lamented. Farah didn't have to tell Lauren that her brother was desired by other women. There was no other man like him. "She's already anticipating her marriage to you."

His eyes, so black and alive, searched hers. "Why are you fighting me on this?"

"Because I'm not going to be the woman responsible

for causing a breach with your father. When you and I were together the other night, I thought you were the king's chief of security. I thought you were emotionally free.

"When you told me you were a pot who still hadn't found its cover, I interpreted that to mean you were a bachelor who enjoyed the life you were living. But now that I know your identity, everything's changed.

"Farah has told me things. She says your father isn't well. One day you'll be taking his place. You have no choice but to carry on certain traditions for which your life has always been destined."

Lines marred his handsome features. "Your argument rings hollow. You're holding back another secret from me. What else did Farah tell you?"

"Nothing."

"That's not true. Why won't you look at me?"

"Rafi—I need to leave."

"You're not going anywhere." He grasped her arms. "I want to know what my sister said to you."

"It was just a passing comment, but it appears to have come true." In fact Lauren was haunted by it now.

She heard him expel an angry breath. "Is your silence intended to be punishment for me because of the way I dealt with you?"

"No—" she cried, hearing the anguish in his voice. She lifted imploring eyes to him. "While we were all at the pool the other day, she made the passing comment you had been too favored. She said your mother feared that because you'd been given every gift there'd be a price to pay.

"I asked her what she thought her mother meant. She said that heaven was jealous of you. One day when something came along you wanted more than anything on earth, it wouldn't be granted."

Rafi bit out an epithet. She didn't have to know Arabic to understand the emotion behind it. "I love Farah, but she's a very dramatic, impressionable person who overstates things at times without realizing it."

"Nevertheless, she was right about this, wasn't she? You and I want something that can't be. I'm going to have to do what my grandmother did. Somehow she found the strength to leave King Malik and never come back. Now it's my turn to do the right thing."

"No," Rafi declared. "That's *not* the right thing for either of us. My nation has come out of the Dark Ages, Lauren. I've been doing everything possible to modernize our way of life and keep up with the new advances, particularly in technology.

"Change has been inevitable and will continue to happen. The point is, I'm not a product of another era. I was born into this one. Some traditions from the past are good and important. Yet I have a different view of many things to make life better for our people.

"Certainly I haven't grown up being in favor of archaic marriage traditions, but until I met you, I was willing to go along with my father's expectations. Now everything has changed. I refuse to be like my grandfather who was so strong in his own beliefs, he gave up the great love of his life and sent your grandmother away. That decision left them no joy."

When Rafi would have kissed her mouth, Lauren hid

her face from him. "Then I'll have to be strong for both of us."

"Why?" he cried.

"Because King Malik was *my* grandfather, too."

Silence shattered everything.

As the revelation computed, his arms tightened around her. "Say that again?" he whispered into her hair.

With tears in her voice she said, "We both have the same grandfather. My grandmother went home not realizing she was pregnant with my mother. *Their* daughter."

His hands tightened in her curls before sliding to her upper arms. He eased her far enough away to look into her eyes. "But that's impossible."

"No. It was very possible, Rafi. They were lovers for a fortnight…i-in the garden suite."

Rafi's skin took on an ashen color.

"Though she never admitted it to me, I'm positive she wanted his child when she realized she couldn't have him."

Unspeakable pain turned his features to a facsimile of his former self. "I don't believe you."

"A DNA test would provide definitive proof, but I have something else that will convince you."

His eyes impaled her. "What proof?" In them she saw grief so profound, she had to look away.

"It's even stronger evidence than the medallion. I'll show you. In my wallet there are some pictures of my mother."

She watched the struggle he was having to swallow. "Let me see them."

Lauren moved out of his arms and reached for her purse. Inside her wallet she kept a packet of pictures. She pulled out the three she'd put in of her parents. The first colored photo she handed him showed a full-length picture of Lana holding Lauren outside on the deck of her grandmother's apartment. At five months Lauren's golden hair had come in curly and gleamed in the sun.

Rafi took the photo in his fingers and looked at it, then at Lauren. "But this is a picture of Samira!"

"It's an amazing likeness of her. When I met your sister, I could see my mother in her. But if you'll look closely, you'll notice Lake Geneva is in the background and she's holding a *blonde* baby. That's me at five months."

"No," he moaned the word.

Gaunt with shock, he looked at the other two pictures she handed him. Both of them showed her blond father holding Lauren, with his arm around her mother.

A lifetime seemed to pass before a haunting groan came out of him filled with soul-deep anguish. He caught her to him. They clung with a desperation that racked them both.

"Tell me this is a nightmare and we're going to wake up," he begged.

"I wish I could," she whispered, her agony beyond tears, "but you had to hear the truth. Celia named my mother Lana, an Arabic name. Our grandfather never knew. Neither did my mother. Celia told her that the man who was her father was just a man she'd met. Ships passing in the night.

"She claimed she never knew what happened to him, but it wasn't important because she and Lana had each other. That was all they needed."

A pulse throbbed at the corner of his mouth. "How could she have kept that news from my grandfather?"

She studied him through glazed eyes. "You of all people should know the answer to that question. His betrothal had taken place years before. He sent Celia away so there'd be no scandal. She loved him too much to cause him any distress.

"My mother had to accept the explanation and let it go. A few minutes ago when I realized who you were, don't you think I wanted to die? Now I've got to let you go the same way."

When she eventually found the strength to ease away so she could look at him, she didn't recognize the man; he seemed to have aged ten years.

"Lauren—"

She forced herself to smile through the tears. "You have a phrase for everything. 'It is what it is.' That's what we have to say now."

"But it *isn't* what it is—" he fired back in pain. "I won't allow it to be." He shook her gently. "No one knows about this but you and me. We'll forget everything because I'm not losing you!" He crushed her mouth beneath his.

For a time she responded, losing track of time and place because she couldn't help herself. But then the reality of what they were doing took hold. Much as she wanted to kiss and be kissed into oblivion by him, the truth was between them and she couldn't keep this up. It was no use.

As soon as he allowed her breath she said, "I could wish you'd told me who you were that first day. Then I would have closed my heart off to you, or broken down and told you we had the same grandfather. You always talk about fate. I'm afraid this time it had something else in mind for us.

"If only you could undo our history, Rafi, you truly would be a god, but you're still mortal and that means I have to go. Every minute I stay here, it's making it that much harder to leave."

"I won't let you." He tightened his arms around her, kissing her with refined savagery.

"We have no choice," she half sobbed the words. "Don't you see?" She caught his face between her hands. "We have two strikes against us. Even if we weren't re- lated, I can't remain here another second and jeopardize the life you were born to no matter what you say. You'll be king one day. Princess Azzah will be your queen. It's written!"

Finding her inner strength, she escaped his arms and flew out of his office. Outside the building, Nazir ran after her, but she didn't stop until she reached the helicopter, out of breath. He helped her inside with a concerned look on his face.

"Tell the pilot to take me to El-Joktor immediately. The prince has set me free. Please do this for me, Nazir. Please," she begged with all the strength of her soul.

"Yes, mademoiselle."

* * *

Since Lauren had fled from his arms like a sand devil spinning away with the speed of light, Rashad had sealed himself in his Raz apartment. Now that it was evening, the helicopter had come back for him.

During the short flight back to Al-Shafeeq, Nazir reported that everything had gone smoothly at El-Joktor. He had walked Lauren on to the jet without problem. Since then, he had had word that her flight had landed in Geneva. Was there anything else he could do for Rashad?

With nothing more to be done, Rashad assured him there'd be a big bonus in his paycheck for services rendered. After thanking the others, he went inside the palace and headed straight for his parents' suite. When he walked in, Farah came flying across the sitting room and threw her arms around his waist.

"I'm so sorry for speaking to you the way I did last night. Please forgive me, Rashad."

"There's nothing to forgive because I know love motivated you." He kissed her forehead. "I deserved it and a host of other things you didn't say."

"This morning I came to say goodbye to Lauren, but she'd already gone."

Rashad closed his eyes tightly. "She's in Geneva as we speak."

"You can pretend all you want, but I know you love her."

He studied his sister who'd always been there for him. "I won't lie to you about that, but she's gone now, so there's nothing more to be said." Their grandfather's blood flowed in Lauren's veins, too. One couldn't jump high enough to get over that camel's hump.

She touched his face. "You look ill."

"It will pass."

"No it won't!" she stamped her foot in a rare show of temper. "Go in to the bedroom and tell our father you can't go through with your marriage next month."

That checked him. "How did you know about the change of date?"

"Father's been looking for you all day and could not find you. No one knew where you were, not even Nazir. Your phone has been turned off. He got so upset he called the entire family and told everyone to look for you.

"I knew you were with Lauren, but I didn't say anything to give you away. When I asked him why he was so upset, he let it slip that you have to let Sheikh Majid know of your agreement about the new date for the wedding by tomorrow night."

"I'll go in to father now. Is mother with him?"

"No. She's still talking to the chef about the meal preparations for our birthday party in a few days. You know how she is." Farah's eyes filled with liquid. "She wants everything perfect for us, for you. So do I, but I know you're never going to know joy. You can't go through with this wedding, Rashad. It won't be fair to you or to Princess Azzah."

Rashad ran a hand over his face in despair. As he'd found out this morning, life wasn't fair. "Bless you for being you, Farah." He kissed her once more, then strode quickly to the bedroom where his father sat on the side of the bed with his bad foot propped on an ottoman piled with cushions.

His father simply stared at him. He didn't need to speak. Rashad already knew every word he would say if he chose to express himself.

"Farah met me in the sitting room. Forgive me for giving you a scare, father. I—"

"You need explain nothing. I have my own eyes and ears around the palace. If I didn't, I wouldn't have lived this long. The American. Is she gone?"

"Yes."

His father's dark eyes pierced through to Rashad's soul. "For good?"

A boulder lodged in his throat. "Yes."

"Good. Did you send her away with your baby?"

Rashad threw his head back in torment. "No. There's no possibility."

"That's even better. The wound that bleeds inwardly is the most dangerous. Tell me what's going on that has you writhing body and soul."

Rashad's pacing came to a halt. "When we buried grandfather four months ago, was he wearing his medallion?"

The change of subject caught his father off guard. "Who told you he wasn't?" he snapped uncharacteristically.

Pain shot through Rashad. Lauren's truth *was* the truth. He was crucified all over again with that knowledge.

"No one," he whispered.

"Since you know he wasn't wearing it, why did you ask me?"

Rashad shook his head. "It doesn't matter. I just wanted you to know it's been found." He reached in his pocket and drew out the medallion and chain. After staring at it for a minute, he put it in his father's hand.

Dumbfounded, his father eyed Rashad strangely. "How did *you* come by it?"

Rashad drew up a chair next to him. "The American woman was wearing it around her neck when I flew her to the palace more dead than alive."

His father's eyes filled with wonder. "Go on."

"Yes. Go on," his mother said. She'd come in the bedroom without Rashad being aware of it. She looked like an older version of Basmah, tall and lovely. She sat down on the bed next to his father.

For the next little while Rashad told them everything from the beginning, leaving nothing out. When he'd finished, his father said, "And throughout all this business, you fell in love."

"Yes." Rashad jumped up from the chair, unable to contain his emotions. "But she has Grandfather's blood in her just as I do." Nothing could have shocked him more in his life. No news could have devastated him more.

His father nodded. "Now I understand why you feel you can never see her again."

Rashad stared at his parents for a long time. "I realize I'm a great disappointment to the two of you, but what I felt for her went beyond honor or duty the moment

I carried her from the sand to the helicopter. It felt as though she'd been delivered to me. For me...

"Before I found out we had a grandfather in common, I planned to come to you and tell you I couldn't go through with the marriage to Princess Azzah because I intended to marry Lauren. When I took her to the Garden of the Moon, I realized I couldn't live without her."

His mother eyed him with tenderness. "That doesn't surprise me. You've always been led by what you believed in your heart, Rashad. I've been listening to everything you've said." She looked at his father. "I think it's time we told him, Umar. Don't you? I know we agreed not to as long as it wasn't necessary, but now I know that it is."

"Tell me what?" He couldn't imagine.

"If you want to know the answer, you need to be patient enough to sit down and listen to a story," his father chastised him.

His mother smiled. "It's a story you'll like."

That's what she'd always said when he was a boy too restless to hear all the words between the beginning and the end.

"Forgive me, Mother, but I'm not eight years old anymore."

"No," she murmured. "That's why you have to listen to your father."

His father cleared his throat. "It begins on the night I was camped on the desert with our patrols because there'd been a raid on one of our villages and we were keeping a watch out for more. I decided to scout around. My right hand, Saud, rode with me."

Yes. He knew. There was no man Umar had loved more than his childhood friend, Saud, but Rashad had heard the story many times of how Saud had protected his father from death before meeting his own, and he couldn't imagine what this was leading up to.

"The assassins had stormed through Saud's village first and killed many of the women and children, Saud's wife included."

Yes, he knew that, too. His father had ridden to that village and had found her lying in a pool of blood.

"What you don't know was that she'd delivered a baby that night who lay under her."

That did surprise, Rashad. His eyes swerved to his father's.

"He was still alive."

CHAPTER EIGHT

ON THE MORNING FOLLOWING her flight from Al-Shafeeq, Lauren drove to the cemetery and put white daisies on all three of the family graves. She lingered over her grandmother's.

"I took the trip you took, Grandmother, and guess what? I, too, fell in love with a great Prince of the desert, but our love wasn't meant to be. Instead of bringing home his baby beneath my heart, I have two cigar boxes, one with his father's image on the top, the other of your beloved Malik. I don't even have a photograph of Rafi." Tears dropped onto the marker.

"Like you, I can't go back to get one. All I could do was leave the medallion. It's in the hands of the man I love. Help me find a way to survive, Grandmother. *Please.*"

Unwilling for people to see her in this condition, Lauren hurriedly left the cemetery and drove back to the apartment. She knew she had to keep busy or go insane and decided she would start some major housecleaning. One day soon she'd phone her friends, but not right now.

After parking her car on the street behind two limos,

she got out, then came to a complete standstill. At least ten men wearing native robes and headscarves blocked the main entrance. Her heart jumped at the sight of them.

"Mademoiselle Viret?"

"Nazir—" she cried, shocked at the sound of the familiar voice.

He walked over to her. "Bonjour, mademoiselle." He smiled. "Please forgive the intrusion. If you would be so good as to come with us, we'll escort you to the plane King Umar has sent for you." The group had surrounded her, leaving her with little room to maneuver.

Her legs felt like water. "Don't you mean Prince Rashad?" Why would he do this now? It was a cruelty she wouldn't have expected of him. There could be nothing between them.

"No, mademoiselle. The king wishes you to return immediately. He would have come, but he can't travel in his condition. He asks if you will be kind enough to spend a few days at Al-Shafeeq with him and his family. He would like to meet Princess Lauren, the American granddaughter of King Malik."

Princess—

This meant Rashad had told his father everything. Lauren couldn't stop her body from trembling. "Much as I would love to meet him, I can't." She needed to root Rafi out of her heart. Of course that would never be possible, but to return to Al-Shafeeq…

"Prince Rashad predicted you would say that. He asked me to tell you that he will be away from the palace while you're there."

Her pain grew worse.

"Since he won't be present, he says there's no reason for you not to come. It will make his father and mother and his sisters very happy, *unless* you can't forgive him for a deception he felt compelled to carry out at the time for the safety of his family."

She rubbed her temples where she felt a headache coming on from all her crying.

"He at least asks you to forgive him as you would one who believes that the ways of his tribe are the laws of nature."

Oh, Rafi. Another one of his unique sayings that made her want to laugh and cry at the same time. This one wound its way into her heart with the rest of them.

She bit her lip. "Are you saying the king wants me to come now?"

"Yes. He hoped it would be a good time since you haven't yet settled back in to your home here."

Rafi might not be at the Oasis right now, but he knew her whereabouts and had eyes in the back of his head. "I would have to pack."

"The prince says that unlike other tourists you are a master at packing lightly. He is very impressed."

Oh Rafi...

"The King urges you to come. He says to remind you he's not well. He may not be your father, but you share the same blood and he already loves you as his half-daughter. He's aware your own father died before you could get to know him. Will you please accept him as your second father and allow him to spoil you a little bit?"

Her eyes smarted. Sheer blackmail.

Like father like son.

Lauren found King Umar to be much like any father and grandfather, surrounded by his family and loving it. The real miracle was that Lauren was a legitimate part of that family. He and his wife accepted her as if she were their long-lost daughter.

For three days they'd gathered at meal times in the king's sitting room to hear the story of her grandmother's great love affair with King Malik.

Naturally the conversation turned to Lauren and the things she'd done with her life. The older children bombarded her with questions about the places she'd traveled, the sights she'd seen when Richard Bancroft had been alive to take her on some of his expeditions.

On the third afternoon, Farah asked Lauren to go on a horseback ride with her around the perimeter of the Oasis. Knowing she'd ridden Zia before, Abdul had the mare saddled and ready for her. The horse made a nickering sound and nudged Lauren in greeting. When she mounted her, the memories were so overwhelming, it was almost debilitating for her.

"The family loves you, Lauren." She and Farah rode side by side. Their bodyguards went along at a discreet distance.

"I love all of you."

"Before you leave, there's something you should know."

Lauren couldn't do this anymore. "Farah—if this is about your brother, I'd rather nothing was said."

"But you need to know he talked to my father on the day you flew to Geneva. Whatever was said, his wedding to the princess was called off permanently."

A moan escaped her lips. "What a sad day for everyone."

"Not for Rashad. He couldn't marry a woman he didn't love."

Lauren gripped the reins so tightly, it cut off the circulation in her hands. "Does this mean your father will allow him to choose the woman he wishes to marry?"

"I don't know. But since he didn't force him to marry Princess Azzah, I have to hope he won't command him to marry someone else who will mean nothing to him."

At the thought of Rashad choosing a woman he could eventually love, physical pain attacked Lauren. "I'm sorry, Farah, but I can't talk about this. I can't."

"I'm sorry if I have distressed you. Come. We'll go back. The family is planning a special farewell dinner for you."

"Everyone has done more than enough for me."

"You still don't understand, do you? My father has asked you to stay here and live with us."

"I know, and I'm very touched, but I couldn't. My life is in Switzerland."

"Life is where your heart is," Farah corrected her.

Lauren had no answer for that. They rode back to the palace in silence.

After a long swim, the two of them parted company so they could get ready for dinner. Once back in the garden suite, Lauren showered and put on a filmy plum-colored sundress with spaghetti straps.

Because of King Umar's poor health, they ate all their meals in his sitting room, this farewell dinner being no exception. Seventeen family members gathered round.

Lauren and her grandmother had been a twosome before Richard had come along to make it three. To belong to such a big family now could have been a real joy except for one thing. One person…

Rafi's absence was the camel in the room no one talked about. Lauren missed him so acutely, she wasn't able to concentrate on the conversations going on around her. Tomorrow couldn't come soon enough to end this pain. The king insisted on flying her back to Geneva in his private jet if she wished to go.

After coffee, he clapped his hands to get everyone's attention. "One of my duties as king is to secure husbands for my daughters, which I have done. Since my father, King Malik, can't be here tonight to secure a husband for his granddaughter, Princess Lauren, the great honor has fallen to me."

Lauren had been eating a sugar-coated almond and almost choked on it.

"As I have the power to act in his stead, I've chosen a man of our tribe who is in every way worthy to be your husband. In a few minutes you will meet him and tomorrow formal negotiations will be made for your marriage."

Her eyes widened. Surely the king didn't mean it, yet

when she looked around, everyone was staring at her with a pleased expression—except Farah.

The princess got to her feet. "You can't do this, Father. She's not used to our traditions."

Lauren loved Farah for defending her. What the king had just said might have made sense to him, but it was impossible!

He nodded his graying head. "Nevertheless, it is not your place to counsel me, Farah," he spoke kindly. "Please sit down. Lauren has no one to protect her. We are her family now and must do what is best for her."

"But—"

"No buts. You've told me on more than one occasion that you have been very happy with my choice of husband for you. Therefore, you trust my judgment, don't you?"

"Yes, but—"

"Silence, my daughter."

He clapped his hands. Lauren heard the doors to the suite open. She jerked around in absolute panic and saw Rafi in the entry wearing a cream silk robe. Her heart turned into a battering ram as he walked into the room and sat down next to his father.

Nazir had assured her Rafi would stay away from the palace during her visit, yet here he was with that tall powerful body, looking more princely than any prince. The king must have insisted his son come to watch, but she couldn't do this, and she jumped to her feet.

She felt Rafi's piercing gaze on her, but she kept her eyes focused on King Umar. "Princess Farah was right, Your Highness. Though the last thing I would ever want to do is offend you, I can't go through with this because I don't wish to be married."

"You would say that to me, knowing I want to take care of a great wrong done to one of my family?"

"Forgive me, Your Highness, but it would be a much greater wrong if I were forced to marry a man I didn't love no matter how much I appreciate your wanting to take care of me."

"You prefer to live a solitary life and die of old age without knowing love or children?"

"Millions of women in the world do it," she stood her ground.

"Not *our* women," he came back.

"Putting aside my feelings for a minute, what about the man you would force to marry me? He would be a stranger to me."

"You will learn to adapt to each other's differences. A lifetime study to make the other person happy is one of the most exciting aspects of marriage. Let me give you an example. When my wife, Tahirah, and I started out, we were blessed with three baby girls.

"But during the pregnancy with Farah—which had taken a long time to happen—there were problems. Dr. Tamam said that once the baby was delivered, my wife would never be able to have another baby.

"We realized it wasn't written in the stars, but deep inside I knew my wife suffered because she could never give me a son. Deep inside *I* suffered because I knew she was suffering and I couldn't take her condition away.

"The night Farah was born, I was away fighting. It was at that same time my best friend Saud died saving my life. That night I learned his wife, Fadwa, had been killed in a village raid. When I found her body, I discovered she'd just delivered a baby boy who was still alive.

"I took him home to my wife, only to discover our little Farah lying in her arms. When I showed her Saud's son, she loved him on sight and asked if we couldn't keep him and raise him as our own. That was the wish of my heart, too, so the two babies became our twins. Only Dr. Tamam knew our secret."

All around Lauren she heard gasps, but none were greater than her own.

"Nothing could have made us happier. A life for a life. Though Saud's and his wife's deaths came at the appointed hour, their child's did not. Together, Tahirah and I vowed to raise him as if he'd been born from our bodies.

"I called him Rashad in honor of his birth father who was a man of flawless integrity. My wife called him Rayhan, the favoured one. His best friend called him Rafi, the exalted one."

Rafi…

"He's headstrong and modern-thinking. Indeed, he's so much like Saud, who always had vision, it has been as if I had my friend back in the form of his perfect son."

His wife nodded. "Rashad has been so perfect, there's been no princess to measure up to him. We feared we'd never find one good enough for him which is why we hadn't forced a marriage before now. But with his thirty-fifth birthday approaching, we picked Princess Azzah in desperation. She had some of the qualities we knew Rashad would admire."

King Umar nodded. "Then fate worked its will once more, and my father's granddaughter suddenly appeared out of the desert, more royal than any princess we could have found for our son.

"You have Shafeeq blood flowing through your veins, Lauren." He smiled at her. "We know Rashad very well and recommend him highly. He will make you a fine husband. Your marriage will secure the sheikhdom for Rashad after I'm gone."

Lauren's gaze fused with Rafi's as he started across the room toward her, but she was feeling light-headed. The last thing she remembered hearing was Farah's squeal of happiness before everything began to spin.

When she regained consciousness, her eyelids fluttered open and she became aware Rafi had brought her to the garden suite. She was lying on her bed.

"Rafi?"

He poured a glass of water for her. "Drink this first," he said emotionally, cradling the back of her head to help her.

Lauren stared at his beloved face while she drank. It was déjà vu for the third or fourth time. She'd lost track.

When he put the glass on the bedside table, she raised up on one elbow. His concerned black eyes made a swift inventory of her features. "Your color's coming back."

"What happened?"

"You fainted when my father said I would make you a good husband. I need to know if you did that because something has changed and you don't want to be my wife. He insisted on handling everything his way. I know it made him happier than he's been in years, but the truth is, I came close to having a heart attack when you slumped in my arms."

"You caught me?" she cried out in wonder.

"I watched your face start to turn white and acted before you slid to the floor. Don't ever do that to me again, darling. I couldn't take it."

"I've never fainted in my life." She looped her arms around his neck and pulled him down. He stretched out on the bed beside her. "I think it might have been because I had been granted the wish of my heart and my body couldn't take in that much joy all at once. A miracle has happened to us," she cried. *"Oh, Rafi—"*

She started kissing him all over his face, his hair, his neck. "Don't move. Don't leave me. I'm going to need till morning to believe this is really happening to us. I love my grandmother for giving me the medallion. I'm crazy about your parents for loving you enough to hold off on finding you a wife until I blew into your life. I love and adore you so terribly, it hurts."

"Even when I was so cruel to you on our campout?" he whispered against her lips.

"I knew there had to be a reason. The more I saw of you, the more I wanted to be with you. I lived for the moments you walked in this suite. Every time I saw you, I couldn't wait to find out what little tortures you had in store for me. At the Garden of the Moon I was shameless with desire for you."

"Do you think a woman with less fire or passion

could ever have held me?" he cried huskily. "Those were gifts I never planned on in this life. Then, when I thought they were miraculously within reach, it was all snatched away by your confession about our grandfather. My heart came close to dying."

"So did mine."

He kissed her deeply, then fastened the chain with the medallion around her neck. "I love you, Lauren. Marry me."

She touched it, feeling the warmth of his fingers against the metal. "I already feel married to you. Does that shock you?"

"No, *kalida*. It thrills and humbles me."

"Kalida?"

"My love, my darling." He sealed the endearment with another kiss that swept her away.

When she could breathe again she said, "I've been thinking about what to do with all my money, my inheritance. I want it to go into a fund for some of your big plans for the kingdom. My grandmother will be entirely approving. Anything you want, but I'll hold a little of it back to hire more bodyguards to protect you. I'm determined to stave off your appointed time until we're old and can die together."

"Your wish is my command."

When Lauren's cell phone rang, she felt too nauseous to turn on her other side and reach for it. But she made the effort anyway because it might be her husband. He'd wanted to make love this morning before leaving for Raz early, but she'd pretended to be asleep so he wouldn't know how sick she felt.

One look at the caller ID and she realized it was Farah calling. Making another superhuman effort, she clicked on and said hello to her sister-in-law.

"Good morning, Lauren. How would you like to go riding with me this morning?"

"Much as I'd love to, I'm feeling a little under the weather. Perhaps tomorrow morning. Please don't tell anyone else. I'm hoping it will pass because I don't want Rafi worrying about me. He has enough on his mind right now winding up the completion of the new smelter."

"Do you feel too awful for a visitor?"

Farah was excited about something. After four months of living at the palace, Lauren was adept at reading her moods. "No. Just walk in. I barely woke up and am still in bed."

"I'll be right there."

No sooner had Lauren hung up, than she had to dash to the bathroom where she was promptly sick. After rinsing out her mouth and brushing her teeth, she felt a little better, but she'd clearly caught some kind of bug. Yesterday morning she'd felt it coming on. Oddly enough tea and a roll suddenly sounded good to her.

She rang the housekeeper and asked that a tray be sent. Enough for two. Then she got back in Rafi's bed. They'd been living in his suite. As soon as he could take a few days off, they were going to fly to Switzerland. She planned to put the apartment up for sale and have all her things shipped to Al-Shafeeq. What they couldn't use, she would put in storage. Rafi wanted her to be completely happy.

While her thoughts were on her fantastic husband, Farah arrived at the same time as the maid and brought the breakfast tray into the bedroom. She put it on the coffee table and flashed Lauren a speculative glance.

"I thought you didn't feel well."

"Right after I got off the phone with you, I was sick in the bathroom. Now I'm hungry."

"How long has this been going on?"

Lauren blinked. "I started feeling queasy yesterday morning."

Farah's dark eyes lit up with excitement. "Both my pregnancies started off exactly like that. I bet you're carrying Rashad's baby."

Lauren slid off the bed and hurried over to hug Farah. "If I thought that were true, I'd fly to Raz and tell him."

"Then get dressed and go to the clinic. Dr Tamam will verify one way or the other. If you're not pregnant, then Rashad will want to know why you're ill because he watches every move you make. Honestly, Lauren, he's so in love with you it's sickening…in the most wonderful way of course."

"I feel the same way about him." She bit into a roll and followed it with several swallows of sweet tea.

Farah smiled. "The whole palace knew the day after you arrived here the first time."

A blush crept up Lauren's neck and cheeks. "I'm sure they do." She finished off her roll. "Before I get dressed and take your advice, tell me what you wanted to talk to me about."

"Well, Abdul and I have made a decision. Since Father and Mother told us Rashad wasn't their blood child, it has convinced us to adopt a baby. At first I was afraid to do it because I didn't think I could be a good mother. But when I see Rashad and Mother together, I know she loves him as if she'd given birth to him."

"Oh, Farah—" Lauren reached out and hugged her again, much harder this time. "That's the most wonderful news I ever heard. Now, come to the clinic with me and we'll see what the wise doctor has to say about me."

While Rashad was inspecting the smelter, he saw three helicopters from his father's fleet headed for Raz. Something had to be wrong, He whipped out his phone and called Nazir to find out what was going on.

"Nothing I've been informed about, Your Highness."

With his heart starting to thud, Rashad rang off and left the smelter for the area where the helicopters were about to land. Soon the doors opened and more guards poured out followed by a golden-haired woman. Lauren!

She jumped down and ran toward him.

He caught her in his arms and swung her around. Her fragrance, the feel of her body intoxicated him. "What are you doing here? You've never flown to Raz to see me before."

Her head fell back so she could look into his eyes. The light green of hers between those dark lashes dazzled him. "Forgive me for intruding, but something important has happened and I couldn't wait to tell you. I'll go inside your office until you can take a break."

"We'll go together. I decided not to eat lunch so I could get home faster to you this afternoon."

With their arms wrapped around each other's waists, they entered the building and hurried toward his office suite. Once inside, he closed the door and locked it.

"It's so hot! You need some water first." She would have gone over to his mini fridge to get him a bottle, but he pulled her back.

"First I need *this!*" His dark head descended and his mouth covered hers, devouring her with shocking hunger, as if they'd never kissed before. "I missed you this morning," he confessed on a ragged breath.

She knew what he meant. "I wanted you more than anything, too, but I didn't feel well. I've just been consulting with Dr. Tamam, actually. It's why I'm here."

In the next instant he took a shuddering breath and his hands tightened around her upper arms. She saw that white ring encircle his seductive mouth; she had come to recognize it as fear. "I've been too happy," his voice throbbed. "Tell me what's wrong with you." She actually saw tears in his eyes.

Lauren stood on tiptoe to kiss his lips, but they refused to cooperate until she gave him his answer. "I'm two months pregnant. We're either going to have a little Saud or a little Fadwa. Your birth parents made the most gorgeous son who ever lived. With you as the father of our child, we'll have to keep him or her scarfed for protection."

An explosion of joy lit up the deep recesses of Rafi's eyes. He picked Lauren up and carried her through to his apartment. Over the last four months he'd taken her to his bed more times than he wanted anyone to know about, but he'd never put her down so gently before. She was a miracle to him. He slid his hand over her stomach to feel her.

Her heart shone out of her eyes. "Rafi, it'll be a few months before we feel the little one kicking, but our baby's in there. The doctor has given me some medicine to help with my morning sickness. I hope that tomorrow morning I'll be able to wake you up first.

"I love mornings with you, Rafi. But then, I love every second of the day and night with you. I told Dr. Tamam I have a sickness because of you. Do you know what he said?"

"What?" he whispered, tracing her delectable mouth with his finger.

"That you were the luckiest of men to have a wife with such a sickness. He said he would pray that I'd go to my grave with it." She kissed his finger. "I told him not to bother. He'd do better to pray that I don't wear you out with my love. That's the reason I haven't come to Raz before now. I haven't wanted to distract you from your work."

He rolled her over carefully on top of him. "I dare you to try."

"You mean now?"

"Now," he growled into her neck.

Lauren's breath caught. "Don't you have to go back to work?"

"No. I've got all the work I can handle right here."
"Hours and hours?" she asked, already out of breath.
"Maybe days."
"Darling."

SECRET PRINCE, INSTANT DADDY!

RAYE MORGAN

This book is dedicated to Ineke
and all my Dutch cousins.

CHAPTER ONE

PRINCE DARIUS MARTEN CONSTANTIJN of the Royal House of Ambria, presently deposed and clandestinely living under the name of David Dykstra, was not a heavy sleeper. Ordinarily the slightest unusual sound would have sent him slipping silently through his luxury penthouse apartment with a lethal weapon in hand, ready to defend his privacy—and his life.

The sense that his life might be under threat was not outrageous. Since he was a member of an overthrown monarchy, his very existence was a constant challenge to the thuglike regime that now controlled his country. And as such, he had to consider himself in constant jeopardy.

But tonight the instinct to defend his territory had been muted a bit. He'd hosted a cocktail party for fifteen rowdy London socialites and they'd all stayed much too long. That had a consequence he didn't suffer from often anymore, but its effects were not unfamiliar to him. He'd had too much to drink.

So when he heard the baby cry, he thought at first that he must be hallucinating.

"Babies," he muttered to himself, waiting to make sure the room had stopped spinning before he risked opening his eyes. "Why can't they keep their problems to themselves?"

The crying stopped abruptly, but by now he was fully awake. He listened, hard. It had to have been be a dream. There was no baby here. There couldn't be. This was an adult building. He was sure of it.

"No babies allowed," he murmured, closing his eyes and starting to drift back to sleep. *"Verboten."*

But his eyes shot open as he heard the little rule breaker again. This time it was just a whimper, but it was for real. No dream.

Still, in his groggy state, it took time to put all the pieces of this mystery together. And it still didn't make sense. There was no way a baby could be in his apartment. If one of his evening guests had brought one along, surely he would have noticed. And if this same ill-mannered person had left that baby behind in the coat room, wouldn't they have come back for it by now?

He tried to shrug the whole thing off and return to peaceful slumber, but by now, that was impossible. His mind was just awake enough to go into worry mode. He'd never go back to sleep until he was sure he was in a baby-free abode.

He groaned, then rolled out of bed, pulled on a pair of jeans he found in a pile on his chair and began to stalk quietly through his set of rooms, checking one after another and wondering grumpily why he'd leased a place with so many rooms, anyway. The living room was littered with cocktail napkins and empty crystal wine goblets. He'd sent the catering crew home at midnight—a mistake, he now realized. But who knew his party guests would stay until almost 3:00 a.m? Never mind, the cleaning lady would arrive in just a few hours and make everything clean and sparkling again.

"No more parties," he promised himself as he turned back to his search, kicking a long feather boa someone had left behind out of the way. "I'll just go to shindigs at other people's homes. I can still maintain my information sources and let others deal with the hassle."

But for now he had an apartment to search before he could get back to bed. He trudged on.

And then he found the baby.

It was asleep when he first saw it. He opened the door to his seldom-used media room and there it was, tucked into a drawer that was serving as a makeshift crib. The little mouth was open, the little round cheeks puffing a bit with each breath. It looked like a cute kid, but he'd never seen it before in his life.

As he watched, it gave an involuntary jump, its chubby little arms lurching upward, then falling slowly back again. But it didn't wake. Dressed in a pink stretch jumper that looked a little rumpled and a lot spit up on, the child seemed comfortable enough for now. Sleeping babies weren't so bad. But he knew very well what happened when they woke up and he shuddered to think of it.

It was pretty annoying, finding an uninvited baby in your home and it was pretty obvious who was to blame—the long, leggy blonde draped rather gracelessly across his cantilevered couch. He'd never seen *her* before, either.

"What in blazes is going on here?" he said softly.

Neither of them stirred, but he hadn't meant to wake them yet. He needed another moment or two to take in this situation, analyze it and make some clear-headed decisions. All his instincts for survival were coming alert. He was fairly certain that this was no ordinary sleepover he'd been saddled with. This must have something to do with his royal past with its messy rebellion history and his precariously uncertain future.

Worse, he had a pretty strong feeling it was going to turn out to be a threat—maybe even the threat he'd been expecting for most of his life.

He was fully awake now. He had to think fast and make sound judgments. His gaze slid over the blonde, and despite his suspicions about her, his immediate reaction was a light frisson of attraction. Though her legs were sprawled awkwardly, reminding him of a young colt who hadn't got its bearings right just yet, they were shapely legs, and her short skirt had hitched up enticingly as she slept, showing the aforementioned legs off in a very charming way. Despite everything, he approved.

Most of her face was hidden by a mass of wiry curls, though one tiny, shell-like ear peeked through, and she'd wrapped her torso up tightly in a thick brown sweater. She wasn't really all that young, but her casual pose made her seem that way and something about her was endearing at first glance. There was an appeal to the woman that might have made him smile under other circumstances.

But he frowned instead and his gaze snapped back to stare at that gorgeous little ear. It was decorated with a penny-sized earring that seemed familiar. As he looked more closely, he could see it was molded in the form of the old Ambrian coat of arms—the coat of arms of the deposed royal family he belonged to.

As adrenaline shot through his system, his heart began to thump in his chest and he wished he'd picked up the weapon he usually carried at night. Only a very select set of people in the world knew about his connection to Ambria, and his life depended on it being kept a secret.

Who the hell was this?

He was pretty sure he was about to find out.

"Hey. Wake up."

Ayme Negri Sommers snuggled down deeper into her place on the couch and tried to ignore the hand shaking her shoulder. Every molecule of her body was resisting the wake-up call. After the last two days she'd had, sleep was the only thing that would save her.

"Come on," the shaker said gruffly. "I've got some questions that need some answers."

"Later," she muttered, hoping he'd go away. "Please, later."

"Now." He shook her shoulder again. "Are you listening to me?"

Ayme heard him just fine, but her eyes wouldn't open. Scrunching up her face, she groaned. "Is it morning yet?" she asked plaintively.

"Who are you?" the man demanded, ignoring her question. "What are you doing here?"

He wasn't going away. She would have to talk to him and she dreaded it. Her eyelids felt like sandpaper and she wasn't even sure they would open when she asked them to. But somehow she managed. Wincing at the light shafting in through the open door, she peered up through her wild hair at the angry-looking man standing over her.

"If you could give me just one more hour of sleep, we might be able to discuss this in a rational manner," she proposed hopefully, her speech slightly slurred. "I'm so tired, I'm hardly human at the moment."

Of course, that was a lie. She was human alright, and despite how rotten she felt, she was having a reaction to this man that was not only typically human, it was also definitely feminine. Bottom line, she was responding to the fact that he was ridiculously attractive. She took in the dark, silky hair that fell in an engaging screen over his forehead, the piercing blue eyes, the wide shoulders and the bare chest with its chiseled muscles, and she pulled in a quick little gasp of a breath.

Wow.

She'd seen him earlier, but from a distance and more fully clothed. Up close and half-naked was better. She recommended it, and under other circumstances she would have been smiling by now.

But this wasn't a smiling situation. She was going to have to explain to him what she was doing here and that wasn't going to be easy. She did try to sit up and made an unconvincing attempt at controlling her unruly hair with both hands. And all the while she was trying to think of a good way to broach the subject that she'd come for. She had a feeling it wouldn't be a popular topic. She would have to introduce it just right and hope for the best.

"You can do all the sleeping you want once we get you to wherever it is that you belong," he was saying icily. "And that sure as hell isn't here."

"That's where you're wrong," she said sadly. "I'm here for a reason. Unfortunately."

Little baby Cici murmured in her sleep and they both froze, staring at her for a moment, full of dread. But she sank back into deep slumber and Ayme sighed with relief.

"If you wake the baby up, you're going to have to take care of her," she warned him in a hushed voice. "I'm in a zombie trance."

He was sputtering. At least that was what it sounded like to her, but she wasn't in good judging form at the moment. He could have been swearing under his breath. Yes, that was probably it. At any rate, he wasn't pleased.

She sighed, shoulders sagging. "Look, I know you're not in the best shape yourself. I saw you when we first got here. You had obviously been enjoying your party a little too much. That's why I didn't bother to try to talk to you at the time. You know very well that you could use more sleep as much as I could." She scrunched up her nose and looked at him hopefully. "Let's call a truce for now and…"

"No."

She sighed, letting her head fall back. "No?"

"No."

She made a face. "Oh, all right. If you insist. But I warn you, I can barely put a sentence together. I'm incoherent. I haven't had any real sleep for days."

He was unrelenting, standing over her with strong hands set on his very tight and slender hips. The worn jeans rode low on them, exposing a flat, muscular stomach and the sexiest belly button she'd ever seen. She stared at it, hoping to deflect his impatience.

It didn't work.

"Your sleep habits are none of my concern," he said coldly. "I'm not interested. I just want you out of here and on your way back to wherever you came from."

"Sorry." She shook her head, still groggy. "That's

impossible. The flight we came on left for Zurich ages ago." She glanced at the baby, sleeping peacefully in the drawer. "She cried almost the whole trip. All the way from Texas." She looked up at him, expecting sympathy but not finding much. She made a face and searched his eyes, hoping for a little compassion at the very least. "Do you understand what that means?"

He was frowning like someone trying to figure all this out. "You flew here straight from Texas?"

"Well, not exactly. We did change planes in New York."

"Texas?" he repeated softly, as though he couldn't quite believe it.

"Texas," she repeated slowly, in case he was having trouble with the word itself. "You know, the Lone Star state. The big one, down by Mexico."

"I know where Texas is," he said impatiently.

"Good. We're a little touchy about that down home."

He shook his head, still puzzling over her. "You sound very much like an American," he said.

She shrugged and looked up with a genuine innocence. "Sure. What else would I be?"

He was staring at her earrings. She reached up and touched one of them, not sure what his interest was. They were all she had left from her birth mother and she wore them all the time. She knew her original parents had come from the tiny island country of Ambria. So had her adoptive family, but that was years ago and far away. Ambria and its problems had only been minimally relevant to her life as yet.

But then, she was forgetting that the Ambrian connection was the reason she was here. So naturally he would notice. Still, something about the intensity of his interest made her uncomfortable. It was probably safer to go back to talking about Cici.

"But as I was saying, she wasn't happy about traveling, and she let everyone know it, all across the Atlantic." She groaned, remembering. "Everyone on that plane hated me. It was hell on earth. Why do people have babies, anyway?"

His eyes widened and one eyebrow rose dramatically. "I don't know. You tell me."

"Oh."

She gulped. That was a mistake. She groaned internally. She really couldn't afford to goof up like that. He'd assumed Cici was her baby, which was exactly what she wanted him to think, at least for now. She had to be more careful.

She wished she were a better actor, but even a professional performer might have trouble with this gig. After all she'd been through over the past week, she really ought to be in a straightjacket by now. Or at least a warm bath.

Just days before, she'd been a normal young first-year lawyer, working for a small law firm that specialized in immigration law. And then, suddenly, the world had all caved in on her. Things had happened, things she didn't dare think about if she was to keep her wits about her. Things she would have to deal with eventually, but not yet…not now.

Still, she was afraid that nothing would ever be sane again. She'd turned around and found herself in the middle of a nightmare, and suddenly she'd had very limited choice. She could give up and go to bed and pull the covers over her head for the duration—or she could try to take care of what was left of her family and get baby Cici to where she belonged.

The question was moot, of course. She was used to doing what was expected of her, doing the responsible thing. She'd quickly decided on the latter course and now here she was, single-mindedly following the path she'd set for herself.

Once her mission was accomplished she would breathe a sigh of relief, go back to Texas and try to pick up the pieces of her life. That would be the time for facing what had happened and deciding how in the world she was going to go on now that everything was gone. But until then, for the sake of this tiny life she was protecting, she had to maintain her strength and determination no matter how hard it got.

In the meantime, she knew she had to lie. It went against her nature. She was usually the type who was ready to give her life story to anyone with a friendly face. But she had to squelch that impulse, hold back her natural inclinations and lie.

It wasn't easy. It was a painful lie. She had to make the world around her believe that Cici was her baby. She hadn't been a lawyer for long, but she knew a thing or two and one of them was that she would put this whole plan in jeopardy if people knew Cici wasn't hers, and that she had no right to be dragging her around the world like this. Social workers would be called in. Bureaucrats would get involved. Cici would be taken away from her and who knew what awful things might happen then.

Despite everything, she already loved that little child. And even if she didn't she would have done just about anything for Samantha's baby.

"Well, you know what I mean," she amended a bit lamely.

"I don't really care what you mean," he said impatiently. "I want to know how you got in here. I want to know what you think you're doing here." His blue eyes darkened. "And most of all, I want you to go somewhere else."

She winced. She could hardly blame him. "Okay," she said, pulling herself up taller in the seat. "Let me try to explain."

Was that a sneer on his handsome face?

"I'm all ears."

She knew very well he was being sarcastic. He didn't seem to like her very much. That was too bad. Most people liked her on sight. She wasn't used to this sort of hostility. She sighed, too sleepy to do anything about it, and went back to contemplating his ears.

They were very nice and tight to the sides of his head. She admired them for a moment. Everything about this man was pretty fine, she had to admit. Too bad she always felt like a gangly, awkward teenager around men like this. She was tall; almost six feet, and she'd been that tall since puberty. Her high school years had been uncomfortable. She'd been taller than all the boys until her senior year. People told her she was willowy and beautiful now, but she still felt like that clumsy kid who towered over everyone.

"Okay."

She rose and began to pace restlessly. Where to begin? She'd thought this visit was going to be pretty straightforward, but now that she was here, it seemed much more complicated. The trouble was, she didn't know all the sorts of facts a man like this was going to want to know. She'd acted purely on instinct, grabbing Cici and heading for London on barely a moment's notice. Panic, she supposed. But under the circumstances, she had to think it was understandable. She'd done the only thing she could think of. And now here she was.

She closed her eyes and drew in a deep, shaky breath. She'd come to this man's apartment for a reason. What was it again? Oh, yes. Someone had told her he could help her find little Cici's father.

"Do you remember meeting a girl named Samantha?" she asked, her voice cracking a bit on the name. Now it was going to be a chore just to keep from crying. "Small, blonde, pretty face, wore a lot of jangly bracelets?"

He swayed just a little and looked to be about at the end of his tether. She noticed, with a bit of a start, that his hands were balled into tight fists at his side. Another moment or two and he was going to be tearing his hair out in frustration. Either that or giving her shoulders a firm shake. She took a step backward, just in case.

"No," he said, his voice low and just this side of angry. "Never heard of her." His brilliant blue eyes were glaring at her. "And never heard of you, either. Though you haven't provided your own name yet, so I really can't say that, can I?"

"Oh." She gave a start and presented herself before him again, chagrined that she'd been so remiss.

"Of course. I'm sorry." She stuck out her hand. "My name is Ayme Sommers. From Dallas, as if you couldn't tell."

He let her stand there with her hand out for a beat too long, still looking as though he couldn't believe this was happening. For a moment, she thought he was going to refuse to respond and the question of what she was going to do next flitted into her head. But she didn't have to come up with a good comeback, after all. He finally relented and slid his hand over hers, then held on to it, not letting her go.

"Interesting name," he said dryly, staring hard into her dark eyes. "Now tell me the rest."

She blinked at him, trying to pull her hand back and not getting much cooperation. She was suddenly aware of his warm skin and hard muscles in a way that stopped the breath in her throat. She tried not to look down at his chest. It took all her strength.

"What do you mean?" she said, her voice squeaking. "What 'rest'?"

He pulled her closer and she gaped at him, not sure why he was playing this game of intimidation.

"What is your tie to Ambria?" he asked, his voice low and intense.

She gasped, her eyes wide, and gazed at him in wonder. "How did you know?"

He inclined his head in her direction. "The Ambrian shield on your earrings pretty much gives it away."

"Oh." She'd forgotten. Her mind was full of cotton right now. It was amazing that she even remembered who she was. She touched one ear with her free hand. "Of course. Most people don't know what it is."

His eyes narrowed. "But you do."

"Oh, yes."

She smiled at him and he winced, and almost took a step backward himself. Her smile seemed to light up the room. It was too early for that—and inappropriate considering the circumstances. He had to look away, but he didn't let go of her hand.

"My parents were from Ambria. I was actually born there. My birth name is Ayme Negri."

That sounded like a typically Ambrian name, as far as he knew. But he didn't really know as much as he should. This girl with the shields decorating her ears might very well know a lot more than he did about his own country.

He stared at her, realizing with a stunned, sick feeling that his true knowledge of the land his family had ruled for a thousand years was woefully inadequate. He didn't know what to ask her. He didn't know enough to even conjure up a quick quiz to test her truthfulness. All these years he'd had to hide his identity, and in the process he hadn't really learned enough. He'd read books. He'd talked to people. He'd remembered things from his early childhood. And he'd had one very effective mentor. But it wasn't enough. He didn't know who he was at his very core, nor did he know much about the people he came from.

And now she'd arrived, a virtual pop quiz. And he hadn't studied.

Her hand in his felt warm. He searched her face. Her eyes were bright and questioning, her lips slightly parted as though waiting for what was going to happen next and slightly excited by it. She looked like a teenage girl waiting for her first kiss. He was beginning to think that the alarm, which had gone off like a whistle in his brain, was a false one.

But who was she really and why was she here? She seemed so open, so free. He couldn't detect a hint of guile in her. No assassin could have been this calm and innocent-looking.

It was pretty hard to believe that she could have been sent here to kill him.

CHAPTER TWO

"Ayme Negri," he repeated softly. "I'm David Dykstra."

He watched her eyes as he said the name. Was there a slight blink? Did she know it was an alias?

No, there was nothing there. No hint of special knowledge. No clues at all. And it only made sense. If she'd wanted to finish him off, she'd had her chance while he was sleeping.

Still, he couldn't let his guard down. He'd been waiting for someone to arrive with murder on his mind since that dark, stormy night when he was six years old and he'd been spirited away from the rebellion in Ambria and across the countryside in search of a safe haven.

The palace had been burned and his parents killed. And most likely some of his siblings had died as well—though he didn't know for sure. But he'd been rescued and hidden with a family in the Netherlands, the Dykstras. He'd been spared.

All that had happened twenty-five years ago, and no one had ever come to find him, neither friend nor foe. Someday he knew he would have to face his destiny. But maybe not today.

"Ayme Negri," he said again, mulling over the name.

He was still holding her hand, almost as though he was hoping to gain some comprehension of her motives just by sense of touch.

An Ambrian woman, raised in Texas. That was a new one to him.

"Say something in Ambrian," he challenged quickly. At least he had a chance of understanding a little of the language if she didn't get too complicated. He hadn't spoken it since he was a child, but he still dreamed in his native tongue sometimes.

But it didn't seem she would be willing to go along with that little test. Her eyes widened and a hint of quick anger flashed across her face.

"No," she said firmly, her lovely chin rising. "I don't have to prove anything to you."

His head reared back. "Are you serious? You break into my apartment and now you're going to take on airs?"

"I didn't break in," she said indignantly. "I walked in, just like everybody else you had here to your party. I…I sort of melted into a group that was arriving and no one seemed to think twice."

She shrugged, remembering how she'd slipped into the elevator with a bunch of boisterous young city sophisticates. They seemed to accept her right to come in with them without a second thought. She'd smiled at a pretty young woman in a feathered boa and the woman had laughed.

"Look, she's brought a baby," she said to her escort, a handsome young man who had already had much too much to drink. "I wish I had a baby." She turned and pouted. "Jeremy, why won't you let me have a baby?"

"What the hell, babies for everyone," he'd called out

as the elevator doors opened, and he'd almost fallen over with the effort. "Come on. If we're going to be handing out babies, I'm going to need another drink."

Laughing, the group had swelled in through the door to this apartment and left her standing in the entryway. No one else had noticed her. She'd seen the host in the main room, dancing with a beautiful raven-haired woman and swaying like a man who'd either fallen in love or had too many rum drinks. She'd sighed and decided the better part of valor was to beat a hasty retreat. And that was when she'd slipped into the media room and found a drawer she could use as a bassinet for Cici.

"I don't remember inviting you," he noted dryly.

"I invited myself." Her chin lifted even higher. "Just because you didn't notice me at the time doesn't make me a criminal."

He was ready with a sharp retort, but he bit his tongue. This was getting him nowhere. He had to back off and start over again. If he was going to find out what was really going on, he needed to gain her trust. Making her defensive was counterproductive at best.

And he did want to know, not only because he was plain curious, but because of the Ambrian connection. There had to be a reason for it. Young Ambrian women weren't likely to just appear on his doorstep out of the blue. In fact, it had never happened before.

"Sorry," he said gruffly, turning away. Taking a deep breath and calming himself, he looked back and his gaze fell on the little child. There had been a period, while living in his huge adoptive family, when he'd spent a lot of time with babies. They didn't scare him.

Still, he could take or leave them. They were often just too much work.

But he knew very well what happened when one of this age was woken from a sound sleep, and the results were never very pretty.

"Listen, let's go to the kitchen and get a cup of coffee. Then we can talk without waking up your baby."

"Okay." She stopped, looking back. "Shall I just leave her here?" she asked doubtfully.

Cici had been practically glued to her body ever since Sam had left her behind that rainy Texas day that seemed so long ago now. And yet it hadn't even been a week yet. She smiled, suddenly enchanted with the way the child looked in the drawer.

"Look at the little angel. She's sleeping like a lamb now."

He frowned. "How old is that baby?" he asked suspiciously.

That was another question she wasn't confident enough to answer. Sam hadn't left behind any paperwork, not even a birth certificate.

"Her name's Cici," she said, stalling for time.

His glare wasn't friendly. "Nice name. Now, how old is she?"

"About six weeks," she said, trying to sound sure of herself and pretty much failing at it. "Maybe two months."

He stared at her. Skepticism was too mild a term for what his gaze was revealing about his thoughts on her answer.

She smiled brightly. "Hard to remember. Time flies."

"Right."

She followed him out into the living room. He snagged a shirt from the hall closet as they passed it, shrugged into it but left it open. She made an abrupt turn so he wouldn't find her staring at him, and as she did so, she caught sight of the view from the huge floor-to-ceiling picture window.

She gasped, walking toward it. It was four in the morning but the landscape was still alive with lights. Cars carried people home, a plane cruised past, lights blinking. Looking down, she was suddenly overwhelmed with a sense of detached wonder. There were so many people below, all with their own lives, going on with things as though everything was normal. But it wasn't normal. The world had tipped on its axis a few days ago. Nothing would ever be the same again. Didn't they know?

For just a moment, she was consumed with a longing to be one of those clueless people, riding through the night in a shiny car, going toward a future that didn't include as much heartbreak and tragedy as she knew was waiting for her once this adventure in Britain was over.

"Wow. You can see just about all of London from here, can't you?" She was practically pressing her nose to the glass.

"Not quite," he said, glancing out at the lights of the city. He liked this place better than most. It was close to the building where his offices were—centrally located and perfect for running the British branch of his foster father's multinational shipping business. "But it is a pretty spectacular view."

"I'll say." She was standing tall, both hands raised, fingertips pressed to the glass to hold her balance as she leaned forward, taking it all in. She looked almost poised to fly away over the city herself.

He started to suggest that she might want to keep her hands off the window, but as he watched her, he checked himself. With her long limbs and unusual way of holding her posture, she had an unselfconscious gawkiness, like a young girl, that was actually quite winsome. But she really wasn't all that young, and in that short skirt, her legs looked like they went on forever. So he kept quiet and enjoyed his own temporary view, until she tired of it and levered back away from the glass.

"Cities like this are kind of scary," she said, her tone almost whimsical. "You really get the feeling it's every man for himself."

He shrugged. "You're just not used to the place. It's unexplored territory to you." His wide mouth quirked. "As the song says, faces are ugly and people seem wicked."

She nodded as though pleased that he saw the connection. "That's the way I felt coming here tonight. A stranger in a very weird part of town."

He almost smiled but hadn't meant to. Didn't really want to. He needed to maintain an edgy sort of wariness with this woman. He still didn't know why she was here, and her reasons could be costly to him for all he knew.

Still, he found himself almost smiling. He bit it off quickly.

"This part of town is hardly weird," he said shortly. The real estate was high class and high-toned, and he was paying through the nose for that fact. "Maybe you miss the longhorns and Cadillacs."

She gave him a haughty look. She'd caught the ill-concealed snobbery in his tone. "I've been out of Texas before, you know," she said. "I spent a semester in Japan in my senior year."

"World traveler, are you?" he said wryly. But he rather regretted having been a little mean, and he turned away. He needed to be careful. The conversation had all the hallmarks of becoming too personal. He had to break it off. Time to get serious.

He led her on into his ultramodern, wide-open kitchen with its stainless-steel counters and green onyx walls. He got down two mugs, then put pods into the coffee machine, one at a time. In minutes it was ready and he handed her a steaming mug of coffee, then gazed at her levelly.

"Okay, let's have it."

She jumped in surprise. "What?" she asked, wide-eyed.

He searched her dark eyes. What he found there gave him a moment of unease. On the surface she seemed very open and almost naive, a carefree young woman ready to take on the world and go for whatever was out there. But her eyes held a more somber truth. There was tragedy in those eyes, fear, uncertainty. Whatever it was that she was hiding, he hoped it had nothing to do with him.

"Who are you and what are you doing here?" he asked again. "Why are you carrying around a very young baby in a strange city in the middle of the night? And most important, how did you even get in here?"

She stared at him for a moment, then tried to smile as she took a shallow sip of the hot coffee. "Wow. That's a lot to throw at a girl who's only half-awake," she noted evasively.

His grunt held no sympathy. "You threw a six-week-old baby at me," he reminded her. "So let's have it."

She took a deep breath, as though this really was an effort. "Okay. I think I already explained how I got in here. I hitched a ride with a party group and no one minded."

He groaned, thinking of some choice words he would have with the doorman later that day.

"As I told you, my name is Ayme Negri Sommers. I'm from Dallas, Texas. And..." She swallowed hard, then looked him in the eye. "And I'm looking for Cici's father."

That hit him like a fist in the stomach. He swallowed hard and searched her gaze again. He knew very well that he was now treading into a minefield and he had to watch his step very carefully.

"Oh, really?" he said, straining to maintain a light, casual tone. "So where did you lose him?"

She took it as a serious question. "That's just the trouble. I'm not really sure."

He stared at her. Was she joking? Nothing she said was making any sense.

"But I heard from a very reliable source," she went on, setting down her mug and putting her hands on her hips as she turned to look questioningly at him, "that you would be able to help me out."

Ah-ha. A very dangerous mine had appeared right in front of him with this one. Careful!

"Me?" he asked, trying not to let his voice rise with anxiety. "Why me?"

She started to say something, then stopped and looked down, uncomfortable and showing it. "See, this is why this is so hard. I don't really know. My source said that you would know where to find him." She looked back up into his face, waiting.

"So you think it's someone I know?" he asked, still at sea. "Obviously, it's not me."

She hesitated much too long over that one and he let out an exclamation, appalled. "You can't be serious. I think I would have noticed a little thing like that, and I know damn well I've never seen you before." He shook his head in disbelief.

She sighed. "I'm not accusing you of anything."

"Good. So why are you here?"

She took a deep breath. "Okay, the person who advised me to look you up is a man associated with the firm I work for."

"In Texas? And he thinks he knows who I know?" He shook his head, turning away and beginning to pace the floor in frustration. "This is absurd. How did he even know my name?"

"He told me you socialize in the same circles as Cici's dad. He said, 'Don't worry. He'll know how to find him.'"

"Oh, he did, did he?" For some reason this entire conversation was stoking a rage that was smoldering inside him. He stopped and confronted her. "So this person who's supposed to be Cici's father—this person I'm supposed to know where to find—what's his name?"

She half twisted away. This had all seemed so easy when she'd planned it out as she made her way to the airport in Dallas. She would dash off to London, find Cici's father, hand over the baby and head back home. She hadn't realized she would have to try to explain it all to someone in between. When you got right down to it, the bones of the story weren't making a lot of sense.

And she realized now that one element would sound really goofy to this man. She was hoping to keep that one under wraps for as long as possible.

She turned back with a heart-wrenching sigh and said dramatically, "Well...you see, that's the problem. I'm not sure what his actual name is."

He stared at her. The absurdity of the situation was becoming clear. She was looking for a man who had fathered her baby. She didn't know where he was. She didn't know his name. But she'd come here for help. And he was supposed to ride to the rescue? Why, exactly?

It was true that he had a reputation for knowing everyone who counted within a certain social strata. He'd made it his business to know them, for his own purposes. But he had to have something to go on. He couldn't just throw out possibilities.

"What are you going to do when you find him? Are you planning to marry the guy?"

"What?" She looked shocked, as though this very mundane idea was too exotic to contemplate. "No. Of course not."

"I see," he said, though he didn't.

She bit her lip and groaned silently. She was so tired. She couldn't think straight. She just wanted to go back to sleep. Maybe things would look clearer in the morning.

"How am I supposed to find someone if I don't know his name?"

She turned and gave him an exasperated look. "If this were easy, I could have done it on my own."

"I see. I'm your last resort, am I?"

She thought for a second, then nodded. "Pretty

much." She gazed at him earnestly, feeling weepy. "Do you think you can help me?"

He gazed at her, at her pretty face with those darkly smudged, sleepy eyes, at the mop of blond hair that settled wildly around her head as though it had been styled by gypsies, at her slightly trembling lower lip.

He had a small fantasy. In it, he told her flat out, "Hell, no. I'm not helping you. You give me nothing and ask for miracles. I've got better things to do with my time than to run all over London looking for someone I'm never going to find. This is insane."

As the fantasy began to fade, he saw himself reaching into his pocket and handing her money to go to a hotel. What a happy little dream it was.

But looking at her, he knew it wasn't going to happen. Right now, her eyes were filling with tears, as though she could read his mind and knew he wanted to get rid of her and her problems.

"Okay," he told her gruffly, clenching his fists to keep from following his instinct to reach out to comfort her. And then he added a touch of cynicism to his tone, just for good measure. "If all this is a little too overwhelming for you in your current state of hysteria…"

"I am not hysterical!" she cried indignantly.

He raised an eyebrow. "That's a matter of judgment and not even very relevant. Why don't we do this in a logical, methodical fashion? Then maybe we can get somewhere."

She moaned. "Like back to bed?" she suggested hopefully.

"Not yet." He was pacing again. "You need to fill in some of the blanks. Let's start with this. What exactly is your tie to Ambria? Give me the full story."

He'd given up wondering if she was here to harm him. The complete innocence she displayed wasn't very likely to be a put-on. And anyway, what sort of an incompetent murder master would send a young woman with a baby to do the dirty deed? It just didn't make sense.

"My parents were Ambrian," she began. "I was actually born there but that was just before the rebellion. My birth parents died in the fighting. I don't remember them at all. I was taken out with a lot of other refugee children and rushed to the States. I was adopted right away. I was only about eighteen months old, so as far as I'm concerned, my adoptive parents are my parents." She shrugged. "End of story."

"Are you kidding? We've barely begun." He stopped and looked down at her, arms folded over his chest. "Who told you about your Ambrian background?"

"Oh, the Sommerses had Ambrian roots, too. Second generation American, though. So they told me things, and there were some books around the house." She shook her head. "But it wasn't like I was immersed in the culture or anything like that."

"But you do know about the rebellion? You know about the Granvilli family and how they led an illegal coup that killed a lot of people and left them in charge of an ancient monarchy that should have been left alone?"

She blinked. "Uh…I guess."

"But you don't know much about it?"

She shook her head.

He gazed at her, speculation glowing in his silver-blue eyes. "So you don't have family still in Ambria?"

"Family?" She stared at him blankly. "Not that I know of."

"I guess they were all killed by the rebels?"

She blinked and shook her head. "I don't know if the rebels killed them."

He raised a cynical eyebrow. "Who do you think killed them?"

She ran her tongue nervously over her lower lip. "Well, to tell you the truth, I really don't know what side they were on."

That stunned him. The idea that someone decent might support the rebels who had killed his parents and taken over his country didn't really work for him. He dismissed it out of hand. But if she were around long enough, and he had a chance, he would find out who her parents were and what role they played. It seemed like something she ought to know.

"Now that we've established who you are, let's get to the real topic. Why are you really here?"

She sighed. "I told you."

But he was already shaking his head. "You told me a lot of nonsense. Do you really expect me to believe you had a baby and don't know the father? It doesn't add up, Ayme. How about giving me the real story?"

She felt like a bird caught in a trap. She hated lying. That was probably why she did it so badly. She had to tell him something. Something convincing. Had to be. She was beginning to see that she would really be in trouble if he refused to help her.

But before she could conjure up something good, a wail came from across the apartment. Ayme looked toward where the sound was coming from, uncertainty on her face. Why didn't this baby seem to want to sleep for more than an hour at a time, day or night?

"I just fed her an hour ago," she said, shaking her

head and thinking of her dwindling stash of formula bottles. "Do you think she really wants to eat again?"

"Of course," he told her. "They want to eat all the time. Surely you've noticed."

She bit her lip and looked at him. "But the book says four hours…."

He groaned. She was still using a book?

"Babies don't wear watches," he noted, feeling some sympathy for this new mother, but a lot of impatience, as well.

"True." She gave him a wry look as she turned to go. "But you'd think they could look at a clock now and then."

He grinned. He couldn't help it. If he really let himself go, he would start liking her and he knew it. And so he followed her into the room and watched as she stroked the little round head rather inefficiently. The baby was definitely crying, and the stroking was doing no good at all. From what he could tell, Ayme didn't seem to have a clue as to what to do to quiet her.

"Why don't you try changing her?" he suggested. "She's probably wet."

"You think so?" That seemed to be a new idea to her. "Okay, I'll try it."

She had a huge baby bag crammed full of things, but she didn't seem to know what she was looking for. He watched her rummage around in it for a few minutes, then stepped forward and pulled out a blanket which he spread out on the couch.

"I can do this," she said a bit defensively.

"I'm sure you can," he said. "I'm just trying to help."

She winced, feeling genuine regret for her tone. "I know. I'm sorry."

She pulled out a paper diaper and laid it on the blanket, then pulled Cici up out of the drawer.

"There you go little girl," she cooed to her. "We're going to get you nice and clean."

David stood back and watched, arms folded across his chest, mouth twisted cynically. She didn't seem very confident to him. Cici wasn't crying hard, only whimpering at this point, but he had the impression that she was looking up at the woman working over her with something close to apprehension.

"Don't you have someplace else you could be?" she muttered to him as she worked, and he could see that she was nervous to be doing this in front of him. Like someone who didn't really know what she was doing.

One thing he knew for sure—this woman didn't know the first thing about taking care of a baby. How crazy was that? And then it came to him. She wasn't the mother of the baby. Couldn't be. In six weeks time anyone would have learned more than she seemed to know.

"Alright Ayme Negri Sommers," he said firmly at last, "come clean. Whose baby is this?"

She looked up, a deer in the headlights.

"Mine."

"Liar."

She stared at him for a moment, degrees of uncertainty flashing across her pretty face. Finally, she threw her hands into the air. "Okay, you got me." She shrugged, looking defeated. "She's not really mine." She sighed. "What was your first clue?"

He grunted, stepping forward to take over. "The fact

that you don't know beans about taking care of a baby," he said, taking the diaper from her and beginning to do an expert job of it in her place. "The fact that you're still reading a book to figure out which end is up."

She heaved a heart-felt sigh. "I guess that was in evitable. It's really such a relief. I hated living a lie." She looked at him with more gratitude than resentment. "How come you know so much about babies, anyway?"

"I grew up in a big family. We all had to pitch in."

She sighed. "We didn't have any babies around while I was growing up. It was just me and Sam."

The baby was clean and in dry diapers. David put her up against his shoulder and she cuddled in, obviously comfortable as could be and happy to be with someone who knew what he was doing. He managed a reluctant smile. It was just like riding a bicycle. Once you knew how to hold a baby, you didn't forget.

He turned back to Ayme. "Who's this Sam you keep talking about?"

She swallowed, realizing the answer to that question was going to be tied to very different emotions from now on.

"My…my sister, Samantha. She was Cici's real mother."

And that was when the horror hit her for the first time since she'd left home. Her legs turned to rubber. Closing her eyes, she sank to the couch, fighting to hold back the blackness that threatened to overtake her whenever she let herself think, even for a moment, about Samantha. It was the same for her parents. The accident had taken them, too. Her whole family.

It was all too much to bear. If she let herself really

think about what had happened and about the emptiness that was waiting for her return to Dallas, the bubble she was living in would pop in an instant. She couldn't think about it and she couldn't tell him about it. Not yet. Maybe not ever. The pain was just too raw to manage.

Steeling herself, she forced out a quick explanation.

"Sam died in a car accident a few days ago." Her voice was shaking but she was going to get through this. "I...I was taking care of Cici when it happened. It was all so sudden. It..."

She took in a gasping breath, steadying herself. Then she cleared her throat and went on.

"Now I'm trying to get her to where she belongs. I'm trying to find her father." She looked up, surprised to find that she'd gone through it and was still coherent. "There. Now you know it all."

He stared at her. Her eyes looked like dark bruises marring her pretty face. The tragedy in her voice was mirrored by her body language, the tilt of her head, the pain in her voice. He didn't doubt for a minute that everything she'd just told him was absolutely true and it touched him in a way he hadn't expected.

The urge was strong to put down the baby and take the woman in his arms. If anyone needed a bit of comfort, Ayme did. But he stopped himself from making that move. He knew it wouldn't work out well. The last thing she wanted right now was compassion. The smallest hint of sympathy would very probably make her fall apart emotionally. He assumed that she didn't want that any more than he did. At least he hoped so. He looked away and grimaced.

But—back to basics—he still didn't understand why she'd come to him.

"Ayme, I'm not Cici's father," he said bluntly.

"Oh, I know. I know it's not you."

He shook his head, still at sea and searching for land-fall. "Then why are you here?"

She shrugged. "You're going to help me find him." She gazed at him earnestly. "You just have to. And since you're Ambrian..."

"I never said I was Ambrian," he broke in quickly. He had to make that clear. As far as the rest of the world knew, he was a citizen of the Netherlands, born and bred Dutch. That was the way it had been for twenty-five years and that was the way it had to be.

"Well, you know a lot about Ambria, which not a lot of people do."

Reluctantly, he admitted it. "True."

Rising from the couch, she began to pace much the way he had a few minutes earlier. She was exhausted and her emotions were spent. But she had more work to do. Glancing over at David, she noticed that Cici's downy head was tucked against his shoulder and the little eyes were closed. She was asleep. Ayme's sigh was from the depths of her wounded soul.

"If only I'd had you along on the flight over the Atlantic," she said.

"Don't try to change the subject," he said, turning to lay the baby down very carefully in her makeshift bed. "If you want my help, you've got to give me more. I can't do anything unless I understand the parameters I'm dealing with."

She nodded. He was right, of course. But what could she say to explain this crazy situation? She moved rest-lessly toward the doorway and leaned against the door-jamb. From there, she could see across the living room and out through the huge picture window surveying the city. The mass of city lights spread out below added a manic energy, despite the time of night.

That made her think—what if all those lights went out one night?

She nodded, realizing that the stars would take their place. And that would be a whole different dynamic. She wasn't sure which she would prefer at the moment— manic energy or soothing starlight. But her preference didn't mean a thing. She had to deal with what she had before her.

Throwing her head back, she began.

"Sam didn't tell me much about Cici's father. Actually, I hadn't seen her for almost a year when she showed up with a baby in her arms. I had no idea..." She put a hand to her forehead as she remembered the shock of Sam's return home. "Anyway, she didn't tell me much, but she did tell me that Cici's father was Ambrian. That she'd met him on a trip to London. And that she wanted nothing more in the world at that moment than to find him and show him his baby."

Of course, there were other moments, even hours, when Sam acted as though she didn't care at all—especially when she took off without her baby. But he didn't have to know about that.

She turned and came back into the room, watching David tuck a blanket in around Cici. It was unusual to see such a strong, handsome man doing something like that. At least it seemed unusual to her. But who knew? Maybe she should get out more.

That sweet little baby was finally getting the sort of care she deserved. She thought of how careless Sam had seemed with Cici. Their mother had been appalled.

But maybe that was because of her precarious circumstances. If she could have found Cici's father and they could have formed a real family, maybe things would have been different.

"Now she'll never get the chance," she murmured softly, then caught herself and frowned. None of that. She couldn't let herself drift off into that sort of sadness. They would never get anything done.

He'd finished with the baby and he came to stand in front of her, looking down. "But she didn't tell you this guy's name?"

She hesitated. "She told me a name, but...."

"Who? You've got to tell me, Ayme. I don't see how I can help you if you won't tell me."

She turned away again and he followed her out to the picture window. "Do you ever see the stars?" she asked.

"Not much," he said impatiently. "Will you stick to the point?"

She drew in a deep breath and looked up at him as though this was a hard thing to do.

"Do you know anything about the lost royals of Ambria?" she asked him.

CHAPTER THREE

FOR JUST a second, David thought he'd heard Ayme wrong. Then the implications of what she'd just said crashed in on him. He could hardly breathe.

"Uh, sure," he said, managing not to sound as choked as he felt. "I've heard of them, anyway. What about them?"

She shrugged and sounded apologetic. "Well, Sam claimed Cici's father was one of them."

"Interesting."

He coughed. He'd heard of sightings before. Mostly, they were nothing, led nowhere. But there had been one that had panned out, and when he'd followed up on it, he'd found his oldest brother, the crown prince. There might be more brothers out there. Could it happen again?

"Which one?" he asked, intrigued, emotionally touched, but not really expecting much.

She gazed up at him with those huge brown eyes. "She said he was the second born, and that his name was Darius."

The room seemed to grow and then contract, as though he'd taken a hallucinogenic of some sort. It took all his strength to stay balanced without reaching for support. She was still talking, telling him something more about her sister, but he couldn't concentrate on what she was saying.

Sam had named him...*him*...as the father of her baby. But that was impossible. Incredible. Wrong. Wasn't it?

He did some quick calculations. Where had he been ten to twelve months ago? Whom had he dated? It was true that he'd spent some time over the years finding love in all the wrong places. There had been a period of his younger life when he'd made conquests first and asked questions later—if at all. He wasn't proud of those times and he was sure he'd put them well behind him. But what had he been doing last year? Why was it that he couldn't really remember?

He thought of Cici's cute little face. Was there anything familiar in it? Had he felt a slight connection? Some magic sense of kinship? A tie? Anything?

He agonized for one long moment, searching his heart and soul for evidence. But he quickly decided there was none. No, he was sure there had been nothing like that. It was crazy to even think this way.

"Have you ever heard of him?" she was asking. "Do you know much about him? Any idea where we can even look to find him?"

"We"? He noted the question and realized what it meant. She really did think he was going to drop everything in his life and start helping her, didn't she? The problem was, he would have to do just the opposite. He needed to melt away and very quickly. She didn't realize how dangerous this could be for him. She was sort of like a grenade someone had pulled the pin on and rolled into his apartment. Things could explode at any moment. The smallest jolt could blow everything up.

"No," he said shortly. "What gave you the idea I would know these things, anyway?"

"I told you, I was given your name as someone who might be able to help me."

She was looking nervous. He hated to disappoint her. But this was serious and now it had his complete attention.

"Given my name?"

As the full implications of that began to come into focus, an icy finger made its way down his spine and all his instincts for survival began to stir.

"Who was this who gave you my name?"

"A man associated with my law firm. He deals with Ambrian things all the time and he knew who you were."

He took that in and considered it carefully. But wait. His Ambrian roots weren't known to more than three or four of his closest associates. To most of the world, he was Dutch. How in hell would someone in Texas know otherwise?

"His name?" he said quickly, staring at her intensely, as though he could draw the information out of her if he tried hard enough.

"Carl Heissman. Do you know him?"

Slowly, he shook his head. He'd never heard the name before, at least, not that he could remember.

She shrugged. "I really didn't know him until…"

"How did you get in touch with him? Did you go to him and ask for his help?"

"No, it wasn't like that." She shook her head. "No, not really. I went to the office and asked for a leave and explained about Cici…."

"So how did he contact you?"

"He must have heard about what I was doing from my boss, so he gave me a call."

His heart was thumping in his chest. "He told you my name over the phone?"

"No. Actually, he wanted to meet at a little wine bar downtown. We sat out on the patio."

"Where he couldn't be recorded," he muttered to himself.

"What?" she asked.

She was beginning to wonder why all this was such a big deal to him. Either he could help her or he couldn't. The man in Texas was a side issue as far as she was concerned. She frowned at him, just to let him know she thought he was going off down a blind alley and that wasn't very helpful.

But he wasn't paying any attention to that. He shook his head, his brow furled, obviously thinking things he wasn't sharing with her.

"Go on."

"Well, I thought he knew you from the way he talked. He gave me your name and address and then he even offered to pay for the trip."

David's eyes flared at that bit of information.

"Why would he do that?"

She shrugged. "I thought it was odd at the time, but I assumed it might have been the law firm that was offering to pay. I didn't take anything from him, but…"

"But you don't really know who he is or what his connection to your law firm is, do you? He just came at you out of the blue."

She gave him an exaggerated glare for the interruption, but she plowed ahead.

"I have a number where I'm supposed to call him

when I find Cici's father." She glanced around, looking for a phone. "Do you think I should give him a call?"

He held back the grunt of exasperation he was tempted to mete out. That was obviously the last thing he wanted her to do.

"You haven't called him yet?"

"No."

"Don't."

She blinked. "Why not?"

He hesitated, then shrugged. "You haven't found Cici's father, have you?"

"Maybe not." She eyed him speculatively, her chin high.

He groaned, turning away. He knew he couldn't let her call the number. That would pinpoint his exact location for sure. But how to convince her of that without giving away the entire background?

Whoever this Carl Heissman was, the man was playing games. Deadly games. He had to think fast and get back to basics and consider all possibilities.

He glanced at her again, studied her, tried to pick up on any details he might have missed so far. Why was she really here? Was this a ploy? A plot to coax him out of hiding?

Whatever. He had to get out of here right away and hope whoever was behind sending her here wasn't already on his trail—or worse, here as well and just hadn't revealed himself as yet. He heard a sound behind him and turned quickly, jumpy as a cat.

There was nothing there—this time. That wary buzz was back in full force. Ayme had invaded his space like the point guard of a small enemy army and he was going to have to be on alert every minute. He couldn't afford to trust her or anything about her. His eyes narrowed as he looked her over and considered every angle.

And then the house phone rang.

They stared into each other's eyes for a long moment as it rang once, twice….

Then David took three steps and picked up the receiver, staring down into the identifying screen. Nothing was there. It was blank.

His face turned to stone and his heart beat so hard he could hardly breath. It was never blank. It always said Private Caller if nothing else. But this time, it was blank.

He couldn't answer. That would give the caller absolute knowledge of where he was at this very moment. There wasn't a doubt in his mind that this person wasn't calling in the middle of the night for a friendly chat. This was the danger he'd always known would come his way—and until he understood the exact threat better, it was something he had to avoid at all costs.

And more than that, he had to get out of here.

He turned to look at Ayme, wondering if she'd caught the connotations of this late night call, if she might even know who it was and why he was calling. But her face was open and innocent and her gaze was shining with curiosity. He couldn't believe she could be an expert liar and con artist with eyes like that. No, she didn't know any more than he did. He would have bet anything on that.

"Okay, you've been begging for sleep," he told her, putting the phone back on its cradle. "Why don't you take the spare bedroom around the corner from where you were? Get a few hours sleep. You'll be better for it in the morning."

"Lovely," she said, pure gratitude shining from her eyes for a few seconds. She only hoped that Cici would have as much compassion and give her a chance to get in some real, sustained sleep. Small dozes had been the rule for days.

She glanced at David. His eyes were clouded with some problem he was obviously working through and his handsome face looked a bit tense. That made her all the more grateful.

She was lucky he was taking her presence with such equanimity. Most people would have kicked her out by now, or at least edged her toward the door. But he was ready to let her stay. Thank God. She wasn't sure she could think clearly enough right now to get herself a room in a hotel on her own, especially carrying a baby around. It was great of him to invite her in. She could hardly wait to throw herself on the bed and let sleep take over.

Then she had second thoughts. He hadn't said anything about getting sleep himself, had he?

"What are you going to do?" she asked suspiciously.

He shrugged rather absently, as though his mind were miles away. "I've got some business to wrap up."

She knew it was an excuse, but she didn't push it. She was just too tired to challenge him. The thought of sheets and a real pillow were totally seductive for the moment. So she followed him to the spare bedroom and waited while he carried Cici in, setting her little bed right beside the real bed without waking her at all. He seemed to have the magic touch.

She smiled, watching him tuck Cici in. So precious.

"I'll see you later," he said gruffly, and she nodded,

waiting just until he closed the door before slipping out of her skirt and sweater, leaving only her underclothes on, and sliding between the sheets. She dropped into sleep instantly, but for some reason, she began to dream right away, and her dreams were full of tall, dark-haired men who looked very much like David.

Meanwhile, David was moving fast, preparing to vacate the premises. He'd been planning for this day from the time he could think through the consequences of being found by the vicious Granvilli family who had taken over his country. He knew they wanted all remnants of the Royal House of Ambria wiped out, wherever they might be hiding. They wanted no lingering threats to their ugly reign of terror over the ancient island people.

And he and his older brother Monte were a threat, whether the Granvilli bunch knew it yet or not. At any rate, they were determined to be one. He was already committed to being in Italy by the end of the week to meet with other Ambrians and begin planning in earnest for a return to power. He might as well leave now. There was nothing keeping him here. He'd already made his office aware of the time off he planned to take. He could begin his journey a little early and make his way to Italy in a more careful trajectory. There was no telling what other obstacles he would find along the way.

"Nothing really worth having is easy." Someone had said that once, and right now it made perfect sense to him. The struggle to get his country back was going to be a rough one and he was ready to get started.

And he had to go on his own, he told himself. There was no way to take Ayme along, no reason to do it. Why should he feel this tug of responsibility toward her? He tried to brush it away. She would be okay here. He hadn't even known she existed two hours ago. Why should he feel he owed her anything?

He didn't. But he did owe the people of Ambria everything. Time to begin paying them back.

He had preparations that had to be dealt with, paperwork that had to be destroyed so that the wrong people wouldn't see things they shouldn't see. It took some time to do all that and he had an ear cocked toward the phone in case the interested party from a half hour before might try again. But the night moved relentlessly forward without any more interruptions. The sky was barely beginning to turn pink as he wrapped up his arrangements.

Completely focused, he pulled on a dark blue turtleneck cashmere sweater and finished dressing at warp speed, then glanced around his bedroom. He hesitated for half a second. Did he have time to grab some things and shove them into an overnight bag? What the hell—he had to have something with him, and he'd taken all this time already. Why not? It was all right there and it took no time at all.

He slid into his soft leather jacket as he headed for the door. Despite all the rationalizing he'd been doing, he felt pretty rotten about leaving Ayme behind this way. She was so all alone in the city. She didn't know anyone but him.

That gave him a quick, bitter laugh. She didn't really know him, did she? Which was what was so ridiculous about all this. Still, he hesitated in the open doorway. Maybe he would call the doorman from his car and ask that he look after her. Sure. He could do that. She would be okay.

Right. He took one more step and then stopped, head hanging forward, and uttered an ugly oath. He knew he couldn't leave her.

There was no telling who that had been on the phone There was no telling who was after him—except that he was rock-bottom sure it was an agent for the Granvillis. What if the assassin came into his apartment after he left? Who would protect her? Not the doorman. That was pure fantasy.

No, he couldn't leave her—even if she was the one who had brought all this down on him. He was almost certain that she didn't know anything about it herself. She was an innocent victim. He couldn't leave her behind.

Giving out a suppressed growl of rage, he turned and went back, opening the door to the spare bedroom and looking in.

"Ayme?" he said tersely. "I'm sorry to wake you, but I've got to go and I don't want to leave you here."

"Huh?" She stared up at him, startled, her eyes bleary. She'd had less than an hour of sleep—not nearly enough. "What?"

"Sorry, kiddo," he bit out. "You're going with me." He glanced around the room. "Do you have any other clothes?"

She blinked, trying to get her fuzzy mind to make sense of the question. "I left my bag in the corner." She nodded her head in its general direction.

He stuck out his hand to her. "Come on."

She took his hand in hers and stared at it as though it were a foreign object. "Where are we going?"

He gave her a little tug and she didn't resist, rising halfway out of bed.

"Away from here."

"Why?"

"Why?" He looked into her eyes, alert for any hint of guile. "Because it's too dangerous to stay."

"Oh."

That seemed to convince her. She tumbled out of bed like a sleepy child, pulled the sheet around herself and began to look for where she'd tossed her clothes. He'd started to turn away in order to leave her to it, but something about the picture she made with the fabric twisted around her torso, leaving one shoulder bare and most of both long, golden legs exposed, had him rooted to the spot. There was a fluid, graceful beauty to her that took his breath away and reminded him of something. What was it? Some picture from history, some long forgotten fable…

Ambria. The legend of the lake. It was the familiar story of loss and earned redemption. He could remember sitting in his mother's lap as she turned the pages of the picture book and read the story to him.

"Look, Darius. Isn't she beautiful?"

The lady sat on a large rock overlooking the lake, weeping into her cupped hands, and the flowing garment she wore was very like Ayme's sheet. Funny. He hadn't thought of that scene in years and yet it came back to him so clearly as he watched Ayme leaning over to retrieve her clothes. He'd felt the same tug of compassion as a boy as he felt now.

Well, not the same, exactly. He wasn't a boy anymore and the pang of sympathy was mixed with something else, something that had to do with how creamy her bare skin looked in the lamplight, especially where the sheet pulled low, exposing the soft curve of her breast just beneath a lacy strapless bra.

For some odd reason his heart was beating hard again, and this time it had nothing to do with a phone call.

Ayme looked up and caught the look. She gave him one of her own, but hers was cool and questioning.

"Where did you say we were going?"

"I didn't. Let it be a surprise."

She frowned, not sure she liked where this seemed to be headed. "I don't like surprises." She bit her lip, then tried another idea. "I could just stay here with Cici until you get back."

"I don't know when I'll be back. If ever."

That startled her. "Oh."

"And we don't know who might be coming for a visit. So you'd better come along with me."

"I see." The seriousness in the tone of his voice finally got through to her. "In that case, can you excuse me for a moment?" she asked, politely but firmly pointing out that she needed to drop the sheet and she darn well wasn't going to do it until he was out of the room.

He had the grace to look just a bit sheepish.

"Of course," he said as he began to walk out into the living area.

But then he stopped and looked at her again. What was he thinking? Too much about what she did to his libido and not enough about what she could do to the preservation of his life and limbs.

"Wait a minute," he said, turning on his heel and walking back. "Listen Ayme, I've got to know, and I've got to know right now. Are you wearing a wire or any kind of tracking device?"

That stunned her. She clutched the sheet against her chest. What was this, spy versus spy? In her groggy state of mind, it seemed very bizarre and she couldn't make heads nor tails of it.

"What? What are you talking about?"

"I'm serious. I'm going to have to check."

She backed away, her eyes huge as she realized what he was saying and what it actually meant. She held tightly to her fabric.

"Oh, no you're not."

"Hold on," he said gruffly. "I have to do this. I'm sorry. If you've got anything on you, we've got to get rid of it."

She shook her head firmly. "I swear I don't."

"That's not good enough." He gestured for her to come closer. "Come here."

"No!"

Her voice was strong but it was determination built on sand. She was struck by his demeanor and her will was beginning to crumble around the edges. He wasn't a pervert and he wasn't kidding around. She wasn't sure how she knew this with such certainty, but she did.

"You might be bugged and not even know it," he said earnestly, holding out his hand. "Let me see your mobile."

That she could deliver.

"Be my guest." She tossed it to him, but pulled the sheet even more tightly around her body and was very sure to stay out of his reach, frowning as fiercely as she could muster.

He slid open the little compartment, flipped out the battery and checked behind it. Nothing. He put the battery back and switched it off, then tossed it back to her.

"I'll have to ask you to leave it turned off," he told her. "A working mobile is a basic homing device."

Funny—and sad, but turning off her cell phone would have seemed like turning off her source of oxygen until very recently. But now it didn't really faze her. Most of the people she might expect a call from were gone. The people most important to her no longer existed in her life. With a shudder, she pushed that thought away.

But her mind was finally clearing and she was beginning to realize this whole security exercise was not the normal routine for overnight guests, at least, not in her experience. What the heck was he doing here?

She set the phone down and glared at him. "Would you like to explain just exactly why it's suddenly too dangerous here?" she asked crisply. "And why you feel the need to search for bugs and homing devices? Are you expecting some sort of home invasion? Or just being friendly?"

The corners of his mouth quirked but there was no hint of humor in his blue eyes. "Just being careful," he said evasively. "Crossing all the t's, dotting all the i's. As they say, better safe than sorry."

"Hmm," she said, cocking her head to the side as she gazed at him. "And yet, here I've been feeling safe for all these years without ever once submitting to a strip search. Just foolishly naive, I guess."

Her tone was mocking and he felt the sting. "Ayme, I don't like this any more than you do."

"Really?" Her tone was getting worse and she knew it, but, darn it all, he deserved it. He took a step forward and she took a corresponding step back, staying just out of reach.

"Can you tell me what exactly you're looking for?" she demanded. "Will you know it when you see it?"

"Yes, I'll know it when I see it," he said, nodding. "Now will you just stay put for a minute?"

"I don't think so." She made a sideways move that put even more distance between them.

"Ayme, be reasonable."

"Reasonable!" She laughed out loud. "Reasonable? You call searching me to see if I'm wearing a bug reasonable? I call it unacceptable. And I'm not going to accept it."

"You're going to have to accept it."

"Don't you think any bugs are more likely to be in my clothing or luggage?" she noted quickly.

He nodded his agreement. She was absolutely right. But there was another element to this situation. Now that he'd alerted her to his intentions, he had to follow through without giving her a chance to go behind his back to get rid of anything she might know about that she had on her. He'd started this train down the track and he had to follow it to the end if this was to be in any way effective.

"I'm planning to search your things. But first I need to search you."

He gave her a stern look as he followed her sideways move.

"Hold still."

Reaching out, she quickly dragged a chair between them and gazed defiantly over it.

"Why are you doing this, David? Who's after you? Whom do you suspect?"

He moved the chair aside and stepped closer.

"We don't have time to go into that."

"No, wait," she said, half rolling across the bed and landing on her feet without losing her sheet. Now she'd put the entire bed between them and she was feeling a bit smug about that.

Not that her success would hold up. She knew that. Still, she hoped it was getting through to him that she was not happy about all this and she was not about to give in.

"David, tell me what's changed," she challenged. "Something must have." She frowned at him questioningly. "When you first found me here, you were annoyed, sure, but now it's different. Now you're on guard in an edgier way." Her eyes narrowed. "It was that phone call, wasn't it?"

He hesitated, then nodded. "Yes," he admitted.

"Do you know who it was?"

He shook his head. "No, but it seemed like a wake-up call. It made me realize I was being too casual about you."

"Too casual! I beg to differ."

He stared at her and growled, "Ayme, enough. We need to get going. But first, we've got to check you out. Someone might have put a bug on you somewhere, somehow."

"Without me noticing?"

"That's what they do, Ayme. They're experts at attaching devices to your clothes or your purse or even your body in ways you wouldn't think of."

"Who? Who do you think would do that?"

"I don't know. Maybe this character who gave you my name."

She shook her head, thinking that one over. It didn't make any sense at all. "But he's the one who gave me your address. He already knows where you live. Why would he…?"

"Ayme, I don't know," he said impatiently. "And when you don't know things, it's best to cover all the bases. Will you stand still and let me look you over? I promise I won't…"

"No." Her voice was a little shaky, but adamant. "It won't do any good, anyway. I've seen those TV shows. They have gotten very inventive about hiding things on people. There's no way you can check it all. There's no way I would let you."

He sighed, shaking his head as he looked at her.

"You think I don't know that? I can only do so much, and probably only find something if it's pretty obvious. But I have to try. Look, Ayme, I'm really sorry, but…"

Her face lit up as she thought of a solution. She looked at him speculatively, wondering if he would go for it. With a shrug, she decided she had nothing to lose.

"*I'll* do it," she said firmly, shaking back her hair.

He stared at her. "You'll do it? You'll do what?"

Her smile was bemused. "I'll do it. Myself. Why not? Who knows my body better?" She gave him a grin that was almost mischievous. "You're going to have to trust me."

He stared. Trust her? But that wouldn't work. Would it?

Why not? asked a voice inside his head. *Look at that face. If you can't trust this woman, you can't trust anyone.*

Which was actually what he'd pledged from the

beginning—don't trust anyone. Still, there were times when you just had to make concessions to reality.

"Okay," he said at last. "Go for it. We'll see how you do."

"*I'll* see how I do," she corrected. "You'll be going over my bags and clothes. With your back to me. Got it?"

"Ayme," he began in exasperation, but she signaled that he should turn away. It was pretty apparent that following her orders was going to be the only way to move things along, and they really needed to get going. So, reluctantly, he did as she demanded.

He went through her things methodically. He'd had some training in this sort of search in some security classes he'd taken lately, so he didn't feel as strange handling her panties and bras as he might have under other circumstances. He had to take it on faith that she was doing her part. She chattered away throughout the entire exercise—and he didn't find a thing.

"I really understand, you know," she was saying. "And I want to do a good job at this because I figure, if I'm going with you, the danger is as much to me and Cici as it is to you."

"You got it," he said. "That's the whole point."

"So I just want you to know, I'm really being meticulous."

"Good."

"Searching every place I can think of."

That gave him pictures in his head he didn't want to dwell on and he shook off a delicious little shiver.

"Are you finished?" he asked at last, waiting for the okay to turn around.

"Just about," she said. "Listen, I saw this one show

on TV where they had these little homing signal things sort of stapled into a man's skin. What do you think? Is that really a possibility?"

"Sure."

She hesitated. "Okay then, I've been going over every inch of skin, feeling for any strange lumps, and I haven't found anything suspicious. But just to be safe…"

He turned and looked at her. She was standing just as before with the sheet pulled around her and clutched to her chest, watching him with those huge dark eyes.

"What?"

She sighed and looked sad. "I can't see my back. I can't reach it, either."

He stood very still, looking at her. "Oh."

She licked her lips, then tried to smile. "You're going to have to do it."

"Oh," he said again, and suddenly his mouth was dry and it felt like he hadn't taken a breath for too long.

"Okay, then."

He was willing.

CHAPTER FOUR

THIS was nuts.

David swore softly, trying to get a handle on this crazy reaction he was having. She was just a woman. He'd been with more women than he wanted to think about. He didn't get nervous around females anymore. He'd gotten over that years ago. He'd made successful passes at some international beauties in his day, film stars, rock singers, even a female bull fighter, without a qualm. So why was his heart thumping in his chest as he approached Ayme to check out her back?

She stood there so demurely, holding the sheet tightly to her chest so that it gaped in back, exposing everything down to the tailbone, but not much else. The entire back was there, interrupted only by the slender scrap of lace that was the band of her bra, but that might as well have been invisible. He didn't even notice it. He reached out to push her hair back off her neck, his fingers trailing across her warm skin, and the flesh beneath his hand seemed to glow.

"Okay, I'll do this as fast as I can," he said, then cleared his throat to try to stop the ridiculous quavering he could hear in his voice. "I'm just going to run my hand across your back a few times."

"Get it all," she said, head tilted up bravely. "I can take it." She drew in her breath as his fingers began to move.

"But don't linger," she warned softly.

Don't linger.

For some reason, those words echoed over and over in his head as he worked. Her skin was buttery smooth, summer-day hot, totally tempting, and every inch seemed to resonate to his touch. But he swore to himself that he wasn't going to notice anything, no matter how crazy it made him. He wasn't going to notice how good she smelled or how sweetly her curves seemed to fill his hand.

So why was his breath coming so fast? Why was his body tightening like a vise? This was insane. He was responding to her like he hadn't responded to a woman in ages. And all he was doing was checking for foreign objects on her back.

And being subtly seduced by her gorgeous body. He closed his eyes as he made a last pass down as low as he dared let himself go, and then drew back, saying, "We'd better check your underclothes, too," and heard his voice break in the middle of it.

He swore angrily, feeling his face turn as red as he'd ever felt it turn, but she didn't look back. She reached under the sheet and pulled off her bra and panties in two quick moves and checked them herself.

"They seem clear to me," she said without turning to look at him. "You can check too if you'd like."

"I'll take your word for it," he said gruffly.

This was unbelievable. He felt sixteen again. How had he ended up here? There was a tension in the room that was almost electric. Was he the only one who felt it, or did she feel it, too? It was probably best not to go there. He turned to leave the room without looking at her again.

"Wait," she said. "Do you think I'm clear?"

Reluctantly, he made a half turn back but didn't meet her gaze. "I didn't find any sign of anything, so I guess you are."

"Good. I'm glad. So now you don't suspect me any longer?"

He turned all the way and looked right into her dark eyes. "I suspect everyone, Ayme. Don't take it personally."

She made a small movement meant to be a shrug but almost more of a twitch. "I'm trying not to. But it's not easy."

His gaze was caught in hers and he couldn't seem to pull it away. There had been a quiver in her voice, a thread of emotion he couldn't quite identify, and it had touched him somehow. Looking at her, he felt suddenly confused, not sure how to respond to her.

"Go ahead and get dressed," he said gruffly as soon as he managed to turn away from her. Not looking her way again, he went through the doorway. "We'll get going in just a minute."

She didn't answer and he went into the kitchen, poured himself a glass of cold water and gulped it down, then took in a deep breath and tried to rationalize away what he'd just done.

It wasn't what it seemed, of course. How could it be? He didn't do things like that. His over-the-top reaction to her body was just a symptom of everything else going on around them—the muted fear, the preparations for running, the memories of his own tragic past. Just natural heightened apprehension. Hardly unusual. Nothing to be alarmed about.

She was just a girl.

Relieved and resolute, he went back into his more normal confident action state and returned to the bedroom with a spring in his step. Luckily, she appeared dressed and ready to go and when he looked into her face, there was nothing special there—no regrets, no resentment, no special emotions making him uncomfortable.

"Come on. We've got to get out of here." He slung his overnight bag over his shoulder and reached for the baby. "I'll get Cici. You bring your bags, okay?"

He led the way to the back steps, avoiding the elevator. It was a long, long climb down, but eventually they hit the ground floor, made their way to the parking garage and found his little racy sports car. He made Ayme and the baby wait against a far wall while he prepared for departure.

He'd done everything right. He'd switched out the license plates on the car. He'd checked under the hood and along the undercarriage for explosives. But even so, he winced as he started the engine with the remote, relieved when nothing went "boom."

Another day, another risky move, he thought to himself as he helped Ayme into the car and began packing baby supplies away in all the nooks and crannies. One of these times the click from the starter just might be the last thing he ever heard.

Now the next dilemma—should he head for a big city where they could get lost in the crowd, or for the countryside where no one would ever think to look? For once he chose the country.

But that was still a long way away. First, he headed into a direction directly opposed to where he actually wanted to go. After an hour of driving, he pulled into a protected area and hustled Ayme and Cici out of the car with all their belongings. Then he hailed a cab and they went in a totally different direction, stopping at a garage where he had arranged for another of his cars to be stored. This car was a complete contrast to his usual transportation, small and boxy and not eye-catching at all.

Ayme carefully maintained a pleasant expression. She didn't want to be a whiner. But she couldn't resist, as they squeezed into the small, cramped car, saying "I like the sports car better."

"So do I, believe me," he told her. "This is my incognito car."

"I can see why. You could probably join the Rose Parade unnoticed in this thing."

Glancing sideways, he threw her a quick smile that had actual warmth and humor in it, and she tingled a bit in response. It was nice to know he could do that. She'd been worried that he might be all scowls and furled brows with very little room for fun. But it looked like there was hope. It might not be all sex appeal with him.

She smiled to herself, enjoying her own little joke. She would love to tease him but she didn't quite dare, not yet. If he was right, they were running from danger here. Not a time for light-hearted humor.

Danger. She frowned out the window at the passing buildings. She wished she knew a little more about this "danger" element. Who was this dangerous person and why was he after David?

For just a moment, her mind went back to what had happened in the bedroom just before they left David's apartment. The way her pulse had surged in response to a few hot looks from the man was all the danger she could deal with right now. Clear and present danger. That's what he represented to a girl like she was.

Woman, she corrected herself silently. *You're a woman, darn it. So act like one!*

"You might as well relax," he said, glancing her way again. "It'll be a few hours before we get to our destination."

"I'm relaxed," she claimed. "Don't worry about me."

"Why don't you try to get some sleep while Cici is taking her nap?"

It was a sensible suggestion, but she wasn't in a sensible mood. Despite her bone-aching weariness, she was too full of adrenaline to sleep now.

"But I'll miss the sightseeing," she told him. "I want to see the countryside."

He glanced out at the gaunt, charred-looking buildings they were passing. "We're not going through a lot of countryside right now. More like an industrial wasteland."

She nodded, her eyes big as she peered out at everything, trying to take it all in. "I noticed that."

"Our route is circuitous and it's not going to take us through many of the nicest parts of England I'm afraid. I'm trying to keep it low key and stay away from places where I might see someone I know."

"It's smokestack city so far," she noted wistfully. "Oh, well. Maybe I will try to sleep a little."

"The views will be better in an hour or so," he promised.

"Okay." She snuggled down into the seat, closed her eyes and went out like a light.

He noted that with a sense of relief. As long as she slept, she couldn't ask questions.

He really had mixed feelings about Ayme. Why had he brought her along, anyway? He'd almost left her behind and it probably would have been the reasonable thing to do. But he felt a strange sense of responsibility toward her and of course he wanted to make sure that she was protected.

On the other hand, she probably wasn't going to thank him in the end for dragging her along on this wild-goose chase. She would be better off in a nice hotel in a touristy part of town where she could while away her time shopping or sightseeing or whatever. At the same time, he would have been free to slip in and out of various cities and countries without having to adjust for a baby. After a day hauling a child all over the landscape, she might be ready to accept a solution such as that.

It was a tempting proposition, but there was a major flaw in his thinking and it came to him pretty quickly. Someone out there in the world was fathering babies under his name. This was not helpful to the world situation or even to his own peace of mind. He had to find out who it was and he had to get it stopped. Until he'd managed that, it might be best to keep tabs on the young woman who'd dumped this particular problem in his lap.

Well, that was hardly fair. The problem had been there all the time. He just hadn't been aware of it until she'd arrived on his doorstep carrying the evidence.

But when you came right down to it, all that might be an excuse to keep her around, just because he liked looking at her. He glanced down at her. She was super adorable when she slept.

He had never been one to be bowled over by a pretty face. After all, there were so many pretty faces and he'd had his share of romantic adventures back when he was indulging in that sort of thing. He wasn't going to let a little fatal attraction get in the way of his plans.

He was hardheaded and pragmatic, as he had to be if he and his brother were going to succeed in getting their country back. Romance wouldn't work in times like these, and even a casual flirtation could cloud a man's mind and get in the way of the goal. What he and his brother planned to do was going to be hard, perilous and very possibly fatal.

Relationships were out. Period.

He wondered, and not for the first time, what Monte would think of what he was doing. He wanted to call him but this wasn't the place—nor the time. He had to be somewhere secure. Later—once they found a place near the coast to stay for the night, he would find a way to contact his brother.

She slept for two hours and then woke, stretching like a kitten and looking up at him as though she were surprised to see him.

"Hi," she said. "You're still here."

"Where would I go?" he asked, half amused.

She shrugged. "Since my life became a bad dream, I expect dreamlike things to happen all the time. Maybe a Mad Hatter at the wheel, or at the very least, an angry hedgehog."

"It's a dormouse," he muttered, making way for another car to merge onto the roadway in front of him.

"All right, an angry dormouse." She smiled, amused that he would know the finer points of the Alice in Wonderland story. "So you're neither?"

"Nope. But I have been accused of White Rabbit tendencies in the past." He gave her a sideways grin. "Always late for that important date."

"Ah." She nodded wisely. "Annoying trait, that."

"Yes. They say habitual lateness is a form of selfishness, but I think it's something else entirely."

"Like what?" She was curious since she was always late for everything herself and would like to find a good new excuse for it.

But he never got to the point of telling her. Cici intervened with a long, loud demand for attention from the backseat.

"Wow, she's hungry," Ayme noted, going up on her knees to tend to her over the back of the seat. She pulled a bottle of formula out of the baby bag, regretting that she couldn't warm it. But Cici wasn't picky at the moment. She sucked on the liquid as though someone had been starving her.

"Don't feel like the Lone Ranger, little girl," Ayme cooed at her. "There's a lot of that hunger thing going around."

"Subtle hint," he commented.

"I can get less subtle if it bothers you," she said, flicking a smile his way. "Do we have any food with us at all?"

"Not that I know of."

"Oh." His answer was disappointing, but pretty much what she'd expected. "Are we planning to rectify that anytime soon?" she asked, trying to be diplomatic about it.

He grunted. "I guess we could stop when we see something promising."

"Good. You don't want me to start wailing away like Cici does. It wouldn't be pretty."

She spent the next ten minutes feeding the baby, then pulled her up awkwardly and tried to burp her. David noted the lack of grace in her efforts, but he didn't say anything. She would learn, he figured. Either that, or she would find Cici's father and head back to Texas, free of burdens and swearing off children for all time. It seemed to be one of those either-or deals.

"We need a real car seat for her," he said as Ayme settled her back into the backseat. "If we get stopped by the police, this makeshift bed won't cut it. We'll probably both get carted away for child endangerment."

She plunked herself back into her seat and fastened the seat belt, then tensed, waiting for the inevitable complaints from the back. After a moment she began to relax. To her surprise, Cici wasn't crying. What a relief!

"When I was young," she told David, "my father would put me in a wash basket and strap me to the seat and carry me all over the Texas Panhandle on his daily route."

"Those were the days when you could do things like that." He nodded with regret. "Those days are gone."

"Pity."

He almost smiled thinking of her as a young sprout, peering over the edge of the basket at the world.

"What did he do on his route. Salesman?"

"No, he was a supervisor for the Department of

Agriculture. He checked out crops and stuff. Gave advice." She smiled, remembering.

"It was fun going along with him. My mother worked as a school secretary in those days, so my father was basically babysitting me and my sister." She laughed softly. Memories.

"Sam's basket was strapped right next to mine. As we got older, we got to play with a lot of great farm animals. Those were the best days." She sighed. "I always liked animals more than people, anyway."

"Hey."

"When I was a child, silly. Things have changed now."

The funny thing was he wasn't so sure all that much had changed with her. From the little bit she'd told him of her life, he had a pretty good idea of how hard she worked and how little she played. Someone ought to show her how to have a little fun.

Someone. Not him, of course, but someone.

They stopped at a small general store and he went in, leaving her in the car entertaining the baby. Minutes later he came out with a car seat in tow.

"This ought to do it," he said, and in no time at all they were back on the road, Cici officially ensconced in the proper equipment.

"She seems to like it fine," Ayme noted. "She's already falling back to sleep."

He handed her a couple of sandwiches he'd picked up in the store and she looked at them suspiciously.

"This isn't going to be one of those strange British things, is it?" she asked. "Vegemite or Marmite or whatever?"

He grinned. "Those are Australian and British, respectively. I'm Dutch. We eat kippers!"

"What's a kippers?"

"Kippers are canned herring, usually smoked."

"Fish?" She pulled back the paper. "Oh, no! What is that smell?"

"It's a great smell," he retorted. "A nice, sea-faring nation smell. Lots of protein. Eat up. You'll love it."

She was ravenously hungry, so she did eat up, but she complained the whole time. He ate his own kipper sandwich with relish.

"Good stuff," he remarked as he finished up. For some reason the fact that she was complaining so much about the food had put him in a marvelous mood. "That'll hold us until we get in later tonight."

She rolled her eyes, but more as a way to tease him than for real. Now that she'd had something to eat, she was sleepy again, but that made her feel guilty.

"Would you like me to drive?" she said. "You must be dead on your feet. You need some sleep."

He shook his head. "Do you have a license?" he noted.

"No," she said sadly. "Only for Texas."

"That won't work."

She sighed. "Sorry."

But in another few minutes, she was asleep again.

Just looking at her made him smile. He bit it off and tried to scowl instead. He wasn't going to let her get to him. He wasn't that easy. Was he?

When he couldn't resist glancing at her again he realized that maybe he was. But what the hell, it didn't mean a thing. It was just that she was so open and natural and so completely different from the women he was used to. For years now, he'd been hanging out with a pretty sophisticated crowd. And that was on purpose. He'd found out early that you could find out a lot if you hung with the right people and learned to listen. He had a very large hole in his life. He needed some very specialized information to fill it in.

Twenty-five years before, he'd been woken in the middle of a terrifying night, bundled up and raced out of the burning castle he'd lived in all six years of his young life. He knew now that his parents were being murdered at about the same time. It was likely that many of his brothers and sisters were killed as well. But one old man whose face still haunted his dreams had come to his room and saved his life that night.

Taken by people who were strangers to him from his island nation and smuggled into the Netherlands, he arrived the next day, a shaken and somewhat traumatized refugee, at the noisy, cheerful home of the Dykstra family. He was told this would be his new home, his new family, and that he must never speak of Ambria, never let anyone know anything about his past. The people who brought him there then melted away into the scenery and were never seen again—at least not by him. And there he was, suddenly a Dykstra, suddenly Dutch. And not allowed to ask any questions, ever.

The Dykstras were good to him. His new parents were actually quite affectionate, but there were so many children in the family, it was easy to get lost in the shuffle. Still, everyone had to pitch in and he did learn to take care of the younger ones. He also learned how to listen and quietly glean information. From the very beginning his purpose in life was to find out what had happened to his family and to find a way to connect with any of them who might still be alive. As he got older, he began to meet the right people and gain the trust of the powerful in many areas, and little by little, he began to piece things together.

At first the socializing had just been a natural inclination. But over time he began to realize that these people did move in circles close to the wealthy and the influential, elements that might prove helpful in his quest to find out what had happened to his family—and his country. Over the years various things half-heard or half-understood sent him on wild-goose chases across the continent, but finally, six months ago, he'd hit pay dirt.

He'd been playing a friendly set of tennis with Nico, the son of a French diplomat, when the young man had stopped his serve, and, ball in hand, had stared at him for a long moment.

"You know," he said, shaking his head, "I met someone at a dinner in Paris last week who could be your twin. It was a fancy banquet for the new foreign minister. He looked just like you."

"Who? The foreign minister?"

"No, idiot." Nico laughed. "This fellow I met. I can't remember his name, but I think he was with the British delegation. You don't have a brother in government?"

By now, David's heart was pounding in his chest as though he'd just run a four-minute mile. He knew this might be the break he'd been searching for. But he had to remain cool and pretend this was nothing but light banter. He took a swing into empty air with his racquet and tried to appear nonchalant.

"Not that I know of. All my brothers are happily ensconced in the business world, and spend most of their time in Amsterdam." He grinned across the net. "And none of them look much like me."

He was referring to his foster brothers, but the fact that he wasn't a real Dykstra was not common knowledge and he was happy to keep it that way.

"The ugly duckling of the family, are you?" teased Nico.

"That's me."

Nico served and it was all David could do to pay enough attention to return it in a long drive to the corner. Nico's response went into the net and that gave David a chance for another couple of questions, but Nico really didn't seem to know any more than what he'd said.

Still, it was a start, and the information breathed new life into his hopes and dreams of finding his family. He got to work researching, trying to find a list of the names of everyone who had attended that banquet. Once he had that, he began searching for pictures on the Internet. Finally, he thought he just might have his man.

Mark Stephols was his name. There were a couple of other possibilities, but the more he stared at the pictures of Mark, the more certain he became. Now, how to approach him and find out for sure?

He could find out where Mark was likely to be at certain public events, but he couldn't just walk up and say "Hi. Are you my brother?" And if he actually was, the last thing he could risk was standing side by side with the man, where everyone could immediately note the resemblance between them and begin to ask questions. So as he waited for the right chance, he began to color his hair a bit darker and grow a mustache. There was no point in making identification too easy.

His highly placed social intimates came in handy, and

very soon he obtained an invitation to a reception where Mark Stephols could be approached. Despite the hair dye, despite the mustache, the moment the introduction was made—"Mr. Stephols, may I introduce Mr. David Dyskstra of Dyskstra Shipping?"—their gazes met and the connection was made. There was instant—though silent—acknowledgment between the two of them that they had to be related.

They shook hands and Monte leaned close to whisper, "Meet me in the rose garden."

A few minutes later they came face-to-face without any witnesses and stared at each other as though they each weren't sure they were seeing what they thought they were seeing.

David started to speak and Monte put a finger to his lips. "The walls have ears," he said softly.

David grinned. He was fairly vibrating with excitement. "How about the shrubbery?"

"That's possible, too, of course. Don't trust anything or anyone."

"Let's walk, then."

"Good idea."

They strolled along the edge of a small lake for a few minutes, exchanging pleasantries, until they were far enough from the house and from everyone else, to feel somewhat safe. They looked at one another, then both jockied comments back and forth for another few minutes, neither knowing just what to say, neither wanting to give the game away, just in case what looked true wasn't.

Finally, Monte said out of the blue, "Do you remember the words to the old folk song our mother would sing when putting us to sleep for the night?"

David stopped where he was and concentrated, trying to remember. Did he? What had that been again?

And then he closed his eyes and began to murmur softly, as though channeling from another time, another place. In his head, he heard his mother's voice. From his mouth came the childhood bedtime song in Ambrian. When he finished and opened his eyes again, he turned to his brother. Mark had been still, but tears were coursing down his tanned cheeks. Reaching out, he took David's hand and held it tightly.

"At last," he whispered. "At last."

CHAPTER FIVE

AYME didn't sleep for long, and soon she was up and reacting to the beauty of the countryside.

"I don't know why I haven't come to Europe before," she said. "I've just been so wrapped up in law school and starting a new career and being there for my family."

Her voice faded on the last word and she had to swallow back her feelings. Every now and then it hit her hard. She had to hold it back. There would be a time to deal with sorrow and pain. The time wasn't now.

"And boyfriends?" David was saying. "I'm sure you've got a boyfriend back home."

She settled down, shaking away unhappiness and trying to live in the moment. "Actually, I don't," she admitted.

"Really."

"Really." She thought about it for a moment. She kept meaning to get a boyfriend. So far her life had just been too busy to have time for that sort of thing. "I've been going to college and going to law school and working, as well. There just hasn't been time for boyfriends."

"You're kidding." So it was just as he'd thought. She was a workaholic who needed to learn how to be young while she still had the chance. "Most women make time."

"Well, I didn't. I was so set on doing the very best I possibly could and succeeding and making my parents proud of me."

"Your adoptive parents, right?"

She nodded, biting her lip.

"Ah." He nodded, too. So it was a classic case of over-compensation. She probably spent all her time working frantically to prove it was a good decision for them to have chosen her. "You're the girl driven to bring home the As on her report card."

She smiled fleetingly, pleased he seemed to understand.

"And your sister Sam?"

"Sam not so much." She winced, wishing she hadn't said that. She didn't ever, ever want to say anything that even hinted at criticism of her adoptive sister ever again. She put her hand over her heart, as though she could push back the pain.

"I came over to Texas with a bunch of kids who'd lost their parents in the rebellion. We were all adopted out, mostly to American families with Ambrian roots."

"So it was an organized rescue operation."

"Sort of. I've told you all this, haven't I? I was adopted by the Sommers of Dallas, Texas, and I grew up like any other American kid." Her parents' faces swam into her mind and she felt a lump in her throat. They were such good people. They should have had another twenty or thirty years. It didn't pay to expect life to be fair.

"You don't remember Ambria at all?" he asked after a moment.

She gave him a look. "I was eighteen months old at the time I left."

"A little young to understand the political history of the place," he allowed with a quick, barely formed grin. "So what do you really know about Ambria?"

"Not much." She shrugged. "There were some books around the house." Her face lit up as an old memory came to her. "One time, an uncle stopped in to visit and he told Sam and me about how we were both really Ambrian, deep down, and he told us stories." She half smiled remembering how she and her sister had hung on his every word, thrilled to be a part of something that made them a little different from all their friends.

Ambrian. It sounded cool and sort of exotic, like being Italian or Lithuanian.

"Other than that, not much."

He thought that over for a moment. He'd had the advantage of being six years old, so he remembered a lot. But when you came right down to it, the rest he'd learned on his own, finding books, looking things up on the Internet. His foster parents had taken him in and assumed he was now one of the family and Dutch to boot. No need to delve into things like roots and backgrounds. That just made everyone uneasy. They had been very good to him in every other way, but as far as reminding him of who he was, they probably thought it was safer if he forgot, just like everyone else.

And if it hadn't been for one old man who had moved to Holland from Ambria years before and lived near their summer home, he might have done just that.

"Too bad your parents didn't tell you more," he mused, comparing her experience to his and wondering why such different circumstances still ended up being treated the same way by the principals involved.

"They were busy with their jobs and raising two little girls, getting us to our dance practices and violin lessons and all that sort of thing."

She moved restlessly. This was getting too close to the pain again. She hadn't told him about her parents yet and she wasn't sure she ever would. She knew she would never be able to get through it without breaking down, and she wanted to avoid that at all costs. Better to stick to the past.

"They were great parents," she said, knowing she sounded a little defensive. "They just didn't feel all that close to Ambria themselves, I guess." She brightened. "But being Ambrian got me a grant for law school and even my job once I passed the bar."

He remembered she'd mentioned something about that before but he hadn't really been listening. Now he realized this could be a factor. "Your law firm is Ambrian?"

"Well, a lot of the associates are of Ambrian background. It's not like we sit around speaking Ambrian or anything like that."

This was all very interesting. The Ambrian connection was going to turn out to be more relevant than she knew—he was sure of it. His jaw tightened as he remembered that he still didn't really know why she had shown up in his apartment or who had sent her.

But of course, there was a very possible explanation. She could, even unwittingly, be a stalking horse for a real assassin. Or she could merely be the one testing the territory for someone who meant to come in and make sure David never reached the strength to threaten the current Ambrian regime. It was hard to know and he was more and more convinced that she didn't know anything more than what she'd told him.

He remembered what she'd said about not knowing which side her parents had been on. Since she had no emotional identification with either side, she was pretty much an innocent in all this. If she was here because an enemy of his had sent her, she wasn't likely to be aware of it.

Still, he shouldn't have brought her along. It was a stupid, amateur thing to do. He should probably find a way to park her somewhere—if it wasn't already too late.

Because he couldn't keep her with him. He was due in Italy by the end of the week for the annual meeting of the Ambrian expatriate community. This would be the first time he'd ever attended. It was to be a gathering of the clan, a coming together of a lot of Ambrians who had been powers, or were related to those who had been, in the old days. He needed to be focused on the future of Ambria, not on Ayme and Cici. He couldn't take them along.

So—what to do with them in the meantime?

He'd promised he would help Ayme find Cici's father and he meant to keep that promise. It was bound to get a bit complicated, seeing as how his name had come into the picture, and he didn't have much time. But he had a few contacts. He would do what he could to help.

The only thing he could think of was Marjan, his adoptive sister who was married with two children and lived in a farming town in a northern area of Holland. It was a good, out of the way place where they could melt into the scenery. Maybe even he could slip in below the radar there.

It was odd how quickly he seemed to have slipped into the cloak-and-dagger mold. But then, he supposed he'd been training for it ever since he left Ambria, in attitude if not in action. It was true that he'd never felt he could fully open himself to others in his life. He always had to hide, not only his real identity, but also his feelings about things.

"So I guess you could say," he said, going on with their conversation, "bottom line, that you don't really care about who runs Ambria?"

"Care?" She looked at him blankly. "I've never given it a second thought."

"Of course not."

He turned away, feeling a surge of bitterness in his chest. Was it only he and his brother who still cared? If so, they were going to have a hard time rallying others to their cause. But it was hardly fair to lay this complaint on her. She couldn't help it that no one had bothered to educate her about her background.

And if he were honest with himself, he would have to admit that the strength of his own feelings had been greatly enhanced by his relationship with his brother. Before he knew Monte, his interest in Ambria was strong, even passionate, but diffused. It had taken an intensive experience with his brother to bring out the nuances.

It had been exciting and a fulfillment of a lifelong dream to find Monte the way he did. But it had been very difficult for the two of them to have any sort of relationship. They couldn't trust most forms of communication, they couldn't appear together anywhere because of how much alike they looked, they had to be aware of the possibility that someone was listening every time they spoke to each other. So Monte finally hit upon the perfect scheme—a six-week sailing trip in the South Pacific.

They met in Bali and proceeded from there, getting to know each other and hashing out the possibilities of being royals without a country to call their own. They had huge arguments, even huger reconciliations, they shared ideas, hopes and dreams and emotions, and they ended up as close as any two brothers could be. By the time the six weeks was up, they had both become impassioned with the goal of taking their country back, somehow, someday. To that end, they quickly become co-conspirators and developed a plan.

They decided to continue to go under their aliases. That was necessary for survival. Monte would travel in international circles he already had access to and try to gain information—and eventually supporters—and David would go undercover in the social jet-setting world he knew so well to glean what he could from business contacts on one side and the inebriated rich drones he partied with on the other. Their primary goal was to find their lost brothers and sisters and begin to work toward a restoration of their monarchy.

So he had a very large advantage over Ayme. He certainly couldn't expect her to share his goals when she'd never even heard of most of them and wouldn't know what to do with them if she had.

Their conversation had faded away by now and she spent some time watching the countryside roll past. Morning had come and gone and afternoon was sending long shadows across the land. The countryside was much more interesting now with its checkerboard fields and beautiful green hedgerows and the quaint little towns. This was more like the England she'd expected to see.

But the unanswered questions still haunted this trip as far as she was concerned. Where were they going? And why?

They stopped for petrol and David noticed a park nearby.

"Want to get out and stretch your legs?" he suggested as he maneuvered the car into the little parking lot next to a large tree. "I need to make a phone call."

They got out of the car and he strolled out of listening range. She let him go. There was no reason to resent his wanting privacy, after all.

He looked back as their paths diverged. He didn't want her to get too far away. But he needed to make contact with his brother.

Once he had Monte on the line, he filled him in on Ayme and the fact that he had her in tow. Monte was not enthusiastic.

"You're not bringing her to Italy, are you?"

"No, of course not. I'm taking her to my sister's. Marjan will take good care of her."

"Good."

"But in the meantime, I'd like you to do me a favor."

"Anything. You know that."

"Just information. First I need to know about a car accident outside of Dallas, Texas, sometime last week. A young woman named Samantha Sommers was killed. I'd like a brief rundown of the facts in the case, the survivors, etc."

"I'm jotting down your info as we speak."

"Good. Besides that I'd like anything you can find on Ayme. Her name is Ayme Sommers. She's an attorney for a law firm in Dallas that has a division which specializes in Ambrian immigration issues."

"Will do."

"And here's another one. There seems to be someone—probably in the greater London area—who is fathering babies under the guise of being Prince Darius."

That gave Monte pause. "Hmm. Not good."

"No. Do you think you can make inquiries?"

"I can do more than that. I can start a full-fledged investigation on that one."

"Without identifying your own interest in the case?"

"Exactly. Don't worry. I can do that easily."

"Good. I figure he's either found a way to make time with the ladies using the royalty dodge, or..."

"Or he's an agent trying to flush you out."

"You got it."

"I'm voting for the latter, but we'll see." Monte's voice lightened. "In the meantime, David...a bit of news. I've found the perfect wife for you."

David's head reared back. Despite his overwhelming respect for his brother, that hadn't sat well with him from the beginning.

"I don't need a wife right now," he shot back. "And if I did, I could find my own."

"You can find your own mistresses, Darius," Monte said, his tone containing just a hint of rebuke. "Your wife is a state affair."

David groaned softly, regretting his reaction. Where had his tart response come from, anyway? He and his brother had already discussed this and he knew very well that he needed a wife to help support the cause. The right wife. It was one of the obligations of royalty.

The two of them had pledged that everything they were going to do from now on was going to be for the benefit of Ambria. No self-serving ambitions or appetites would be allowed to get in the way. They were both ready to sacrifice their private lives—and even their actual lives if it came to that. He was firmly committed to achieving their goals. Nothing else mattered.

"Families are the building blocks of empires," Monte was saying blithely. "We need you to be married and to have a solid relationship. We've talked about this before. I thought you were on board."

"I am," David put in hastily. "Sorry, Monte. I'm just a little tired and short tempered right now. Don't pay any attention."

"Good. Wait until you meet her. She's beautiful. She's intelligent. And she's totally devoted to overturning the Granvilli clan's totalitarian regime. She'll fight by your side and rule there, too, when we achieve our goal." He chuckled. "I'm not worried about how you'll react. She'll knock you out when you see her."

"I'm sure she will."

But David grimaced, wondering if Monte wasn't perhaps overselling the case. He'd known a lot of bright, gorgeous and astonishing women in his time. So this was another one of them. Readiness to fight for the cause would be just the icing on the cake. He'd seen it all before.

But he couldn't completely discount Monte's opinion. He'd spent so many years adrift, not knowing where he was going or what he wanted to do with himself. He'd done well in his Dutch father's business, but his heart wasn't in it.

Once he and Monte had found each other, their future trajectory became clear. Now he knew what he was on earth to do. He had a new seriousness and a sense of purpose. His life had meaning after all. Finding the rest of his family and restoring them all to power was all he lived for.

"Keep me apprised as best you can. Let me know where you are if you can."

"I will."

Ringing off, he started back to join Ayme and the baby, stopping only to toss the cell phone into a trash can. You couldn't be too careful and he had a stock of extras, just in case.

The park was pretty and green and centered on a pond with a small bridge over it, creating a lovely vantage point for watching small silver fish swim by below.

"Look, Cici. Look at the fishies," Ayme was saying, holding the baby precariously at the rail and making David laugh. Still, he moved in quickly to avoid disaster.

"She's a little young for a swim," he commented. "Here, I'll take her."

And he did so easily. Ayme sighed. It seemed to come naturally to him and she was having such a hard time with it.

She watched him for a moment. He glanced up and caught her eye, but she looked away quickly, still uneasy, still not sure what the point of all this was. The questions just kept bubbling up inside her and she needed some answers.

"Okay, here's what I don't understand," she challenged him as they walked through the grass. "If you're Dutch, how come you care so much about Ambria? What is your tie to the place?"

He looked startled, then like a man trying to cover something up. "Who says I care so much about Ambria?"

"Oh, please! It resonates in everything you say."

Hmm. That wasn't good news. He was going to have to be a bit more guarded, wasn't he? Still, it did seem churlish to keep such basic information from her. It would all be common knowledge soon enough. Once he got to Italy, all would very likely be revealed anyway. He decided she deserved to be among the first to know. Just not quite yet.

"We can talk about this later," he said evasively.

"Wait a minute," she said, stopping in front of him and putting her hands on her hips. "I'm staging a small rebellion here."

Her dark eyes were flashing and her pretty face was set firmly. He knew better than to laugh at her, but it was tempting. She did look damn cute.

"What are you talking about?" he asked instead.

She sighed, shaking her head. "I don't get it. What the heck are we running from?"

"Danger."

"What danger? From whom?" She threw her hands up. "I don't see what I've done to put myself in danger. All I did was hop on a plane and come to England looking for Cici's father. How did that put me in danger?"

He raked fingers through his hair and looked uncomfortable. "It hasn't exactly. It's put *me* in danger." He took in a deep breath and let it out again, slowly. "And because you're currently attached to me, it's put you in danger, too."

Her chin rose and she watched him with a hint of defiance in her gaze. "Then maybe I should unattach myself."

She was just throwing that out there, waiting to see what his reaction would be. When you came right down to it, the thought of "unattaching" from him filled her with dread. At this point, she didn't have a clue what she would do without him. And she really didn't want to find out.

"Maybe you should," he said calmly, as though it didn't mean a thing to him. "It's a good idea, really. Why don't you do that? We can find you a nice hotel and get you a room…."

She observed the way he was holding the baby, so casual, so adept, and she looked at his handsome face, so attractive, so appealing. Did she really want to trade this in, danger and all, for the sterile walls of a hotel room on her own? Wouldn't she just end up trudging from place to place, trying to find someone who could help her?

Hmm. Good luck with that.

Maybe she ought to reconsider before this went too far. She wasn't going to detach herself from him until she had to. Who was she kidding, anyway? She was going to stick around and see what happened. She knew it. He probably knew it, too.

"On the other hand," she said in a more conciliatory tone, as they began to walk again, "if you would just let me know what's going on so I could understand and be prepared, it would be nice. I'd like to be able to make plans for myself once in a while." She searched his face hopefully. "It would be a big help."

His jaw tightened. "You want to know what's going on."

"Yes, I do."

He nodded. She was really a good sport. She deserved more information than he'd been giving her. He couldn't tell her everything. But he could do a better job than he'd been doing so far. He shifted the baby from one arm to the other, stood in one spot with his legs evenly spaced, like a fighter, and looked into her eyes. He was taking a risk in telling her. But what the hell—life was a risk. And despite everything, his gut feeling was that he could trust her.

"Okay Ayme, here's the deal. I am Ambrian. You guessed right from the beginning."

"I knew it!" Her eyes flared with happy sparks and she wanted to grab him around the neck and give him a triumphant kiss, but she restrained herself admirably.

"There's more."

He glanced at her, his intensity burning a hole in her skin and as she realized how seriously he was taking this, her victorious satisfaction faded.

"I've been working with other Ambrians determined to overthrow the usurpers and get our country back."

She gaped at him, suddenly feeling as though her bearings had been yanked away.

"No kidding," she said softly, feeling shaky. "No wonder there are people after you."

No wonder. That was a choice he'd made. But she hadn't made that choice, so what the heck was she doing putting herself and the baby in this sort of jeopardy?

Maybe she was going to have to tell him thanks, but no thanks, after all. Time to say goodbye?

His face was hard and serious and his tone was low and intense as he went on.

"The people who run Ambria right now have spies everywhere. They are very much interested in trying to destroy any opposition they see beginning to crop up. That's why I have to be careful and why I'm afraid of being tracked."

"Okay." She folded her arms across her chest and hugged herself worriedly. "Now I get it. Thank you for telling me that." She blinked up at him, her eyes wide, a picture of pure innocence. "Believe me, I won't betray your confidence."

He wanted to kiss her. Looking down, the urge swept over him. Her face was so fresh and honest, her lips full and slightly parted, her cheeks red from the outdoor air and he didn't think he'd ever seen anyone look prettier. The urge passed. He didn't act on it.

But it left behind another feeling—guilt.

She trusted him.

Ah, hell, he thought.

Guilt filled his throat. He was still lying to her, still leaving things out. She didn't know he was actually the man she was seeking. Well, that wasn't exactly the case, but close. If she knew who he really was, she would be able to focus better on finding the real father. On the other hand, maybe she would just believe he had fathered the child himself. Then what?

There would be no time for DNA tests. He had to be in Italy in less than a week. And he couldn't tell her about that—not yet. Probably not ever. After all, she wasn't going with him, so why did she have to know?

They went back to the car and packed everything away, including the now-sleeping baby, then climbed in themselves and started off. But all the while, he was thinking about their conversation.

There was still so much he couldn't tell her, but he could tell her a bit more than he had.

"Here's some more truth, Ayme," he told her after a few miles. "The truth is, I'm just like you."

"Like me?"

"Yes. I'm an Ambrian orphan, too. I was adopted by a Dutch family right after the rebellion. Just like you."

She thought about that for a moment. It seemed to fit the scheme of things nicely and it gave her a warm feeling of bonding with the man. Though when she glanced at his face, she didn't see any reciprocating on the bonding thing. He appeared as much as ever as though his profile had been hewn in stone.

So now she had some important information and she could use it to fill in the blanks. She knew why David was afraid someone was after him. And she knew why he felt such deep feelings for Ambria. And she knew why he might have connections in the Ambrian community that would help her find Cici's father. But she didn't know...

Turning to face him again, she confronted him with a steady gaze.

"Okay, mister," she said firmly. "Let's have it. More truth. I understand why you might have felt you had to take off from your apartment. And why you want to keep on the move. But what I don't understand is this— why did you bring me along?"

CHAPTER SIX

THAT was a very good question and David wasn't sure he had the guts to answer it, even to himself. He looked at Ayme.

He'd meant a quick glance, but something in her pretty face held him for a beat too long and he had to straighten the car into the proper lane when he put his attention back on the road.

That was a warning—don't do that again.

For some reason Ayme's allure seemed to catch him up every time. He didn't know why. She was pretty enough, sure, but it was something else, something in the basic man-woman dynamic that got to him, and he didn't seem to be able to turn it off.

"Come on, David," she was saying. "Tell me. Why did you bring me along?"

He shrugged and tried to look blasé. "Why do you think?"

She made a face. "My charm and beauty?" She managed to put a sarcastic spin on her tone that made him grin.

"Of course."

She rolled her eyes. "No, really. What was the deciding factor?"

He glanced at her, then looked back at the road and put both hands firmly at the top of the wheel.

"Okay, if you want me to be honest about this, I'll tell you." He hesitated and grimaced again. Since this seemed to be the time for truth why not go a little further? She could handle it.

"This won't be easy for you to understand. You'll think I'm overstating things. You might even think I'm a little nuts. But just hear me out and then decide."

"Of course."

"There are a couple of things going on here. First..." He took a deep breath and went on. "I've always had good reason to expect that someone would try to get to me and kill me someday and I'm not going to talk about why."

She sat very still, but she made a small grating noise, as though she were choking. He ignored it.

"When you arrived on my doorstep I had to consider the possibility that you, or someone who sent you, might be involved in something like that."

"David." Her voice was rough. "You thought I could be a killer?" The idea shocked her to her core.

He looked her full in the face and shrugged. "You bet. Why not?"

She sputtered and he went on.

"But it's more likely to be your Carl Heissman person. Don't you see that? And if I have you with me, you can't contact him and let him know where I am."

She made a gasping sound. "David, what have I done that would lead you to think—"

"Not a thing. And believe me, Ayme, I don't suspect you of anything at all. It's the people who sent you who have me on guard."

"Sent me?" She shook her head, at a loss. "Nobody sent me. I came on my own."

"Someone found out your plans, sought you out and gave you my name. Why?"

She stared at him, realizing he had a point. She remembered that she had been surprised when Carl Heissman contacted her and wanted to meet. He'd been friendly, concerned, charming and her doubts had quickly evaporated. But now that David brought them up again, she had to acknowledge them.

She could see that but, still, this all seemed crazy to her. People killing people was something she just wasn't used to. Assassinations. Killers. Spies. Those things were on TV and in movies, not in real life.

Was he for real or just some insane paranoid? But the more she studied his beautiful face, the more she was sure he believed every word he said.

Did that make it all true? Who knew?

"There's one little problem with that whole scenario," she pointed out right away. "If you left me behind, I wouldn't have known where you were within minutes of your leaving. So how could I tell anyone anything?"

His mouth twisted sardonically. This was obviously not a new thought to him. But all he said was, "True."

She waited a moment, but he didn't elaborate and she frowned.

"Anyway, I thought you were just protecting me from the bad guys, whoever they may be. Isn't that what you said?"

"I did say that, didn't I."

She frowned again, watching him as though she was beginning to have her doubts. "But we don't know who the bad guys are. Do we? I mean, we know they're these

Ambrian rebel types, but we don't know what they look like or what their names are. Right?"

"You're absolutely right. Rather a dilemma, don't you think?"

"Kind of nuts, that's what I think." She shook her head. "Maybe we should have stayed in the apartment. Maybe if we just stayed in one place and waited for them to show up, we'd find out who they are."

"We'd find out more than that. Not a good idea."

"Maybe. But you can't live your whole life just running all the time. Can you?"

"I don't know. I've only just begun."

She made a sound of exasperation and he grinned.

"We have a destination, Ayme. We're not just running for the fun of it."

"Oh. How about letting me in on where that destination is so I can share that feeling of comfort?"

"Not yet."

Her sigh had a touch of impatience to it. "In that case, I'm just useless baggage. So I still don't see why you brought me along."

"Because I feel some responsibility toward you. You came and you asked me for help. Isn't that enough?"

"So you're really planning to help me?" she asked as though surprised that such a thing might be the case.

"Of course. I told you I would."

She settled back and tried to think. What was the old expression, jumping from the frying pan into the fire? That was pretty much what she felt like. She'd been feeling vulnerable enough just searching for Cici's father. Now she was still searching for the man and being tracked by assassins, as well. And everyone knew what happened to people who hung out with people who were being tracked by assassins. Nothing good.

It was like reaching the next level in a video game. Suddenly the danger was ratcheted up a notch and you had to run that much harder.

From what she could gather going over the information he'd relayed, he was part of a revolt against the current regime in Ambria. Too bad she didn't know more about it so that she could decide if he was a good guy or not. From his point of view, he was obviously the "goodest" of the good guys, but that sort of thing tended to be a biased assessment. A strange thought came to her unbidden. What if he considered her a hostage?

The beginnings of a wail from the backseat interrupted her musings and gave notice that Cici was awake again.

"Uh-oh, here we go," Ayme said with apprehension.

David gave her a look. "You seem to live in dread of this baby waking up. She's barely announced her presence. And actually she's been quite good all day."

She sighed. She knew she shouldn't be taking it out on the baby. Still. "You don't know what it was like on that airplane crossing," she told him.

"Babies on planes." He nodded, thinking it over. "Yes, I have to admit that is not a pleasant prospect. But it was probably the pressurized cabin. It probably hurt her little ears."

"You think so?" That put Cici in the category of someone transgressed against instead of the transgressor. She looked back at the baby and gave her a thumbs-up.

"Sure," he said. "It's not likely she's going to cry that way all the time."

He was right. She hadn't been all that fussy lately. But Ayme attributed it to David's calming influence. It certainly had very little to do with her. She only wished she knew the secrets of how to reassure a baby and get it to stop howling.

Cici was awake but gurgling happily as they came into the seaside area where they were going to spend the night.

"Where are we going to stay?" Ayme asked, looking longingly at the Ritz as they cruised past it. Then there was the Grand with its long, sweeping driveway and uniformed attendants standing ready to help guests as they arrived at the huge glass doors. They zipped right by that one, too.

"It's just a little farther," he said, leaning forward to read a street sign.

She noticed that the farther they went from those elegant hotels, the farther they also went from the bright lights and sparkling entryways. Soon they were surrounded by gloom.

"Here we are," he said at last, pulling into a driveway that immediately plunged them down a dark tunnel and into a broken-down parking lot. "This is the Gremmerton."

She took note of the oily puddles and stained walls. "Might as well be the Grimmer-ton," she muttered softly to herself.

"What was that?" he asked, glancing at her as he parked and shut off the engine.

"Nothing," she said, feeling sulky and knowing she was being a brat. "Nothing at all."

He grimaced. He knew exactly what she was thinking but he didn't bother to explain why they were staying here. She would have to figure it out for herself. When you were trying to travel below the radar, you had to stay in places where people would never expect to find you. And at the same time, you had to be low key, so that people wouldn't look at you and sense the incongruity and say among themselves, "Hmm. What is someone like that doing here? You would think someone like that would be over at the Grand."

"We're running low on formula," he noted as they unloaded the car and prepared to carry things up into the room.

"I saw a small market on the corner when we drove up," she said. "If you'll watch her for a while, I'll run out and get some. After we get settled in."

"Good."

They climbed two flights of stairs and found their room. It wasn't really too bad, although it did have wall-paper peeling from one corner and a single light bulb hanging down from the ceiling.

It also had only one bed.

She stared at it for a long moment, then turned to look at him, perplexed. "What are we going to do?" she asked. "Maybe we can order in a rollaway."

"No," he said calmly. It was fascinating watching the sequence of emotions as they played across her face. "We're pretending to be a family. We'll share the bed."

Her eyes widened. "I don't know if we ought to do that," she said, gazing at him with huge eyes.

That one statement, along with her horrified look, told him everything he needed to know about the state of her innocence—as well as the state of her media-fed imagination. He bit back a grin and coughed a bit before he could respond.

"Ayme, do you think I'm not going to be able to control myself? Do you really think I'm going to attack you during the night?"

She looked very stern. Evidently that was exactly what she was worried about.

"Okay," she said. "Here's the honest truth. I've never slept in a bed with a man."

"No!" He pretended to be surprised, then wished he hadn't. He didn't want her to think he was mocking her. It was really very cute that she was so concerned. Compared to most of the women he'd become accustomed to, it was delightful.

"No, really," she was saying earnestly. "I don't know what will happen. I...I don't know men very well." She shook her head, eyes troubled. "You read things..."

"Ayme, don't pay any attention to what you read."

He reached for her. It seemed a natural enough instinct to comfort her. He took her pretty face between his hands and smiled down at her.

"Pay attention to what I tell you. I won't pretend I'm not attracted to you. I am. Any man would be. But it doesn't mean a thing. And anyway, I can handle it. I'm not going to go mad with lust in the middle of the night."

She nodded, but she still seemed doubtful. What he didn't realize was that she was reacting to only one of the things he'd mentioned: the fact that to him being attracted to her didn't mean a thing.

He'd realized by now that he shouldn't have touched her at all and he drew back and shoved his hands into the pockets of his jeans. Then he frowned, watching emotions play over her face and wishing he'd never started down this road.

But now she could add missing the wonderful feel of his warm hands on her face to the fact that to him, she didn't mean a thing. He'd actually said that. Any attraction between them was a biological urge, nothing more. She could have been any woman, it would have been the same.

Wow, she thought sadly. *Talk about crushing a girl's spirits. Didn't mean a thing.*

But what did she expect? She looked at him, at how large and beautiful he was. He was an exceptional man. He probably dated a lot of exceptional women. And he probably thought she was young and silly. Meanwhile, she'd begun to think that he was pretty wonderful.

He cleared his throat, wishing he understood women. She appeared unhappy and he didn't know if it was because of the bed situation or if something else was bothering her. "So let's just play this by ear, okay?" he tried hopefully.

"Okay," she said softly.

"You sleep on your side, I'll sleep on mine. If it would make you feel better, we can make a barrier down the middle with pillows."

Her smile was bright but wavering. "Like an old Puritan bundling board?" she said.

"If you want."

She seemed to be somewhat reassured, but he wasn't. He could still feel the softness of her face against his hands. He shouldn't have touched her.

"Where's the bathroom?" she asked, looking about the room.

"Down the hall," he said. "You can't miss it."

"What?" Ayme shuddered. This on top of everything. "Down the hall?"

"That's right."

"Oh, no, I can't share a public bathroom." She was shaking her head as though this were the last straw. "Are you crazy?"

"This is the way old hotels are set up," he told her. "You'll have to get used to it. You'll be okay."

"I won't," she cried dramatically, flopping down to sit on the edge of the bed. "Bring me a chamber pot. I'm not leaving the room."

She bit her lip. Deep inside, she was cringing. That hadn't really been her, had it? Couldn't be. She didn't play the drama queen, didn't believe in it. But it seemed a combination of circumstances had come against her all at once and for just a moment, she'd cracked.

She was tired, she was scared, she was exhausted, and she didn't know where she was going or what was going to happen once she got there. It was no wonder she was on edge.

But she didn't have to take it out on David. When you came right down to it, he was being very patient. In fact, he was a super guy. Which made it that much worse that she was having a silly tantrum. She could feel her cheeks redden.

Slowly she raised her gaze to his.

"Okay," she said. "I'm done."

"You sure?"

She nodded.

"I'm sorry," she said, trying not to cry. "I'll go check out that powder room now. I'm sure it will be lovely."

It took all his strength to keep from laughing at her

sweet, funny face. He pulled her to her feet by taking both hands in his.

"Come on. You can do it. Others have and lived to tell the tale."

He smiled down at her as she looked up. He was so close. For a fleeting second or two, she had a fantasy, just the flash of an image, of what it might be like if he would kiss her.

But that was ridiculous. There was no reason for him to kiss her. This was not a kissing situation, and anyway, they weren't in a kissing relationship. And never would be. Besides, any feeling between them didn't mean a thing. Hadn't he said so?

Get it out of your head, she scolded herself silently.

Sure, there had been a couple of hot looks between them when they had struggled over the body search incident. And certainly, his hands on her skin had sent her into some sort of sensual orbit for a moment or two. But that was just natural sexual attraction stuff. It might have happened with anyone.

Maybe.

She had to face facts here. She knew her own nature and was inclined to try to find a little romance in almost anything that happened. When she saw a film or a TV show and there was no love interest, her attention would wander. She wasn't a deep thinker. Speculative theories could hold her interest for just so long and no longer. What she wanted to see and to think about was people loving each other.

Maybe it was because she'd never had a real romance of her own. She kept hoping, but no one really wonderful had ever come her way.

Until David, a little voice inside was saying.

Well, she couldn't deny he was pretty darn good. Still, he could never be for her and she knew it. Right now they were thrown together. They were hiding. They were running from someone. They were both taking care of a baby. There wasn't much romantic in all that, but it did keep them involved. She was just going to have to learn to keep his theory in mind at all times.

No matter what happened, it didn't mean a thing.

And then, gritting her teeth, she made her way down the hall and found that the bathroom wasn't nearly as bad as she'd expected. In fact, it was rather cozy, with newer decorations and more accessories than the hotel room itself.

The worst thing was the huge mirror set over a vanity area with a chair and small table. There she was in living color, looking even more horrible and haggard than she'd thought. She was a mess. Her hair resembled a bird's nest. Her eyes were tired and the dark circles beneath them were epic. She groaned and immediately went to work, splashing water on her face and pinching her cheeks to get some color in them. As she tried to comb her hair into a more pleasing tangle, she realized what she was doing and why she was working so frantically to make herself look a bit better. She cared what David thought of her.

"Doggone-it," she whispered, staring into her own eyes in the mirror. There was no hope. He'd already seen the worst of her.

She made her way to the corner market and found a brand of formula that looked like it would do. She was standing in line at the cashier when it occurred to her that she didn't have the right money.

"Uh-oh." She made a pathetic face to the bored-looking young woman behind the counter. "All I have are American dollars. I don't suppose…"

The cashier shook her head, making all her many piercings jangle at the same time. "Nah. We've had some bad experiences. We don't accept American money after six."

Ayme stared at her wondering what difference the time made. "Uh…what if I…?"

"Sorry," the girl said dismissively, pursing her brightly painted lips and looking toward the customer behind her.

Ayme sighed, starting to turn away. She might as well go back, climb the two flights of stairs, get some proper money from David, and do this all over again. But before she could vacate the premises, someone else had intervened, stepping forward to stop the clerk from going on to the next customer.

"Allow me, madam," he said with a gracious nod of his head. In his hand was exact change. He gave it to the clerk with a flourish.

Ayme gasped.

"Oh. Oh, thank you so much." She smiled at him, thoroughly relieved. What a nice man. He looked like her idea of what a composer or conductor should look like—eyes brightly seeing something over the horizon, white hair flying about his head, seeming to explode out from under a smallish felt hat, a supernatural smile as though he could hear music from the heavens. All in all, she thought he looked delightful, and she was so grateful she was bubbling with it.

"You are so kind. This is incredible. I wouldn't accept it but I'm just so tired tonight and the baby is out. But

I do have the money. If you'd like to come with me to the hotel room where we're staying..."

Even as she said the words she realized this wasn't a good idea. They were supposed to be in hiding, not inviting in strangers. She made a quick amendment to her suggestion.

"Please, give me your name and address so I can make sure you get repaid."

He waved all her protestations away. "Don't think twice about it, my dear. It's not a problem." He tipped his hat to her and turned to go. "I hope you have a safe journey to the continent."

"Thank you so much."

She smiled, but as he disappeared into the crowd on the street, her smile faded. How did he know she was on her way to the continent? She barely knew that herself. But this seaside town was a bit of a launching location for trips across the channel. So maybe she was taking his words too seriously.

Still, it did give her pause.

"I assume we're going to the continent?" she said as she returned to the room and began to unpack the little bottles of formula. David already had Cici sound asleep in her new car seat, tilted back and rigged as a bed. "Is that our next move?"

"Yes. Tomorrow we'll be crossing the channel," he told her. He gave her a quick glance to make sure she was suffering no lasting damage from the earlier trip into a public facility, and the fact that she looked calm and pleasant seemed to confirm that all was okay.

"Heading for France?" she asked hopefully.

France! Paris! She would love to see it all.

But he gave her an enigmatic smile and avoided the issue.

"Possibly," he said.

"Or possibly not," she said mockingly, making a face.

He grinned.

"I almost didn't get the formula," she told him as she began to set up a feeding for Cici. She explained about the cashier and the white-haired man.

"It was so nice of him," she said.

Alarms went off in David's head but he quickly calmed himself. After all, she was a very attractive woman. Any man worth his salt would have stepped forward to help her in a moment of need. He would have done it himself. Hopefully that was all there was to it.

Still, he was wary.

"What did he say?" he quizzed her. "Tell me every detail."

"Oh, he was just a nice old man," she insisted, but she told him everything she could remember, and he couldn't really find anything extraordinary in it.

"Let me know if you see him again," he told her. He briefly considered changing hotels, but then he decided he was being a bit paranoid. There was really no reason to suspect the man of anything at all. "Right now I want you to lie down on that bed."

"What?" she said, startled.

His mouth twisted. She was so predictable on certain subjects.

"I want you to get some sleep. I'm going out for a while, but when I get back, I'll take care of Cici should she waken. We may have to take off at an odd hour. I want you to take this chance to get the rest you need."

She turned to look at him. He was handsome as ever, but his eyes did look tired.

"But what about you? You're the one who's been driving and you need some sleep yourself."

He gave her his long, slow smile that he only handed out on special occasions. "I never sleep."

She laughed, charmed by that roguish smile. "Oh, please. What are you, a Superhero?"

"Not quite. But close."

It occurred to her that she knew precisely what he was—wary and mistrustful of something. What exactly did he think was going to threaten them? What was it he was running from? He'd given her a brief sketch of his theories, but not many specifics. She wished he would tell her so she could worry, too.

"Ayme, do what I say," he said firmly when she still hadn't moved. "We don't have time for long, drawn-out discussions."

"Aye aye, sir," she said, sitting on the edge of the bed.

"That's the spirit," he said approvingly. "Consider this a quasi-military operation. I'm the superior officer. You do what I say without questioning anything."

She rolled her eyes dramatically. "Oh, that'll be the day!"

"Indeed." He shook his head and turned to go. "I have to go out to make a phone call."

"Why can't you do it from here? Don't you have your cell phone?"

"I've got my mobile," he responded. "But it's not the phone I want to use for this call."

"Oh." More likely, she thought, it was a call he didn't want her to overhear.

"I'll be back."

She didn't bother to ask again. It was confusing at times. For whole moments he would seem to warm to her, and that special connection would spark between them. Then, in an instant, it was gone again. She wished she knew how to extend it.

But she had other things to think about. She got up off the bed and puttered for a bit, putting clothes away in the closet and cleaning off the dresser of things David had thrown there. Cici still slept. Maybe she would be able to get that nap in as David had suggested she do.

Something drew her to the side window, and peering down into the gathering gloom, she could see the walkway along the front of the hotel. Suddenly, she caught sight of David. He had a cell phone to his ear and seemed to be carrying on an energetic conversation with someone. She could see him gesticulating with his free hand. As she watched, he ducked into the side alleyway beside the hotel and she lost sight of him. She wondered who he was talking to. Hopefully it was someone who knew Cici's father.

Funny how she always thought of him that way— Cici's father—instead of Darius, the Ambrian Prince, or the lost royal. Was that because, deep down, she was pretty sure that either Sam had been fooling her or someone had fooled Sam. The story didn't really seem to hold together. But maybe David would find out the truth.

It was interesting how she trusted him and she really didn't want to analyze why that was. She had a feeling it had something to do with a deep need for a sense of stability in her life. She wanted him to be good. Therefore, he had to be good. Simple as that.

She looked at Cici. Babies were so adorable when

they slept. She was starting to get a handle on how to care for a baby. At least, she thought she was. She was trying to copy everything that David did. It was obvious that a strong, steady hand, a soothing tone of voice and a sense of confidence made all the difference. Cici hadn't been crying much at all and that was certainly a relief.

"I'm a fast learner," she muttered to herself. "I will survive."

Turning from the window, she lay down on the bed and fell instantly to sleep.

CHAPTER SEVEN

DAVID had made a couple of calls, but now he was talking to his brother again. Monte had some information on the requests he'd made earlier. Ayme's background checked out perfectly. She did have an adoptive sister named Sam who had a few teenage arrests for petty crimes and who had died in a car accident just days ago. But that wasn't all. The girls' parents had died in the same accident.

"That's odd," David said almost to himself, reacting to the horror of what Ayme must have gone through. "I wonder why she would have held that back from me?"

"Never trust a woman, David. You aren't falling for her, are you?"

"Hell, no. Give me some credit, okay?"

"Sure, I'm only kidding. I have no doubt about your ability to hang tough. But on to other matters, there is nothing new on the impostor pretending to spread your love about the land. I'll let you know as soon as I hear anything."

"Thanks."

"In the meantime, there's news. Our Uncle Thaddeus has died."

"Oh, no." David felt real remorse. He was the last of

the old guard. "That's a shame. I was looking forward to meeting him someday, and hopefully hearing stories about our parents and the old days."

"Yes, so was I. It is not to be. But his funeral is another matter. We must go to it."

David frowned "Are you serious?"

"Yes. As luck would have it, the ceremony will be held in Piasa during the clan reunion gathering. It will be a huge affair. He's considered the patriarch of the Ambrian expat community. Everyone who means anything to Ambria will be there. It's our chance to begin to step forward and take the reins of the restoration movement. Whoever takes charge at the right time is going to rule the future." He paused, letting the importance sink in.

"Darius, you must come. I need you by my side."

"Of course. If you need me, I'll be there."

Monte gave him the details. "The town will turn Ambrian for a few days, it seems."

"Our covers will be blown."

"Yes."

David smiled. "Thank God."

"Yes."

They both laughed.

"Don't forget. Italy. Be there or be square."

"You got it."

He rang off, bemused and filled with conflicting emotions. He was looking forward to Italy. It was bound to be an exciting, important lesson about his own past, as well as a chance to lay the foundations for a new future. But as he turned back toward the hotel, it was Ayme and the information he'd heard about her parents that filled his thoughts.

He went back up to the room and opened the door quietly. Ayme and Cici were both sound asleep. There was only one light on in the room, in the far corner, and he left things that way, pulling off his sweater and unbuttoning his shirt but leaving it and his jeans on as he came to the bed he was going to share with Ayme.

Looking down, his gaze skimmed over her pretty face, her lovely bare shoulder, the outline of her leg beneath the sheet. She appealed to him, no doubt about it. He waited as the surge of desire swept through him. That he expected. But what surprised him was another feeling that came along with it, a tightening in his chest, a warmth, an unfamiliar urgency. It took a moment to understand what it was, and when it came to him, he closed his eyes and swore softly.

Everything in him wanted to protect her. Every instinct wanted to make sure no one could hurt her.

Where had that come from? He didn't think he'd ever felt that before. He'd spent so much of his life protecting himself, he hadn't had the capacity to worry about others. In other words, he was a selfish, self-centered jerk. And he could accept that. So where had this new soft-headed urge to nurture come from?

Maybe it was just because of the baby. Maybe he was blurring the lines between them in a visceral way he couldn't control. He knew he needed to watch that. It could put him in unnecessary trouble. He didn't want to go doing anything stupid.

More likely the facts that he'd just learned about Ayme's parents' fate had something to do with it. And maybe it was just that he was so damn tired. Could be. He knew he needed sleep. And there was a bed right in front of him. Too bad it was already occupied.

She'd been so shocked by the thought of them sleeping together this way, he sort of hated to spring it on her with no warning, no time for her to prepare. But he wasn't a predator. He was just a sleepy guy right now. And the bed was just too tempting to pass up. With a sigh, he began to prepare for getting some sleep.

Giving a half turn, Ayme gasped.

There was a man in her bed!

Luckily, it was David. This was just what she'd been afraid of. Could she really allow this? Didn't she have to make a stand or something?

But maybe not. He still had his jeans on, but his chest was bare. Still, he was fast asleep and completely nonthreatening. She relaxed and went up on one elbow to look at him in a way she hadn't been able to do before.

She'd been telling the truth when she'd said she'd never had a serious boyfriend. She'd done some dating in college, but it never seemed to come to much. Most men she'd met had either disappointed or annoyed her in some way. The type of man she attracted never turned out to be the sort of man she thought she wanted in her life.

So far David hadn't annoyed her. But he wasn't trying to hit on her, either. Her mouth quirked as she realized that if his disinterest went on too long, that in itself might get to be annoying.

"You're never satisfied," she accused herself, laughing at the paradox. "Picky, picky, picky."

No doubt about it, he was about the most handsome man she'd ever been this close to. She liked the way his lustrous coffee-colored hair fell over his forehead in a sophisticated wave that could only have come from a high-end salon. Then she laughed at herself for even thinking that way. This was no time to dilute her Dallas roots.

"Hey," she whispered to herself. "He's got a good haircut."

But the rest of him was purely natural and didn't depend on any artifice at all. His features were clear and even, his brows smooth, his nose Roman, his chin hard and newly covered with a coat of stubble that only enhanced his manliness. He looked strong and tough, but he also looked like a good guy.

And then there was the rest of him. He had a build to make any woman's heart beat a little faster—something between a Greek statue and an Olympic swimmer. His skin was smooth and golden and the tiny hairs that ran down from his beautiful navel gleamed in the lamplight. His jeans were the expensive kind and his shirt was crisp and smooth, despite all it had been through in the day. His hands were beautiful, strong but gentle. She leaned a little closer, taking in his clean, male scent and the heat that rose from his body, feeling a sudden yearning she didn't really understand. It was tempting to lean down and touch her lips to his skin. She leaned a little closer, fantasizing about doing just that, about touching that belly button with her tongue, about running her hand along those gorgeous muscles.

Then she looked back up into his face and found his blue eyes wide open and staring right at her.

"Oh!" she gasped, ready to jump back away from him, but his hand shot out and stopped her.

"Don't make any sudden moves," he whispered. "Cici is stirring."

She stayed right where she was, just inches from his face.

"So," he said softly, his eyes brimming with laughter. "I guess I caught you checking me out."

She gasped again and turned bright red on the spot.

"I was doing no such thing," she whispered rather loudly, her eyes huge with outrage.

"Oh, yes, you were." He was almost grinning now. "I saw you."

"No, I was just…" Her voice faded. She couldn't think of anything good to pretend she'd been doing.

"Hey, it's only human to be interested," he said softly, still teasing her. "Come on, admit it. You were interested."

"I'm not admitting anything," she whispered back. "You're not all that wonderful, you know. I mean, you may be tempting, but I can resist you."

Somehow that didn't come out quite the way she'd meant it and she was blushing again. His iron grip on her wrist meant she was trapped staying close. So close, in fact, that she could feel his breath on her cheek. It felt lovely and exciting and her mouth was dry. The laughter in his eyes was gone. Instead something new smoldered in his gaze, something that scared her just a bit. She couldn't stay here against him like this. She pulled back harder and this time he let her go.

She swung her legs off the bed and sat up, looking back at him. "I…I think I'll get up for now," she said. "I think you should get some sleep and…and…"

He pulled up and leaned on one elbow, watching her. "I think sleep is going to be hard to find for a while," he said dryly as Cici began to whimper. "We might as well both get up."

She rose and went to the baby and by the time she'd pulled her up and turned back, he was up and putting on his sweater.

"I'll go down and get some food," he said. "I'm sure you're hungry by now. Fish and chips okay for you?"

"More fish?" She wrinkled her nose.

"It's good for you." He hesitated. "I could probably find an American hamburger somewhere, if that's what you want."

"No, actually I like fish and chips just fine. As long as the fish isn't kippers."

He grinned. "Don't worry. They don't make them that way too often."

He left the room and she sighed, feeling a delicious sort of tension leave with him. He'd said it didn't mean a thing, but she was beginning to think he'd been fooling himself. For her, it was meaning more and more all the time.

The fish and chips were okay and so was the pint of ale he brought back with them. But now it was time to tend to Cici and hope to convince her to go back to sleep so that they could get some rest, as well. After a half hour of pacing back and forth with a baby softly sobbing against her shoulder, Ayme had a proclamation to make.

"I've decided I'm not going to have any children," she said with a flourish.

"Oh." David looked up from the evening paper he'd picked up with the fish. "Well, it might be best to hold off until you get married."

She glared at him. "I'm not going to do that, either."

He smiled. "Right."

"I'm serious about this," she insisted. "Babies take over your life. It's unbelievable how much work they are."

"It's true." He had some sympathy for her state of mind. He'd been there himself. "They do monopolize all your time. But that doesn't last forever."

"It certainly seems to last forever on the day you're doing it."

He leaned back. "That's just for the moment. Before you know it, they're heading out the door with their friends and don't need you at all anymore."

She gave him a long-suffering look. "How long do you have to wait for that lovely day?"

"It takes a while."

"I'd be marking off the days on my calendar."

He grinned. "It can be hard, but think of the rewards."

"What rewards?"

Cici stirred in her arms, stretching and making a kitten sound. He watched as Ayme's fierce look melted.

"You see?" he said softly.

She smiled up at him ruefully. "Yeah, but is it all really worth it?"

He shook his head. How the hell had he become the family practices guru here? Still, she seemed to need some sort of reassurance and he supposed he could do that at least.

"Once you have one of your own," he told her, "I think you'll figure that out for yourself."

He rose and took Cici from her, and as he did, he thought of what Monte had told him. He'd thought from the beginning that there was a sense of sorrow lingering in her gaze, something deeper than she was admitting to. Why hadn't she told him about her parents? She must have a reason. Or maybe, as Monte hinted, it was a sign that he shouldn't trust her.

But what the heck—he didn't trust anybody, did he?

"Ayme, you've said you don't know much about your birth parents and you don't know much about Ambria. What exactly do you know?"

She scrunched up her nose as she thought about it. "Just a few things I've picked up casually over the years."

"You should know more."

She looked at him and made a face. "How much do you know?"

"I don't know as much as I should, either. I should have learned more."

"So we're both babes in the woods, so to speak."

He nodded, though there was obviously a vast gulf between what he knew and what she did. "Why weren't you more curious?"

She didn't answer that one, but she had something else on her mind.

"You were adopted just like I was," she noted. "Didn't you ever feel like you had to...I don't know. To prove to your parents that they should be glad to have picked you?"

He stared at her. "Never," he said.

She shrugged. "Well, I did. I was always trying so hard to make them proud of me."

He could see that. He could picture her as a little girl in her starched dresses with patent leather mary janes on her little feet.

Cici had finally fallen asleep and he laid her down in her little car seat bed before he turned toward Ayme again.

"And were they?" he asked softly, his gaze taking in every detail of her pretty face. "Proud of you, I mean."

"Oh, yes. I was the perfect child. I made straight As and won awards and swam on the swim team and got scholarships. I…I think I did everything I possibly could." A picture swam into her head. She'd entered the school district Scholars' Challenge, even though she was the youngest competitor and she was sure she had no chance. Jerry, a boy that she liked, had tried out and hadn't made it. He mocked her, teased her, made her miserable for days, saying she'd only made it on a fluke, that she was going to be the laughing stock of the school.

By the time the night of the competition rolled around, she didn't like him much anymore, but he had succeeded in destroying her confidence. She went on stage shaking, her knees knocking together, and at first, she didn't think she could hear the questions. She panicked. Jerry was right. She wasn't good enough. She looked to the side of the stage, ready to make a run for it.

Then she looked out into the crowd. There was her mother, looking so sweet, and her father, holding a sign that said Ayme Rocks. They were clapping and laughing and throwing kisses her way. They believed in her. There was a lump in her throat, but she turned and suddenly she knew the answer to the question, even though she thought she hadn't heard it right. She was awarded ten points. She wasn't going to run after all. A feeling of great calm came over her. She would do this for her parents.

She won the trophy for her school. Her parents were on either side of her as they came up the walk at home. Suddenly, her mother stepped ahead. She threw open the doors to the house, and there inside were friends and neighbors tooting horns and throwing confetti—a surprise celebration of her win. It was only later that she realized the celebration had been planned before her parents knew she would win. They were going to celebrate her anyway.

Thinking of that night now, tears rose and filled her eyes and she bit her lip, forcing them back.

"I think I made them very happy. Didn't I?"

Her eyes were brimming as she looked up into his face as though trying to find affirmation in his eyes.

He couldn't answer that for her, but he took her hands in his and held them while he looked down at her and wished he knew what to say to help her find comfort.

She took in a shuddering breath, then said forcefully, holding his hands very tightly, "Yes. I know I did." She closed her eyes, made a small hiccupping sound and started to cry.

He pulled her into his arms, holding her, rocking her, murmuring sweet comforting things that didn't really have any meaning. She calmed herself quickly and began to pull back away from him as though she were embarrassed. He let her go reluctantly. She felt very good in his arms.

"Sorry," she murmured, half smiling through her

tears. "I don't know what made me fall apart like that. It's not like me to do that."

"You're tired," he said, and she nodded.

He waited, giving her time, wondering when she was going to tell him her parents had died in the accident, but she calmed down and began to talk about a dog she had found when she was young.

"And what about Sam?" he asked at last, to get her back on track.

Now that she had unburdened herself this far, he felt as though she might as well get as much out in the open as she could bear. A catharsis of sorts.

And she seemed to want to talk right now. There was a little couch in the room and they sat down side by side and she went on.

"See, that's the flip side of it," she said. "The dark side, I guess. The better I did, the worse Sam seemed to do." She tried to smile but her face didn't seem to be working right at the moment. "The more I seemed to shine, the more Sam rejected that path. She became the rebel, the one who didn't succeed, on purpose. She got tattoos against our father's orders and got her nose pierced and ran around with losers."

"That sounds pretty typical. I've seen it before."

"I guess so." She shrugged. "Funny, but I can see it so much more clearly now than I ever did then. I knew she resented me." She looked up quickly and managed half a smile. "Don't get me wrong. We shared a lot of good times, too. But the undercurrent was always resentment. I used to think if she would just try a little harder... But of course, she felt like I'd already taken all the love slots in the family. There was no room for her to be a success. I'd already filled that role. She had to find something else to be."

"That must have been hard on your parents."

"Oh, yes. But in some ways, they didn't help matters. They weren't shy about telling Sam what they thought of her."

"And comparing her to you?"

"Yes, unfortunately. Which didn't help our relationship as you can imagine."

"Of course."

"So Sam left home as soon as she could. By the time she showed up with Cici, she'd been mostly gone for years, off with some boyfriend or another and only coming back when she needed something. She broke our parents hearts time and time again. And then, suddenly, there she was with a baby in her arms. Of course, part of us was thrilled. A new member of the family. But at the same time, my parents were horrified. Where was Cici's father? Had there been a wedding? I'm sure you can guess the answer to that one."

"I think I can."

"She was penitent at first. I think she'd been under a lot of stress trying to deal with a baby on her own. But once she got some good sleep and some good food, she quickly became defiant again. And when Mom tried to get her to make some realistic plans she had a tantrum."

"That was helpful."

"Yes. It was later that night that she told me who Cici's father was. She came to my room to ask me to take care of Cici. She claimed she'd tried motherhood and it didn't agree with her. So she was taking off."

"Just like that."

"Just like that."

"What did you say?"

She turned to him. "What do you think I said? I got hysterical." She threw up her hands. "I couldn't take her baby. I…I refused and I yelled a lot. I told her either our parents would have to raise her…or we'd have to put her up for adoption."

"Ouch."

"Oh, yes. I said horrible things." She looked at the sleeping baby. Was she looking at the situation any differently now? "Things I didn't mean. But I was trying to get her to face reality. She had the responsibility. She couldn't just shrug it off."

"And yet, somehow that is the way it worked out."

She nodded.

"She took the keys to my mother's car and drove off into the rainy night."

"And your parents went after her?"

"Yes. And they found her quickly enough."

"And?"

She flashed him a stiff smile. "There was an accident. And Cici became my problem."

He watched her, puzzled. Why not take that next step and tell him her parents had died in that accident, too? What was holding her back? It was a horrible thing and she was probably still reeling from the shock of it. But surely it would be better to open up about it, work through it, put it in some sort of context with her life. Until she did that, he was afraid she would have that look of tragedy deep in her eyes. And what he wanted most for her—wanted with a deep, aching need—was happiness.

CHAPTER EIGHT

CICI was fussy during the night and Ayme and David took turns walking her. That way, they both got enough sleep and in the morning they were actually feeling rather refreshed and ready to face another day.

And it was a beautiful morning. They ate a quick breakfast and then went walking along the stone path that led to the marina, watching the morning sun glint over the silver sea and the breeze shuffle some puffy white clouds across a cerulean sky. Cici was good as gold, her big blue eyes wide as she looked out at the world, so new and fresh in her young gaze.

Ayme had found a little stash of cute clothes in the bag, things she hadn't packed and didn't remember, so she'd been able to dress the baby very stylishly for their morning walk.

"This is the fun part, putting them in cute clothes," she told David.

"I never knew that," he said doubtfully. "Somehow that never appealed to me."

"Live and learn," she advised him with a sassy smile.

He grinned. He liked her sassy smile. In fact, he was beginning to realize he liked a lot about this young woman. Too much, in fact. But he wasn't going to think about that this morning. He was going to enjoy the weather, the scenery—and her.

They watched ships and boats sail in and out of the harbor, watched the fishermen come in with a catch. They listened to the sounds, smelled the sea odors and breathed in the sea air. Then it was time to go back and they walked slowly toward the hotel. David felt a strange contentment he wasn't used to. Cici made a cute, gurgling sound and they both laughed at her. He smiled. What a cute kid.

But whose kid?

Was there really a chance that he could be Cici's father? He'd racked his brain trying to remember who he'd been dating almost a year ago. He was afraid it was rather emblematic of his lifestyle that he was having so much trouble. What did it prove? Maybe nothing. But it did mean he'd had encounters with women that meant nothing to him, didn't it? And that wasn't anything to be proud of.

He was virtually certain he couldn't be the baby's father. And yet, one tiny little doubt kept nagging at him. It was the kind of thing where you woke up in the middle of the night and stared at the ceiling as the thought whirled in your brain, larger than life. During the day, it faded into irrelevancy, hardly noticeable. And yet, it wouldn't fade completely away and leave him totally alone.

He was thinking about it when Ayme suddenly whirled and pointed toward a man disappearing around a building.

"Look! There's the man from the little store last night."

He turned and looked but the man had disappeared. "What man?"

"The white hair…didn't you see him?"

"No. Who is he?"

"I don't really know, but he was very sweet to me last night at the convenience store. Remember? I didn't have enough money and he paid for me. Actually, I owe him some money. Keep a look out, maybe we can flag him down and I can pay him back."

The entire incident put David on alert. In his current frame of mind, seeing anyone twice on their itinerary was seeing them too often. He swore softly.

"Damn," he said as reality flooded back. "We're going to have to go."

"Go?" She turned to look at him. "Go where? Why?"

There was no point in trying to explain to her. She would just ask more questions. Besides, they didn't have the time.

"Come on, hurry. We've got to get going."

"Okay, but tell me why."

"I wanted to wait until dark," he said instead. "Everything's easier in the dark."

"Or harder, as the case may be."

"True." He flashed her a quick grin. "Let's pack up and get out of here post haste."

Ayme was hurrying along, but rebellion was smoldering in her heart.

"David," she said softly. "Tell me what we plan to do."

"Get away from your white-haired man."

"What? Why? He was very nice."

"Most assassins are great guys to go bowling with,"

he told her from the side of his mouth. "You can look it up. It's in the statistics."

She looked at him and shook her head. He wasn't taking her request seriously and it was beginning to make her angry. Swinging around in front of him, she blocked his path into the hotel and confronted him, hands on her hips.

"You know what? You need to give me a reason for all this. I can't do things without a reason. I'm a methodical, logical thinker and I really need to know why I'm doing things."

He seemed annoyed but tried to be patient. "I will. I promise you. Just give me a little more time."

She threw up her hands. "For all I know, we could be on our way to rob a bank or knock over a candy store or kidnap a famous hockey star or...who knows?"

"None of the above," he assured her, though he knew she was just using those as examples. "Ayme, we don't have time for this. We'll talk once we're on the road."

She sighed. She knew she wasn't going to be able to stand her ground. Not yet. But if he kept this up...

"Oh, all right," she said, and they raced for the stairway.

They were able to get a slot on the service that packed cars in for the trip through the tunnel, and they made it in record time. A short time later, they were back on the highway, on the French side of the channel.

Ayme was excited. After all, this was part sightseeing trip for her. But when David made a left turn where she was expecting a right one, she protested.

"Hey, the sign says 'Paris, that way'."

He glanced at her warily. "But we're not going to Paris."

Her heart sank. "Where are we going?"

"You'll see."

She bit her tongue. She'd had just about enough of this "you'll see" stuff. If he didn't trust her enough to let her know their destination at this point, what was she doing with him?

And then she had a brief moment of self-awareness and she realized she really ought to stop and think about what she was doing, period. Why was she running around the countryside with this man she barely knew? It was bad enough that she'd dropped everything to race to London with Cici on a mere address and a whim. But what was she doing now? This was crazy. His apprehension of being in danger was obviously sincere or he wouldn't be taking these measures to stay hidden. And here she was going right along with him—as though she were meant to. Insanity!

But she knew very well why she was doing it. Of course, his being such a gorgeous hunk of male humanity didn't hurt. There was a spark between them; she wouldn't deny that.

But there was something more, something deeper, something worse. She was doing it to avoid reality.

Funny, that—she'd jumped headlong into a dangerous chase in order to avoid her real-world situation. It seemed a contradiction. But she knew it was pretty accurate. Anything beat sitting around and thinking about her life. The longer she stayed on this journey to nowhere, the longer she could put off dealing with what had happened to her sister and to her parents. And the longer she could put off facing what the rest of her life was going to be like.

Okay, so she knew why she was doing this. And she

knew why he was doing this—at least she had a good idea. But that didn't mean she had to sign on to this "you'll see" business any longer. Either she was a partner in crime, or she would bail out of this situation. Well, maybe not bail exactly. But she would let him know she wasn't happy and insist on better treatment.

She settled back and looked at him, at his beautiful profile and his sexy day's growth of dark beard, at the way his gorgeous, shiny hair fell over his forehead. He glanced her way and frowned.

"What?" he said. "What's the matter?"

She didn't answer. She just kept looking at him. He glanced her way a few more times, and finally, with an exclamation of exasperation, he pulled over to the side of the road and turned to face her.

"What's wrong?" he demanded crankily. "You're driving me crazy with this silent routine. Tell me what you want."

She stared hard into his starry blue eyes. "Trust," she said at last. "I want to be trusted."

From the puzzled look on his face, she could see he had no idea what she was talking about.

"I trust you," he protested.

"No, you don't. If you trusted me, you'd tell me the truth."

A wary look suddenly clouded his gaze.

"Ah-ha!" she thought. There was evidence of guilt if she'd ever seen it.

"The truth about what?" he asked carefully.

"Everything," she said firmly.

Everything. He let his head fall back against the headrest and chuckled softly. If she only knew how much more complicated that would make it all.

"Ayme, Ayme, what makes you think I actually know the truth about anything?"

"You know more than I do. And that's all I want." She moved closer, touching his arm with her hand, trying to make him understand just how important this was to her. "You see, this is what I hate—you knowing and me not knowing. You guiding and me following without a clue. I need to be in control of my own destiny. I can't just sit here and let you control my fate. I have to have some free choice in the matter." Her fingers tightened on his arm. "Give me facts, let me make my own decisions. Let me make my own mistakes. But don't treat me like a child, David. Please. Let me be your partner."

He looked into her earnest face and felt a wave of emotion different from anything he'd ever felt before. He liked her. He liked her a lot. Too much, in fact. But he didn't care. There was something so good and true and valuable in her. Reaching out, he cupped her cheek with the palm of his hand and smiled into her eyes. The urge to kiss her bubbled up in his chest. Another urge competed. He wanted her to have whatever she wanted in life and he wanted her to have it right now. He wanted to protect her and be there for her and, at the same time, to let her fly free.

But mostly, he wanted to kiss her. He was moving closer, looking at her pretty lips. He could already taste her….

But wait. Swearing softly, he pulled himself up short. Someone had to. Taking a deep breath, he slipped his hand from her face and looked away and pulled himself together. What the hell was he doing here?

Frowning fiercely, he got tough.

"You want some facts, Ayme? Okay, here you go. I've

had word that there definitely are people following me. It's not all in my mind after all."

An early morning call to Monte had given him that information.

"I think your white-haired man may be one of them."

"Oh."

"Right now I'm trying to think of a way to get us to a safe place I know of without the bad guys knowing for sure where we are. So we are headed for a nice Dutch farm area to the north. My sister lives there. If we make it there without something bad happening, we're going to stay with her for a bit."

She sighed. That was all she wanted, a little sign that he trusted her, at least a little.

"Thank you," she said earnestly. Then she smiled. "That sounds nice. I always like people's sisters."

He watched her face light up and he groaned inside. The temptation to kiss her was with him all the time now. Every time he looked at her, he could feel what her body would be like against his and all his male instincts came to life. He had to find a way to ratchet his libido down. The whole sexual attraction thing was a new way to complicate his life and he had to resist it.

"I'm sure she'll like you, too," he said gruffly.

She nodded happily. "Okay then. Lead on."

And he did.

But he knew very well that the information he'd given her would only be the beginning. It was human nature. Once you had a taste, you wanted more. They hadn't driven for half an hour before she was asking questions again.

"So who exactly are these people who are following you?"

He shrugged. "I assume they are agents of the regime in Ambria. But I don't know that for sure."

"Because they know you are working against them?"

He nodded. This was no time to get into the rest of the reason.

She frowned thoughtfully, biting her lip. "We need something to call them. The Bad Guys is too generic."

"You think?"

"Yes, I do." She thought for another minute or two. "I've got it. Let's call them the Lurkers."

He shrugged, amused by her urge to organize everything. "Sounds fair."

She smiled, obviously pleased with her choice.

And she was pleased with Holland, too.

"It's so beautiful here," she said after a few hours of watching the landscape roll by. "It's like a fairy tale. Everything is so cute and clean."

"That's the Netherlands," he agreed. "It's quite a nice place."

"And you grew up here."

"That I did."

"Did that make you into a nice person?"

He grinned at her. "It's good to see you've noticed," he told her.

She smiled back at him. That spark thing happened and they both looked away quickly. But Ayme was warmed to her toes and floating on a cloud.

By late afternoon, they had arrived at the outskirts of the town of Twee Beren where David's sister lived.

"Here's another news flash for you, Ayme," he said

as he began to navigate the tiny streets. "If my current plan works out, we'll be making our way to my sister's house in a farmer's hay wagon. How's that for local color?"

"Oh. That's interesting." Though she was a bit taken aback at the prospect.

"I thought you'd like that. Hope Cici can take all the straw."

"The straw?" Ayme blinked at him. "What straw?"

"We'll be in hay. Straw." He gave her a puzzled glance. "You do know what a hay wagon is, don't you?"

"I…I think so. In fact, I think I've been on one before when I was a little girl and going around to the different ranches with my father."

"There you go. You should be an old hand at this."

"Hmm."

"The thing is, I'm sure the people following us…."

"The Lurkers, you mean."

He nodded, his wide mouth twisted in a half grin. "The Lurkers. They have the license number on this car, so we have to ditch it somewhere unobtrusive in the town. Then we'll switch over to the hay wagon. That ought to throw them off."

"I know it does that to me," she muttered, shaking her head, wondering what on earth he was thinking.

He pulled into a parking space near a vacant lot, switched off the engine, and turned to her. "Okay, here we go. We have about two blocks to walk. I'll carry Cici. Try to look inconspicuous."

She gazed at him, wide-eyed. "How do I do that?"

He looked her over. She was right. She was gorgeous with the afternoon sun shining in her golden hair.

Everyone within a half mile would be craning their neck to see her.

"Think ugly," he said, knowing it was no use. "Here, wear this wool cap."

She put it on and now she resembled a ragtime street urchin. He smiled. He couldn't help it. She was so darn adorable.

But someone else walking by was smiling at the picture she made, too, and he frowned.

"Come on. We're becoming a spectacle just trying not to be one. It's no use. We'll have to hurry along and hope we blend in."

They gathered their things, packed in a sleeping Cici and made their way down the street and around the corner to where a rather mangy-looking horse stood hitched to a relatively flat farmer's wagon. Hay was piled on it high as a hay stack and it had been left right in front of a small, friendly seeming pub.

David nodded with satisfaction.

"Good. Some things never change. Old farmer Shoenhoeven has been stopping here for his afternoon drink for as long as I can remember. When he leaves for home, he goes right past my sister's farm." He grinned at his own memories. "It's been fifteen years since I last did this. And to think the old man is still going strong. How old must he be? He seemed ancient back when I was a kid."

"You know him? Do you think he'll give us a ride?"

"He'll give us a ride but he's not going to know about it," David said, scanning the street. There weren't many people out and about. "We can't sit up there with him for all to see. We're going to hide in the back of his wagon."

"We're going to do what?" She came to a screeching halt and whirled to face him, appalled. "Even in Texas we don't do stuff as goofy as that."

"Well, here in Holland, we do." He looked around the quiet street again. There was no one in sight.

"Come on. As you walk past, turn in a little. There's a place where you can climb up. See the foothold? Just swing yourself up and make a dive under the straw."

She turned to face him, horrified. "Are you kidding me?"

"Hurry, Ayme," he commanded in a tone that brooked no debate. "Before someone comes around the corner."

"But…"

"Now!"

She threw her hands into the air but she did as he said. He came right behind her, handing off the baby and pushing back the straw so that they would all fit beneath it. They scrunched in, lay side by side under the straw and stayed very still. Ayme was holding her breath, listening intently, but no one came along to challenge their right to jump aboard.

"Is Cici okay?" David asked in a low voice at last.

Ayme looked at the baby, then blew a small piece of straw out of her mouth before she answered. "She's still asleep. Can you believe it?"

Carefully, she laid the baby down on a blanket between two wooden boxes, making sure no straw was touching her face. Then she turned back to David. They'd made a little cave in the straw and it was actually rather cozy. The corners of her mouth quirked.

"This is really silly," she whispered to him. "I feel like my feet are sticking out the bottom. Like the witch in *The Wizard of Oz*."

He grinned at her, leaning on his elbow and looking incredibly handsome with his eyes dancing and hay in his hair.

"Do I look like a farm boy?" he asked her, chewing on the end of a long straw.

"Uh-huh."

"Hush," he told her. "Or we'll have people calling in to the police about checking out a talking hay stack."

She couldn't meet his gaze without giggling. "Here we are in the back of a hay wagon." She was laughing out loud. Then she hiccuped and laughed harder.

"Shh," he hushed warningly, reaching to quiet her.

"This is just so funny, it's so ridiculous," she said between hiccups. "I mean, what are we doing here?" She was laughing again.

"You're getting hysterical," he warned near her ear.

"I'm not hysterical. You're tickling me."

"I'm not tickling you."

"Your breath. It tickles my skin."

Somehow that very concept sent her into new gales of laughter that she tried to stifle, but couldn't. He was on the verge of laughing, too, just from watching her. But she had to be quiet and stop making the haystack move if they were going to get away with this. And she showed no inclination to do so.

So he kissed her. As far as he could see it was the only option, short of throttling her.

It was meant to be a quick shock to her system, a way to stop the laughter in its tracks. A warning. A suggestion. A way to keep her from harming them all. But it turned into much more than that.

When his mouth covered hers, her lips parted immediately and her tongue flickered out as though to coax him inside. He took that invitation and made his move and then everything began to blur. His senses went into red-velvet mode. Everything about her felt soft and plush and everything he touched seemed to melt before him. He'd never felt anything this wonderful before. He never wanted to stop.

And neither did she. Every other man she'd ever kissed had been a wary exercise in testing waters that she hadn't found very warm, nor very tempting. This was so different. She felt as though she'd reached for a ripe fruit and had fallen over a cliff just as she grabbed it. It was a fall that had her spiraling from one level of delicious sensation to the next. She never wanted to reach the bottom of that canyon. She wanted to fall forever, as long as she was in David's arms.

She stretched. She reached for him—she was begging for more. His embrace was such a comfort to her, such a warm, safe place to be. She sank into the kiss as though she'd finally found a place where she really belonged.

But not for long. He pulled back, cursing himself silently for being such an idiot. This was exactly what he'd been warning himself against. He couldn't do this. It was stupid, but most of all it wasn't fair to her.

"I'm sorry," he said, hair falling over his eyes as he looked down at her. "I didn't mean to do that."

"Shh," she said, eyes wide. "He's coming."

They listened, quiet as mice, while the man called out his goodbyes and started to sing as he came toward the wagon.

Ayme gasped. "David, he's drunk!"

"Nah."

"Yes, he is," she whispered near his ear. "Listen to him."

"He's not drunk-drunk. Just a little tipsy. He's had his evening Bols and he's floating a bit. That's all."

The farmer climbed up into the driver's seat and called the horse to attention, and they started off. The wagon creaked loudly. The horses hooves clanged against the pavement. And the farmer sang at the top of his lungs.

"He's definitely had too much to drink!" Ayme hissed at David.

"Yes," he admitted. "Yes, he has. But it's okay. This isn't like a car. The horse knows the way. He'll take over."

"The horse!" She shook her head at the concept.

"You can always count on the horse. Out here in the country, you can fall asleep at the wheel...or the reins, I guess it is...and the horse will still get you there."

She wasn't sure she bought that one. "How do you know all this?"

"I used to live out here. Every summer, we spent at least a month in the country."

The wooden wheels hit a rock and they all bounced into the air.

"Ouch. This is bumpier than I remember. I guess my bones are older now."

Ayme was laughing again, which made him laugh. She was right. This whole thing was crazy. But at least they might be losing the Lurkers, leaving them in the dust. He certainly hoped so. He didn't know for sure what they wanted, but he knew he didn't want to give it to them. And he had a feeling it probably had something to do with an effort to keep him from showing up in Italy at the end of the week. That only made sense.

He was glad he'd thought of going to Marjan's. She was the closest to him in age of all his adoptive siblings. They'd been quite close growing up. She was married now and living a mile or so outside the little village of Twee Beren. He hadn't been able to call ahead, but he knew she would be happy to see him. She always was. Hopefully, she would be happy to take in Ayme and Cici until he could find Cici's father. That would leave him free to maneuver, and free to meet Monte in Italy. And that would get him away from the temptation Ayme was beginning to represent. The sooner the better for that.

They didn't have to be as sneaky bailing out as they had been climbing in. The farmer was singing so loudly, he wouldn't have noticed a brass band piling out from under the straw.

And then the farmhouse was right before them. David rang the bell and a pleasant-looking, slightly plump woman answered, took one look at them and threw her arms around her brother's neck without a word.

Ayme watched, just a step away, and then she followed them into the large, comfortable house while Marjan explained that her family was away and she was alone.

"Hans takes the children to see his mother every year for her birthday, and usually I go, too. But this time I had promised to make pies for the cheese festival in town, so here I am, rolling out pie dough all day instead."

David was glad he only had one person to try to explain things to. He'd been wondering just what he was going to say to her about why he was on the run, and why he wanted Ayme to stay with her. But he got a reprieve while the women chatted happily with each other and Marjan fixed up a bedroom for Ayme and the baby. Cici was being fussy and his sister helped quiet her with a practiced touch.

"You do that as easily as David does," Ayme told her with admiration as she watched.

"Oh, we all grew up taking care of babies. I sometimes think my whole life has been nothing but babies, from beginning to end."

David coughed discreetly. "There were those years at the Sorbonne."

Marjan grinned "Yes, but we don't talk about those." She rolled her eyes. "Massive waste of time."

David raised an eyebrow. "Didn't you have fun?"

Marjan gave him a look. "Fun is overrated. It often leaves behind a large mess that is very hard to clean up." She turned to Ayme. "You'll want your baby with you, won't you?"

"Oh! Of course."

"We still have a little crib that will be perfect."

She gave them both some soup and sent Ayme, who looked dead on her feet, off to bed. Then she turned to her brother.

"It's not her baby, is it?"

David smiled, waving a soup spoon at her. "You could tell that quickly?"

She nodded. "It wasn't just the fact that she doesn't have a smooth way of caring for her. There was something in the way she looked at the child." she shrugged. "That total depth of feeling just wasn't there."

David nodded slowly. "You're right. But she's actually

a lot better at hiding it than she was when she first burst into my life."

"Oh?"

"At that point she was practically holding the poor thing by one leg."

Marjan laughed. "She was claiming the baby was hers?"

"Yes. But when she constantly referred to a book on child care I knew pretty quickly that she was a fraud."

Marjan frowned. "That's a harsh word to use, don't you think?

"You're right," he said ruefully. "Fake is much more accurate."

Marjan laughed. "Are you going to tell me the story? Or do I just have to wait and read about it in the papers?"

He looked at her ruefully, not sure how much he should tell her.

"Maybe we could start with this—just tell me where you two are headed."

"We're not 'you two'," he said defensively. "We're not a couple."

"No?"

"No. I'm going to Italy. And she's…" He sighed. "I was hoping she could stay with you for a few days."

"Of course." She nodded wisely. "I just read in the paper about the last of the old Ambrian royal family dying. Thaddeus, isn't it? I saw that his memorial service is scheduled to be held in Italy."

David stared at her. "Interesting," he said carefully.

"Yes." Her smile was guileless. "Will you be going to that?" she asked.

David's heart was beating a little harder.

"Why do you ask?" he said.

"No reason." She rose. "Would you like some more soup?" she asked him with a smile.

He didn't answer. He stared at her for a long moment. "How did you know?" he asked at last.

CHAPTER NINE

"OH, DAVID." Marjan ruffled his hair affectionately. "I've long had my own ideas about who you are and why you came to live with us in the middle of the night so long ago."

He stared at her. He'd never known she knew. "I hope you keep those ideas to yourself."

"Oh, I will. I understand the danger." She sat down next to him and reached out to hold his hand. "I figured it out years ago. Remember the summer you were fifteen? Suddenly you were too busy reading to go for a nice bicycle ride by the canals as we used to. You were always with your nose in a book, like you were possessed. I couldn't understand why, so I looked into what you were reading. Ambria. That funny little island country almost nobody knows anything about. But you were crazy for the place, and I was jealous. My buddy was hooked on something new and leaving me behind."

He squeezed her hand and she smiled at him.

"So I started reading about it, too, and I found information about the lost princes. The dates matched the time when you came to live with us. Then I looked at pictures of the royal family." She shook her head, smiling at him. "Then I knew. It was such a great story. My brother, the prince."

He sighed. "Do the others know?"

She shook her head. "I don't think so. I don't think of any of them ever stopped to wonder why you were with us or where you came from, or why a family who already had five children and more on the way would want another one. They just assumed your family were close friends with our parents and we took you in when you needed us to." She laughed softly.

"Do you remember? We spent long summer evenings talking about what was and what could be. I knew there was something more to you than mere happenstance. Besides, I remembered that night you arrived, everyone whispering and acting like something very scary was about to happen." She nodded. "So when I read about that death, I thought you might be going to Italy for the memorial service. I would think it is time for you to take up the cause."

"Are we going to Italy?" Ayme's voice cut into the kitchen's warmth.

They both jumped, realizing Ayme had come into the room behind them. David quickly scanned her face, looking for evidence that she might have heard more than he would want her to. But her eyes were clear. He didn't think she'd heard anything much.

"I have to go to Italy," he told her. "Marjan has said that you can stay here until I get back."

Her eyes suddenly filled with tragedy, imploring him. "Oh, no," she said softly. "But we haven't found that Darius person yet."

He got up from his chair and went to her, reaching

out to take both her hands. She was dressed in a long white nightgown Marjan had loaned her and she looked like an angel. A lump rose in his throat. She was so beautiful, it made his heart hurt.

"We'll talk about it tomorrow," he told her. "Get some sleep. Your eyes are like bruises on your face, they're so dark."

She searched his eyes, then nodded. "All right," she said. "I just came out to get Cici's warmed bottle, but…"

"Here it is," Marjan said, handing it to her. "Good night, Ayme. Let me know if you need anything else."

Ayme gave her a wavering smile. "Good night. And thank you so much."

She gave David one last look and turned to go.

Marjan looked at David's face and her eyes got very round. She nodded knowingly. "Not a couple?" she murmured.

But he was watching Ayme leave and he didn't seem to hear her.

Ayme fed Cici, put her back into her cute little crib and slipped back into the huge fluffy bed. It felt warm and luxurious. Maybe if she just closed her eyes and let herself go limp she would fall asleep right away—and not have to think.

She tried it. It didn't work.

Her eyes shot open and she stared into the darkness. But she wasn't going to think about Sam or her parents. She would never sleep if she let that happen. Better to think about David. She snuggled down into the covers and closed her eyes and imagined David in the bed with her. She was asleep in no time.

* * *

The next day dawned a bit blustery. David made a careful survey of the area from his window on the second floor, but he didn't see any sign of surveillance activities anywhere in the neighborhood. Ayme and Cici came out looking fresh and rested and Marjan cooked them all a wonderful breakfast.

Ayme and David lingered over coffee.

David was trying once again to figure out what had started this race across the continent, and why he'd suddenly known he was in danger and had to flee. Was it really Ayme showing up the way she had? Or the phone call in the night? Or just that it was time to leave for Italy and the sense of a gathering storm had become his reality?

"Have you tried to call that man in Dallas?" he asked her.

She shook her head.

"Has anyone tried to call you?"

She gave him a crooked smile. "How would I know? You made me turn my phone off."

"Check your voice mail," he said.

She checked, but there was nothing. Just the absence of the usual cheery greeting she could expect daily from her mother—a lump formed in her throat, but she shook it off.

He pulled out a leather case that had four cell phones in neat pockets and took a moment to choose one.

"Why do you have so many phones?" she asked.

"Just in case. I like to be prepared." He set a phone up and looked at her. "Okay, give me the number."

"What number?"

"That Carl guy. I want to check him out."

She opened her own phone again and retrieved it,

reading it off to him while he clicked the numbers in. In a moment, there was a snap and a voice answered.

"You've reached the number for Euro Imports. Mr. Heissman is out at the moment. Please leave your name and number so that he may call you back. Thank you for calling Euro Imports."

"Euro Imports," he muttered, getting out his laptop and going on the Internet. There it was. It seemed to be legit.

He looked at Ayme who had been watching all this with interest.

"I guess your friend Carl is at least a real businessman in Dallas," he said. "So if that was him calling the other night, maybe it wasn't such a threatening call after all."

She nodded.

"Or maybe it was something else entirely." He gave her his best Humphrey Bogart impression. "You just never know. The problems of three little people like us don't matter a hill of beans in this crazy world."

She laughed, warmed to think he was talking about the very three people she was thinking of. It almost made it seem like they were a family of sorts.

They finished up their coffee and David asked his sister to watch Cici for an hour so that he could take Ayme along on a pilgrimage of sorts. He wanted to see if old Meneer Garvora, the man who had taught him some of the fundamentals about Ambria, still lived in the area.

They set off down the lane between hedgerows and David told her how the old man had caught him fishing in a landowner's fishpond one day when he was about ten, and as punishment, he'd made him read a book about Ambria and come by to give him a report.

"I have no idea how he knew about my ties to that country, or if he even did know. But he insisted I learn a lot about the place. I owe him a debt of gratitude for that."

He realized now how much the old man had husbanded the flame in him, making sure it didn't go out in the cold wind of international apathy. How had he known how important that would be to David's future?

"I wish someone had taught me a thing or two," Ayme said in response.

He looked over at her and smiled. "I'll teach you everything you need to know," he said.

But she gave him a baleful look and he realized she was brooding about his plan to leave her with his sister.

They reached the little cottage where David's mentor had lived, but the place seemed a bit deserted.

"This looks like a place where hobbits might live," Ayme noted. "Or maybe the seven dwarves."

David knocked on the door but there was no answer. Walking about in the garden, they found a stone bench and sat together on it, gazing into a small pond and enjoying the morning sunshine, and he told Ayme about some of the lessons the old man had given him when he was a boy.

Memory was a strange thing. Now that he'd opened his mind to that past, a lot came flooding in that he hadn't thought of in years. He especially remembered how lost and lonely he'd felt as he tried to make sense of his situation. He'd spent years wondering about his family, wondering what had happened to them.

At one point in his childhood, he'd asked his foster mother. Neither of this second set of parents ever brought up the fact that he was an addition to their thriving nest. They treated him as though he'd come the same way the others had come, and looking back now, he was grateful. But at the time, it made it hard to bring up the subject of his old life. He felt as though he was betraying their kindness in a way. Still, he had to find out whatever he could.

When he'd finally built up the courage to ask, his foster mother had looked sad and pulled him onto her lap and given him a hug. She told him how sorry she was for the tragedies in his life. She gave him sympathy and a tear or two. But what she didn't give him was the truth.

Maybe she didn't know anything else. He realized that now. But at the time, he'd resented the lack of information. He'd felt as though he had to operate blind in a seeing world. He wanted to know about his siblings. He wanted to know what his parents had been like. He had a thousand questions and his foster parents gave him sympathy but not much else.

As he grew older he tried doing research on his own, but he couldn't find much. Most of the world seemed to assume that his entire family had been wiped out in the rebellion, but since he knew different, he didn't take that seriously. He knew there was hope that more royals had survived. Still, he was always aware, just as he'd been aware that dark, stormy night, that the wrong move or a careless word could bring on disaster.

And then he had been found by Meneer Garvora. The old man, in his crusty way, had opened up the world of

Ambria to him. Looking back, he realized now what a resource he had been.

"So he gave you what your new parents just couldn't," Ayme noted. "How lucky that you had him in your life."

He nodded. "My adoptive parents were very nice to me. I thoroughly appreciate all they did for me. And I've had a nice career working for my father's company." His gaze clouded. "But they were never my real parents the way yours seem to have been with you—we never had that special closeness." He shrugged. "Maybe it was because I could still remember my birth parents, and that made it more difficult to attach to new ones. But it was also because there were just so darn many of us kids, it was pretty hard to get much individual attention."

Ayme sighed. "I had all the attention in the world. I was the fair-haired child and I enjoyed every moment of it. Analyzing it now, I can see that their joy in my accomplishments pushed Sam to the sidelines, and I regret it so much."

Tears shimmered in her eyes. David reached out and put an arm around her shoulders, pulling her close. She turned her face up to his and he kissed her softly on the lips.

She smiled. "I like you," she said softly.

He'd only meant to comfort her. He only wanted to shield her from pain. But when she looked up at him and said that so sweetly, he lost all sense of reality in one fell swoop.

He wanted to speak, but his throat was too choked for him to say anything. He more than liked her. He wanted her, needed her, felt an overpowering urge to take her in his arms and kiss her lips and kiss her breasts and make her feel his desire until she was ready to accept him, body and soul.

The thought of taking her body with his set up an ache and a throbbing in him that threatened to blow away all his inhibitions. He was all need, all desire, all urgent hunger. He felt, for just a moment, like a wolf who'd caught sight of the prey that destiny had been saving just for him—how could he be denied?

He took her face in his hands and saw acceptance in her eyes. He could hardly breathe, and his heart was beating so hard he didn't hear the sound of the back gate opening until a voice called out, "Who's here?"

He froze. His body rebelled. Closing his eyes, he forced himself back into a sense of calm, and as he did Ayme slipped from his hands, rising to meet the elderly woman coming around the corner.

"Well, hello," she said. "I've just come to pick up the mail from the box."

David rose as well, feeling like a man who had just avoided the pit of stark, raving madness. He was breathing hard, but he managed to smile and ask "Doesn't Meneer Garvora live here anymore?"

"Oh, certainly, he still lives here just as he has for thirty years," she responded in a kindly manner. "But he's gone on a trip right now. First time I've known him to go anywhere for years and years. He said he might be gone for quite some time." She waved an arm expansively. "I'm watering his pots for him while he's gone."

"I see. I'm sorry to have missed him." Turning, he looked down into Ayme's clear brown eyes. There was a question in them. And why not? What he'd almost done was insane and she was wondering whether he should be committed, no doubt. Internally he groaned. He was going to have to control himself better if he didn't want to bring down the whole house of cards on his own head.

Man up! he told himself silently. *Think of Ambria. Think of Monte.*

"Yes," the lady was saying. "Aren't you one of the Dykstra clan? I seem to remember seeing you visiting here years ago. Am I right?"

"You're right. Meneer Garvora gave me some important geography lessons in the old days. I just wanted to come by and thank him for that."

"I'll tell him you came by."

They started to go and David turned back. "By the way, did he say where he was going?"

"Yes, of course. He went to Italy."

David's eyebrows rose at that news. Thanking the woman, he nodded to Ayme and they started back down the path to the farmhouse.

"Hmm," Ayme said, noting his reaction to hearing his old mentor's destination. "Are we going to Italy, too?" she asked, just a bit archly.

He growled but didn't really answer.

"If I could just find this Darius person," she murmured.

He looked at her and frowned. "Listen, we need to talk about that." He hesitated, but there was no time like the present. "You do realize it is not very likely he was ever planning to marry your sister."

"Oh, I know that." She waved his statement away. "Knowing Sam, I doubt she was ever planning to marry him." She smiled sadly, remembering her sister. "Sam wasn't one to yearn for marriage. In fact, she wasn't one to stick with one man for more than a weekend."

He made a face. "Ouch."

"Well might you say that." She nodded, remembering the painful past. "I'm expecting him to be a sort of male version of Sam, if you know what I mean." She gazed at him earnestly as they walked along. "I just think he has a right to know about Cici and she has a right to the chance that her Dad might want her."

He winced. He was only just beginning to realize how hard this was all going to be. "I know. It's been bothering me, too."

"I don't know how much you can blame him. I mean I'm sure he's the sort of man who has women throwing themselves at him constantly. Being a handsome young and eligible prince and all."

He had to give her that. He nodded with a half smile he couldn't hold back. "Of course he does. But that doesn't mean he has to accept them, does it? Not if he has any integrity."

She gave him a bemused smile. "Celebrities with integrity? I'm sure there are a few, but..." She shrugged. "Hey, I've had men throw themselves at me all my life. Some seem to think I do have certain charms."

His sideways glance was warm. "I'll second that emotion."

She felt a glow of pleasure but she didn't want to lose her equilibrium. "But I would never let it go to my head. That way lies the pit, and once you fall over the edge, you're done for."

He grinned at her melodramatic tone. But then his grin faded as he remembered how he'd almost lost control just a half hour before. He hadn't even known it was possible. He'd never felt anything like that before, so strong, so overwhelming, so irresistible. It was almost scary—his own private "pit."

"So anyway, I think I should give him a chance to make a case for himself. Mostly for Cici's sake."

He had to admire her for that. If only he wasn't pretty sure that this guy was a rat, and maybe even needed exterminating.

Something stopped him just before they got back within sight of his sister's house. Some natural-born instinct for survival, perhaps. Whatever it was, it told him right away that danger lurked, and he had Ayme follow him as they stayed behind the bushes and traveled down along the hedge at the edge of the canal instead of walking in on the road. They kept out of sight and sneaked in through the back gate, surprising Marjan in the kitchen.

"Oh, I'm so glad you came in that way," she said as soon as she saw them. "I've just heard from my friend Tilly Weil that there is a man watching the house. He hangs out in that little stand of trees over there, across the way, pretending to be a bird watcher."

David went to the window, standing to the side. "How long has he been there?" he asked.

"Tilly thought he was there early this morning, then seemed to go have breakfast somewhere and is now back, binoculars in hand. So you see, you didn't get away with your ride in the hay wagon."

"Maybe," David said. "And maybe he's just watching my sister's house in case I might show up there. You can't tell." He looked at Ayme. "But I'd better go."

Ayme turned to look at him, her eyes huge. He felt

an ache in his heart. It was going to be hard to leave her behind.

"First of all," his sister said, "I know you're going to be anxious to go, but from what we've seen, I think you're right, that they don't know for sure whether you are here or not. And I say you wait until morning. If you do that, you'll have a place to stay tonight, and tomorrow I may have a way to get you out of here completely unseen by the outside world."

David thought for a moment. She had a point. If they left now, they would just have to find another place to stay for the night and it was getting late for that.

"All right," he said at last. "We'll go in the morning. Early."

"Ayme, I hope you'll be staying here with me," Marjan said, trying to help David do the right thing. She turned to him. "She'll be a big help, and at the same time I could teach her some practical things about babies."

He studied his sister's pleasant face for a moment, feeling a warmth for her he didn't feel for many other people. But he couldn't look at Ayme. He knew she was holding her breath, waiting to see what he would say.

Various and sundry thoughts ranged through his head as he stood there, thoughts about his brother's plan to match him up with the woman who was perfect princess material, about how his brother had warned him against getting entangled with Ayme, about how much easier it would be to sneak around on his own if she stayed behind. He had to keep his eye on the prize. He knew that. Ayme being with him tended to diffuse his focus at times.

His head knew all these things and agreed with them.

But his heart and soul had other ideas. He couldn't keep her with him forever, but he wanted her close right now. He needed her. Why? He wasn't ready to verbalize that just yet.

But he also wanted to make sure she was protected. For now. Not for always—that was impossible. But for now. For now.

He'd made up his mind. He was taking her to Italy with him. Monte wasn't going to like it, but he didn't care. Monte wasn't king yet.

"Thank you for your offer, Marjan. I appreciate it and love you for it. But I can't take you up on it. Ayme has to come with me."

Ayme's heart leaped in her chest. Yes!

Marjan's smile was understanding. "Well, then, how about the baby? You can leave her here. I'll take care of her. You need to be able to slide through the world without the baggage a baby entails."

Ayme's heart was beating as fast as a bird's, making her feel faint. She held her breath. Deep inside, she knew there was no way she would ever leave this helpless little baby behind. But what would David say?

He turned slowly. He looked at her and then he looked at Cici.

"That's up to Ayme," he said, then glanced at her. "She would be safe here," he suggested. "What do you say?"

She searched his gaze, looking for clues as to what he really thought. Did he want the freedom that being without the baby would bring? She could understand that he might. But she couldn't accept it. She needed Cici to come with them.

She drew in a deep breath. She was going to insist,

even if that meant David decided to have her stay instead of go. That was the way it had to be. She closed her eyes and said a little prayer.

Then she opened them and said, loud and clear, "Cici needs to go with us. That's where she belongs."

David smiled. "Good," he said firmly. "Thank you, Marjan, but we'll keep Cici with us."

Ayme felt a glow of happiness in her chest. It seemed to be settling right where her heart should be. She raced off to pack for the trip.

They had a lovely dinner. Ayme helped Marjan cook it, stopping to tend to Cici in between her duties. They ate heartily and laughed a lot. That night, they slept well.

When they were ready to go, they found that Marjan had set up a special plan for them.

"Okay, Mari. Tell me. What's your idea?" David asked her.

"Here's the scenario. You said you wanted to throw them off by going back to where you left the car and taking it."

"Yes."

Marjan frowned. "Won't they know?"

He shrugged. "I doubt it. They'll already have checked it out for any information they could use. There would be no reason for them to keep watch on it when they think we've abandoned it."

Marjan nodded, but suggested, "You could take my car."

"Thanks, Mari, but they probably have it pegged too, just in case. I think my idea is the best."

She nodded again, thinking. "All right then. Now, as for my plan, my friend Gretja takes her canal boat in to town every other morning. Today she is stopping by in half an hour to pick up my pies to take to the Cheese Fair. How would you like to ride back to town in a canal boat?"

David was all smiles. "That would be perfect."

"Good." She gave him a hug, then turned to Ayme and did the same. "I want you both to be safe and happy. So be careful!"

Forty minutes later they were on Gretja's canal boat, tucked away inside the little open cabin in a place where no one could see them from the shore. Gretja enjoyed the whole event more than anyone. As they were skimming along the waterway, the older woman grinned at them from above, her eyes sparkling as though she were carrying smugglers out of Kashmir.

"Oh, isn't this fun? I'm trying not to move my lips when I talk so they can't see me. Just in case anyone should be watching from the side, you know. I think I'll pretend to be singing. Yes, that should work just fine. Don't you think so?"

They humored her. The trip didn't take long, but it was fun while it lasted. They thanked her profusely when she dropped them off in town, choosing a crowded dock where they wouldn't be noticed. A few minutes later they were back in David's "incognito" car and driving toward France.

"I don't know how much more of this craziness I can take," Ayme said as she settled in and began to give Cici her bottle. "I'm just a stay-at-home girl from Dallas. I'm not used to all these shenanigans."

"Don't forget that semester in Japan," he reminded her sardonically.

"Well, yes, there was that." Her eyes narrowed as she

thought that over. "But we had escorts and chaperones everywhere we went. It was very controlled. Here I feel like I keep getting aboard a crazy train that's running wild. What if it goes off the tracks?"

He watched her, his eyes slightly hooded in a way she considered exceptionally sexy.

"Don't worry. You've got me to catch you if you fall off."

"Do I?"

He was kidding but she smiled at him anyway. At the same time, she wished she could ask him: *"But who are you?"*

She didn't ask it aloud, but it was always there in the back of her mind. She knew there was more to him than he was giving her. She just didn't know what it was.

She had caught a word or two between David and his sister, but she was in the dark. Bottom line, she didn't really care. She just wanted to be with David. She'd had to throw caution to the wind to go with him in the first place, and that was what she was doing again.

Was she falling in love with the man? How could she tell when she didn't really know who he was. She certainly had a pretty strong crush, stronger than any attachment she'd ever felt for any man—or boy— before. Was that love? She needed more information. Finally, she screwed up her courage and asked him the question.

"David, when are you going to tell me who you really are?" she asked, watching closely for his reaction.

His gaze flickered her way and she had the distinct impression he was looking to see just how much she thought she knew. What did that mean?

"I mean, I know most of the world thinks you're a

Dutchman named David Dykstra, but you're really not him at all. So who are you?"

"No, Ayme, you've got that wrong," he said with exagerated patience. "I really am David Dykstra. It's just that I'm someone else, as well."

"Someone Ambrian."

"Right."

"And what is that someone's name?"

He shook his head and didn't look her way. "Later."

"Oh!" She growled. "I hate that answer."

"It's the only answer I can give right now."

"It's not acceptable." She waited and when he didn't elaborate, she added, "When is later, anyway?"

He glared at her, not smiling. "I'll let you know when I feel I can."

"Why can't you do it right now?"

"Ayme…"

She held up a hand. "I know, I know, it's too dangerous."

"Well, it is. I don't want you to get hurt because you know too much."

"Sure." Her mouth twisted cynically. "They could come and kidnap me. Where would I be then? They might put me on the rack and pull me apart until my bones snap." She punched a fist into the upholstery. "But I'll never talk. I'll say, 'No, you blackguards, you won't get anything out of me!'"

She sighed, dropping the phony accent. "Or I could tell them everything I know, which is more likely. So I understand why you won't tell me. You think I'll fold under pressure." She turned to give him a knowing look. "But what happens when I figure it out for myself? Then what? Huh?"

"You're making jokes, Ayme," he said calmly. "But your being tortured for information is no laughing matter. It could happen." He frowned. "Which makes me wonder why I let you come along."

"Okay," she said quickly. "Let's stop speculating. I won't beg for information anymore. I swear."

He looked at her earnest face and laughed. "Liar," he said softly.

"Okay, then how about this old chestnut? Where are we really going?"

"To Piasa, Italy. My uncle died. I need to attend his memorial service."

"Oh."

Wow. That was a lot more than she'd expected and it took her a moment of two to digest it.

"Your Ambrian uncle?" she asked.

He nodded.

She opened her mouth to ask more about that but he silenced her with a quick oath.

"No more, Ayme," he said. "That's enough for now."

"Okay." Suddenly, she remembered something.

"I forgot to tell you. I saw the white-haired man again."

His head turned quickly. "What? Where?"

"When we were transferring from the canal boat to the car. I couldn't warn you because we were sort of occupied at the time, the way we were sneaking around to find the car. But I saw him, or somebody who looked just like him, going into a store across the square. I don't think he saw us."

"Damn." He thought for a moment, then shook his head. "Okay, hang on."

Soon they were flying down the road at breakneck speed and Ayme was hanging on for dear life. She took a few minutes of this, then called out, "Hey, slow down. They can drive fast, too. You're not going to avoid them this way."

He let up a bit on the speed, but they were still going too fast. "You're right," he said. "I just wanted to feel like I was doing something, making some progress."

"With a little bit of luck, they don't know where we are and won't be coming up behind us," she said. "You never know." She sighed. "I never realized before how much of what happens to you in life is just based on dumb, blind luck."

He nodded, slowing even more. "Sure, to some extent. But there's also grit and determination and how much you're willing to put into life."

"One would hope. I've always used that as my template. Work hard and ye shall reap the rewards thereof, or something like that. But…" She threw up her hands. "Look at how much luck smoothed the way for me in life. I was adopted by a wonderful set of parents who adored me and did so well for me. What if I'd ended up with some other people? I was so lucky to get the Sommerses."

"So lucky, it almost balanced out the bad luck of losing your birth parents to begin with," he noted dryly.

"You're right." She frowned. "There's as much bad luck as there is good, isn't there?"

"At least as much."

She thought for a long moment, then ventured a look his way. "That last day in Dallas, I was alone with Cici. She slept all day. I was terrified she would wake up and

I would have to hold her. I had no clue what to do with babies. My parents had raced off to find Sam and bring her home without telling me anything except, 'take care of Cici.'" She sighed.

"If only Sam hadn't run away. If only my parents hadn't found out so quickly where she'd gone. If only... If only..." She closed her eyes for a moment, then opened them again.

"But when I opened the front door and found a policeman standing there, I knew. Right away, I knew. It was like the end of the world had come to my door. The end of my world, for sure."

He peered at her sideways, wondering if she was finally going to tell him about her parents' deaths.

"But consider this," she went on. "I was in shock, and it was just luck that I was so overcome that I didn't think to mention Cici to them. If I'd had her out at the time, or if she'd begun to cry, I would have remembered to tell them about her. They probably would have taken her away. Instead, there I was with Sam's baby and no family left."

There it was. He waited, poised. No family left. Maybe now she would go on and tell him about her parents. He looked at her, waiting for her to amplify. But she was staring out the window, brooding, so he coaxed her to continue.

"So that was bad luck?"

"No. No, not really. When I was able to think straight again, I realized Cici was now my responsibility. I couldn't let some social agency take her. I had to find her father."

He shrugged. "Perhaps if you'd told the authorities about her, *they* would have found her father."

"Maybe. But because of Sam's lifestyle and the crazy things she did, I have a feeling there would have been entanglements and problems. And delays. And red tape. No, I knew from the beginning it would be better if I could find a way to take care of it myself. Besides, I needed..." Her voice faded away.

He glanced at her. "Needed what?"

"Nothing." She cleared her throat. She'd needed to have something to do, somewhere to go, so that she wouldn't have to deal with her parents' deaths. "I was talking about Cici. At first, I didn't know anything about babies. My main concern was just to get her to someone who could take care of her and give her the love she needed. And that was why I dashed over here as soon as I found someone I could go to—and that was you."

"And here you are."

"Look at the blind dumb luck in you turning out to be the sort of man you are." She was looking at him with unabashed affection. "You actually cared. You gave me shelter from the storm."

"Some shelter," he said gruffly. "I threw you into a car and we've been racing across Europe ever since."

There was a quivering thread of passion in her voice when she said, "You made all the difference."

He looked away, steeling himself. He knew what was happening here. Her words were reaching into his heart and soul and touching his emotions like they'd never been touched before. If he wasn't careful, he was going to fall for it.

Not that she was trying to fool him. She wasn't. It was obvious that she was totally sincere. But Ayme's sincerity was already messing with his mind and he knew how much he already cared about her. He couldn't afford any more. If he let her into the secret places where his real feelings lay buried, he'd be done for.

CHAPTER TEN

DAVID had always known he was royal. He wasn't Monte. Monte would probably have been king right now if they were back in Ambria where they belonged. He was glad that responsibility was his older brother's and not his. Still, he knew if anything happened to Monte, he would be more than ready to take his place. It was the natural order of things.

Sometimes he wondered why he seemed to know this so instinctively. He hadn't had a family to pound these things into him, like most royals would have. He didn't have years and years of tutors teaching him about his place, years and years of servants treating him like he really was someone special. But he knew anyway. He knew it was both a special advantage and a special danger—as well as a responsibility.

"Uneasy lies the head that wears a crown," as Shakespeare wrote so long ago. He accepted that. It was part of the role as he'd always envisioned it. But that didn't mean it was a simple thing to deal with.

And romance certainly complicated matters. For a long time he'd assumed that casual romance came with the territory. It seemed all the royals he read about in the gossip papers were naturally promiscuous. He'd given that a try himself, but he hadn't really taken to it. Something in him seemed to be searching for that special someone who would complete his life.

Where he had gotten such a mundane, ordinary idea he wasn't sure. Maybe it had to do with the good, solid Dutch family that had raised him with morals and values that he couldn't seem to shake, even if he'd wanted to. Maybe it was something more basic. He wasn't sure, he only knew it made it hard to treat love as casually as people seemed to expect.

And now there was Ayme.

Wait. Why had he thought of that? What did this woman who had appeared out of nowhere and parked herself and her baby in his apartment have to do with anything? He wasn't falling in love with her. Of course he wasn't because that would be nuts.

"Where are we going next?"

He smiled. Her questions didn't even annoy him anymore. He expected them, like a parent expected the inevitable "Are we there yet?".

"As I told you, our ultimate destination is in Italy," he said to her.

"Are we going through Paris?" she asked hopefully.

"No. We're sticking to the back roads."

"Oh." Her disappointment was obvious. "I've always wanted to sip a glass of wine in a Parisian café," she said, her head tilted dreamily. "Preferably a sidewalk café. With a man playing an accordion and a woman singing torch songs in the background."

"Edith Piaf, no doubt."

"If possible." She grinned at him. "Why not?"

"I don't think she's around anymore."

"I know. Only in dreams."

He looked at her. More than anything, he wanted her to be happy.

"We'll do it," he said softly.

She looked at him in surprise. "But we're in a hurry."

He nodded. "We can't go to Paris. But don't worry. I'll find us a sidewalk café. Just have faith."

"I've got nothing but faith in you," she told him happily.

He took one look at her face and pulled over to the side of the road. In one smooth move, he had his arms around her and was kissing the heck out of her. She kissed him back once she was over her surprise. And when he pulled away, he touched her cheek and said, softly, "I thought you needed kissing."

She nodded. "You were right. I did."

He grinned and turned back to the wheel. They were back on the road in no time at all.

It was a couple of hours later when he turned onto a rutted road and told her what their next stop would be.

"We'll find you that sidewalk café very soon," he said. "But right now, I want you to see Ambria."

"Ambria!" She sat up straighter. Suddenly she was terrified.

"Yes. Ambria."

She swallowed a sudden lump in her throat. "How am I going to do that?"

"Under the right conditions, you can see her from the shore. I've done it. It's just a few miles ahead."

She pulled her arms in tightly around her chest and looked worried. "I'm not sure I want to see Ambria."

He gazed at her levelly. "Why not?"

"I...I don't know. I'm afraid it will change things."

He looked out the window and frowned, thinking. "You may be right," he said at last. "But I think you should see it, anyway."

She was silent for a long time and he didn't push her. Finally she said, "I'll do it, as long as you stay with me."

"Of course." He looked at her again. "Don't forget, you were born there. Deep down, you're Ambrian."

That didn't sit well with her. "I'm an American," she told him. "And I'm a Texan. And maybe I'm an Ambrian, too. But I don't feel it."

He nodded and his smile was pure affection. "That's why I'm taking you there."

She took in that affection like a flower took in sunshine. And in her own way, she bloomed a little. "Okay. I'll try to see what you want me to see. I'll try to like it."

"That's all I ask."

She gave a little hiccup of a laugh. "Just remember," she said. "In the immortal words of the Supremes, you can't hurry love."

He nodded. He knew what she meant. "Even love of country."

"Exactly."

They stopped along the way to get a couple of cold lemonades and then to let Ayme give Cici a bottle. The baby wanted to play so the stop took longer than they had expected. It was early afternoon by the time they got to the seashore.

What Ayme saw was unimpressive. If she looked carefully, she could just make out a sort of somber lump of land hidden behind a wall of melancholy fog. The entire aspect was grim and cheerless, like a prison off shore. She looked at David, hoping he couldn't read her disappointment in her face. But he was staring out at it, so she went back to staring, too.

As they watched, the clouds began to part above the gloomy, fog-shrouded island nation. Ayme reached out and took David's hand but she didn't meet his gaze. Instead, she was staring straight out to sea.

They watched for a long time. Eventually, the sun broke through and shafts of silver-gold sunlight shot down, illuminating the place. The fog lifted and there it was. And suddenly, she was transfixed. She'd never seen anything so beautiful before.

"That's Ambria?" she asked, breathless.

"That's Ambria," he said, satisfaction in his voice. "I haven't been there since I was six years old but it lives in my heart every day."

She shook her head and looked back. The vision was so brilliant, she almost had to shield her eyes.

"It's not in my heart yet," she said, "but it's knocking on the door."

David started talking in a low, vibrant voice. He talked about their Ambrian ancestors, about what it must have been like for their parents, about lives lost and dreams deferred. She listened and took in every word. She began to feel what had been lost. He spoke of how her parents had probably died there, and tears began to well in her eyes.

She wanted to tell him to stop, but somehow she couldn't. He went on and on and she listened, and soon her tears became sobs. He took her into his arms, but he didn't stop talking. And then he mentioned the loss of her sister, Samantha, and finally, of her adoptive parents.

She didn't even stop to wonder how he knew about that. He knew everything, it seemed. He was her everything. She trusted him and she loved him. And finally, the dam within her let go and she could mourn.

She had a lot to mourn about. Her birth parents, Sam, her Texas parents. It hardly seemed fair that one young woman should have to bear the weight of so much suffering on her slender shoulders. And she had avoided it for a long time. But finally, it was here, and she had David beside her. She could mourn.

He held her tightly and he rocked her and whispered comfort in her ear. She clung to him. She needed him. He was all that was keeping her from being swept away by a river of grief.

And when her crying was spent and the torrent was over, she told him about the accident—about how her parents had found Sam and how Sam had jumped into the car and driven off, and how her parents had given chase. And Sam had made a hard turn that had sent her skidding the wrong way, and her father, unable to stop in time, had smashed into Sam's car. All three dead from one stupid accident that shouldn't have happened. And at first she'd thought she might as well have died with them. Her life was over.

Things didn't look quite that way any longer, but still, it was a black cloud that might never leave her.

She wasn't sure what she wanted anymore. In some ways she felt like her emotions had been tugged in too many different directions in the past few days. She couldn't take much more. She'd had it. The only place she wanted to be right now was in a nice warm bath, with candles set around for good measure.

Back at the car, she drank the rest of the lemonade and kissed Cici and felt a bit revived, and then they were off. David was determined to find a nice sidewalk café for her, and he did just that in the next little town. It was as cute and quaint as she could have asked for and the three of them left the car and sat at a table, and David and Ayme drank wine and ate lovely biscuits. The torch songs were on the radio, but they did just fine. It was wonderful.

And then, Ayme saw the man again, riding past on a bicycle.

"Oh, David, look. The white-haired man."

David spun around. "The man from the first place we stayed?"

"Yes. Did you see him?"

"Yes." He stared down into his wine. "I've seen him before."

"Where? When?"

It was odd how he'd never really remarked on it before, but the man had popped up along the sidelines of his life in the past. Now that she'd pointed him out, he saw that clearly. Was he a threat? How could he take it any other way?

"We've got to get out of here," he said, rising. "We'd better go."

"The car?"

"No. We can't take the car. We'll have to do something else. Come on."

They left the table and began to walk quickly down the street. And then a van drove up beside them and two men jumped out and life became a jumbled, violent mess.

It all happened so fast. The men grabbed David. He struggled, but Ayme saw blood and knew he'd been hit with something. Her first impulse was to stand still and scream at the top of her lungs, but that wouldn't have helped anyone. There was another man getting out of the van and she was pretty sure he would be coming for her next.

David was hurt. She knew it. She couldn't do anything about it, but maybe she could save Cici. She turned and ran as she'd never run before, down between buildings, across railroad tracks, through a yard, over a fence, down an alley, into a field and back between buildings again.

She couldn't breathe. She felt as though there was a stone on her chest. And still she ran, holding Cici as tightly as she dared, adrenaline rushing through her veins. If she could just find some place to hide, a hole in the wall, a little cave, a wooden box, something.

But she ran out of luck before she found it. She was never sure if it was the blow to her head or the cloth soaked with chloroform under her nose that knocked her out, but suddenly there were people at both ends of the alley she'd run down.

"End of the line, little lady," said a burly man, just before they put the cloth over her face and something hit her just above the temple. She was out like a light.

She woke up in a hospital bed. There were voices all around but at first she couldn't focus on what they were saying. She drifted off and when she woke again, she was a bit more alert. A man was sitting beside her bed.

She turned her head to look at him. It was the white-haired man.

She gasped and looked for an escape, but he leaned over the bed with a sweet smile, shaking his head.

"I'm not one of the bad guys, Ayme," he told her. "Believe it or not, I was the one who rescued your little group before the Granvilli thugs could cart you off to Ambria, which seemed to be their objective."

She stared at him. Should she believe him? She scanned the room, which seemed to be a normal hospital room, not some dungeon or hideout. She began to relax.

"David is in a room down the hall. I'm sure you want to know how he is. Well, he's doing fairly well, though his injuries are much more extensive than yours. You have a lump on your head and will probably have a headache for a while, but the doctor says you're doing fine."

"Cici?" she asked, as she reached up to touch the lump he was referring to.

"Not hurt at all. They have her in a crib in the children's ward, but that's only because they don't know what else to do with her right now."

She narrowed her eyes, looking at him. He seemed nice. But then he always had. Could she trust him?

"Who are you?"

He smiled again. "My name doesn't matter. I'm allied with the Ambrian restoration team. We want to restore the royal family to its rightful place on the throne of our country."

"Then, why were you following David everywhere?"

He leaned closer and spoke as though in private.

"The truth is, I've been following David for years, trying to make sure nothing threatened him until he was ready."

"Ready?" She was getting confused again. "Ready for what?"

He smiled. "I see David needs to explain a few things to you. But I'll let him do that." He rose from his chair. "And now that you're awake, I'll go back to David, if you don't mind. Have the nurse contact me if you need anything, my dear." He nodded his head in her direction and left the room.

She stared after him, still not sure what was going on. When the team of men had driven up in the van and they'd been attacked, she'd thought it was exactly what David had been guarding against all this time. At least, from what he'd told her, that was what she assumed.

But the white-haired man had been a part of that threat—hadn't he? Now it seemed David had been wrong about that. But she really didn't understand. How had she let herself get involved, anyway?

She had to get out of here and she had to get Cici out. Rolling out of the bed, she clutched the hospital gown around herself and made her way to the door. She was dizzy, but it wasn't bad enough to stop her. She had to know how David and Cici really were, not just what someone she didn't really trust was telling her.

Up and down the hallway all seemed clear and she started toward the room across the hall. In the third room she checked, there was David. He had a big bandage on his head and appeared to be regaining consciousness. The white-haired man was there. But the strange thing was, he was bowed over from the waist and seemed to be kissing David's hand.

"Your Highness," he was saying. "I'm at your service, always."

She pulled back so that she couldn't be seen and tried to catch her breath.

Your highness? Your highness?

But hadn't she suspected this? Hadn't she known it all along? It all fell together. The pieces just fell into place. David was royal. Of course.

The white-haired man left the room, walking off down the hall without seeing where she was standing, half-hidden by a bank of oxygen tanks. She waited until he was out of sight, then slipped into David's room and approached him.

He looked as though he'd been through a meat grinder. Her heart flipped in her chest as she saw his most obvious wounds.

"Oh, David," she said, reaching for his hand.

He looked up and tried to smile around a swollen lip.

"Hi, Ayme," he said. "Hey, nice little frock you've got on there."

She ignored that. "Are you okay?" she asked anxiously.

"I'm okay. I'm still groggy from pain medication, but once I get that out of my system, I'll be good to go." His smile was bittersweet and his voice was rough. "I didn't protect you very well, did I?"

"What?" She shook her head, then grimaced. It hurt to do that. "I'm just so glad you're not badly injured," she said. "It all happened so fast."

"Yes. Thank God for Bernard and his men."

She looked at him questioningly. "The white-haired man?"

"Yes. He said he'd talked to you."

"Yes."

"Did he tell you how he and his men swooped in and saved my butt?"

"No."

He nodded slightly. "Let's reserve that story for later," he said, obviously starting to lag a bit. "Just be thankful they were there, keeping an eye on the situation. Without them, we'd be…" He let his voice trail off. He didn't really want to speculate right now.

"So, let me get this straight," she was saying. "There were bad guys following us. But there were also good guys following us?"

"That's about it."

And that left the question of why. But she knew that now, didn't she? She studied his face for a moment and then gave him a sad smile.

"You're one of them, aren't you?"

His eyes had been drifting shut, but they opened again. "One of whom?"

"The lost royals." Her heart was hammering in her chest. "Which one are you?"

He closed his eyes and turned away.

"Don't tell me you're Darius. Are you?" She wanted to grab him and shake him, but she knew she couldn't do that. "Are you Cici's father?" she asked, her voice strangled.

He opened his eyes again and looked at her. "No. That I am not."

She shook her head, feeling as though she were drowning in unhappiness. "How do you know?"

"Ayme, I never met Sam. Believe me, I've thought long and hard about it, just to make sure. It's not me."

"But you're Prince Darius. And at the same time, you're looking for him? I don't get it."

He tried to pull up to a seated position, but it was beyond him at this point. "Don't you see? I'm not looking for Darius. I know where he is. I'm looking for the man who's pretending to be me. That's the one we need to find."

"Why is he pretending?"

"Why not? If it helps him with the ladies, why not?"

She lowered her head and thought about that. She had to admit, Sam had been just crazy enough to fall for something like that.

"Of course, there's another theory. He might have been pretending to be Darius in order to try to lure me or any of my siblings who may have survived out of hiding. That's why we've got to find him."

"So either way, he's probably a jerk."

"Looks like."

Her sigh came from the depths of her soul. "And what if he wants Cici? Do I have to give her up to a jerk who might even be a criminal?" She searched his eyes, desperate for a good answer.

But he didn't have one for her. He could barely keep his eyes open. She gave up.

"I'm going to go see if I can get checked out of here," she told him. "I'll be back later."

He didn't answer. He was sound asleep.

A few minutes later she was dressed and ready to leave. Luckily, no one seemed to be paying much attention to her and she'd managed to prepare to check out without having to fill out any forms. All she had to do was find

Cici. She started down the hall, then hesitated. David's room was like a magnet. She wanted to see him one last time. Walking softly, she looked into the room. There was a man she didn't recognize talking to David.

"You've still got the Ambrian girl with you," he was saying.

"Ayme?" David asked groggily.

"Yes. What do you want me to do about her?"

"Do about her?"

"Your brother, the Crown Prince, has asked that you not bring her to Piasa. He has someone he thinks would make a perfect match for you waiting there to meet you and it would be…"

Pulling back, she began to walk on down the hall, pacing quickly, thinking, thinking. Her mind raced with plans. The pain of being cast aside would overwhelm her if she let it. She had to push it away and ignore it for now.

What was she going to do? She had to get out of here and she had to take Cici with her. It was obvious that she would never have David. She had to shut that off, not think about losing him. She had lost so much lately. And then, as though fate had lead her to the right place, there was Cici, alone in a room with only one little crib.

"Oh, my baby!" she cried as she rushed to hold her.

Was that a smile? Yes! Her heart filled with love as she held the child close and murmured sweet things to her. At the same time her mind whirred with ideas of how she could take her away before people asked questions and began to require official forms to be signed. If she could just get her back on a plane to Texas, she would be in a position to make a claim on her. Once she lost control of her here in Europe, there was no telling what would happen next. She might have no chance of ever getting her back.

At the same time, she knew what she was about to do was probably illegal. If she got caught, it could be all over for her. But if she just let Cici slip away, the last thing she loved in this world would be gone. Some choice she had. The pit or the pendulum.

She was going to risk it.

David was on the phone with Monte.

"We found him."

David had to concentrate and be sure he understood. His mind was still fuzzy. "Okay, you've got the guy who was pretending to be me? Is that right?"

"Well, in a manner of speaking. He's dead, has been for a few weeks, but we know who he is."

"Dead? How?"

Monte's voice lowered. "It looks like an assasination. He was shot by a sniper."

"Oh, my God."

"Yes. We assume whoever shot him thought he was you. He'd been using that story about being one of the lost royals to seduce young women off and on for a couple of years. It finally caught up with him."

They were both silent for a moment, taking that in.

Finally, Monte said, "You know what this means, don't you?"

"You tell me."

"This means that, however much we're tempted to say 'aw, forget about it, let's just go on and live our lives like everyone else,' that's not going to work. Because there are people out there who feel threatened by our very existence, and until we find a way to take back our country and get rid of those people, we're in danger. We'll never be safe, and neither will the ones we love."

He was right. David closed his eyes and swore softly. He didn't have a choice. He was Prince Darius of Ambria and he was going to have to deal with it.

"So, I guess I'll see you in Piasa on Friday? You're good to go?"

"Yes. I'll be there."

Monte hesitated. "About this Ayme person," he began.

David was fully awake now. "She'll be there, too," he said firmly. "She's with me."

There was a pause. "You do realize how important this is," Monte reminded him. "Every Ambrian who can make it will be there. This is our time to claim our heritage."

"I understand that, Monte, and I'll be there right beside you. I'll fight to the death for you and for our cause. For our place in history. But I'll be the one to decide on my private life, on what I need and what I don't."

Monte let his breath out in a long sigh. "Okay," he said. "That's your call. But I wish you'd reconsider."

David smiled, thinking of Ayme, thinking of Cici. There would be no problem with them keeping the baby now. "I've gone beyond the point of no return," he told his brother. "Take it or leave it."

"Okay. I'll take it. See you in Italy."

David was fully awake now. He looked around the sterile hospital room.

"Enough of this," he said, ripping the IV out of his arm and easing off the bed. He took it slowly. He was weak and he didn't want to end up on the floor. But he was going to find Ayme if it killed him.

He found his clothes and put them on, then headed out into the hallway. He knew that finding Cici would be the key to Ayme's location, and he knew where Cici had been put. He passed three separate nurses and a doctor, each of whom gave him curious looks, but didn't try to stop him. But when he arrived at his destination, the room was empty.

Alarm shot through him. If she'd already left, would he be able to find her again? He looked out the window. From the third story where he was, he could see Ayme heading down the walkway, Cici in her arms.

He couldn't run, but he moved faster than he would have thought possible and caught up to her before she got off the grounds.

"What are you doing?" he called to her as he got close.

She whirled, holding Cici to her chest. "Uh…uh…" Her eyes were huge and she looked guilty as hell.

"You're kidnapping Cici," he said, trying to keep the amusement hidden in his eyes. "Do you know you could be put in prison for something like that?"

"I'm not!" She gasped. "Oh, no. That's not what I'm doing." Her eyes filled with tears. "Oh, David," she wailed.

"Ayme, darling," he said, laughing as he pulled her into his arms. "Why are you running away?"

She gazed up at him, tears streaming down her face. "David, I've lost everything I ever loved. And now I've lost you. I can't bear to lose Cici, too."

He looked down into her pretty face. "Why do you think you've lost me?"

"You're royal. I…I'm not from that world."

"Neither am I. Not really. I didn't grow up preparing to be royal." He dropped a kiss on her nose. "Oh, Ayme, I want you with me. We can learn about being royal together."

"But, Cici…"

He pulled back and got serious. "They found Cici's father. I'm afraid he's dead."

Quickly, he told her what Monte had told him.

"So your search is over." He touched her cheek. "But I'm hoping our journey together has just begun."

She searched his gaze. "Do you mean that?"

"With all my heart."

"Oh, David!"

He kissed her, then pulled back.

"Come on. Let's get a cab and find a nice hotel."

"But, don't we need to tell the hospital?"

"Don't worry about it. This is the good side of being royal. We have people who take care of these little details for us."

"Like the white-haired man?"

"His name is Bernard. Get used to it. I have a feeling we'll be seeing a lot of him."

"Really?"

"And that Carl Heissman who first sent you to me? He's an associate of Bernard's. He wasn't sure if Sam's claim that Prince Darius was Cici's father would hold up, but he thought it best to send you to me to find out. You see, there are wheels within wheels. I'm sure we don't know the half of it yet."

He sobered.

"Do you understand?" he asked her. "I love you, Ayme. I want to marry you. But I don't want to sugarcoat this. It's something you're going to have to consider going forward. I want you with me, but you have to be willing to take the risks involved."

She shook her head, ready to be supremely happy, but warned against it by the tone of his voice. "What are you talking about?"

"We're about to start a major push on Ambria to win our country back. If we go ahead with it, there will likely be fighting. There will be danger. There may be dying. You will be risking a lot just by being associated with me. You must think this through and decide if it's worth it."

Reaching up, she flattened her hand against the plane of his handsome face. "David, my life was over until I met you. Now it's about to begin again. I'll risk it. I'll risk anything to be with you."

He kissed her again. After all these years of wondering what the big deal about love was, it seemed like a miracle that he had found a woman he couldn't live without, a woman he had to spend his life with.

"We'll be together."

"And Cici?"

As if on cue, the baby gurgled happily. They looked at each other and laughed.

"I think she'll probably be with us, too."

Ayme sighed with pure happiness, looking down at the child she'd come to love with all her heart.

"Good. Let's go to Italy."

ARRANGED MARRIAGE, BEDROOM SECRETS

YVONNE LINDSAY

There are so many people who enrich my life but foremost are the members of my incredible family, so I dedicate this book to them.

One

"Isn't that you?"

Mila shoved an unruly lock of her long black hair off her face and looked up in irritation from the notes she'd been making.

"Is what me?" she asked her friend.

"On the TV, now!"

Mila turned her attention to the flat screen currently blaring the latest entertainment news trailers that so captivated her best friend and felt her stomach lurch. There, for all the world to see, were the unspeakably awful official photos taken at her betrothal to Prince Thierry of Sylvain seven years ago. Overweight, with braces still on her teeth and a haircut that had looked so cute on a Paris model and way less cute on an awkward eighteen-year-old princess—especially one who was desperately attempting to look more sophisticated and who had ended up, instead, looking like a sideshow clown. She shuddered.

"I know it doesn't look completely like you, but that *is*

you, isn't it? Princess Mila Angelina of Erminia? Is that really your name?" Sally demanded, one finger pointing at the TV screen while her eyes pinned Mila with a demanding stare.

There was no point in arguing. Hiding a cringe, Mila merely inclined her head. She looked back down at her notes for a thesis she'd likely never be permitted to complete, but her concentration was gone. How would her friend react to this news?

"You're going to marry a prince?"

Mila couldn't be certain if Sally was outraged because Mila was actually engaged to a prince, or because she'd never thought to let her best friend in on the secret of her real identity. She sighed and put her pen down. As an uncelebrated princess from a tiny European kingdom, she'd flown under the radar in the United States since her arrival seven years ago, but now it was clearly time to face the music.

She'd known Sally since their freshman year at MIT and, while her friend had sometimes looked a little surprised that Mila—or Angel as she was known here in the States—had a chaperone, didn't date and had a team of bodyguards whenever she went out, Sally had accepted Angel's quirks without question. After all, Sally herself was heiress to an IT billionaire and lived with similar, if not quite as binding, constraints. The girls had naturally gravitated to one another.

It was time to be honest with her friend. Mila sighed again. "Yes, I am Mila Angelina of Erminia and, yes, I'm engaged to a prince."

"And you're a princess?"

"I'm a princess."

Mila held her breath, waiting for her friend's reaction. Would she be angry with her? Would it ruin the friendship she so treasured?

"I feel like I don't even know you, but seriously, that's so cool!" Sally gushed.

Mila rolled her eyes and laughed in relief. Of all the things she'd anticipated coming from Sally's rather forthright mouth, that hadn't been one of them.

"I always had a feeling there were things you weren't telling me." Sally dropped onto the couch beside Mila, scattering her papers to the floor. "So, what's he like?"

"Who?"

It was Sally's turn to roll her eyes this time. "The prince of course. C'mon, Angel, you can tell me. Your secret's safe with me, although I am kind of pissed at you for not telling me about him, or who you really are, any time in, oh, the last seven years!"

Sally softened her words with a smile, but Mila could see that she was still hurt by the omission.

How did you explain to someone that even though you'd been engaged to a man for years, you barely even knew him? One formal meeting, where she'd been so painfully shy she hadn't even been capable of making eye contact with the guy, followed by sporadic and equally formal letters exchanged by a diplomatic pouch, didn't add up to much in the relationship stakes.

"I...I don't really know what he's like." Mila took in a deep breath. "I have Googled him, though."

Her friend laughed out loud. "You have no idea how crazy that just sounded. You're living a real life fairy tale, y'know? European princess betrothed from childhood—well, okay, the age of eighteen at least—to a reclusive neighboring prince." Sally sighed and clutched at her chest dramatically. "It's so romantic—and all you can say is that you've *Googled* him?"

"Now who sounds crazy? I'm marrying him out of duty to my family and my country. Erminia and Sylvain have hovered on the brink of war for the last decade and a half. My marriage to Prince Thierry is supposed to end all that—unite our nations—if you can believe it could be that simple."

"But don't you want love?"

"Of course I want love."

Her response hung in the air between them. Love. It was all Mila had ever wanted. But it was something she knew better than to expect. Groomed from birth as not much more than a political commodity to be utilized to her country's greatest advantage, she'd realized love didn't feature very strongly alongside duty. When it came to her engagement, her agreement to the union had never been sought. It had been presented to her as her responsibility—and she'd accepted it. What else could she do?

Meeting the prince back then had been terrifying. Six years older than her, well-educated, charismatically gorgeous and oozing confidence, he'd been everything she was not. And she hadn't missed the hastily masked look of dismay on his face when they'd initially been introduced. Granted, she hadn't looked her best, but it had still stung to realize she certainly wasn't the bride he'd hoped for and it wasn't as if he could simply tell everyone he'd changed his mind. He, too, was a pawn in their betrothal—a scheme hatched by their respective governments in an attempt to quell the animosity that continued to simmer between their nations.

Mila rubbed a finger between her eyebrows as if by doing so she could ease the nagging throb that had settled there.

"Of course I want love," she repeated, more softly this time.

She felt Sally's hand on her shoulder. "I'm sorry. I know I shouldn't joke."

"It's okay." Mila reached up and squeezed her friend's hand to reassure her.

"So, how come you came here to study? If peace was the aim, wouldn't they have wanted you two to marry as soon as possible?"

Again Mila pictured the look on Prince Thierry's face when he'd seen her. A look that had made her realize that if she was to be anything to him other than a representation of his duty, she needed to work hard to become his equal. She needed to complete her education and become a worthy companion. Thankfully, her brother, King Rocco of Erminia, had seen the same look on the prince's face and, later that night, when she'd tearfully appealed to him with her plan to better herself, he'd agreed.

"The agreement was that we'd marry on my twenty-fifth birthday."

"But that's at the end of next month!"

"I know."

"But you haven't finished your doctorate."

Mila thought of all the sacrifices she'd made in her life to date. Not completing her PhD would probably be the most painful. While her brother had insisted she at least include some courses in political science, the main focus of her studies had been environmental science—a subject that she'd learned was close to the prince's heart. After years of study, it was close to hers now, too. Not being able to stand before him with her doctorate in hand, so to speak, was a painful thought to consider, but it was something she'd just have to get over. She certainly hadn't planned on things taking this long, but being dyslexic had made her first few years at college harder than she'd anticipated and she'd had to retake a number of courses. As Mila formed her reply to her friend, Sally was suddenly distracted.

"Oh, he's so hot!"

Mila snorted a laugh. "I know what he looks like. I've Googled him, remember."

"No, look, he's on TV, now. He's in New York at that

environmental summit Professor Winslow told us about weeks ago."

Mila looked up so quickly she nearly gave herself whiplash. "Prince Thierry is here? In the US?"

She trained her gaze onto the TV screen and, sure enough, there he was. Older than she remembered him and, if it was humanly possible, even better looking. Her heart tumbled in her chest and she felt her throat constrict on a raft of emotions. Fear, attraction—longing.

"You didn't know he was coming?"

Mila tore her eyes from the screen and fought to inject the right level of nonchalance into her voice. "No, I didn't. But that's okay."

"Okay? You think that's *okay*?" Sally's voice grew shrill. "The guy travels how many thousand miles to the country where you've been living for years now and he can't pick up a phone?"

"He's obviously only in New York for a short while and I'm sure he'll have a strict timetable set in place. I'm over here in Boston—he can't exactly just drop in." She shrugged. "It's not like it matters, anyway. We're getting married in a little over four weeks' time."

Her voice cracked on the words. Even though she played at being offhand, deep down it had come as a shock to see him on the TV. Would it have killed him to have let her know he was coming to America?

"Hmph. I can't believe you're not seeing each other while he's here," Sally continued, clearly not ready to let go of the topic yet. "Don't you even want to see him?"

"He probably doesn't have time," Mila deflected.

She didn't want to go into what she did or didn't want when it came to Prince Thierry. Her feelings on the subject were too confusing, even for her. She'd tried to convince herself many times that love at first sight was the construction of moviemakers and romance novelists, but ever since the day of their betrothal, she had yearned for him with a longing that went deep into the very fabric of her being. Was that love? She didn't know. It wasn't as if she'd had any stellar examples during her childhood.

"Well, even if he hadn't told me he was coming here, I'd certainly make time to see him if he was mine."

Mila forced herself to laugh and to make the kind of comment Sally would expect her to make. "Well, he's not yours, he's mine—and I'm not sharing."

As she expected, Sally joined in with her mirth. Mila kept her eyes glued to the screen for the duration of the segment about Prince Thierry—and tried to ignore the commentary about herself. The reporters were full of speculation as to her whereabouts, which had been kept strictly private for the past several years. Though she realized, if Sally had put two and two together as to who she was, what was to say others wouldn't, also?

She clung to the hope that no one would think to connect the ugly duckling of her engagement photo with the woman she had become. No longer was she the timid young woman with a mouth too large for her face and chubby cheeks and thighs. Somewhere between nineteen and twenty she'd begun a miraculous late-blooming transformation. The thirty extra pounds of puppy fat had long since melted from her body—her features and her figure fining down to what she was now, still curvy but no longer overweight. And her hair, thank goodness, had grown long and straight and thick. The dreadful cropped cut and frizzy perm she'd insisted on in a vain attempt to look sophisticated before meeting the prince was now nothing more than a humiliating memory. And she'd finally developed the poise that had been sadly lacking when she was just a teenager.

Would her soon-to-be husband find her attractive now?

She hated to think he'd be put off by her, especially given how incredibly drawn *she* was to *him*.

Sally had been one hundred percent right that Prince Thierry was hot. And all through the broadcast she saw evidence of that special brand of charisma that he unconsciously exuded. Mila watched the way people in the background stopped and stared at the prince—drawn to him as if he was a particularly strong magnet and they were nothing but metal filings inexorably pulled into his field. She knew how they felt. It was the same sensation that had struck her on the day of their betrothal—not to mention since, whenever she'd seen pictures of him or caught a news bulletin on television when she was home on vacation back in Erminia.

She'd return there in just a few weeks. It was time to retrieve the mantle of responsibility she'd so eagerly, even if only temporarily, shrugged off and reassume her position.

She should be looking forward to it. Not only because of the draw she felt toward the prince, but because of what the marriage would mean to both of their countries. The tentative peace between her native Erminia and Sylvain had been shattered many years ago when Prince Thierry's mother had been caught, *in flagrante delicto*, with an Erminian diplomat. When both she and her lover had died in a fiery car crash fingers had pointed to both governments in accusation. Military posturing along the borders of their countries ever since had created its own brand of unrest within the populations. She'd understood that her eventual marriage to Prince Thierry would, hopefully, bring all that turmoil to an end—but she wanted something more than a convenient marriage. Was it too much to hope that she could make the prince love her, too?

Mila reached for the remote and muted the sound, ready to turn her attention back to her work, but Sally wasn't finished on the subject yet.

"You should go to New York and meet him. Turn up at the door to his hotel suite and introduce yourself," Sally urged.

Mila laughed, but the sound lacked any humor. "Even if I could get away from Boston unchaperoned, I wouldn't get past his security, trust me. He's the Crown Prince of Sylvain, the sole heir to the throne. He's important."

Sally rolled her eyes. "So are you. You're his fiancée, for goodness' sake. Surely he'd make time for you. And, as to Bernadette and the bruiser boys," Sally said, referring to Mila's chaperone and round-the-clock bodyguards, "I think I could come up with a way to dodge them—if you were willing to commit to this, that is."

"I couldn't. Besides, what if my brother found out?"

Sally didn't know that Mila's brother was also the reigning king of Erminia, but she was aware that Rocco had been her guardian since they lost their parents many years ago.

"What could he do? Ground you?" Sally snorted. "C'mon, you're almost twenty-five years old and you've spent the last seven years in another country gaining valuable qualifications you'll probably never be allowed to use. You have a lifetime of incredibly boring state dinners and stuff like that to look forward to. I think you're entitled to a bit of fun, don't you?"

"You make a good point," Mila answered with a wry grin. As much as Sally's words pricked at her, her friend was right. "What do you suggest?"

"It's easy. Professor Winslow said that if we wanted he could get us tickets to the sustainability lecture stream during the summit. Why don't we take him up on it? The summit starts tomorrow and there's a lecture we could *attend*," she said the latter word with her fingers in the air, mimicking quotation marks, "the next day."

"Accommodation will be impossible to find at this short notice."

"My family keeps a suite close to where they said the prince is staying. We could fly to New York by late afternoon tomorrow—Daddy will let me use his jet, I'm sure, especially if I tell him it's for my studies. Then we check into the hotel and you could suddenly *feel ill*." Sally hooked her fingers into mimed quotation marks again. "Bernie and the boys wouldn't need to be with you if you were tucked up in bed with a migraine, would they? We'll take a blond wig so you can look more like me. After a couple of hours, I'll pretend I'm going out but instead I'll go to your room and go to bed and pull the covers right up so if she checks on you she'll think you're out for the count. We'll swap clothes and you, looking like me, can just slip out for the evening. What do you say?"

"They'll never fall for it."

"It wouldn't hurt to try, though, would it? Otherwise when are you going to get a chance to see the prince again? At your wedding? C'mon, what's the worst that could happen?"

What was the worst that could happen? They'd get caught. And then what? More reminders of her station and her duty to her country. Growing up in Erminia constant lectures about her duty and reputation had been all she'd known, after all. But after living and attending college in the States for the past few years, Mila had enjoyed a taste—albeit a severely curtailed one—of the kind of freedom she hadn't even known she craved.

She weighed the idea in her mind. Sally's plan was so simple and uncomplicated it might just work. Bernadette was always crazy busy—even more so since she'd begun making plans for Mila's return to Erminia. A side jaunt to New York would throw her schedule completely out—if she even agreed to allowing it. But Mila still had the email from the professor saying how valuable attending the lecture would be. Mila knew she could put some emotional pressure on the chaperone who'd become more like a mother-figure to her and convince her to let her go.

"What's it going to be, Mila?" Sally prompted.

Mila reached her decision. "I'll do it."

She couldn't believe she'd said the words even as they came from her mouth, but every cell in her body flooded with a sense of anticipation. She was going to meet Prince Thierry. Or, at least, try to meet him.

"Great," Sally said, rubbing her hands together like the nefarious co-conspirator she was at heart. "Let's make some plans. This is going to be fun!"

Two

Dead.

The king was dead. Long live the king.

Oblivious to the panoramic twilight view of New York City as it sparkled below him, Thierry paced in front of the windows of his hotel suite in a state of disbelief.

He was now the King of Sylvain and all its domains—automatically assuming the crown as soon as his father had breathed his last breath.

A flutter of rage beat at the periphery of his thoughts. Rage that his father had slipped away now, rather than after Thierry had returned to his homeland. But it was typical of the man to make things awkward for his son. After all, hadn't he made a lifetime hobby of it? Even before this trip, knowing he was dying, his father had sent Thierry away. Perhaps he'd known all along that his only son would not be able to return before his demise. He'd never been a fan of emotional displays.

Not that Thierry would likely become emotional. The

king had always been a distant person in Thierry's life. Their interactions had been peppered with reminders of Thierry's duty to his country and his people and reprimands for the slightest transgression whether real or imagined. Yet, through the frustration and rage that flickered inside him, Thierry felt a swell of grief. Perhaps more for the relationship he had never had with his father, he realized, than the difficult one they'd shared.

"Sire?"

The form of address struck him anew. Sire—not Your Royal Highness or sir.

His aide continued, "Is there anything—?"

"No." Thierry cut off his aide before he could ask again what he could do.

Since the news had been delivered, his staff had closed around him—all too wary that they were now responsible for not the Crown Prince any longer, but the King of Sylvain. He could feel the walls closing in around him even as he paced. He had to get out. Get some air. Enjoy some space before the news hit worldwide headlines which, no doubt, it would within the next few hours.

Thierry turned to his aide. "I apologize for my rudeness. The news…even though we were expecting it…"

"Yes, sire, it has come as a shock to everyone. We all hoped he would rally again."

Thierry nodded abruptly. "I'm going out."

A look of horror passed across the man's features. "But, sire!"

"Pasquale, I need tonight. Before it all changes," Thierry said by way of explanation even though no explanation was necessary.

The reality of his new life was already crushing. He'd been trained for this from the cradle and yet it still felt as though he had suddenly become Atlas with the weight of the world on his shoulders.

"You will take your security detail with you."

Thierry nodded. That much, he knew, was non-negotiable, but he also knew they'd be discreet. Aside from the film crew that had caught him arriving at his hotel yesterday, his visit to the United States had largely gone untrumpeted. He was a comparatively small fry compared to the other heads of state from around the world who had converged on the city for the summit. That would all change by morning, of course, when news of his father's death made headlines. He hoped, by then, to be airborne and on his way home.

Thierry strode to his bedroom and ripped the tie from his neck before it strangled him. His elderly valet, Nico, scurried forward.

"Nico, a pair of jeans and a fresh shirt, please."

"Certainly, sire."

There it was again. That word. That one word that had created a gulf of distance between himself and his staff and, no doubt, the rest of the world with it. For the briefest moment, Thierry wished he could rage and snarl at the life he'd been dealt, but, as always, he capped the emotions that threatened to overwhelm him. He was nothing if not controlled.

A few moments later, after a brief shower, Thierry was dressed and waiting in his suite's vestibule for his security detail—all ready to go.

"It's cool out this evening, sire. You'll be needing these," Nico said.

The older man's hands trembled as he helped Thierry into a finely woven casual jacket and passed him a beanie and dark glasses. At the visible sign of his valet's distress, Thierry once again felt that sense of being crushed by the change to his life. Now, he was faced not only with his own emotions at the news of his father's death, but with those of his people. So far, his staff had only expressed their condolences to him. It was time he returned that consideration. He turned and allowed his gaze to encompass both Pasquale and Nico.

"Gentlemen, thank you for all your support. I know you, too, have suffered a great loss with the death of my father. You have been in service to my family for longer than I can remember and I am grateful to you. Should you need time to grieve, please know it is yours once we return home."

Both men spluttered their protestations as they assured him that they would take no leave. That it was their honor to serve him. It was as he'd expected, but that didn't mean they wouldn't carry a sense of loss deep inside.

"I mean it," he affirmed. "Nico, will you see to the packing? I believe our plane will be ready by 8 a.m."

The head of his security, Armaund, entered the suite with three of his team.

"Sire, when you're ready."

With a nod of thanks to Pasquale and Nico, Thierry headed for the door. Three security guards fell in formation around him as one went ahead to the private elevator that serviced this floor.

"We thought the side entrance would be best, sire. We can avoid the lobby that way and hotel security have swept for paparazzi already."

"Thank you, that's fine."

He felt like little more than a sheep with a herd of sheep dogs as they exited the elevator downstairs.

"Some space, please, gentlemen," Thierry said firmly as he picked up his pace and struck out ahead of his team.

He could sense they didn't like it, but as long as he didn't look as if he was surrounded by guards, he was relying on the fact that in a big city such as New York he'd soon become just another person on the crowded sidewalk. It was the team who would likely draw attention to him rather than his own position in the world.

Thierry rounded the corner and headed for the exit. Not far now and maybe he could breathe, really breathe for the first time since he'd heard the news.

"'Fun,' she said," Mila muttered under her breath as she walked the block outside the hotel for the sixth time that evening.

Once she'd overcome the sheer terror that had gripped her as she'd escaped Sally's family's hotel suite, anticipation had buoyed her all the way here. But she'd yet to feel that sense of fun that Sally had mentioned. Leaving the suite had been nerve-racking. She'd been sure that Bernadette or one of the guards would have seen past the blond wig she wore and realized that it wasn't Sally leaving the suite, but they'd only given her a cursory glance.

The walk to the prince's hotel hadn't been too bad, but it had given her too much time to think about what on earth she was doing here. And far too much time to begin to regret it—hence the circuits around the block. Any minute now she'd be arrested, she was sure of it. She'd already started getting sideways glances from more than one person.

She took a sip from the coffee she'd bought to steady her nerves and ducked into a doorway at the side of the hotel just as the skies opened with a sudden spring shower of rain. Great, she thought, as she watched the rain fall, making the streets slick and dark and seeming to emphasize just how alone she was at this exact moment, even with the tens of thousands of people who swirled and swelled around her. One of those people jostled her from behind, making her lurch and sending her coffee cup flying to the pavement. She cried out in dismay as some of the scalding liquid splashed on her hand.

"Watch it!" she growled, shaking the residue from her

stinging skin and brushing down the front of her—no, she corrected herself, Sally's—jacket.

So much for making a good impression, she thought. Wet, bewigged and now coffee-stained—she may as well quit and go home. This had been a ridiculous idea from start to finish and there'd be hell to pay if she got caught out.

"My apologies."

The man's voice came from behind her. It was rich and deep and sent a tingle thrilling down her spine. She wheeled around, almost bumping into him again as she realized he was closer to her than she'd anticipated.

"I'm sor—" she began and then she looked up.

The man stood in front of her, an apologetic smile curving sinfully beautiful lips. A dark beanie covered the top of his head, hiding the color of his hair, and he wore sunglasses. Odd, given the late hour but, after all, this was New York. But then he hooked his glasses with one long tanned finger and slid them down his nose, exposing thick black brows and eyes the color of slate. Everything—all thought, all logic, all sense—fled her mind.

All she could focus on was him.

Prince Thierry.

Right there.

In the flesh.

Mila had often wondered if people were exaggerating when they talked about the power of immediate physical attraction. She'd convinced herself that her own initial reaction to the prince years ago had been largely due to nerves and a hefty dose of overactive teenage hormones. Now, however, she had her answer. What she'd felt for him then was no exaggeration, since she felt exactly the same way now. Her mouth dried, her heart pounded, her legs trembled and her eyes widened in shock. Even though she had come here with the express purpose of meeting him, the reality was harder to come to terms with than she'd anticipated.

Sally had said he was hot. It had been a gross understatement. The man was incendiary.

Mila lowered her eyes to the base of his throat, exposed by an open collar. A pulse beat there and she found herself mesmerized by the proof he was completely and utterly human. A shiver of yearning trembled through her.

"I'll get you another coffee."

"N-no, it-it's okay," she answered, tripping over her tongue.

Think! she commanded herself. *Introduce yourself. Do something. Anything.* But then she looked up again and met his gaze, and she was lost.

His eyes were still as she remembered, but what had faded from her memory was that they were no ordinary gray. They reminded her of the color of the mountain faces that were mined for their pale slate in the north west of her country, and the north east of his. She'd always thought the color to be mundane, but how wrong she had been. It was startling, piercing, as if he could see to the depths of her soul when he looked at her. His irises were rimmed with black and lighter striations of silver shone like starlight within them. And his lashes were so dark they created the perfect frame for his eyes.

Mila realized she was staring and dropped her gaze again, but it did little to slow the rapid beat of her heart or to increase her lung capacity when she most needed a deep and filling breath.

"Si—?"

A man loomed beside them and angled his body between the prince and herself. One muttered phrase from the prince in his home language stopped the man mid-speech and he slipped back again. Security, obviously, and none too happy about their prince mixing with the natives.

Except she wasn't native, was she? And, she realized with a shock, he didn't seem to recognize who she was.

The prince turned his attention back to her and spoke again, his voice laced with concern. "Are you sure you're okay? Look, your hand is burned."

Mila started as he took her hand in his and held it so he could examine the pinkness left by the hot coffee. Her breathing hitched a little as his thumb softly traced around the edges of the tender skin. His fingers were gentle and even though he held her loosely—so she could tug herself free at any time—they sent a sizzle of awareness across the surface of her skin that had nothing to do with hot coffee and everything to do with this incredibly hot man.

"It's nothing, really," she said, knowing she should pull her hand loose but finding herself apparently unable to do so.

Nothing? It was everything. This was the magnetism she'd seen in action on TV earlier today. She was as helpless against it as everyone else had been.

"Please," he said, letting go of her and gesturing down the sidewalk. "Allow me to buy you another coffee."

His simple request was her undoing and she searched his face, seeking any sign that he knew who she was, and fighting back the disappointment that rose within her when he didn't. Of course he wouldn't expect to find himself face-to-face with a princess on the streets of New York, let alone *his* princess, she rationalized. But in spite of herself, Mila felt annoyance quickly take disappointment's place. Was he so disinterested in her and their eventual union that she wasn't on his mind at all?

But perhaps she could use this to her advantage. The plan she'd made with Sally had been for her to reintroduce herself to the prince, but what if she didn't? What if she let herself just be another anonymous person on the streets of New York? Without the weight of their betrothal making them formal or awkward with each other, she could use this chance to get to know him better. To see for herself who this man was, while he was emotionally unguarded and not on show, and to gauge for herself what kind of man she would be marrying.

"Thank you," she said, quelling her irritation and drawing on every gram of serenity and inner strength that had been instilled in her since her birth. "I would like that."

His lip quirked up at the corner and, just like that, she found herself mesmerized once again. His eyes gleamed in satisfaction, the faintest of lines appearing at their corners. She forced herself to look away, to the street, to the rain, to basically anything but the man who guided her to walk at his side.

Ahead of them, one of his security team had already scoped out the same small coffee shop where she'd bought her cup earlier, and discreetly gestured an all-clear. It was done so subtly that if she hadn't been so used to looking for it for herself, she wouldn't even have noticed.

They entered and went to the counter to order. Mila was struck by how surreal this all felt. He was acting as if he did everyday things like walk down the street for coffee all the time, when she knew he certainly did not. His security team were dotted around the premises, two by the door and one near a table to which the prince guided her once they had their orders.

"Friends of yours?" Mila commented, nodding in the direction of his shadow team.

He made a sound that was something between a snort and a laugh. "Something like that," he acknowledged. "Do they bother you? I can ask them to leave."

"Oh, no, don't worry. They're fine."

She settled in her chair and looked at the tray Prince Thierry placed on the table, noticing he'd also ordered a small bowl of ice. She watched in bemusement as he took a pristine white monogrammed handkerchief from his pocket and wrapped some of the ice inside it.

"Give me your hand," he commanded.

"Really, it's not that sore," Mila protested.

"Your hand?" he repeated, pinning her with that steely gaze and Mila found herself doing as he'd bidden.

He cradled her hand in his while gently applying the makeshift ice pack. Mila tried to ignore the race of her pulse as she watched him in action. Tried and failed.

"I apologize again for my clumsiness," he continued. "I wasn't looking where I was going."

"Seriously, it's okay," she answered with a smile.

"Let me be the judge of that," he said firmly, smiling to take the edge off his words.

Clearly he was a man used to being in command. The idea sent another thrill of excitement coursing through Mila's veins. Would he take command in all things? She pressed her thighs together on a wave of need that startled her with its intensity.

He looked up. "I'm Hawk, and you are?"

"A-Angel," Mila answered, defaulting to the diminutive of the name she was known by here in the United States. If he could use a moniker, then why shouldn't she also? Why shouldn't they just be two strangers meeting on the street just like anybody else?

"Are you in New York on business?" she asked, even though she knew full well why he was here.

"Yes, but I return home in the morning," he replied.

She was surprised. The summit was scheduled to last for four days and only started tomorrow. He had just arrived here yesterday and now he was already returning to Sylvain? She wanted to ask why but knew she couldn't. Not when he was supposed to simply be a stranger she'd just met on the street.

He lifted the makeshift ice pack from her hand and gave a small nod of satisfaction. "That's looking better."

"Thank you."

The prince let go of her hand and Mila felt an irrational sense of loss. His touch had been thrilling and without it she felt as though she'd been cast adrift.

"And you?" he asked.

Mila looked up and stared at him. "Me, what?"

"Are you in New York on business or do you live here?"

The skin around his eyes crinkled again. He was laughing at her, she was sure of it, but not in an unkind way. For a moment she was struck by the awful and overwhelming sense of ineptitude that had marked her first meeting with the prince. She recalled how embarrassed she'd felt back then. How she'd found herself so unworthy of this incredibly striking, self-assured man.

She wasn't that girl anymore, Mila told herself firmly. And tonight, incognito, she could be anyone she wanted to be. Even someone who could charm a man like Prince Thierry of Sylvain. The thought empowered her and bolstered her courage. She could do this.

"Oh, sorry," she laughed, injecting a note of lightheartedness to her voice. "You lost me there for a moment."

"But I have you now," he countered.

Warmth flooded her as his words sank in.

"Yes," she said softly. "You do."

Three

The air thickened between them—conversation forgotten for the moment as they stared into one another's eyes.

Thierry found himself willingly drawn into her gaze. Her brows were perfect dark arches, framing unusual amber eyes fringed by thick dark lashes. Their coloring seemed at odds with her long blond hair, but she was no less beautiful for it. If anything, it made her even more striking. Her cheekbones were high and gently sculpted, her nose short and straight. But it was her lips to which his eyes were most often drawn. They were full and lush and as she parted them on an indrawn breath he felt a deeply responsive punch to his gut. Arousal teased at his groin. It was as if he was in a spell of some kind. A spell from which he had no desire to break free.

It was only as someone walked past their table, bumping it and spilling some of her coffee, that the enchantment between them was broken.

Angel laughed and sopped up the mess with a paper

napkin. "Seems I'm destined not to finish my coffee this evening. And in answer to your question, no, I live in Boston. I'm only visiting the city."

"I didn't think your accent was from around here," Thierry commented.

With elegant fingers, she balled the napkin and picked up her cup to take a sip of what was left of her drink. He found himself captivated by her every movement. Enthralled by the flick of her tongue across her lip to taste a remnant of the topping of chocolate and milk foam that lingered there. Thierry swallowed against the sudden obstruction in his throat. It was as if his heart had lodged there, hammering wildly.

He shouldn't be here with this woman. He was engaged to another—someone he barely knew, even though he would be married to her by the end of the month. And yet, not in all his years of bachelorhood had he felt a compulsion to be with someone as he did with the enchanting female sitting opposite him. It was almost as if he knew her already, or felt as if he should. Whatever the sensation was that he felt, he wanted more of it. Hell, he wanted more of her.

Angel put her cup back down. "Actually, I'm in New York to attend a lecture on sustainability initiatives."

Thierry felt his interest in her sharpen. "You are? I was scheduled to attend that lecture tomorrow myself."

"And you can't delay your return home?"

The dark pull of reality crept through him and with it the reminder of what tomorrow would entail. Eight and a half hours by air to Sylvain's main airport, then another twenty minutes in his private helicopter to the palace. All of which to be followed by meetings with his household and the heads of government. His time wouldn't be his own until after his father was buried in the family vault near the palace. Maybe not even then.

"Hawk?" Angel prompted him.

He snapped out of his train of thought and gave her his full attention. "No, I must return home. An urgent matter. But enough of that. Tell me, what takes a beautiful young woman like yourself to a dusty old lecture hall?"

She looked affronted by his question. "That's a little sexist, don't you think?"

"Forgive me," he said quickly. "I did not mean to undermine your intelligence, or to sound quite so chauvinistic."

He was disappointed in himself. It seemed the apple hadn't fallen far from the tree, after all. Thierry's father had been nothing but old-fashioned in his view that women were for the begetting of heirs and to be a faithful and adoring ornament by his side. His consort had failed miserably at the second part. Instead of considering that he might have made a mistake in his treatment of her, the king had clung more fiercely to his opinions about a woman's role in the monarchy and it was obvious in palace appointments that his chauvinism guided his choices.

Thierry had recently begun to wonder if part of the reason for his mother's infidelity had been a lack of self-worth caused by her husband's condescending treatment. Maybe his actions had meant that she'd desperately sought meaning for her life anywhere but within her marriage. But that mattered little now. She and her lover had died in a fiery car wreck many years ago. The resulting scandal had almost brought two nations to war and it was one of the reasons Thierry had vowed to remain chaste until marriage and then, after he was wed, to remain faithful to his spouse. He also rightly expected the same in return. While he wouldn't marry for love, his marriage would last. It had to. He had to turn the tide of generations of marital failure and unhappiness. How hard could it be?

Across the table, Angel inclined her head in acknowledgment of his apology. "I'm glad to hear it. I get quite enough of that from my brother." She softened her words with another smile. "In answer to your question, my professor recommended the lecture."

For the next hour they discussed her studies, particularly her interest in developing sustainable living solutions, equal opportunities for all people and renewable energy initiatives. He found her fascinating. Her enthusiasm for her causes made her quite animated and he relished the pinkish tinge of excitement that colored her cheeks. The subjects they discussed were dear to his heart as well, and topics he wished to pursue further with his government. His father had seen little point in breaking away from the methods that had been tried and true in Sylvain for centuries, but Thierry was acutely aware of the need for long-term planning to ensure that future generations would continue to benefit from and enjoy his country's many resources—rather than plunder them all into oblivion. Their discussion was exhilarating and left him feeling mentally stimulated in a way he hadn't anticipated.

The clientele of the coffee shop had thinned considerably during their talk and Thierry became aware that the members of his security team were beginning to shift uncomfortably at their tables. Angel appeared to notice it, too.

"Oh, I'm sorry to have taken so much of your time. When I get on my pet subjects I can be a little over-excited," she apologized.

"Not at all. I enjoyed it. I don't often get to exchange or argue concepts with someone as articulate and well-versed as you are."

She looked at her watch, its strap a delicate cuff of platinum and, if he wasn't wrong, diamonds. The subtle but obvious sign of wealth made him even more intrigued about her background.

"It's getting late. I guess I'd better head back to my

hotel," she said with obvious reluctance. "This has been really nice. Thank you."

No. Every cell in his body objected to the prospect of saying goodbye. He wasn't ready to relinquish her company yet. He reached out and took Angel's hand.

"Don't go, not yet." The words surprised him as much as they appeared to surprise her. "Unless you have to, of course."

Damn. He hadn't meant to sound so needy. But in the face of the news he'd received tonight, Angel was a delightful distraction in what was soon to be a turbulent sea of chaos. He looked deep into her eyes, struck again by the beauty of their unusual whiskey-colored hue. He'd seen that color before, he realized, but he couldn't quite remember where. Thierry looked down to where their hands were joined. She hadn't pulled away. That had to be a good sign, right? He certainly hoped so. He wasn't ready yet to relinquish her company.

"No, I don't have to, exactly..." Her voice trailed away and she looked at her watch again before she said more firmly. "No. I don't have to go."

"No boyfriend waiting for you at home?" he probed shamelessly, running his thumb over her bare fingers.

Angel chuckled and his heart warmed at the sound.

"No, no boyfriend."

"Good. Shall we walk together?" he suggested.

"I'd like that."

She rose with a fluid grace that mesmerized him, and gathered up her coat and bag. He reached for her coat and helped her into it, his fingertips brushing the nape of her neck. He'd felt a shock of awareness when he'd touched her hand, but that was nothing compared to the jolt that struck him now. It was wrong, he knew, to feel such an overpowering attraction to Angel when he was engaged to another woman. Was he no different than his mother, who had been incapable of observing the boundaries of married life?

Thierry pulled his hands away and, balling them into fists, he shoved them deep into his pockets. A sense of shame filled him. This was madness. In a few weeks' time he'd be marrying Princess Mila and here he was, in New York, desperate to spend more time with someone whose first name was almost the only thing he knew about her. Well, that and her keen intelligence about topics dear to his heart. Even so, it didn't justify this behavior, he argued silently.

And then she turned to look at him and smiled, and he knew that whatever else was to come in his life, he had to grasp hold of this moment, this night, and make the most of the oasis of peace she unwittingly offered him.

They headed out of the coffee shop and turned toward Seventh Avenue. His security detail melted into the people around them. There, ever vigilant, but not completely visible. The rain had stopped and Thierry began to feel his spirits lift again. This felt so normal, so unscripted. It was a vast departure from his usual daily life.

"Tell me about yourself," he prompted his silent companion. "Any family?"

"I have a brother. He's in Europe right now," Angel said lightly, but he saw the way she pressed her delectable full lips together as if she was holding something back. "How about you?" she asked, almost as if her question was an afterthought.

"An only child."

"Was it lonely, growing up?"

"Sometimes, although I always had plenty of people around me."

Angel gestured to the guard in front and the others nearby. "People like them?" she asked.

"And others," he admitted.

They stopped at a set of lights and she lifted her chin and stared straight ahead. "Sometimes you can be at your most lonely when you're surrounded by people."

Her words struck a chord with him. There was something about the way she'd made her statement that made him think she spoke from personal experience. The thought made something tug inside him. He wished he could remove the haunted, empty tone from her voice and fill it with warmth. *And what else*, a voice inside him asked. He pushed the thought aside. There could be nothing else. Come morning he would be a different man to the rest of the world. A king. This interlude of normality would be nothing but a memory. One, he realized, he would treasure for a long time to come.

"So what do you do?" Angel asked him after they'd crossed the street.

"Do?"

"Yes, for a living. I assume you do work?"

Yes, he worked, but not in the sense she was probably expecting. "I'm in management," he said, skirting the truth.

"That's a very broad statement," she teased, looking up at him with a glimmer of mischief in her tawny eyes.

"I have a very broad range of responsibilities. And you, what do you plan to do once you have completed your studies?"

Her expression changed in an instant—the humor of before replaced with a look of seriousness. Then she blinked and the solemnity was gone.

"Oh, this and that," she said airily.

"And you accused me of being vague?" he taunted, enjoying their verbal sparring.

"Well, since you asked—I want to go home and make a difference. I want people to listen to me, to really listen, and to take what I have to say on board—not just dismiss me out of hand because I'm female."

He raised his brows. "Does that happen a lot?"

"You did it to me," she challenged.

"Yes, I did, and I apologize again for my prejudice. I hope you get your wish." He drew to a halt beside a food truck. "Have you eaten this evening?"

"No, but you don't have to—"

"I'm told you haven't been to New York until you try one of these rib eye sandwiches."

She inhaled deeply. "They do smell divine, don't they?"

"I'll take that as a yes."

He turned to the head of his security and gave an order in Sylvano. The man grinned in response and lined up at the food-truck window.

They continued to walk as they ate, laughing in between bites as they struggled to contain their food without spilling it.

"I should have taken you to a restaurant," Thierry said as Angel made a noise of disgust at the mess she had left on her hands when they'd finished.

"Oh, heavens no! Not at all. This is fun…just messy." She laughed and gingerly extracted a small packet of tissues from her bag so she could wipe her fingers.

Thierry felt his lips pull into a smile again as they had so many times since he'd met her. What was it about her that felt so right when everything else around him felt so wrong?

"I can't get over this city," Angel exclaimed. "There's never a quiet moment. It's exhilarating."

"It is," he agreed and then looked over at her. "Do you dance?"

"Are you asking me if I'm capable of it, or if I want to?" Angel laughed in response.

Thierry shrugged. "Both. Either." He didn't care. He suddenly had the urge to hold her in his arms and he figured this would be the only way he could decently do so without compromising his own values.

"I'm not exactly dressed for it," Angel said doubtfully.

"You look beautiful. I've heard of a quiet place not far from here. It's not big and brash like a lot of the clubs. More intimate, I suppose, and you can dance or talk or just sit and watch the other patrons if that's all you want to do."

"It sounds perfect."

"So, shall we?"

She grinned back. "Okay, I'd like that."

"Good." He took her hand in his, again struck by the delicacy of her fingers and the fine texture of her skin.

What would it feel like if she touched him intimately? Would her fingers be firm or soft like a feather? Would she trace the contours of his body with a tantalizing subtlety, or would her touch be more definite, more demanding? He slammed the door on his wayward thoughts. It seemed he had more of his mother in him than he'd suspected. Still, there was nothing wrong with dancing with a woman other than his betrothed, was there? He had to do it at state functions all the time.

He tugged her in the direction of a club he'd visited on his last trip to New York and sent Armaund ahead to ensure they'd gain entry. The night was still young and he wasn't ready for it to end yet.

Drawing her into his arms on the dance floor was everything he'd hoped for and more. The only problem was that it made him *want* more—and that was something he'd forbidden himself until marriage. He was determined to hold sacred the act of love and making love. It was something he would share with his wife and his wife alone. He hadn't remained celibate purely for the hell of it. Sometimes it had been sheer torment refusing to acknowledge the demands of his flesh. But he'd promised himself from a very young age that he would not be that person. He would not allow physical need to cloud all else. Over the centuries his family had almost lost everything several times over because of a lack of physical control.

He'd always believed his forebears' susceptibility to fleshly pursuits to be a mark of weakness, and nothing had happened in his thirty-one years to change his mind. Except perhaps the young woman dancing with him right now. Even so, he denied himself any more than the sensation of her in his arms—the brush of her breasts against his chest as he held her close, the skim of her warm breath on his throat—they were torments and teases he could overcome. When he boarded the plane a few short hours from now, to return to Sylvain, he would do so with the full knowledge that he had honored his vow to both himself and to the woman he was to marry.

But until then, he'd enjoy this stolen night as much as his duty and honor would allow.

The night had been magical—something even her wildest imagination could never have dreamed up. In fact, Mila doubted even Sally, with all her romantic ideas, could have come up with something like the night she'd just had. She felt like Cinderella, except in her fairy tale the prince was seeing her home and it was well past midnight. As the limousine, which had been waiting outside the club when they'd left it, pulled up outside her hotel she turned in her seat to face the prince. Tonight, she'd seen a side of him she'd never anticipated—and she was utterly captivated by him.

Maybe it was the champagne they'd drunk at the club, or maybe it was simply the knowledge that at month's end she'd be standing next to him beneath the ancient vaulted ceilings of the Sylvano palace cathedral and pledging her life to him, but right now she felt as if she was floating on air.

At least now she knew what Thierry was like away from the pomp and ceremony that was attached to his position in the world. Once they were married and had the chance to spend time together alone, without all the trappings and formality of their official lives, she believed that they could become important to one another beyond what their marriage would gain for their respective nations. Tonight she'd had a chance to get to know the man beneath the crown. The man who would be her husband— who would share her days and her nights. And, given the fierce attraction between them, she looked forward to getting to know him even better. In every way.

He'd been the consummate gentleman tonight and, for the first time in her life, she'd *felt* like a desirable woman— one who could be confident that she would be able to make him happy in their marriage, too.

She turned to face him in the seat of the limo. "Thank you, Hawk. Tonight was incredible. I will never forget it."

He took her hand and lifted it to his lips, brushing them across her knuckles in a caress that sent a bolt of longing straight to her center.

"Nor I."

Thierry leaned forward, his intention to kiss her cheek obvious, but at the last minute Mila turned her head, allowing their lips to brush one another. It was the merest touch, sweet and innocent, and yet in that moment she felt something expand in her chest and threaten to consume her. It shook Mila to her core.

Words failed her and she pulled away, blindly reaching for the door handle and stumbling slightly as she left the private cavern of the vehicle. She didn't look back. She couldn't. If she did she might ask for more and it wasn't the time or the place to do that.

She moved swiftly through the hotel lobby and to the elevator and swiped her key card to head for the penthouse.

In the elevator car she reached up and tugged the blond wig loose and locked her gaze with her reflection in the mirrored walls. She'd been a stranger to Thierry tonight and he'd enjoyed her company. But would he enjoy it quite so much when he met the real Angel, or would he remember the gauche and chubby girl for whom he'd shown a moment of disdain? Only time would tell.

Four

"Of all the stupid, irresponsible, brainless things to do! What if the media catches wind of this? Did you even stop to think about that? You'll be crucified and all of Sylvania will reject you before you even cross their border."

Mila sat back in her chair waiting for her brother's tirade to subside. It didn't look as if it would be soon, though. He was working up another head of steam as he paced the priceless Persian carpet on his office floor. She kept her head bowed, her tongue still in her mouth. It was no easy task when she'd become used to offering her opinion—and having it respected.

"You were raised to behave better than this. What made you sneak out like nothing more than a common tramp? Was this idea concocted by that friend of yours in America? Sally what's-her-name?" Anger and disgust pervaded his tone.

That got her riled. "Now wait a minute—!" she protested, but Rocco cut her off with a glare.

"You are a princess of Erminia. Princesses do not sneak out of hotel rooms in the dead of night and stay out until dawn with strangers."

Unless you live in a fairy tale, Mila amended silently, remembering her favorite bedtime story about the twelve dancing princesses. But this, her life, was no fairy tale. Besides, Prince—no, *King*, she reminded herself—Thierry wasn't a stranger to her anymore. At least, not completely. But she'd endure Rocco's lecture. For now, it suited her not to tell her brother whom she'd spent her night with. The secret was hers to hold safely in her heart. She didn't want to share it with her brother who would no doubt worry about the political ramifications of her and Thierry's impromptu date. Ramifications that would sully her memory of that wonderful, magical night.

Rocco strode to the large arched window set deep into the palace wall, which offered a view of the countryside beyond it. Mila looked past him to the outside—to freedom. A freedom she'd never truly taste again. The anonymity of life in the United States had been a blessing, but now that she was back home for good she was expected to kowtow to protocol—and that meant doing whatever it was her brother decreed. She began to wonder if perhaps it might not have been better not to have known the freedom she'd experienced after all. The comparison made coming home this time so very much harder.

"So, Rocco, what are you going to do? Throw me in the dungeons?"

Her brother turned and she was struck by how much he'd aged since she'd last seen him a year ago. As if stress and worry had become his constant companions, leaving lines of strain on his face and threads of gray at his temples. And some of that strain, and no doubt several of those gray hairs, were due to her, she acknowledged with a pang. She loved her brother dearly, and had no desire to hurt him or cause him distress, but she just wished he'd listen to her once in a while—really listen as if she and what she had to say had value.

"Don't think I won't do it," he growled. "Such flippancy is probably all I can expect from you after allowing you so much leeway these past seven years. I should never have been so lenient. Our advisers recommended that you marry the prince immediately when you turned eighteen but no, I had to allow you to persuade me to send you away—for an education, not so you could bring our family name into disrepute." He pinched the bridge of his aquiline nose and drew in a deep breath before continuing. "I felt sorry for you back then, Mila. You were no more than a schoolgirl, entering into an engagement with an older man—someone you had barely met, yet alone knew. I understood that you felt stifled by that and, I hazard to say, somewhat terrified at the prospect of what came next. You were so much younger than your years, so innocent."

He sighed and turned away for a moment. Mila bristled at his description of her. Innocent? Yes, of course she'd been innocent. Given her strict and restrictive upbringing there had been little opportunity to learn anything of the ways of the world and the people within it. It was part of why she'd begged her brother for the chance to study abroad. What kind of ruler could she be if she couldn't understand her people and the struggles and challenges they lived with every day? Rocco continued to speak.

"And so I agreed when you asked me for time until your twenty-fifth birthday. I thought it was the best thing to do for you and that it might help to make your eventual union a happier one. I should have known it would come to this—that the lack of structure in your life overseas would corrupt you and deviate you from your true path."

Lack of structure? Mila bit her tongue to keep herself from saying the words out loud. While her life in Boston had not been like her life here in the castle, how on earth did Rocco think she'd attained the measure of academic recognition she'd achieved without structure? And even aside from her scholastic successes—won through hard work and discipline—she'd also dealt with the social restrictions of a team of bodyguards, not to mention a chaperone who vetoed nearly every opportunity to relax or try to make friends. She had barely even socialized with any of the other students on campus.

But her brother was on a roll now. If she tried to explain, he would not listen, and she knew it. To say anything while he was still so angry with her would be a complete waste of time. Instead, she let his words flow over her, like the water that, during a heavy downpour, spouted from the gargoyles positioned around the castle gutters.

"Even I cannot turn back time. You are home now and you will prepare for your marriage. Your wedding takes place four weeks from today. And there will not be one wrong move, one misstep, or one breath of scandal from you. Do you understand me? Too much rides on this, Mila. The stability of our entire nation depends on your ability to do the job you were raised to do."

The job she was raised to do. There it was—the millstone around her neck. The surety that she had no value as a human being beyond that of being a suitable wife for a powerful man.

"And the late king's funeral this week? Am I not to attend that with you as a mark of respect?"

"No. You will stay here."

She wanted to argue, to say she had every right to be there at her fiancé's side as he bid a final farewell to his father, but she knew the plea would fall on deaf ears. Mila shifted her gaze to look her brother straight in the eyes. She hated seeing him like this—so angry and distraught—so she said the words he was expecting to hear.

"I understand you, brother. I will do as you ask."

But he hadn't asked, had he? He'd ordered it from her. Not once, at any stage during this audience with him—for it couldn't be deemed anything else—had Mila felt as if he was pleased to welcome his baby sister home. Instead she'd felt like nothing more than a disappointment. A burden to be off-loaded. A problem to be corrected.

There hadn't been a single word of congratulations on her achievements while she'd been away. No mention of her honors degree or the publication of her treatise on Equal Opportunity and Sustainable Development in European Nations. Her only value was in her ability to play the role of a proper fiancée and wife. She was merely a pawn on her brother's chessboard.

She kept her eyes fixed on Rocco and she saw the minute the tension that held his body began to ease from his shoulders. His eyes, amber like her own, but several shades deeper, softened.

"Thank you. You understand, don't you? I don't ask you to do this for myself, but for our people. And for your sake as well, since I couldn't bear to see you do anything to jeopardize your chance at winning your husband's trust and respect."

And there it was. The glimpse of the brother she'd grown up loving more than life itself—the brother who had been her protector and defender all throughout her childhood. But that was all she was permitted to see because the veil of command he perpetually bore took up residence once again on his visage.

"I understand," she answered with an inclination of her head.

And she did. Even though, inside, her emotions spun in turmoil. It was entirely clear that her value—to her brother and her future husband—came from her chastity and unimpeachable honor. Her knowledge, her insight, her plans to better society and improve conditions for her people, and even the grace, poise and confidence she had gained in her years abroad mattered little to their society compared to her reputation.

Nothing had changed in all the time she'd been away. She didn't even know why she would have expected it to. Erminia was still locked in the old days where a woman's place was not beside, but behind her husband, or her father or brother or whichever male figure led her household—her thoughts and ideas to be tolerated but not celebrated or given any respect.

Even in the Erminian parliament women were a rare breed. Mila wanted to see that change, and for their government to acknowledge women's intelligence and their value as vital members of the very fabric of Erminian society as a whole. But she knew that change would be very slow to come...if it came at all.

"You don't sound excited about your wedding," Rocco prompted. "I thought you would be full of chatter about it."

Mila sighed. "Rocco, I'm not a little girl about to go to a tea party in her favorite dress. I am a full-grown woman with a mind and thoughts of her own, about to enter into a marriage with a man I barely know."

He stepped closer to her and placed a finger under her chin, lifting her face up to his. "You've changed."

"Of course I've changed. I've grown up."

"No, it's more than that." A frown furrowed his brow and his eyes narrowed. "Are you still...? Did you...?"

Mila held on to her temper by a thread. "What? You're actually asking me if I've kept myself chaste? Do you really think I'd compromise the crown by throwing my virginity away on a one-night stand?"

Her brother paled. "You will not speak to me in that tone. I might be your brother but, first and foremost, I am your king."

Mila swept down into a curtsey. "Sire, I beg your forgiveness."

"Mila, don't mock me."

She rose again but did not look directly in his eyes. "I do not mock you, Your Majesty. I am well aware of my position in this world. I will do my duty and you can rest assured that by my wedding day no man will have touched me, with even so much as a kiss, before my future husband does. But, just in case you don't believe me, please feel free to have the royal physician examine me to ensure that I am indeed a woman of my word."

"Mila—"

"I believe I have an appointment for a dress fitting now. If you'll excuse me?" she said, turning before his reaching hand could touch her.

She knew that, deep down, he probably hated the exchange they'd just shared even more than she did. But duty drove him now, and that meant the needs of the country always came first. He couldn't be the doting older brother who had sheltered her for so many of her younger years. Ten years her senior, Rocco had been forced to prematurely take the crown after their father's assassination when Rocco had been only nineteen. Mila could barely remember a time since when his shoulders hadn't borne the weight of responsibility that had descended with the crown. Almost overnight, he'd gone from the teasing and protective older brother she'd adored, to the domineering sovereign she knew today. The man who showed no signs of weakness, no chink in the armor that shrouded his emotions.

As she let herself out of his office and barely held herself back from storming down the ornately decorated corridor of the castle to her suite of rooms, a part of her still mourned the boy he'd been while another continued to rail internally at how he'd spoken to her just now. He still saw her as a silly, empty-headed child; that much was clear. And no matter what she did or said, that would probably never change. She had to learn to accept it as she'd had to learn to accept so much about her life. But maybe, just maybe, she would be in a position to effect change once she was married.

Later, as she fidgeted under the weight of the elegant silk-dupion-and-lace gown that was being fitted to her gentle curves she couldn't help but think back to that moment when she and Thierry had kissed good-night—or perhaps it had been good morning, she thought. She couldn't hold back a smile as she remembered the exquisitely gentle pressure of his lips upon hers. If she closed her eyes and concentrated she could almost feel him again, smell the subtle scent of his cologne—a blend of wood and spice that had done crazy things to her inside—and sense the yearning that there could be more. A tiny thrill of excitement rippled through her—a ripple that was rapidly chased away by the sensation of a pin in her thigh.

"I'm so sorry, Your Highness, but if you'd just keep still for me a moment longer…" The couturier's frustration was evident in her tone.

"No, it is I who should apologize," Mila hastily assured the woman. "I wasn't concentrating. It is not your fault."

She focused on a corner of a picture frame on the wall and kept her body still, turning or lifting and dropping her arms when asked—like a marionette. And that, essentially, was all she was to her brother, she realized with a pang. A puppet to be manipulated for the benefit of all of Erminia. There wouldn't have been such pressure on her if he had married by now himself. But, when faced with a royal proposal, the girl he'd loved through his late teens and early twenties had decided royal life was not for her, and since then he'd steered clear of romantic entanglements.

Rocco's crown might sit heavily on his dark curls, Mila

thought with a sad sigh, but hers was equally burdensome. But, there was a silver lining, she reminded herself. Her night with Thierry showed they were intellectual equals and he had at least appeared to respect her opinion during their discussions.

If he could give a total stranger his ear, why wouldn't he extend the same courtesy to his wife?

It was 2:00 a.m. and Mila was still wide awake. Never a good traveler, she struggled to adjust to the change in time zones. While most of the good people of Erminia would be fast asleep in their beds about now, Mila's body was on Boston time and for her it was only seven in the evening. Granted, it had been an exhausting day with the hours of travel followed by that awful meeting with her brother. Given how she always suffered severe motion sickness, which left her physically wrung out, logically she should be more than ready to sleep. Sadly, logic was lacking tonight, she accepted with a sigh as she pushed back the covers on her pedestal bed and reached for the light robe she'd cast over the end of her mattress before retiring.

Maybe some warm milk, the way Cookie used to make it for her back when she was a child, would help. After donning her robe, Mila headed for the servants' stairs toward the back of the castle. Sure, she knew that all she had to do was press a button and someone would bring the milk to her, but a part of her craved the inviting warmth and aromas that permeated the castle kitchens and that were such an intrinsic part of her happier childhood memories.

Her slippers barely made a sound on the old stone stairs and, as opposed to the usual daily busyness that made the castle hum with activity during normal waking hours, the air was still and serene. She could do with some of that serenity right now.

To her surprise, the sound of voices traveled up the

corridor toward her. Obviously some staff was on duty around the clock, but it was unusual for the senior household steward to still be afoot at this time of night. Mila recognized Gregor's voice as it rumbled along the ancient stone walls. For a second she was prepared to ignore it, and the younger female voice she could barely hear murmuring in response, but her ears pricked up when she caught Thierry's name mentioned.

Mila slowed her steps as she approached the open door of the steward's office and listened carefully.

"And you're certain of this?" the steward asked.

Mila was surprised Gregor's voice sounded so stern. While the man held a position of extreme responsibility, he was well-known for his warm heart and caring nature—it was part of why the royal household ran so smoothly. His brusque tone right now seemed at odds with the person she remembered.

"Yes, sir. My second cousin assists the king of Sylvain's private secretary. He saw the document soliciting the woman's—" the young woman hesitated a bit before continuing "—services."

"What does your cousin plan to do with this information he so willingly shared with you?"

"Oh, sir, he didn't do so willingly. I mean, it wasn't meant as gossip."

"Then what did he mean by it?"

Mila heard the younger woman make a sound, as if holding back tears. "Oh, please, sir. I don't want him to get into any trouble. It troubled him that the king would seek the services of a courtesan so close to his marriage, especially when it is known within the Sylvano palace that the prince is—was—saving himself for marriage."

A courtesan? Mila's ears buzzed, blocking out any other sound as the word reverberated in her skull. Her stomach lurched uncomfortably and she fought the nausea that swirled with a vicious and sudden twist.

A sound from the steward's office alerted her to the movement of the people inside. She couldn't be caught here, not like this. Mila turned back down the corridor and slipped into another office, this one dark and unoccupied. With her arms bound tight around her middle, she stared at the closed door framed by a limning of light. Her mind whirled.

Thierry had procured a professional mistress? Why would he even do such a thing? How had she misjudged him so badly? Their time together that night in New York had been wonderful, magical—and entirely chaste, without the slightest hint that he was seeking physical intimacy. It had thrilled her to think that he was staying untouched for her, just as she had done for him. None of what she'd learned about him in the hours they'd spent together made sense against what she'd just overheard.

Mila stiffened as she heard a light pair of footsteps walk briskly down the hallway—the maid, leaving Gregor's office by the sound of it. She waited, wondering if she'd hear Gregor leaving the same way, and as she waited her mind spun again. What should she do now she had this knowledge? She couldn't refuse to marry Thierry. That would cause upheaval on both sides of the border. And she didn't want to, not really. But how could she consider a future with a man who was already in the process of installing a mistress in a home they were meant to share? She had toiled long and hard to make herself into a worthy wife for the man she thought he was. Had she been wrong about him all along? Was he just another ruler who treated marriage as nothing more than a facade—like so many royal marriages that had taken place in the past? Had he already given up on the idea that Mila could possibly make him happy?

Was their marriage really to be nothing more than a peace treaty between neighboring nations? Were they not to share the communion of two adults with shared hopes and dreams for the future? Tears burned her eyes, but she blinked them back furiously. She would not succumb to weakness in this. There had to be a way to stop him from taking a mistress, a way to somehow circumvent this. *Think!* she commanded herself. Here she was, well educated, astute about women's issues and keen to do something about them, and yet, when faced with a problem all she could do was hide and then fight back tears? How clichéd, she scolded silently. Mila loosened her arms and let them drop to her sides and lifted her chin. She was a princess, it was about time she started to think and act like one.

An idea sprang into her mind. An idea so preposterous and far-fetched it almost took her breath away with its audacity. Even Sally would be proud. But could she do it? Thinking about it was one thing, undertaking it quite another—and it would involve far more people than just herself.

Just how important was a happy marriage to her? Was she prepared to accept a union in which she was merely a figurehead and lead her own separate life, or did she want Thierry as her husband in every way, emotionally and physically? The answer was resoundingly simple. She wanted it—*him*—all.

Mila reached for the door handle and entered the corridor and resolutely trod toward Gregor's office.

Five

"But, Your Royal Highness!" Gregor protested. "What you're suggesting…it borders on criminal. In fact, kidnapping *is* criminal."

She'd expected resistance and she'd hoped it wouldn't have to come to this. Mila had long believed the pledge of absolute obedience made by staff to the royal household to be archaic and, frankly, ridiculous. Who in their right mind would vow to serve their royal family *unquestioningly* in this day and age—especially if it meant doing something illegal? But tradition still formed the foundation of everything in Erminia and, in this case, the end justified the means. It had to. Her happiness and that of any children she might bear depended on it. She couldn't allow Thierry to begin their marriage with a professional courtesan already in place as his mistress—not without making every effort to win his love for herself, first.

"Gregor, it is your princess who asks this of you," she said imperiously. She hated herself for having to act with such superiority. She'd never been that person—never had to be. In fact, she'd never believed she could be, but, it seemed, when pushed hard enough she was no different from her forebears. "I have no desire to take another woman's leavings when I meet my groom at the altar," she said, taking the bull directly by the horns.

Before her, Gregor blushed. One didn't discuss that sort of thing in front of a member of the royal family—especially not a princess. He looked as if he was about to protest once more, but Mila held her ground, staring directly into his eyes. The man never faltered. He held her gaze as if he could change her mind by doing so but then it appeared that he realized she was set on her course of action—whether he helped her, or not.

"I understand, ma'am."

And he did. She could see it in his eyes. No one who lived and worked within these walls understood her dilemma better. In his position he'd seen one generation after another form marital alliances that had been alternately mediocre and miserable—which, Mila guessed, was only to be expected when people were picked for their pedigree alone and not their compatibility. Thierry's family had been little different, even though his parents purportedly married for love—and look how that had ended. Deep in her heart she knew that she and Thierry could have better than that. They deserved it.

"Then you'll assist me?" she pressed.

"Your safety is paramount, ma'am. If at any time you are under threat—"

"There will be no risk of that," Mila interrupted. "First, however, we must find out who this *courtesan*—" she said the word with a twist of distaste on her lips "—is, and what her travel plans are. Everything hinges on that."

"It won't be easy, ma'am."

"Nothing worthwhile ever is," Mila said with a twinge deep down inside. "And, Gregor, thank you."

"Your wish is my command, ma'am," Gregor said with a deep bow. "Your people only wish for your happiness."

Her happiness. Would she be happy, she wondered? She'd darn well better be if this plan to kidnap the courtesan and take her place worked. If not, well, the outcome did not bode well for any of them.

Thierry ripped the ceremonial sword belt from his hip and cast the scabbard onto his bed with a disrespectful clatter.

"Nico!" he commanded. "Assist me out of this getup immediately, would you?"

His valet scurried from the dressing room and helped Thierry from the formal military uniform he'd worn to his father's funeral this afternoon. The weight of the serge and brass and loops of braid was suffocating and Thierry wanted nothing more than to divest himself of it and all it signaled for his life to come.

The day had been interminable. First the lengthy procession from the palace to the cathedral, following his father's coffin on foot through streets lined with loyal, and some not so loyal, subjects crowding the pavements. One step in front of another. It had gotten him through the ghastly parade of pomp and ceremony and through the endless service at the cathedral and finally through the gloomy private interment in the royal tomb back here at the palace. The entire event had been sobering and a reminder of the years of restrictive duty that stretched before him and what was expected.

It was nothing more than he had been brought up to do, and nothing more than his children would be brought up to do after him, God willing. Children. He'd never stopped to think about what it might be like to be a parent. He only remembered his own dysfunctional childhood where his parents had been distant characters to whom he was always expected to show the utmost respect and reverence. Even to his mother, who'd thrown her position and her responsibilities to the wind long before she'd embarked on her final, fatal affair.

"Is there anything else you require, sire?" Nico asked, as he took the last of the heavy raiments on his arm.

"Not this evening, thank you, Nico. I'm sorry I was so short with you just now."

"No need to apologize. It's been a trying day for you."

Trying. *Yes, that was one word for it*, Thierry thought as he stalked in his underwear toward the massive marble bathroom off his bedroom. He stripped off his boxer briefs and turned on the multiheaded shower in the oversize stall and set the jets to pulse. He had a meeting scheduled with King Rocco of Erminia in an hour. An appointment dictated by duty, although if they could shed their various hangers-on, one that could prove fruitful as they both wished for the same outcome. Peace between their countries and an opening of the border, which was slated to improve both their economies.

Of course, there were still plenty of the old-school holdouts in their respective governments who wished to maintain the status quo. Trust no one, was their motto—and Thierry could see how that motto had been earned. But that era needed to end and it was time their nations grew with positive change rather than remain forever entrenched in the old ways.

Water pounded against the tension in his neck and shoulders, slowly loosening the knots. Thierry wished he could escape to his hunting lodge in the mountains tonight, but he had to abide by the protocols set by others before him. The meeting with King Rocco needed to be a productive one. After all, the man was set to become his brother-in-law in only three weeks' time.

Later, in his library, Thierry lifted the heavy crystal

stopper from a decanter and looked across to the power-fully built dark-haired man who lounged comfortably in one of the armchairs by the window.

"Brandy?" he asked.

"Actually, I'd kill for a beer," his guest, the King of Er-minia, said with a dazzling smile that lifted the darkness of his expression.

Thierry replied with a smile of his own. "Glass or bottle?"

"The bottle is made of glass, isn't it?" Rocco replied.

A man after his own heart, Thierry decided as he opened the fridge door, disguised as a fourteenth century cupboard, and snagged two longnecks from the shelf. No doubt their respective protocol advisers would have a fit if they could see them now. Well, let them. Thierry twisted off the tops and handed Rocco a bottle. They drank simultaneously, sighing their satisfaction after that first long pull.

"A local brew?" Rocco asked.

Thierry nodded.

"I don't believe we carry it in Erminia. We might need to do something about that, among other things."

And there they were, at the crux of their meeting. His forthcoming marriage to Rocco's sister. Thierry tried to summon the interest he knew the subject was due—it was his duty after all—but it had been a long time since his first meeting with Princess Mila and it had not gone well at all. Though he supposed, it had gone better than if she'd thrown up on his shoes, and from the look he'd seen on her face, that had certainly been a possibility.

No, he castigated himself. He wasn't being fair to her. She'd been a child still, brought up in a sheltered environment, nervous at meeting her future husband for the first time. What else had he expected? A beautiful woman of the world? Someone he could converse with at length on topics near and dear to his heart?

For a moment he was caught by a flash of memory of

a woman who'd been exactly that. That brief moment in time with Angel was less than a week ago, but it felt as if an entire lifetime had passed since then. He pushed the memory from his mind but he couldn't hold back his body's response. Just a thought of Angel and excitement rippled through his veins. For the briefest instant he wished he could have been an ordinary man. One who might have been permitted to pursue, to court, to bed his Angel. But he shoved the thought unceremoniously from his mind. His was no ordinary life. He was no ordinary man. And, he was soon to marry a princess.

And just like that the thrill that had coursed through him was gone. Thierry took another slug of his beer and turned to his guest.

"How is Mila? Did she enjoy her time in the United States?"

And, pow, there it was again. The memory of his own time in the United States, with Angel. The scent of her skin as he held her while they slow-danced. The sweet, *sweet* taste of her lips as they bade one another farewell.

He realized that Rocco had spoken and was awaiting a response. "I'm sorry," he apologized swiftly. "Could you repeat that?"

"Daydreaming about your bride already," Rocco said with a tight smile. "A promising start to your forthcoming nuptials. I said that she has returned both well-educated and well-polished. Provided you look after her, she will make a most suitable consort for you, I'm sure."

There was a thread of protectiveness in Rocco's tone that was unmistakable. Rocco could rest assured that Thierry had no intention of harming his new bride. In fact he was taking steps to ensure that she was well-satisfied in their union, both in bed and out of it. But that wasn't the kind of thing one shared with the brother of your fiancée, Thierry thought as he schooled himself to make a suitable response to Rocco's comment.

Before long they turned their discussion to broader topics relating to their two nations, and how they hoped to mend the rifts between them. By the time Rocco withdrew from their talks three hours later, they'd reached an accord—one underpinned by an implicit understanding that while Rocco's sister's happiness was of the utmost importance, of equal magnitude was the well-being of both of their countries, starting with reconciliation and moving on toward growth and prosperity. In fact, if pushed, Thierry wasn't certain if Rocco did not give the latter even more weight and consequence than his sister. Perhaps the two went hand in hand, he reasoned as he saw his guest from the room. One thing had been made adamantly clear, however. If relations between him and his new bride failed, the uneasy peace between their nations would shatter, causing a return to the economic instability that currently gripped his country and possibly even early stages of war. It was a sobering thought.

As the door closed behind his visitor, Thierry reached for the brandy decanter and poured himself a measure. Taking it over to one of the deep-set windows, he looked out toward Erminia. What was his bride doing now? Brushing up on Sylvano protocol, perhaps?

He hoped she was well prepared for the life she would soon face. There was only so much sheltering he could do for his new wife. She had duties already diarized for when they returned from their honeymoon and he wouldn't be able to continue to protect her from the glaring lens of the media as she had been to date. Still, he considered, as he took a sip of the brandy and allowed it to roll on his tongue, he had excellent staff who would assist her in her transformation from princess to queen consort if that was necessary. Perhaps he needed to focus less upon Princess

Mila and what she needed to do and more upon himself and what he needed to do to keep her happy.

His upbringing had made one thing absolutely clear to him—if the royal couple were not united in everything, the entire country suffered. And so he had taken steps to ensure his education in the delights of the marital bed. Before his wedding day, he would learn how to keep his wife satisfied—and those lessons would be undertaken well away from any media spotlight. He looked forward to it. Of course, his personal vows meant that the instruction would be strictly hands off, with no actual physical intimacy between himself and his instructor. But even without direct demonstration, he knew there was still so much he could learn that would help him start his marriage on the right foot. He wanted to know exactly what it was that a woman needed to be seduced—not only physically, but emotionally and spiritually as well—into remaining committed to her union with him.

Neither the example his parents had left him, nor several generations of grandparents before them, was conducive to the kind of future he sought to achieve with his wife. He wanted to be happy and stable in his marriage, and he wanted his children to know the same happiness and stability. Was that too much to ask? He didn't believe so. It wouldn't necessarily be easy to achieve, since he and his bride would be entering marriage as strangers, but that was where his lessons would help.

Thus, his employment of the services of a discreet courtesan. Who else could educate him on the subtleties of what gave a woman the ultimate in pleasure? Being prepared had always been vital to him. He hated surprises. He would go into this marriage educated and ready, and he would take any steps necessary to make his wife love him enough to offer him the same commitment and fidelity that he was prepared to offer her.

He would do what he had to do.

Six

"This is beyond preposterous! I'm traveling on diplomatic papers. Why have I been brought in here?"

From the room where she was hiding, Mila could hear the woman arguing with the Erminian border official in a back office. She looked up as Gregor hastened through a side door.

"You have her documents?" Mila asked, rising to her feet.

"I do." He started to hand her the papers but then hesitated. "Are you certain you wish to go through with this, ma'am? The risks—"

"Are outweighed by necessity," Mila said firmly.

She held out her hand for the papers and took a moment to check the woman's passport. Long dark hair like her own, similar shape to her face. As long as no one looked too closely at eye color or height she would get away with this. An advance scouting party had already informed her of the clothing the woman had been wearing and Mila was dressed identically, right down to the large-lensed sunglasses she held in her hand and the Hermès scarf already tied over her hair. It was a relief to know that the documentation that had been confiscated from Ottavia Romolo ensured direct passage through the border crossing into Sylvain. Mila supposed that it was unlikely the prince would want his newly procured mistress to be delayed.

Nerves knotted in her stomach and she slipped on her sunglasses. Hopefully the Sylvano driver was more focused on the officials examining the contents of the trunk of his car than on the exact identity of the passenger who was about to enter the rear compartment of the limousine.

"Wish me luck, Gregor."

"Good luck, ma'am," he responded automatically, but the expression on his face was woeful.

Mila shot him a smile. "Don't worry so much, Gregor. I'm not going into enemy territory under live fire."

"You may not be under fire, ma'am, but rest assured I most certainly will be if your brother discovers what you've done and my part in it."

"Then we must make sure that doesn't happen. You have the hotel suite and security team organized for Ms. Romolo?"

"We do. She will be quite comfortable while you're away."

"Right," Mila said and straightened her shoulders. "Let's do this."

"As we discussed, I will stand on your left as we go through the outer office. Hopefully everyone will be too busy outside to pay us much attention."

"You are certain the border official is fully compliant with this?" Mila checked.

"He is, ma'am."

"Good." Mila nodded. "Let's go."

Their passage through the outer office went smoothly until they reached the main door. Someone coming through from outside bumped into Mila hard enough to knock the sunglasses from her face. She caught them in her hand before they fell far and immediately slid them back into place, briefly acknowledging the apology of the elderly gentleman who had just entered. She was so busy concentrating on getting out the door without further mishap that she didn't notice when the man did a double take before bowing deeply in her direction—his movement attracting the attention of the woman still arguing at the counter.

Outside the air was cool and redolent with the crisp scent of pine. Mila inhaled deeply and walked with confidence toward the waiting limousine. Beside her, Gregor gave a nod to the official overseeing the examination of the vehicle and he barked an order in Erminian to the border guards who promptly stepped away from the car and instructed the driver to resume his journey. Mila sank onto the wide leather seat and fastened her seat belt, surprised to find her fingers were quite steady. A minor miracle considering how fast her heart was beating, she thought. She looked up to Gregor with a smile and removed her sunglasses for a moment.

"Thank you, Gregor. I won't forget this," she said softly.

He gave her a brief nod of acknowledgment and then closed the door.

"I apologize for the waste of time, Ms. Romolo," the driver said through the intercom. "You can never trust these Erminians. Rest assured that heads will roll over this."

Mila stifled her reflexive desire to defend her people and merely murmured, "Oh, I hope not."

"I will attempt to make up the time lost through the rest of our journey. We should reach our final destination by seven-thirty this evening."

"Thank you. I think I will try to rest now."

"Certainly, Ms. Romolo. I will let you know when we are nearer the lodge."

In the last few days Mila had done her best to discover where Thierry's lodge was, but its location remained a well-kept secret. Which only served her purpose even better, of course, since it was highly unlikely they would be interrupted. But it was just a little worrying that no one who was in on this escapade with her would know exactly where she was. Her personal staff had been sworn to secrecy about her mission and her brother was still away from the palace and not expected back for another week, at least. Still, what did it matter that nobody would be able to find her? As she'd said to Gregor, it wasn't as if she was going into enemy territory.

Although, the chauffeur's comment did raise a question. He'd been very clear about how he felt about the people of her country. Was that indicative of how most Sylvanos felt? If that was the case, it would make her role as Thierry's wife that much more demanding. Not only did she have to win over her husband and his people, she would have to do so on behalf of all of the people of the land she would be leaving behind. There was a weight of responsibility on her shoulders. Maybe she should not have stayed so long in America. Not only had she distanced herself somewhat from her own people, but she'd missed the opportunity to build a rapport with Thierry's.

Mila bit pensively on her lower lip and stared out the window at the passing countryside. She'd been so determined to better herself—to become the person she thought she should be for her future husband—that she'd lost sight of other, equally important, matters. While she'd thought she was being so mindful of her duty, she'd also been terribly remiss. But it was too late to change any of that now. All she could do was try to make wise decisions going forward. But was this current plan truly wise?

She wanted to build a strong marriage with Thierry, and surely that would have to start by making herself the only woman her husband would want in his bed. Still, she'd taken a massive risk doing this. If she'd made a mistake, there was no going back now. She simply had to make this work. She had to be the courtesan Thierry was expecting and she had to make him fall in love with her so that he would never look outside of their relationship again. She was unwavering in her determination not to become a casualty of the past.

But did that mean she'd become a casualty of the future?

They'd been driving beside a massive stone wall for some time now, the road narrow and winding as it crept higher and higher into the mountains. Mila had napped on and off, but for the last half hour she'd been wide awake—too nervous to close her eyes even though weariness and anxiety pulled at her every nerve. Her mouth was dry and her head had begun to throb. Tension, that's all it was. Once she saw Thierry again she knew she'd be all right. Wouldn't she?

Of course she would, she told herself firmly. She was there to do his bidding. What man would turn that away? Her body warmed as she thought about the intensive cramming she'd done since making her decision to kidnap the courtesan and take her place. Things like, what on earth did a courtesan do?

A surge of longing swept through her body at the thought of some of the duties, making her clench her legs on the unexpected spear of need. Inside her French lace bra her breasts swelled, exerting a gentle pressure against the delicate cobwebs of fabric that barely restrained her and which teased her hardened nipples to sensitive points. She ached to feel pressure against them—the pressure of large, strong fingers or a hard, naked male chest perhaps?

Heat flooded her cheeks. Clearly her research had been quite thorough if she could react like this only based on thinking about what she'd learned. Books—both fiction and not—romantic films and even those less romantic and more blatantly erotic, had filled her days—and her nights. She'd tried to approach the information as she would any research project she'd been assigned, but she hadn't factored in her own response, or the sheer physical frustration the research engendered. While she was no stranger to her body, to say that imagining herself and Thierry engaged in the acts she'd seen had left her painfully unfulfilled would be an understatement. Right now she felt like a crate of nitroglycerin used to blow tunnels through mountains—fragile, unstable and ready to blow at the least provocation.

The car began to slow down while at the same time her pulse rate increased. Before them stood iron gates that were at least twelve feet high. Twin guard boxes stood at each side. One guard, in a Sylvano army uniform, came to the car. Mila shrank back in her seat. The driver opened his car window, said but a few words and the gates began to slowly open. They were through within seconds and, as they began to ascend the steep, winding driveway, she looked back. The gates clanged shut and a tremor passed through her body. Fear, she wondered, or anticipation of what was to come? Slowly, she turned around and faced forward. Hopefully facing her future and not failure.

Thierry stirred from the deep leather button-back chair in his study as Pasquale materialized beside him and cleared his throat.

"Sire, the guard at the gate has alerted us that Ms. Romolo's car is about twenty minutes away."

"Thank you, Pasquale, that will be all."

Thierry stared into the flames set in the ancient stone fireplace a moment longer, then rose to his feet.

"Pasquale, one more thing," he called to his departing assistant. "Please see to it that we are not disturbed this evening. In fact, please dismiss the staff until further notice."

"All the staff, sire?"

"All of them—yourself included."

"But your meals?"

"I think I can survive seeing to my own needs for a week or two," Thierry replied, with a hint of a smile on his lips. "We are well provisioned, are we not?"

"Whatever you say, sire," Pasquale said. "But I must insist that the security staff remain on the perimeter and throughout the grounds."

Thierry nodded. "Of course. And, Pasquale?"

"Yes, sire?"

His assistant gave him a look that almost begged Thierry not to make any additional scandalous requests. Thierry summoned a smile and chose his words carefully, knowing that Pasquale would not be pleased with what he had to say next.

"Please see to it that all forms of communication within the lodge are disabled. There is to be no internet, no radio, no television. In short, no distractions."

Pasquale visibly paled. "And the telephones, sire?"

"And the telephones. Obviously, for security, the radios can continue to be used."

"I must advise you against this, sire. It is foolish to leave yourself so vulnerable."

"Vulnerable? No, I don't believe so. As we just discussed, the royal guards will still be on duty. But the fewer eyes and ears that are party to this, the better. As for myself, I wish to be completely off the grid, as they say. I want no communications coming in here, or going out. Privacy, through the next week, is paramount. If necessary, you can make a statement on my behalf that I have sequestered myself in mourning for my father."

Pasquale's shoulders dropped. "Whatever you say, sire."

"Thank you, that is all. Enjoy your time off."

His assistant looked as if the man would rather suffer a root canal without pain relief than take time away from his king, but he merely gave Thierry a short bow and left the room.

Thierry walked to the mullioned windows at the end of the study and looked out over the drive. It was already busy below. Even though he'd had just a skeleton staff here since his arrival, their leaving caused a momentary upheaval as they exited the property. He watched as the last car pulled away, Pasquale's censorious expression still visible even from this, the second floor, as he was driven away.

Silence reigned. Thierry took in a deep breath and absorbed the reality of being alone. It was such a rare commodity in his life and felt strange, at odds with the norm. It excited him, along with the knowledge that shortly his guest would be here. His education would begin, in absolute privacy—only the two of them and nothing and no one else to observe.

He turned from the window, strode to the door and headed downstairs so he could wait near the front entrance for her arrival. The driver had already been instructed to leave his passenger and her luggage at the door. Thierry would welcome her and see to her things himself. He fought back a grin. This was becoming quite the adventure.

Downstairs, he waited in the great hall. In the massive fireplace, logs crackled and burned bright and warm. Even though it was spring, the air still held a bite to it up here in the mountains, and he was warmly dressed in a cream merino wool sweater and jeans. He held his hands to the heat of the flickering flames and was startled to find his fingers shook a little. Anticipation, or trepidation, he wondered. Probably a little of both.

Expectancy rolled through him like a wave. These next

days would make all the difference to the rest of his life. No wonder he was a bit nervous.

He heard the faint sound of tires on the graveled turning bay in front of the lodge. Thierry listened to the slam of a car door and the crunch of footsteps on the gravel before another door slammed closed. There was a shuffle of movement up the wide stone stairs that led to the front porch, then the sound of footsteps moving away, followed by a car door again and then the sound of the vehicle being driven away.

This was it. He straightened and moved toward the door as he heard the heavy knocker fall against the centuries-old wood. He reached for the handle and swung the door open, for a moment blinded by the low slant of evening light as it silhouetted a feminine form standing in the entrance. Every nerve in his body sprang to full alert, his blood rushing through his body as if he was preparing for battle.

His vision adjusted as the woman lifted her head and looked him in the eyes. Shock rendered him temporarily speechless as he recognized her.

"Angel?"

Seven

Thierry's pulse throbbed as his eyes raked over her. It had only been a matter of days since he'd seen her last, yet it had felt like an eternity. He hadn't expected ever to see her again, let alone here at his hunting lodge—a location so zealously guarded that no one could enter unless it was at his specific invitation. He barely believed his eyes, and yet, there she stood.

He swallowed against the questions that rose immediately in his throat, the need to know who she really was. Was she the Angel he'd met in New York or the courtesan whose services he'd contracted for the next week? Of all the people...

He realized that Angel had not yet spoken, in fact, she looked anxious, unsure of herself. Did he have it wrong? Was she not the woman he'd already met in a city so distant from the country they were now in? He began to notice the differences—the hair that was black instead of blond, the clothing she wore so vastly different from what she'd worn that evening in New York. Even the way she held herself was different—more confident and assured, although the innocence on her face was at complete odds with the way she was dressed in a figure hugging garment that both concealed and revealed at the same time. A dress designed, no doubt, to entice and intrigue a man. And the four-inch spikes she wore on her feet aided in defining the lines of her calves and making her slender legs look incredibly long and alluring.

Then she lifted a delicate hand to her face and removed her sunglasses, exposing the deep-set amber eyes that had so intrigued him. It was her. Positive recognition flooded his mind and his body. He knew her. He wanted to know her better.

This wasn't what he'd bargained for at all. He'd requested a courtesan to educate him, believing he could separate his emotions from the tutelage. That he wouldn't even think about breaching his own vow of chastity until he was with his wife for their first time together. But judging by the sensation coursing through his body, the hunger clawing with demand at the very basis of his being at the mere sight of his Angel, this was not going to be a series of easy lessons.

Thierry stepped forward and offered a hand to his guest. "Welcome to my lodge. I hope you will be comfortable here."

The formality of his words was at complete odds with the chaos of his emotions. Angel. He still couldn't believe she was here.

"Thank you, Your Majesty. I have looked forward to this time," she replied, dipping into a curtsy.

As she rose to her full height again, he realized he still held her fingers in his.

"Come inside," he said, dropping her hand and standing aside to let her pass.

As she did he caught a whiff of fragrance and felt a

moment of disillusion. The heady spicy scent was not the same as the lighter, enticing fragrance she'd worn in New York. This one spoke of experience, of sultry nights and even hotter days. It suited her, and yet, did not. It was as if his Angel was two different women. And, dammit, he was painfully attracted to both.

Why did she make him feel so intensely? Why her? He'd met hundreds, possibly thousands, of attractive women over the years. Women of aristocratic and royal birth as well as those from the people. Many had attempted to entice him into bed. But never had he felt like this. It was confusing and disturbing at the same time.

"M-my bags—shall I bring them in?" Angel asked, bending to grab the handle of a large case.

"I'll see to them myself in a moment. They will be safe there."

"Y-yourself?"

Again, that slight stutter. Could it be his courtesan was nervous? The idea fascinated him. Why would a woman like her be nervous? Surely she was used to such situations—meeting a client for the first time. Did he dare hope that her response to him left her as unsettled as he felt at the sight of her?

He smiled and gestured for her to precede him into the great hall. "I am quite strong. I think I can manage a few cases."

His words were teasing, but he saw the way her body tightened in apprehension. This wasn't how he had imagined his first meeting with a courtesan to be going at all. She was dressed like a siren, smelled like sin and seduction and yet her expression still hinted at naïveté. Perhaps that was her stock in trade, he realized. In her line of business she could be no innocent. But the appearance of it would be a highly prized commodity. He closed the door behind her and noticed her flinch at the resounding thud it made.

Discontent plucked at him, making his voice harsh when he spoke. "Why did you say nothing of this when we met in New York?"

"I—I was not engaged for your service that evening. When I am not working, I prefer to maintain discretion about my particular career. And if you recall, you were the one who bumped into me and began our conversation. I didn't seek out your company. We were simply strangers enjoying a visit to a foreign city, nothing more. I'm sorry if it disturbs you to see me again," she said in a voice so soft he wasn't even certain she'd spoken.

Her eyes were on the floor beneath her exquisitely shod feet, her hair a dark fall that almost curtained her face. He stepped closer and lifted her chin with a thumb and forefinger.

"Disturb me? No, you don't disturb me," he lied.

Hell, she disturbed him on every level but he wouldn't tell her that. Not now and probably not ever. She couldn't know quite how deeply she affected him. He was King of Sylvain and he was about to be married. He would not yield so much as a gram of his power to another. Weakness was always exploited by others less honorable. He would not give anyone the satisfaction of providing them with an "in" or a point of leverage that might lead to even wider cracks in a monarchy he was determined to preserve and to rebuild its long-lost glory. He would not be played for a fool.

"It's a good thing, isn't it? That I don't disturb you," she said, looking up beneath her lashes.

"That quite depends on whether we met by accident last week, or by design. If the latter, I should probably have my security team escort you from here immediately."

Shock slammed into Mila's chest and stole her breath away. Be taken away? Already? No. She couldn't allow that to happen. She *had* met Thierry by design, but not in the manner he thought. What was another lie on top of the gigantic one she perpetrated already? She lifted her head and straightened her shoulders, staring him directly in the eyes.

"I had no idea that I would meet you in New York," she said as boldly, and as honestly, as she could.

"But you recognized me, didn't you?" When she nodded, he added, "And you didn't see fit to introduce yourself as who you really are?"

"I did not. Meeting you like that was a bonus. A chance to see you unguarded. To understand the man behind the title, if you will."

It wasn't a lie—she meant every single word of what she'd just said. She'd treasured every second of the time they'd spent together that night. The chance to know Thierry as a man, not a prince or a king.

"And, Angel? Why go by that name?"

"It's a name I'm known by from time to time."

Again, not a lie.

Thierry studied her and she fought not to shift uncomfortably under that steely gaze. Mila allowed her gaze to take in the beauty of the man standing before her. From the second he'd opened the front door he'd taken her breath away.

Even though he was dressed casually, she couldn't help noticing the lean but powerful build of his shoulders beneath the knitted sweater. The cream wool offset the olive tone of his skin to perfection and highlighted the stubble on his jaw, making him seem dark and dangerous. A wolf in sheep's clothing? She almost laughed out loud at the irony. His jeans sat snugly on his hips, with well-worn creases at his groin that made her mind boggle on the idea of what hid beneath the fabric.

A piercing streak of need plunged to her core. Physical awareness warred with a combination of apprehension and a desire for the discovery of what making love would be like with this man. How she kept her body and her voice calm was a testament to her years of training in decorum. She wanted nothing more than to step forward. To inhale the scent of his skin at the hollow of his throat. To feel the rasp of his stubble on the tender skin of her neck, her breast, her thighs.

She had to stop this or she'd be melting into a puddle of craving helplessness. For a second she silently cursed the reading and viewing she'd done—for the want it aroused within her. But then she remembered why she was here, what she planned to do and what was at stake. Summoning every thread of control tightly to her she focused her eyes on his once more. Calming the clamor of body and forcing herself to become the worldly woman she was here representing herself to be.

Thierry appeared to come to a decision and gave her a brief sharp nod of his head.

"It seems I will have to trust you on what you say."

He hesitated as if waiting for her to say something, but Mila held her silence. One thing she had learned from a very young age was that it was often better to say nothing at all than to open your mouth and step straight into a minefield. You learned a lot more in silence than by making a noise.

Apparently silence was the right choice. Thierry continued, "You must be tired after your journey. Would you like to freshen up before having an evening meal?"

She inclined her head. "Thank you. That would be lovely."

"I'll show you to your rooms."

Her rooms? A moment of confusion assailed her. She'd expected to be staying in *his* rooms, in his bed. Was that not what he'd summoned a courtesan for? As she ascended the wide wooden staircase beside him her thoughts whirled in confusion. Perhaps he preferred to keep his own rooms and to visit his courtesan in hers. Either way, it wasn't exactly what she'd expected.

Mila reminded herself it was the end goal in sight that was paramount. She'd travel whatever route it took to get there. After all, hadn't most of her life been one act or another?

Thierry led her down a long, wide wood-paneled corridor, the darkness of the walls broken here and there with paintings or hunting trophies. She shuddered as they passed one of the latter, the points of the antlers on the deer head intimidating and imposing at the same time.

"You're not a fan of hunting?" Thierry remarked as they reached the end of the corridor.

"Not especially. Not when it's for trophies alone."

"Is that a note of censure I hear in your voice?"

She stiffened, unsure of what to say next. She didn't want to criticize or to alienate. Not when she'd only just arrived. "Not censure, Your Majesty. Never that."

"Don't!" he said, the word sharp in the air between them.

"Your pardon—" she began.

"No, don't do that. Here, I am Thierry, not Your Majesty. I am simply a man."

"I beg to differ. You are not simply a man. In fact, I doubt you're *simply* anything."

He pierced her with another of those looks. But she held her ground. And then he smiled, the expression on his face easing as mirth crept into his gaze and softened the imperiousness of his stare.

"You're probably right, Ms. Romolo. However, I would prefer that you not use my title while we are within the walls of this estate. If you will not use my first name, perhaps you will continue to call me Hawk, as you did in America?"

"If you will continue to call me Angel," Mila suggested.

"Angel," he repeated, lifting his hand and stroking the curve of her cheek with the back of his index finger. "Yes, it suits you better than Ottavia."

She was glad he thought so, since she didn't think she could stand to hear him call her by another woman's name when they were intimately engaged. "Then we are agreed?"

"Yes." She offered him her hand. "It's a deal."

He took her hand in his and she felt the heat of his palm against her own. The sensation made her catch her breath, her imagination already working overtime imagining that dry heat on other, more sensitive, parts of her body.

Thierry let her hand drop and turned to open the door before them. They entered a tastefully furnished ladies' sitting room. It looked as if it had barely changed in the past hundred years.

"It's beautiful," she said, walking toward the deep-set window and looking out over the lawn and gardens. As far as she could tell the outlook here was the only manicured part of the property, the rest had been left in its natural forested state. The lush foliage now appearing on the trees afforded the lodge its own special brand of privacy, locked as it was in a wooded cocoon. They could almost be the only two people in the world. "You must love it here. It's so isolated."

"I do," Thierry answered. He crossed the sitting room and opened another door. "This is your bedchamber."

She smiled at the old-fashioned term, but as she stepped through the doorway she acknowledged that the phrase far better fit the opulence and beauty of the furnishings than the term "bedroom."

"And you call this a hunting lodge?" Mila commented as she reached to touch the lovely, feminine silk drapes that hung at the window. "I thought hunting lodges were generally a male domain?"

"This suite has always been reserved for the mistress of the house."

Was it her imagination or did his lips curl somewhat over the term mistress? And did he mean mistress as in the female head of the household, or as another word for a temporary paramour, such as she was pretending to be?

"It's lovely. Thank you. I shall be very comfortable here."

"Fine, I shall get your bags. Your bathroom is through there. Please, take your time and come downstairs to the great hall when you're ready."

He was gone in an instant. For a big man he moved with both elegance and stealth, she realized. Mila rolled her shoulders and forced herself to relax a little now that she was alone. She'd take a shower, she decided, and change into something fresh—provided he brought her bags up as he'd promised. Strange that so far she'd seen no staff at the lodge. Why would he fetch and carry for her himself, when he should have a full complement of staff to complete his every wish?

She stepped through to the bathroom and began to disrobe, deciding that she would find out all that, and no doubt more, about him in due course. While the guest sitting room and bedroom were exquisite examples of old-world elegance and femininity, the bathroom was a tribute to unabashed luxury. Gold-veined cream marble surfaces abounded and the heated tiled floor was warm beneath her bare feet. The shower was a large glassed-in area with multiple showerheads and settings. She chuckled to herself as she figured out how to do the basics and lathered up beneath the generous spray of hot water, luxuriating in the sense of feeling fresh and clean again after her journey.

After her shower she dried herself off with a thick soft towel and shrugged into the pristine white robe that hung on the back of the bathroom door. If Thierry hadn't brought her bags up yet, she would have to attend their supper together dressed just as she was. Or maybe that had been his intention all along? A frisson of nervousness prickled across her nape. Was she well enough prepared for this charade? Could she be convincing enough? She had to be, she told herself as she tightened the sash around her waist. That was all there was to it.

In the bedroom she found her luggage—well, Ottavia Romolo's luggage. She felt like little more than a trespasser as she opened a case and began to sort through its contents. It really didn't sit comfortably with her, touching the other woman's personal things this way, but Mila steeled herself to do it. She couldn't have switched out the woman's luggage for her own without alerting the driver. The end had to justify the means. She uttered a silent thank-you to Gregor, who had suggested she pack her voluminous handbag with her own specially-purchased intimate apparel—undergarments that were far racier and far more enticing than what she would usually wear—because, while she was virtually slipping into another woman's skin, she absolutely drew the line at using her underwear.

Mila put the lace confections that were Ottavia's lingerie to one side and concentrated on unpacking the rest of the garments from the large cases. Looking at the variety of clothing, she wondered just how many changes per day the courtesan had planned for the short duration of her stay. Several, by the looks of things—or perhaps Ottavia was just the kind of woman who preferred to have multiple choices at hand.

She held up a pair of wide-legged pants in amethyst purple and a matching tunic that was deeply embroidered and beaded around the neckline and at the ends of the three-quarter-length sleeves. This outfit would do for this evening, she decided. She dressed quickly and shivered a little as the silk trousers skimmed the surface of her buttocks. She was unused to wearing such scant underwear as the G-string she'd pulled on, but she had to admit the sensation of the finely woven fabric against her skin was a sensuous pleasure in its own right. She quickly finished unpacking and shoved the cases away in the small box room she discovered off the sitting room.

Once dressed, Mila reapplied her makeup, darkening her eyes with thick black eyeliner and a charcoal-colored shadow and applying a sultry ruby-red gloss to her lips. She brushed out her hair, leaving it to swing loose over her shoulders and slid her feet into a pair of black sandals with a delicate heel. Thank goodness she and the courtesan shared the same shoe size.

She took a final glance in the mirror to ensure she was quite ready—and a stranger looked back at her. If anything, looking at this altered version of herself gave her a sense of strength. She could be whatever she needed to be, whomever she needed to be—and do what needed to be done. A wave of desire rolled slowly through her as she contemplated the night ahead. Would they make love tonight? Would it all begin here and now? Her eyes glittered and her cheeks flushed in anticipation.

She was ready for him—oh, so very ready.

Eight

Mila tried to steel herself for what lay ahead as she descended the stairs. As she reminded herself, nothing ventured nothing gained. But how much did she stand to lose if this went wrong? Her fingers tightened on the shiny wooden balustrade. In a word, everything. Which is exactly why she had to make it work, she told herself as she reached the bottom of the staircase and entered the great hall.

Thierry stood by the fire, apparently mesmerized by the dance of flames across the massive log of wood set deep in the wide stone fireplace. She took a minute to simply take in the sight of him. Tall and upright, dressed casually still in his jeans and sweater, and yet still with that incredible air of regal command sitting so comfortably on his broad shoulders. Again she felt a pull of attraction and wondered how she would initiate their first encounter. And, what he expected of it. If, as rumor had it, he was as chaste as she, it should be a breathtaking experience for them both.

Mila focused on her surroundings. Rich, jewel-bright, hand-knotted carpets scattered across the flagstone floor, lending warmth to the hall. Comfortable furniture stood in groupings, creating nooks for conversation or privacy or simply somewhere to curl up and read a book. And then there was the massive fireplace that dominated the room. In front of it sat a long, low coffee table while comfortably worn leather couches stood in a horseshoe shape around the table, facing the fire. It looked inviting—even more so because of the man standing there with his back to her.

She drew in a breath and stepped forward. Thierry turned as her sandals made a sound on a bare patch of flagstone floor.

"You found your way back here all right," he said with a smile. "Good. Are you hungry?"

Her stomach growled in response to his question, the sound echoing in the large room and making them both laugh. "I think you can take that as a yes," she said.

A flush of embarrassment heated her cheeks. She was ravenous. She'd been far too nervous to eat breakfast this morning, or lunch. Now, she was almost light-headed with hunger. Or perhaps it was more her reaction to the nearness of her future husband that made her feel this way—as if every nerve in her body was hypersensitive and attuned to his every movement and every expression.

"I have a platter of antipasto here," Thierry said, gesturing to the coffee table. He pulled several cushions down off the leather couches and piled them on the floor by the table. "Will this do to get started?"

"It looks delicious," Mila answered and slipped off her sandals before lowering herself to the cushions as gracefully as she could. "This feels like a picnic of sorts."

"You'd prefer to sit on the sofa?" he asked, settling down beside her.

"Oh, no! I like this. It's very relaxed."

"Good," Thierry replied with a firm nod. "I want you to feel relaxed."

Mila looked at him and raised a brow in surprise. "Shouldn't I be the one making you feel that way?"

For a second Thierry looked startled and then he let loose a laugh that came from deep inside. When he settled again he gave her a piercing look. "Humor. I like that in a woman."

Mila held her tongue. She had no idea what to say in response to that. As it turned out, speech wasn't necessary. Thierry handed her a small white plate and indicated to her to help herself to the platter.

"Please, eat," he instructed.

"What do you like best?" she asked, her hand hesitating over the selection of cold meats, cheese and vegetables.

"This isn't about me," he said, a quizzical expression on his face.

"Isn't it?" she replied, looking him square in the eye. "I beg to differ. Our lessons may as well begin with this. Have you ever been fed by someone before?"

"Not since infancy," he countered.

"There's a great deal of intimacy in the act of feeding another person, don't you think? And it speaks volumes as to the give and take required in a relationship—the learning and the understanding of what pleases your partner."

She selected some slivers of artichoke heart and finely sliced salami. Wrapping the salami around the artichoke, she held it to him, silently inviting him to taste. He hesitated, then leaned forward, his lips parting. Mila's heart hammered in her chest so hard she wondered if he could hear it, and when his mouth closed around the morsel she offered—his lips brushing against the tips of her fingers— she forgot to breathe.

The sensation was electric and sent a buzz of excitement through her, making her tremble ever so slightly. He noticed and caught her with one hand, his fingers curling around her slender wrist with a gentle touch.

"I see what you mean," he said, looking at her from below hooded eyes. "It appears to affect you also. Are you okay? You don't need to be nervous with me. I'm not a king here. I'm simply…Hawk."

The man wasn't *simply* anything, Mila decided. He was *everything*, and right now that everything was just a little too much. She tugged free of his hold and inclined her head in acknowledgment.

Seeking distraction from her racing pulse and erratic breathing, she scooped up a little hummus on a slice of roasted red pepper and offered it to him. He smiled in response, just a sweet curve of his lips, before opening his mouth to take the morsel. He nodded and made a sound of approval at the combination of flavors before reaching for some food, which he then offered to her. Mila found it disconcerting to be on the receiving end of his attentions, but as the piquant flavor of the tomato relish on the sliver of garlic bread he'd chosen for her burst on her tongue she gave herself over to the delight of flavor and texture even as she tried to distance herself mentally from the man in front of her.

Tried, and failed.

"What would you like to drink?" Thierry asked. "Do you prefer red wine, or white? Or, perhaps, you'd prefer champagne to celebrate our coming together?"

There was something in the way he'd said those last two words that made Mila's inner muscles squeeze hard on a piercing hunger that had nothing to do with food and everything to do with him.

"Champagne, I think," she said.

He rose to his feet. "I'll be right back."

Why did he not summon a staff member to pour for

them, she wondered. Her question must have registered on her face because Thierry hesitated a moment.

"Is there something wrong?"

"No, not at all. I was just wondering, where is your staff? They seem to be absent tonight?"

"They are absent altogether."

"I beg your pardon?"

"I have dismissed my staff for the duration of your stay. I'm sure you understand. I had no desire for an audience, or for distractions, during our time together."

They were completely alone? The idea both thrilled and terrified her.

"I believe I can make my own bed," she said with a small laugh, then realized that she'd brought their conversation immediately to her sleeping arrangements.

"I'm sure you are as resourceful as you are beautiful. Now, I'll get that champagne."

He was gone in an instant and Mila leaned back against the sofa behind her wondering what to make of it all. Of course he wouldn't want witnesses to their liaison, why hadn't she considered that before? Not so much for her protection as for his, she understood, but in its own way it worked out even better for her. There was less chance that someone might recognize her—not that she expected anyone to. She'd been overseas for such a long time and during her childhood she had all but melted into obscurity as the awkward, unattractive younger sister of the Erminian king. Looking back she barely recognized herself sometimes. And yet, deep inside, there still remained the girl who simply wanted to please and to know she was loved. Would Thierry fall in love with her?

She could tell he was definitely attracted to her. The warmth in his gaze when it drifted over her body was clearly the interest of a man toward a woman. The knowledge gave her a sense of power and she wondered again when they would begin to put her research to practice. He did not seem to be in any hurry to take her to bed. And as for her, she knew she wanted him, but she wanted all of him, not just physically. How would she be able to ensure that?

"You look deep in thought," Thierry said, returning to the hall with an ice bucket in one hand and two crystal champagne flutes in the other.

"I was," she admitted, shifting a little on the bed of cushions. "To be honest, I was wondering what it is you expect of me. After all, I am here to please you, am I not?"

Thierry halted halfway through removing the foil from the bottle of one of France's finest vineyards.

"You are, and I believe your brief was made clear to you in our correspondence."

Damn, Mila thought. Of course there would have been correspondence between Thierry and the courtesan. Why had she not thought this through further? She pulled her scattered thoughts in order and smiled back at him before speaking.

"I would like to hear, in your own words, exactly what you expect of me."

"You are to instruct me in the art of seduction. It is important to me that my future wife be well satisfied in the bedroom," he said, pouring the champagne adeptly.

Mila felt her eyes open as wide as saucers. That wasn't what she had been expecting. He was doing this for *her*?

"That is very noble of you, Hawk," she said, accepting one of the flutes and holding it up in a toast. "Perhaps we should make a pledge, to each strive to do our best to ensure you have a very long and a very happy marriage."

Thierry lifted his glass and clinked it against hers. "To my long and happy marriage," he repeated.

The bubbles fizzed over the surface of her tongue in much the same way that anticipation now sparkled through her veins. A new thought occurred to her, and she voiced it without filtering the words in her head.

"And what about when you're out of the bedroom? Do you plan to keep your wife satisfied in all things?"

Thierry took a long drink of his champagne before nodding. "If I can. I want you to know that the success of my marriage is paramount in my mind. I do not want to be the object of pity or gossips or to repeat any of the mistakes of the past that my parents and theirs before them perpetuated."

His words came through loud and clear. There was no mistaking the emotion or the intent behind them. It was something Mila had not expected. It seemed that they both wished for the same in their marriage.

"I understand."

He turned to her. "Do you? I wonder. I imagine for a woman such as yourself that it is hard to understand that a man should want a happy marriage."

"Not so impossible," Mila countered. "I would like to believe that deep down it is every man's desire—and every woman's also. It's my greatest wish to have a happy and fulfilling union with my husband one day."

Thierry did not reply, simply looked toward the fire, and Mila watched as the reflection of the flames etched sharper lines on his face. She leaned forward and placed a hand on his forearm.

"You speak of giving your wife satisfaction. Tell me, Hawk, exactly what you mean. Right here, right now, what you expect of me to achieve this?"

"I want you to tell me what will make my wife happy. I want to know how to understand everything about her—her moods, her needs, her desires. All of it."

"Don't you think you would have been better served to have talked to *her* about those things?"

He shook his head. "It has been impossible. She has

lived overseas for the past seven years and she was such a frightened rabbit the first time I met her I doubt she would have welcomed any overtures from me in the interim. I am afraid that she will consider our marriage to be a duty, and nothing more."

"But the two of you *are* marrying for duty, are you not?"

It felt weird to be talking about herself to him like this, as if she were another person.

"Yes, we are. But our marriage need not be entirely based on duty."

"So, you want to take your relationship with her slowly?"

He barked a cynical laugh. "That will be impossible when we are to be married at the end of the month."

"And you cannot court her once you are her husband?"

He shook his head. "There will be…expectations put upon us from the start. It will be difficult to court her with the eyes of every man, woman and child in both Sylvain and Erminia upon us."

She understood, perfectly. Since she'd been home she had struggled with the knowledge that there were eyes upon her all the time. It had made it difficult to disappear on this quest but, thankfully, not impossible. With her brother away on official business she'd only had to inform his immediate staff that she would be taking some time to herself and retiring for some privacy before the pomp and ceremony of her wedding.

Thankfully, no one had questioned it and with the vow of deference to her will that her staff had taken, they basically had no choice but to accede to her commands and go through the motions of transporting her to the royal family's summer lake house. It still sat uncomfortably on her shoulders that she'd had to go to such lengths, but being here with Thierry like this, she knew she'd done the right thing. When else would she have had the opportunity to get to know him like this?

"So, as you see, I need to fast-track our courtship," Thierry commented, selecting another morsel from the platter and offering it to her. "Let's begin with foreplay, hmm?"

Mila shook her head. As hungry as she'd been before, she could barely think about eating now. Her mind was in overdrive. She'd totally underestimated Thierry—taking on face value alone the idea behind him requesting the services of a courtesan. Not for a moment had she considered that he had done so for her benefit. There still remained the ugly stain of jealousy, though, that he had not planned to come to his marriage as virginal as she, that he had chosen to learn seduction from a stranger rather than seeking to learn together with her, as husband and wife. Getting to understand him, even in the tiny slice of time they'd had together today, she knew she wanted to be the only one to give him pleasure. To show him the kind of physical love that melded hearts together forever.

"I think it is safe to say that a woman wants to be made to feel special all the time. Not just when you're going to bed."

Thierry cocked his head at her and feigned a look of complete shock. "Really?" he said, as if she'd just disclosed a secret of monumental importance.

Mila reached over and gave him a playful shove. "Yes, really. Are you prepared to listen to me, or not?"

"Of course I am prepared to listen to you," he said, stretching lazily in front of the fire.

Mila couldn't help but watch him. Not for the first time she was reminded of a jungle cat. Long and lithe and powerful. Seductive by virtue of its leashed power and strength alone, but when combined with its beauty a woman could become totally and irrevocably lost. And she was. Lost in him. She ached to tell him the truth about who she was but she couldn't. Not yet, not until she felt certain that he cared for her the way she did for him.

Cared? The word was an insipid descriptor for the way her emotions churned in a constant roil of awareness in his presence.

She snapped her attention back to their discussion.

"It is not enough to simply smile lasciviously at your wife at bed time and tell her how sexy she looks."

"That is something I should not do?"

"No, you misunderstand me. Or, perhaps, I misrepresent what I'm trying to say." She sighed and tried to get her thoughts in order. Not an easy task when he lay on display in front of her, looking sinfully appealing. Mila cleared her throat and directed her gaze beyond him, to the flames that flickered and danced over the log in the grate. "What I mean is that you can find opportunities to seduce your wife every single day. From first waking until you go to sleep at night. You need to season her day with expressions of love, with touches that show her you're thinking of her."

"I'm to grope her at every occasion?" Thierry smiled with a glint of mischief in his eyes.

"Even you should know that's not appropriate. Sure, a gentle brush of her buttocks or her breast from time to time occurs in a natural day, but it's the other touches. The smoothing of a strand of hair, the tangle of fingers as you walk together. Intimacy grows in the little things. Something as simple as making eye contact when you both witness something that you each know the other will find amusing. Or something more concrete, like the note you leave on her pillow or the text you send when you're apart to say you're thinking of her, or the picture you take and message to her because you know she would appreciate it. It is all the things like that which show you care."

"Involving her in my day-to-day moments, you mean. And when she physically shares those with me, I should show her I'm glad she is with me. That sort of thing?"

Mila smiled in approval. "Yes, exactly that sort of thing.

Seduction—particularly when your goal is to win over her heart as well as her body—is a constant thing, not just a something to use when you want to get into a woman's pants."

"Even if I do?"

"I guess there's a time and a place for that. I just know that for many women, myself included, I can't simply turn my libido on and off with a switch. We generally don't compartmentalize like that. Our thoughts and responsibilities are a nest of interconnected strands. I would respond best to my senses being wooed throughout the day, with repeated reminders that I am valued and desired. To small indications that someone is thinking of me and, if I'm not with them, that they wish I was."

"So, first I need to seduce my bride's mind?"

"Basically. It is a shame that the two of you have not had any contact since your betrothal."

Thierry got up and stretched before settling on the deep leather chair opposite hers. "What would be the point? Our marriage has been preordained. It's not as if I need to convince her to accept my proposal."

"But you say you want a happy marriage. Don't you think your bride deserves to get to know you—to understand you?"

"She doesn't seem to think so. I have had nothing but a series of stilted correspondences from her. No photos, no calls. Getting better acquainted is a two-way street, is it not?"

Mila felt the color drain from her cheeks. Of course he was right. It was unfair of her to expect him to do all the work, to make all the effort. It seemed that in matters of the heart she was as immature as she was in matters of the body. If she'd ever doubted her decision to undertake this crazy mission, she could cast such thoughts aside. This was an education, all right. For them both.

"It most definitely is, which brings me to another question. How can your bride court you? What things can you do so she knows you welcome her into your life and your daily affairs?"

Thierry chuckled. It was a warm sound that made Mila feel happy inside and it coaxed a smile from her.

"Are you planning to spend some time educating my fiancée as well?" he asked, then laughed again at the ridiculousness of the idea.

"Would that I could," Mila murmured and avoided making eye contact. "Do you think it would work in terms of couples counseling?"

"Oh, yes, definitely." His smile died and his face grew serious again. "But the princess and I are no ordinary couple, are we? We are two strangers who will be making a life together under the strain of uniting two countries at the same time."

Mila played with the stem of her wineglass. That fact had not escaped her. So much hinged on the successful outcome of their marriage. The reopening of trade between the countries, the relaxation of military positions along the border, the widening of educational opportunities, not to mention what they could achieve in matters of ecological significance through the pooling of resources. It was true that not every couple faced the same hurdles and some would say that their hurdles were taller than most. But they could be overcome. They could be tackled if they were unified as husband and wife in more than just ceremony. Which was why it was so important that she get this right.

"Your fiancée, she is well educated, isn't she?" she asked, going through the motions of pretending to not fully understand who his fiancée was.

"Indeed. Her brother very proudly informed me of her achievements at our recent meeting, before warning me not to hurt her feelings."

Mila fought back a grin of sheer delight. Her brother had done that? She would never have believed it of him. Not the stern man she'd met with when she'd arrived home.

"And do you think you two will be compatible, mentally?"

"Of course, why wouldn't we be?"

"So what is it that worries you most? Why do you fear you will not be able to truly bond as man and wife? Is she not attractive enough?"

"Looks are not the key issue here."

"Is it the physical side of your relationship that concerns you?" Mila pressed curiously.

"Only in that I wish to learn how to please her. She will be my consort, the mother of my children. My partner, I hope, for a lifetime. I want to be able to hold her interest. To share respect for one another. To share dreams for our future. Nothing too outstanding, I suppose, but these things, they are important to me."

As they were to her also. "Then why are you so worried? Don't you think she'll want the same from your marriage?"

"I don't know. I barely know her. In fact, I barely know anything of her. I need to know how to seduce my wife—not just physically, but emotionally, too. I never want to see loathing in her eyes when she looks at me, as my mother did so often when looking at my father. And I never wish to treat her with the disdain my father showed to my mother. They could barely tolerate one another toward the end. I will not have a marriage like that."

A vein pulsed at the side of Thierry's brow, and while his voice had remained level, Mila could see the strain in his eyes as he turned to face her again.

"These are the reasons why I have employed you. I want you to teach me how to make my wife fall in love with me so deeply she will never look to another man for her fulfillment. Can you do this?"

Nine

Thierry stared into the glowing amber of Angel's eyes and willed her to give him the answer he craved.

"Let me get this clear," she said softly. "You want me to teach you to seduce your fiancée's mind and her senses, and then her body?"

"I do."

She looked surprised for a moment, but then her face cleared and her eyes shone bright as she smiled.

"Your demand is not quite what I expected but I will do what you ask."

"How do we begin this?" he asked.

"Well, when seeking to win someone over, it is customary to ask a person about the kinds of things they like, and to look for common ground amongst those things. For example, what do you like to do in your spare time?"

"Spare time? Perhaps it would be better if I understood more fully what spare time was."

Angel laughed and the sound made him feel lighter inside for the first time in days.

"Perfect!"

Thierry tried to hide his confusion. "Perfect?"

"Yes, humor is a wonderful icebreaker when you're trying to get to know someone."

Except he wasn't trying to be funny. His time was always filled with something—other than when he was here, up in the mountains. This was where he recharged for the year ahead, where he learned to calm his mind and prepared it for the demands that would be made upon him the next time he surfaced. Thierry inclined his head.

"I see. So, shall we try this? Pretend we've never met before? What if I get it wrong?"

Angel shifted on the cushions, angling herself to face him fully, and rested one elbow up on the seat of the sofa behind her. "Hawk, this is no different from when we met in New York. You did not seem to suffer from any fear of failure then."

"I was not speaking to my betrothed then," he said bluntly and was surprised to see her expression change to one of shock.

Or maybe he imagined it. Her eyelids fluttered down and when she looked up again her expression was composed once more.

"I see. Let's pretend, then, that I am your fiancée. What is it that you want to know about me?"

For a few seconds Thierry was flustered, wondering where to begin. Angel let go of that enticing laugh again and leaned forward to give him a gentle shove with one hand.

"Oh, come on! It's not that hard. What's wrong? Are you scared of her? Is she such a dragon?"

"No, of course not." Dammit, but he sounded like just the kind of stuffed prig he hated talking to. How could he expect his courtesan, let alone his bride, to enjoy talking with him and learning about him when he could barely stand the sound of his own voice right now?

"Then relax, Hawk. She probably won't bite you."

Thierry stared back at Angel, at the smile currently on her exquisitely beautiful face. At her straight white teeth. And he wondered what it would be like to feel those teeth upon his skin. Desire clawed at him, shocking him after his years of carefully honed restraint.

This had been a crazy and foolish idea. He wanted to learn how to know and understand Princess Mila, not feel hopelessly drawn to another woman. This wasn't the first time he'd experienced desire, but this was the first time he'd truly been tempted to act on it. He pushed himself upright and took a few steps closer to the fireplace. He reached for the mantel and gripped the rough-hewn wood as if his life depended on its stability, as if he could anchor himself somehow to the fact it had remained here for several hundred years. Battered and scarred but still whole and strong. The way he needed to be.

"I find it impossible to relax tonight," he announced. "Perhaps it would be best if we started anew in the morning. When we're both fresh."

He heard a rustle of movement behind him, then felt her move up close. Her scent was sultry, but subtle, and stole its way past the barriers he was trying so hard to maintain.

"I'm sorry, Hawk. I didn't mean to—" Her voice trailed off before she finished her sentence.

"No, it's not you. I expected too much from tonight. I have so little time and—"

She interrupted, "And I can see how important this is to you. It's okay, I understand. I will see you in the morning."

She moved away and he fought the urge to try and stop her, reminding himself he needed some time and space to shore up his strength against the enticement she presented.

"Yes, the morning. Do you ride?" he asked abruptly and spun around to face her.

"It has been a while but, yes, I am capable of riding."

"We'll ride before breakfast, then. Meet me in the stables out back when you wake."

"I'm an early riser," she said, cocking her head to one side. "Are you?"

He couldn't help it. He sensed innuendo in every word that fell from those lush and inviting lips, and God help him but he wanted to act on it. Only half a dozen steps would take him from where he was now to where she stood. Six strides and he could have her in his arms. Could press his mouth to hers and taste again the nectar that he'd tasted all too briefly when they had kissed in New York. He felt his body begin to move, took one step, then stopped himself from going any further.

"Yes," he bit out. "I am awake with the birds most mornings."

She inclined her head gracefully, her hair falling forward to expose the gentle curve of her neck. His fingers itched to caress that fall of hair. His lips tingled in anticipation of placing a kiss, just there on that exposed section of skin. Thierry shoved his hands into the front pockets of his jeans to stop himself from reaching for her.

He watched as she ascended the stairs, her sandals dangling from her fingers. The fabric of her tunic drifted over her body in places he should not be looking. But he looked. And he craved.

With a muttered epithet Thierry spun on his heel and made for the front door and, flinging it wide open, he strode outside into the evening. He made a sharp left and headed for the woods. He would work this out of his system somehow.

* * *

The moon's silvered light filtered across the edges of the mountains as he made his way back to the lodge. Even the birds had ceased their chatter and had settled down for the night. There were few lights on at the lodge as he approached, a stark reminder that he had dismissed his staff and that inside only one person remained. A person he had summoned here without realizing how alluring she would be.

How stupid could a man be? Calling upon the services of a courtesan without realizing that he would be lured into her web of temptation.

It was simple, he'd decided on his tramp through the woods. He would send her on her way in the morning. Forget the horse riding. Forget the education. Forget everything. He had made up his mind.

Right up until he stepped inside the lodge. Thirsty after his walk, he made his way into the expansive kitchen at the rear of the building. There, perched on a chair at the kitchen table was the woman who had unwittingly become his Achilles' heel. Dressed in a diaphanous robe which barely concealed the slip of satin and lace beneath it, she was biting into a chunk of bread, layered with what looked like cheese and cold meat, as if she hadn't seen a meal in a week.

She looked up, startled, as he burst into the kitchen, and fought to swallow the bite of food in her mouth. He looked at her in surprise, but then understanding dawned.

"Forgive me. I knew you were hungry and I didn't see to your needs. I am a terrible host."

She shook her head. "It's okay. I'm a big girl. I am quite capable of looking after myself."

"Do you have enough there?"

He gestured to the antipasto platter which she'd obviously brought through from the hall.

"Yes, do you want some? You must be hungry, too."

He had an appetite all right. But not for food. He shook his head in reply to her question and grabbed a glass from the cupboard and filled it with icy cold water from the kitchen faucet.

"The water here is from a mountain spring," he said, trying his best not to watch her mouth as she took another bite of her open sandwich. "Would you like a glass?"

Angel shook her head again and gestured to the glass of milk she had before her. He found a smile tugging at his lips. She was such a study in contrasts, dressed in gossamer-fine silk and eating a meal with the vigor of a farm hand after a hard morning in the fields. Earlier, she'd sipped her champagne with elegant nonchalance, but now she drank down her milk with the enthusiasm of a child. Her face was clean of makeup and she looked younger than she had before. He liked this side of her better, he decided, although he'd prefer her to be in less of a state of undress even if only for his own barely constrained sensibilities.

"Did you enjoy your walk?" she asked when her mouth was once again empty.

Enjoy it? He'd been too angry at himself to enjoy anything. The time had been utilized to rid himself of the overwhelming need to touch the woman who now sat so innocently in his kitchen. And while he had been successful in repressing his feelings for that moment in time, it seemed he only needed to be within a meter or two of her to be reduced to the same state of neediness once again.

"The woods are always lovely this time of year."

She tipped her head and studied him carefully. "You're avoiding the question. Do you do that a lot in conversation?"

"Perhaps. It is often easier than giving a straight and honest response," he admitted grudgingly.

"And do you plan to be evasive with your new wife also?"

"No," he said emphatically. "I wish to be able to be honest with her in all things. Deception is a seed of discontent. I won't have that between us."

Angel nodded slowly and selected an olive from the platter, then studied it carefully as if it was the most important thing in the room right now. She popped it in her mouth and chewed it thoughtfully before answering him.

"I'm pleased to hear it," she said simply. "So I'll ask you again. Did you enjoy your walk in the woods?"

He sighed a huff of frustration. "No. I barely noticed the woods. I went out angry and I didn't stop to enjoy the beauty that should've calmed me and now I'm angry at myself for that, too."

Angel laughed gently. "Well done. I applaud your honesty. There, now. That wasn't so hard, was it?"

"It was hell," he admitted, then unexpectedly found himself laughing with her.

"Clearly we need to work on that, hmm?" she said, slipping from her chair and picking up her plate.

He watched as she took it across to the dishwasher and put it inside before going to clear the rest of the table. Every movement silhouetted the lines of her body—the fullness of her breasts as they swayed gently with her actions, the curve of her hips and buttocks, the length of her thighs. Honesty wasn't the only thing he needed to work on. He turned and poured himself another glass of cold water. Self-control was definitely very high on that list, too, he acknowledged as his jeans became more uncomfortable by the second.

"Leave the mess. I'll clean up. It's the least I can do as your host," he said gruffly after downing the cool clear liquid in his glass. If only it was as quenching to the fire deep within him as it was to his thirst.

"Okay, I will," she said with a cheeky grin. "I'm always better at making a mess than clearing it."

"Somehow that doesn't surprise me."

Her smile widened. "Well, I think I'm quite safe in saying that I doubt you have to clean up after yourself on most occasions, hmm? After all, why would you when you normally have a bevy of staff at your beck and call."

"It's not always everything it's cracked up to be. I have little privacy."

"I can quite believe it," Angel said, solemnity replacing the fun on her face. "Well, I'll leave you to it and see you in the morning."

"Sleep well, Angel."

"Thank you. You, too, Hawk. Sweet dreams."

She turned and left the kitchen and once again, for the third time since he'd met her, he realized, he watched her walk away from him. His gut twisted and something deep in his chest pulled tight. He didn't want her to leave. It was ridiculous. He barely knew the woman. One night in New York, a brief time together tonight, and he was smitten.

Perhaps his personal vow of chastity hadn't been the right thing to do for all these years. Perhaps, if he'd been a little more free with his wants and needs, this desperate hunger would be less consuming.

She was a courtesan, he reminded himself. Her job was to entice, to be alluring. To make a man feel important and wanted and needed and desired. Clearly, she was *very* good at her job. The reminder should have been sobering— should, at the very least, have dampened the fire that simmered and glowered beneath his facade of normality. It wasn't and didn't.

Thierry turned his attention to the platter left on the table and decided to finish off the remnants. Not that there was much left. It seemed his courtesan had quite the appetite. Did that appetite for food extend to everything else she did? He groaned out loud. Damn, there he went again. Letting his mind travel along pathways that were forbidden to him.

He'd always believed himself to be a patient man. One who'd made restraint an art form. Now, it seemed, he was to test that restraint to the very edge of its limits. Somehow he had to get through the next seven days without breaking.

Ten

Mila sprang from her bed before 6 a.m. and raced through her shower. She hadn't expected to sleep well after the turmoil of last night, but the moment her head had hit the pillow she'd been lost in a deep sleep. Now, however, she was fully revitalized and ready to go.

The discussions with Thierry last night had been a complete eye-opener for her. Even now she could scarcely believe his intentions toward the courtesan—toward her. A cheery grin wreathed her face as she played his words over in her mind yet again. He was doing this all for her—the princess. It was as astounding as it was unbelievable...and it had raised one big question in her mind. Why was he so committed to doing this for her?

Maybe today she'd get to discover his reasons for his decision.

After dressing and tying her hair back in a tight ponytail, Mila riffled through the drawers, wishing she remembered better exactly where she had put everything.

She knew she'd seen a pair of riding pants amongst Otta-via Romolo's things—ah yes, here they were. She eased into them and drew on a snug T-shirt and a sweater, then grabbed the riding boots that had been packed. Ms. Ro-molo had been exceedingly well prepared, Mila conceded. She had something for every possible eventuality, which made Mila wonder whether the woman might have been equally as surprised as she was upon discovering that Thierry was more concerned with learning about how to seduce his future wife's mind than her body.

She shoved all thoughts of the other woman from her head. She didn't want to think, or to worry about her right now. It was enough to know her staff would be taking very good care of her. Surely it would make little difference to Ms. Romolo to be paid to have a luxurious holiday rather than to be with a client?

Mila headed downstairs in bare feet, gasping as her soles hit the flagstone floor at the foot of the stairs. She plonked her butt down on the bottom step and quickly pulled on a pair of woolen socks, then the boots, huffing a little as she did so. Man, she was out of condition if pull-ing on a pair of fitted boots made her breathless. Or maybe it was just the idea of seeing Thierry again so soon that made her heart skip and her lungs constrict.

She went through to the kitchen, grabbed an apple from the fruit bowl on the tabletop and crunched into its juicy sweetness as she found a corridor that led to a door at the rear of the lodge. Outside, the morning air was crisp and cool, but the sun had begun its ascent in the clear blue sky and the day promised to be warm.

She crossed a wide courtyard and walked toward a large stone barn. Inside she could hear the nicker of horses and the sound of hooves shifting on the barn floor. It was warm in the building and the scents of horses, hay and leather all combined to make one of her favorite aromas. She paused a moment in the doorway and simply inhaled, a wide smile spreading on her face. She loved this environment. It was one of the things she'd missed most while in America. Of course there had been plenty of riding stables available, but it wasn't the same as being in her own place with her own animals. Neither was this, she reminded herself. But it would be, once she and Thierry were married. And then, she'd have her own horses here, too.

"Good morning. You weren't kidding about being an early riser," Thierry said, coming out of a room at the side of the stables carrying a saddle.

He wore riding pants and boots with a fitted polo shirt. His skin was tanned and his bare arms strong and beautifully muscled. Not too much, and definitely not too little. He hefted the saddle onto a waiting tall bay gelding as if it weighed no more than the saddle blanket that already lay on the horse's back.

"Why waste a beautiful day like this in bed?" she answered.

She hadn't meant a double entendre, but it hung in the air between them as thick and as potent as a promise. Oh, she could spend a day in bed with him and not consider it wasted in the slightest, she realized. Hot color suffused her cheeks and her throat and she turned away from his direct gaze, searching for something to do or say that would distract him from her discomfort.

"Can I help you get the horses ready?" she squeaked through a constricted throat.

"I'm almost done," he replied, turning away from her and focusing his attention on cinching the girth strap and checking the stirrups. "I thought you might like to take a ride on Henri, here. He's big, but he's gentle with women."

Like you? she almost asked, but instead she stepped forward and reached out to stroke the blaze on the gelding's forehead.

"That's good," she answered, offering Henri the remains of her apple. "As I said last night, it's been a few years since I've ridden."

"He'll take good care of you, don't worry," Thierry said, dropping his hand to the horse's rump and giving him a gentle slap.

Was it Thierry's turn for double entendre now, she wondered? Would *he* take good care of her also? Before she could ask, Thierry unhooked the reins from the hitching post and began to lead Henri outside through the other end of the barn. There, another horse—this one a majestic gray stallion—waited, already saddled up.

"Oh, he's beautiful," Mila exclaimed.

"Don't tell him that, he'll get too big for his shoes," Thierry said with a laugh.

But even so, he patted the horse's neck and leaned in to whisper something to the animal that only it could hear. The horse whickered softly in response. The sight warmed her and Mila felt Thierry ease just that little bit deeper under her skin and into her heart as she observed the relationship between man and beast. Oh, he was so easy to love, especially when he was sweet and relaxed like this. He straightened and turned to face her.

"What's his name?" she asked.

"Sleipnir, it's—"

"Norse, I know. What a noble name for a noble steed. Have you had him long?"

Thierry looked taken aback at the fact she knew the origin of his horse's name. "About five years. I raised him from a colt."

"He suits you," she said, saying exactly what was on her mind.

She had no doubt the two of them would make a formidable sight paired together.

"Shall we get on our way? Perhaps I can help you mount?"

"Thank you. I wouldn't normally ask, but it's been a while."

"No problem," Thierry answered without further preamble. "Let me give you a hand."

He came around to the side of her horse and bent down, cupping his hands for her to step one foot into. His shirt stretched tight across the breadth of his shoulders and the bow of his back. Her fingers itched to reach and touch him, to stroke those long muscles along his back, to trace the line of his spine down to its base. Thierry turned his head.

"Are you ready?"

She flushed again at being caught staring at him— woolgathering and wasting time while he patiently waited for her.

"Yes, thank you," she said and hastily placed her foot in his cupped hands.

He gave her a boost and she flung her leg over the saddle to seat herself comfortably, her feet finding the stirrups and her hands gathering the reins up so she was ready to go.

"That length okay for you?" Thierry asked, one hand on her thigh as he once more checked the girth strap and the stirrups.

"Y-yes," she answered, barely able to concentrate on his question with the warmth of his hand resting so casually on her leg.

Just a few more inches inward and upward, she thought—no! She slammed the door on the wayward idea before it could bloom in her mind and get her into even more trouble.

"Yes," she said more firmly and urged Henri forward. "This is perfect, thank you."

Thierry made a grunt of assent, then swung up onto his own mount and drew up alongside her. "I thought we could take a path through the woods at first and then let the horses have their heads through the meadows on the other side. Are you up for that?"

"It sounds great. I'm up for whatever you want to do."

He gave her another of those penetrating looks and Mila wondered if she was going to have to filter every word from her mouth from now on. She hadn't meant that to come out quite the way it had…or had she? She didn't even seem to know her own mind right now. Instead, she dropped her head and stared at Henri's ears and then urged him to follow as Thierry and Sleipnir led the way out of the courtyard and toward the woods.

Birdcalls filtered around them as they entered on the bridle path. It looked well used and Mila wondered how often Thierry had the time to come up here to this private hideaway. The tranquility that surrounded them seemed worlds away from the life of a ruler she knew Thierry now lived. She'd seen firsthand what her brother's life was like—how his time was not his own. How it had changed him when he'd ascended to the throne. Would that be Thierry's fate also now that he was King of Sylvain? She hoped not. Thierry would, at least, have her by his side. Someone to share the weight of his crown when he was out of the public glare.

They rode through the woods in silence, the horses happy to simply amble along, and Mila relaxed in her saddle. No doubt she'd be a little stiff from the ride tomorrow, but for now she was loving every creak of the leathers, every scent of the woods and every sound of the awakening forest.

After about twenty minutes, the trees began to thin.

"You can give Henri his head now if you want," Thierry called from a few meters ahead of her and then did just that with his horse.

Mila and Henri were hard on their heels as they burst from the woods and into an idyllic hillside meadow, the grass interspersed with dots of color from wildflowers beginning to bloom. Mila laughed out loud as she and her mount began to gain on Thierry and Sleipnir, but it was soon apparent they were outclassed. When she eventually caught up with him, he'd dismounted beside a brook—the scene so picture-perfect it was almost cliché.

She said as much as she dismounted from Henri. Thierry came swiftly up behind her, his hands at her waist before her feet could even touch the ground.

"You think I'm cliché?" he asked with one eyebrow cocked.

She shook her head. "No, not you, just…this!" Mila spread her arms wide. "It's all so impossibly beautiful. How on earth do you stand going back to the city?"

Thierry was silent for a moment. "It's my favorite place on earth and knowing it's still here waiting for me is what makes me able to stand it."

She put a hand on his chest and stared him straight in the eyes. "Is it so hard, being royal?"

"It's my life. I don't know any different."

The words were simplistic, but there was a wealth of unspoken emotion behind them. Mila let her hand drop again and opted to attempt to lighten the mood a little.

"So it's not all tea parties and banquets?"

The corner of Thierry's mouth kicked up and she ached to kiss him, just there.

"No, it is not. Which is for the best. If it were, I would be the size of a house."

"True," she said with a considering glance his way. She poked him in the belly, her finger finding no give against his rock-hard abdomen. "You're getting a little soft there, Your Majesty."

He grabbed her hand. "Hawk. Here I am Hawk and nobody else."

She nodded, all mirth leaving her as she studied the serious expression on his face.

"Do you ever wish all of Sylvain could just be like this spot here?" she asked as they walked over to the brook to allow the horses a drink.

"Yes and no. Obviously industry is required for our country to continue to move forward and for our economy to support our people. But I am encouraging our government to always consider sustainable practices when they discuss lawmaking and our constitution. Regrettably, my direction often falls on deaf ears. It isn't always easy to persuade people to change, especially when additional cost is involved."

"I think we stand a better chance to effect change if we start at school level, so all children grow up with the idea that sustainable development is the right way—the only way—to move forward. With education and understanding, things will become easier."

"But will it happen soon enough?" Thierry mused, his gaze locked on a distant mountain peak. "Up here everything is so simple, so clean and pure. And yet, past those mountains, you can already begin to see the haze of civilization as it hangs in the air."

"I'm not convinced you'll ever see great change in our lifetime, but essentially you're not effecting change simply for change's sake, are you? You're doing it for the future, for your grandchildren and their grandchildren."

"Grandchildren," he repeated. "Now there's a daunting thought when I'm not yet married."

"They are a natural progression, are they not?" she probed.

Mila knew that she wanted children, three or four at least. She had grown up as one of a pigeon pair with an age gap that had meant she and her brother had never had as close a relationship as she would have liked. Thierry had been an only child.

"Yes, they are. To be honest, I hadn't considered children as being a part of my marriage just yet. I know I have a responsibility to my position to ensure the continuation of the line, but I want to know my wife—truly know her—before we take that step."

"Those are honorable words."

"I mean every one of them. I look at the world my forebears have created and sometimes I ask myself if I should even marry—if I should have children—or whether I should simply let the monarchy die with me."

"No! Don't say that!" Mila protested.

"Let's be honest. Monarchy is an outdated concept in this day and age."

"But you still have a role to play. You remain a figurehead for your people. A guiding light. Look at your work so far on the Sylvano waterways, how you've spearheaded campaigns to ensure clean, safe water throughout your country," she argued passionately.

"It's a step in the right direction," Thierry conceded.

"It's more than a step. You are seen to be doing the things that matter to you. You don't just pay lip service to them. You lead from the front. You give your people someone to look up to and aspire to emulate. You can't throw that away."

"And I will not. I will continue the royal line, as is my duty. I am promised to Princess Mila and I honor my promises. We will marry."

There was a note in his voice that dragged a question from deep inside her. "And if you were not already promised to her? Would you still marry the princess?"

Thierry remained silent for several seconds before answering. "I don't know."

"Well, that's honest at least," Mila muttered.

"Ah, Angel, you sound so disappointed. Have I shown to you I have feet of clay?"

"No, you've shown me you're a man. Like any man.

With the same weaknesses and worries, but with strengths, too." She paused for a moment before continuing. "I am glad you are an honorable man and that you will marry the princess, whether you think you want to or not."

And she was. Because the more she got to know the complex man who was soon to be her husband, the more she knew she would spend the rest of her life loving him.

If only she could help him to love her, too.

Eleven

"Whether I think I want to, or not?" Thierry repeated.

It was an odd way for her to phrase such a sentence, he thought as he studied her.

"Yes, although I think you probably do your princess a disservice."

"How so?"

"Perhaps her feelings are not so distant from your own. Perhaps she, too, is mindful of her duty to her king and her country—and your country, as well—and, perhaps, all she wants to do is find a common ground between you so that you can have a full and happy life together."

He felt his lips pull into a smile. Angel's speech on behalf of an unknown woman was supportive and compassionate. He really liked that about her. In his experience, the women in his circles were never invested in each other's well-being in the way that Angel apparently was for Princess Mila. It showed another side to her that pulled strongly at him. If only he had the luxury of marrying a wife of his own choosing, he would definitely have chosen a woman such as Angel. But then again, he rationalized, if he wasn't who he was with an arranged marriage ahead of him, he would never have had cause to meet his courtesan beyond their stolen evening in New York, would he?

He looked at her, really looked this time. In the early morning light she appeared fresh and invigorated. Eager to seize the day they had ahead of them and all that it offered. Her long dark hair was drawn tightly off her face in a ponytail, exposing delicate cheekbones and a jaw that was made for a line of sensual kisses that would lead a man directly to those invitingly full lips. If he wasn't mistaken, she didn't wear so much as a slick of lipgloss this morning. Her naked face was even more beautiful than the visage of the seductress who'd joined him for antipasto yesterday evening.

The simmering sense of awareness that sizzled through his veins whenever he was near her burned a little brighter and his body stirred with longing.

"You make an interesting point," he eventually conceded, dragging his gaze from her face and looking long into the distance as if that could erase the growing need for her that unfurled inside him.

"Of course I do. I'm a woman. I know what I'm talking about," Angel said lightly, then punctuated her words with a small shove at his shoulder. "You should listen to me."

He laughed. "I'm listening. Now, tell me more about how I am to seduce my bride's mind."

"Be interested in her, genuinely interested."

Thierry was taken aback. "It's that simple?"

Angel groaned in response. "Of course it is. What do women do when they meet someone?"

He looked at her blankly. How was he supposed to know that?

"They ask questions," Angel said, a thread of irritation

evident in her voice. "They show an interest. Like this for example. Your horses are beautiful, do you buy them yourself or does your stable master do that for you?"

"The horses here at the lodge are all handpicked by me or bred through the breeding program I have established at the palace stables."

"See? It's as easy as that. With my question and your answer, we've opened up a dialogue that could keep us in conversation, discovering similar interests, for some time. And it branches off from that. For example, did you get that scar beside your right eyebrow while riding? It's so faint as to barely be noticeable but—" she lifted her hand and caught his jaw with her fingers, turning his head slightly to one side "—when the light catches you just so, it's visible."

Thierry tried to ignore the sensation of her fingers on his jaw. He hadn't shaved this morning and the rasp of her skin across his stubble sent a tingle through him. If he moved bare millimeters, he would catch her fingertips with his lips. He slammed the door on those thoughts before he could act on them. A lifetime of analyzing his every thought and action gave him the strength he needed right now to bear her touch without showing her how it affected him. He drew in a breath, waited for her to release him and let the breath go in a long steady rush of air as she did so.

His voice was calm when he answered, "Very observant of you. Yes, I wasn't paying attention one day when out riding. My mount was a rascal, prone to dropping riders whenever he felt like it. I was so busy talking to my companions as we rode that I didn't notice a low-lying branch. It collected me and dumped me quite unceremoniously on my royal behind. Of course, there was a major panic when everyone saw the blood, but, despite the scar it left, the wound was minimal and the experience taught me to be more aware of my surroundings at all times."

"How old were you when it happened?"

"I was eight years old. My father scolded me soundly for being so careless even while my mother fussed over me as if I had a life-threatening injury."

"I'm sorry."

"Sorry? Why?"

"The contrast in the ways they treated you tells me that you were probably left very confused afterward."

Confused? Yes, he had been confused and sore. But how had she known that? Most people asked him how many stitches he'd had or joked about him making a royal decree to have the tree chopped down or, worse, have the pony destroyed. No one had ever come to the conclusion Angel had just now. Something in his chest tightened as her care and understanding worked its way past his defenses.

Angel lifted her hand again, one finger tracing the silvered line that ran from his eyebrow to his hairline. Her eyes were fixed on the path of her fingertip, her expression one of concern and compassion, but all of a sudden her expression changed and she let her hand drop once more. This time her fingers curled into a fist before she crossed her arms firmly around her, almost as if she couldn't trust herself not to touch him again. The thought intrigued him and made him step forward a little, closing the distance between them to almost nothing.

"And you?" he asked. "Do you have any interesting tales to tell about any scars you might have hidden upon your body?"

Angel lifted her chin, her lips parted on a breath. "I…"

Suddenly she stepped away and walked over to where Henri was now grazing and gathered up the reins.

"You're getting the hang of it," she said.

"The hang of it?" He was momentarily confused.

"Getting to know someone. Shall we carry on? We can talk while we ride."

Why was she creating distance between them all of a

sudden? he wondered. It was she who had suggested he ask questions and probe his conversational partner to discover more about her. And yet, when he asked one simple thing she backed away as if she was afraid to answer. The thought intrigued him and he stowed it away to explore further another time.

"Certainly, if that's what you want. We can head back to the lodge for breakfast."

"That sounds like a good idea."

He drew close beside her and squatted down to offer her a boost onto the horse. This time he couldn't help but notice how the fabric of her riding pants clung to her thighs and buttocks as she bent her leg and put her foot in his hand. She sprang up into the saddle and gently guided Henri away from him, as if she was determined to create some distance between them.

Thierry wasted no time in mounting Sleipnir. "We'll take a different path back," he called to Angel, leading the way again.

Back at the lodge she dismounted quickly and led Henri into the barn and began to undo the girth strap of his saddle. Thierry hastened to her side and put his hands at her waist to gently pull her aside.

"Leave that. It will be taken care of."

"I'm not a delicate flower, you know. I can help."

"Fine," he replied, letting her go before he did something stupid like give in to the urge to pull her hard against his body and rediscover what it would feel like to hold her in his arms. He nodded toward the tack room. "Get the brushes while I remove the saddles."

She did as he asked and he took the opportunity to watch her walk away. She held herself straight and tall and moved with an elegance that was at odds with her attire. He tore his gaze away from the ravishing picture she made and put his attention back toward the horses.

* * *

In the tack room Mila took a moment to steady herself. Being with Thierry was proving insightful and immensely difficult at the same time. She ached to tell him the truth about who she was and remove the veils of subterfuge she'd wreathed between them, but she couldn't. She doubted he'd take too kindly to being tricked like this but she wished—oh, how she wished—she could be herself with him. There'd be time enough for that once they were married, she reminded herself, and looked around the room for the brushes he'd sent her to find.

Grabbing two, she went back out into the barn. Together they finished tidying up and grooming the horses before returning them to their stalls. Once they were done, Mila dusted her hands off on her pants. The atmosphere between them had been easy enough while they attended to the horses, but right now she felt awkward.

"Shall I go and see what I can put together for breakfast?" she asked.

"You don't trust me to cook?" Thierry lifted one eyebrow, as if punctuating his question. Her heart did a little flip-flop in her chest.

"It's not that," she protested.

"It's okay. I am man enough to take advantage of your offer. I'll go and shower while you do your thing in the kitchen."

Mila narrowed her eyes at him. "Are you being sexist again?"

"Again?"

"Like you were in New York."

He snorted a laugh. "Not at all, at least I didn't mean it to come across that way. To make up for any offense I may have caused, I'll provide the rest of our meals today. Is that punishment enough for my apparent lapse of manners?"

She couldn't help it—she smiled in return and inclined her head in acceptance. "Thank you. That would be lovely."

"And that is the perfect example of how I should have responded," he commented.

"You're a quick study," she teased, feeling herself relax again.

"I'll need to be if I'm to ace all my lessons with you."

And in an instant, there it was again. The sensual tension that drew as tight as an overstretched bow between them. Mila felt as if every cell in her body urged her to move toward him. Did he step closer to her? Or she to him? Whether it was either or both of them, somehow they ended up face-to-face. She felt his hands at her waist again, hers suddenly rested on his chest. Beneath her palms she felt the raggedness of his breathing, the pounding of his heart. And when he bent his head and pressed his lips to hers, she felt her body melt into him as if this was what they should have been doing all along.

No more skirting around the subject of getting to know a person. Simply a man responding to a woman. And what a response. She flexed her body against his, relishing the hard muscles of his chest and abdomen against her softness, purring a sigh of pure feminine satisfaction when she felt the hardness at his groin. The concrete evidence that he found her attractive.

All the years of feeling as though she'd never be anything to him but the gauche teenager she'd been all those years before fell away as if they were nothing.

His hands were at her back, pressing her more firmly to him. Her breasts were pressed against his chest and she welcomed the pressure, felt her nipples harden into painfully tight points that begged for more of his touch. The restrictions of her bra and clothing were too much, and too little at the same time.

Thierry's lips were firm against hers, coaxing. She opened her mouth and gave a shudder of delight as he gently sucked her lower lip against his tongue. The heat of his mouth against that oh-so-tender skin made her fingers curl against his chest, her nails digging into the fabric of his shirt as if she needed to anchor herself to him, to anything that would stop her from floating away on the tide of responsiveness that coursed through her.

And then, in an instant, there was nothing but air in front of her. Mila almost lost her balance as she opened her eyes and realized Thierry had thrust her from him and taken several long steps away.

"H-Hawk?" she asked, reaching out a hand.

"Don't!" he snapped in return and wiped a shaking hand across his face. "Don't touch me. I should not have done that. I apologize for my actions."

"But…why not? What is wrong? I'm here as your courtesan, am I not?"

Confusion swirled through Mila's mind as she fought to understand.

"I must remain faithful to my promise. I cannot touch you like that again. This was a mistake. Being here with you, of all people—it's making me weak."

There was genuine pain in his voice. Pain laced with disgust. At himself, she recognized, not her.

"Your promise to marry the princess?" she probed, seeking more clarity.

"Yes, my promise to her. And my promise to myself."

"Tell me of your promise to yourself," she asked softly.

"I can't—not right now. Please, go inside the lodge. I just need some time to recompose myself." He looked at her, his eyes as stormy as a mountain lake on a cloudy, windswept day.

But she didn't want to let it go. Not when her entire body still hummed with the effect of his kiss.

"No, tell me now. I'm here to help you. How can I do that

if you shut me out?" She walked toward him and caught him by the hand. "Hawk, let me understand you. Please?"

She watched the muscles in his throat work as he swallowed. He held himself so rigid, so controlled, that she feared he would reject her overture. But then, millimeter by scant millimeter she began to feel him relax. He drew in a deep breath and then slowly let it go again. His voice, when he spoke, was raw, as if his throat hurt to let go of the words.

"Fidelity is everything to me."

"As it should be," she said softly.

"No, you don't understand." He shook his head.

"Then tell me. Explain it to me," Mila urged.

"I grew up watching my parents live side by side but I never saw them as a couple, not in the true sense of the word. By the time I was old enough to notice, they barely even liked one another, but they couldn't live apart because of their position. They spent years barely tolerating one another, with my father putting every other obligation and concern ahead of his wife's happiness until my mother could no longer put up with it. She followed her heart into a relationship with someone who she believed would love her—and it destroyed her. I will not put my wife through anything like that."

"And yourself? What about what you want?"

"I just want to be the best I can be, at everything, and ensure that no harm comes to my people...including my wife."

"Hawk, that is admirable, but you have to realize that you can't control *everything*."

He pulled away. "I can. I am King of Sylvain. If I cannot control the things within my sphere of influence, what use am I? I won't be my father. I won't just stand by and allow my inadequacies as a person to lead to others' misfortune. I will have a successful marriage and my wife will love me."

"And will you love your wife equally in return?"

Twelve

Thierry felt her words as if they were a physical assault.

"I will respect her and honor her as my consort and I will do everything in my power to make sure she is happy. Isn't that enough?"

Angel looked at him with pity in her eyes. "What do you think, Hawk? If you loved someone and respect and honor was all you could expect from them for the rest of your life, do you think that would be enough for you? Isn't that no more than your father offered your mother?"

Thierry snorted. "He did not respect her nor did he give a damn for her happiness. She was a vessel for his heir—no more, no less—and when she refused him and wouldn't share his bed he found others more accommodating."

She looked shocked. Clearly she had not heard the rumors about his father's many affairs. None of them proven, of course, but Thierry knew they had happened. Discreetly and very much behind closed doors. Where else had the idea of a courtesan come from but his father? Hell, the man had even offered to arrange one for Thierry. He studied Angel carefully.

"I would never treat my wife so cruelly," he assured her. "I will ensure that she is always treated with the dignity due to a princess."

"But you want more than that from her," she argued. "You want her to love you. Yet you won't offer her love in return?"

"I…cannot promise her that," he choked out.

The shock had faded from her face, but now it was replaced with disappointment.

"Then I am sorry for your bride," she said eventually, her voice hollow. "Because I could not live without love."

She turned and went inside the lodge and he watched her every step feeling as if, piece by piece, slices of his heart were being torn from him. She could not live without love? He didn't even know what love was. He'd never experienced it firsthand. But he did understand attraction and how it could lead to trouble.

He turned and walked away from the lodge and headed back into the woods, stopping only when he could no longer feel the pull that urged him to follow her. To apologize for the things he'd said and to tell her that—

That what?

That he loved *her*? The idea was ridiculous. He was drawn to her, but that was all.

He should have stuck with his decision last night and sent her away. This whole exercise was a waste of time. He was not achieving his objectives, only complicating matters. With the thought firming in his mind, he returned to the lodge. The words telling her that her services were no longer required hovered on his tongue until she turned to face him and he could see she'd been crying.

Pain shafted him like an arrow straight to his heart and

he crossed the floor to gather her into his arms. She resisted a little, at first, then gave in to his embrace.

"I am sorry," he murmured as he pressed his lips to the top of her head. "I didn't mean to upset you."

"Y-you didn't," she hiccupped on a sob. "It was me and my stupid ideals."

"It isn't stupid to want to be loved," he countered.

As he said the words, he realized that he meant them. That they weren't the hollow uttering of a man so jaded by his parents and so many of the people in his sphere that he'd lost all belief in love. When he was with Angel, he *wanted* to believe that love was possible. But he couldn't even begin to contemplate such a thing with her. She was his courtesan, not his princess. Which begged the question, why did she feel so right in his arms and why did every particle in his body urge him to simply follow his instincts and to revel in all she could offer?

Angel pulled loose from his arms and stepped back.

"It isn't the role of a courtesan to be loved," she said bleakly. "But I do think you should at least be open to loving your wife if you expect to have a long and happy marriage. You seem to have this idea that you must keep her happy, which is admirable. But should she not also provide that same service to you?"

Her question raised an interesting point. "I hadn't considered that necessary until now," Thierry conceded.

"So now you believe it is necessary?"

He nodded. "I do. You have a lot to teach me, Angel. I'm glad you're here."

She hesitated before speaking. Her eyes raking his face—to see, perhaps, if he was telling her the truth. He would not have thought it possible, but every word he'd told her had been truthful. And now, having begun to understand how he felt, he realized just how much he wanted what she had suggested. Could he hope to achieve that with Princess Mila?

He cast his mind back and tried to assimilate how he felt now with the young woman he remembered. Try as he might, the ideas of love and intimacy did not spring immediately to mind. And yet, when he turned his attention back to Angel, he had no difficulty at all.

"So you're not going to send me away?" Angel asked, lifting that softly rounded chin of hers in a challenge.

"How did you—?"

"It was only natural you would consider it. You are a king. I opposed your thinking, contested what you said. You could do with me whatever you wanted."

Thierry felt a flush of shame color his cheeks. "It crossed my mind," he admitted ruefully. "I would like to think that I am man enough to withstand a bit of criticism, but it seems that I am a little different from everyone else when it comes to that."

"Your wife may not always agree with you, but she will still be your wife. How do you plan to cope with that? You can't exactly throw her down an oubliette these days, or banish her to a convent."

There was a thread of humor in Angel's voice, but beneath it he detected a genuine concern for the woman he was intending to marry.

"I hadn't considered my marriage in those terms. But you can rest assured that I will neither imprison nor banish my queen consort."

"Well, that's reassuring," she commented with a touch of acerbity. "She has much to look forward to then, doesn't she?"

"I will do my best," Thierry said firmly. "And you will help me to deliver that, won't you?"

Again there was that hesitation, as if she was turning over his request in her mind before reaching her conclusion.

"Yes. I will," she promised.

Angel crossed the kitchen to the massive double refrigerator that hummed energetically.

"Eggs and bacon?" she asked over her shoulder after giving the contents a cursory glance.

"Sure. What can I do to help?" he offered.

"Nothing. Just leave it to me."

"Leave the cleanup to me, then. If you don't mind I'll go and shower."

She smiled, but it didn't reach her eyes. "That's fine."

Thierry started to leave the kitchen and hesitated a second in the doorway. He was burning to ask her why their earlier encounter had made her cry. The memory of seeing her tears sent another shock of pain through him, reminding him that he was allowing himself to become too emotionally attached to this woman.

He resolutely continued on his way upstairs, determined not to think about Angel and how she had so easily inveigled her way beneath his barriers. Somehow he had to find a way to keep her in her place—to keep things simple and straightforward between them. Teacher—to—pupil—and that was all.

It had been several days since that first ride in the woods, and she and Thierry had settled into a pattern, of sorts. They spent their early mornings riding or walking in the woods. Together they had covered a wide variety of conversational topics and Mila took every opportunity to encourage him to do so—hoping that he would continue to seek her opinion once they were married. It began to weigh upon her that he would probably not be too thrilled when he discovered her deception, but she rationalized that with his own desire to know how to please her. Who better to instruct him than herself?

Their evenings, on the other hand, were a lesson in

torture. After that first day, Thierry had begun to ask her advice about the physical side of a man and a woman's relationship. About the gentle touches that a couple might enjoy together in a nonsexual way to reinforce their togetherness. It had seemed only natural for Mila to steer their conversation toward more intimate and sensual matters and last night, by the time she ascended the stairs to her rooms, every nerve in her body had been screaming for release. Satisfying her frustration in the deep spa bath in her en suite bathroom had left her feeling physically gratified but emotionally empty and strung out. Judging by Thierry's bear-headedness this morning, he had been left feeling much the same way.

When she'd told him she would not be riding with him this morning, but planned instead to take advantage of the beautiful library, with its floor-to-ceiling shelves, on the ground floor of the lodge, he'd been short with her to the point of rudeness. She'd let him go without comment, even though his words and manner had left her feeling as if she'd done ten rounds with an angry wasp's nest. The skies had opened shortly after he'd left on Sleipnir and he hadn't returned for several hours.

It was hard to concentrate on the book she'd selected from the shelves as she waited for him to return. She'd lit the fire set in the grate and the library was warm and cozy, a wonderful retreat on what had rapidly turned into an unpleasant day. Mila had totally given up on reading by the time she heard the clatter of hooves on the courtyard outside. She looked out the window and saw Thierry dismount and lead Sleipnir into the barn. It was half an hour before he came inside the lodge and went straight upstairs.

She put the book she'd taken back on its shelf and composed herself in a chair in front of the fire—keeping her focus on the dancing flames and wondering what type of mood Thierry would be in for the balance of the day. She would need to be able to recognize and handle them all, she reminded herself, even though she had shrunk from attempting to appease him this morning. And why should she appease him, she asked herself. A man was entitled to his moods as much as she was. And she'd certainly been in a terrible mood this morning. Had he tried to appease her? Not at all, in fact he'd done his level best to exacerbate her frustration. It seemed they both had a lot to learn about living with one another, she reflected with the benefit of hindsight.

The door to the library flung open and, even though she had expected Thierry, she started in surprise.

"Oh, you're back," she said, forcing nonchalance into her voice as if she hadn't been counting every tick on the centuries-old clock that hung on the library wall. "Did you have a nice ride?"

"I did not," he answered in clipped tones.

She quieted the sense of unease that built in her stomach. If he was going to be in a mood all day then it might be best if they didn't spend any more time together just yet. She watched him as he stalked to the fireplace and spread his hands in front of him, absorbing the heat as if he was chilled to the bone.

"I'm sorry to hear it," she said as lightly as she could, and rose from her seat. "Would you like me to leave you alone?"

Thierry whirled around and grabbed her hand, jerking her around to face him as she began to walk away. "No, I would not."

She wasn't certain exactly what happened next, but within seconds she was pulled up against the hardness of his body and his lips had descended upon hers. This kiss was vastly different from the one they'd shared in New York, and equally so from the one after their first morning ride. This embrace was about him dominating her, using the kiss to express his anger and frustration. She knew it would be impossible to pull away when he held her so tightly, so she did the opposite. She became unresponsive in his arms—her hands still by her side, her mouth unmoving as he attempted to plunder her lips.

She wanted nothing more than to wrench herself from his embrace and to leave this room, leave him to his wrath, but within seconds she felt a change begin to come over him. In an instant his arms loosened around her, allowing her the freedom to pull free, and his mouth lifted from hers. Instead of stepping away, however, she held her ground.

"Do you feel better now?" she asked in as level a voice as she could muster.

Somehow it seemed more important to her to face up to him than to walk away. They needed to do this, to face the demons that had raised his ire and to deal with them.

Shame filled his face and Mila felt a wave of compassion sweep over her. He was a man in so very many ways and yet, when it came to his emotions, he was as untutored as a child.

"I should not have done that. Angel, I'm sorry. If you wish to leave I won't stand in your way. I'll arrange for a car immediately."

"That won't be necessary. You contracted me to do a job, and I won't leave until I have finished my contract. However—" she allowed a small smile to pull at her lips "—it seems I have been remiss in my duties if that is the best you can do."

She watched his eyes as disgrace at his behavior warred with the pride of a sovereign born. Eventually both were replaced with something else, humility.

"Again, I apologize. Perhaps you would afford me another opportunity to show you how much I have learned."

She didn't have time to speak before he drew her more

gently against him. One hand lifted to her chin and tilted her face upward so her eyes met his and nothing else existed between them.

"Angel? May I kiss you?" he asked.

She nodded ever so slightly, but it was all the encouragement he needed. This time, as his lips claimed hers he did so with infinite care, coaxing a response from her that made her blood sing along her veins while her body unfurled with desire and heat. He traced the seam of her lips with the tip of his tongue, making her open her mouth on a sigh of longing that went soul deep.

This was what she wanted from him. A sharing of connection that opened them both up to one another—that stripped everything bare and left them each vulnerable and exposed and yet safe in the knowledge that they each had only the other's best interests at heart.

Mila cupped his face with her hands and deepened their kiss, her tongue sweeping into his mouth and stroking the inside of his lips, his tongue, until her senses were filled with the texture and taste of him. Thierry groaned into her mouth, the sound giving her a sense of power and yet making her recognize his susceptibility toward her was a gift beyond measure.

Thierry's hands swept beneath the sweater she'd pulled on this morning, his fingertips touching her bare skin and leaving a trail of fire in their wake as he stroked the line of her spine then splayed his fingers across her rib cage as if he couldn't get enough of her. His mouth left hers and he peppered the edge of her jaw with tiny kisses that tracked toward the curve of her throat. Mila shivered as he kissed the hollow at her earlobe then followed the line of her throat to the curve of her shoulder and down the deep *V* of her sweater.

Her breasts ached for his touch, for the tug of his lips at the taut, sensitive peaks. And then his hands were cupping her, the clasp of her bra undone without her even realizing it and the coarse strength of his fingers gently kneaded at her fullness. The pads of his thumbs brushed across her nipples so sweetly and gently she couldn't hold back the moan of longing that had built from deep within her core.

Mila's legs shook and she felt a combination of heat and moisture at the juncture of her thighs, intermingled with an ache that she knew only Thierry could assuage. She flexed her hips against him, felt the hard evidence of his arousal pressing back in return.

She drifted her hands down his strong neck, over those broad shoulders and down, down, down until she could pull at the hem of his shirt and tug it from his jeans—could finally feel the satin smoothness of his skin as she stroked him, her fingertips tingling as she encountered the smattering of hair on his belly, just above the waistband of his jeans. Her fingers were clumsy as she reached for his belt, guided by instinct and desire over expertise.

And then his hands were at her wrists, tugging them away from their task, lifting them upward to his mouth where he kissed first one wrist then another before letting her go. She was speechless and shaking with need, unable to speak to voice any objection when he reached under her sweater and refastened the clasp at her back. When it was refastened, he drew her back into his arms in a hold that, in its innocence, defied all logic of the passion they'd just shared.

Beneath her ear she could hear his heart beat in rapid staccato and his breath came in short, sharp bursts—much the same as her own. She felt the pressure of his lips on the top of her head and then his arms loosed her again and he stepped away.

For endless seconds they could only stare at one another. She had no idea what he expected of her now. What he thought she might say. She only knew that their embrace had ended all too swiftly and that the physical hunger that clawed at her was nothing compared to the way he'd beguiled his way into her heart. That kiss had been an exhibition of what their relationship could have been, had it been given the chance to be nurtured and grow in a normal manner. Instead, they faced one another with untruths between them—her untruths, her manipulation, her lies.

How could she ever come back from this and expect him to trust her? She'd believed that the end justified the means, but how wrong had she been? He'd said that fidelity was everything to him. Wasn't honesty a part of that? Hadn't he kissed her just now with his soul laid bare? A sob rose in her throat but she forced it back down. Reminded herself she was not Princess Mila right here and right now. She was a courtesan—a woman experienced in joys of the heart and pleasures of the body.

Her mind scrambled for the right words, the right level of insouciance that might lessen some of the awful tension that gripped her. She settled for a shaky smile and drew in a long breath.

"If you plan to kiss your wife like that, I'm sure you will find no complaint coming from her quarter. That was—"

"That was dangerous," Thierry interrupted, releasing her and shoving a shaking hand through his short cropped hair. "When I am near you I am incapable of restraint. I didn't expect this. I can't want this and yet I do."

"You are a man of great passions. I saw that already in New York when we spoke together that night. It only makes sense that your physical passions should be equally as strong as your intellectual ones." She rested a hand on his chest and let the radiant heat of his body soak up through her palm. "Hawk, do not worry. Everything will be all right."

But even as she said the words she wondered, would it? Could it, when what lay between them was a thick web of lies?

Thirteen

Thierry had prowled the lodge like a restless tiger for the balance of the day, unable to settle into anything. Following their encounter in the library he could hardly blame Angel for steering out of his way. Something had to give, but what?

Angel had kept herself scarce, although he'd smelled the scent of baking coming from the kitchen at one stage during the afternoon. He'd been tempted to see what it was that she was making, but the thought of seeing her in such an environment would just make him want more of what he couldn't have.

He'd learned from a young age not to want the things that were out of his reach. A cynical smile twisted his lips at the thought of how people would react if he ever said such a thing. As if anyone would ever believe that anything was truly out of reach for a young prince. But there were many things that money and influence couldn't buy. Things that, despite so many years of schooling himself to quell the yearning, he still craved, though he kept his desires buried beneath the surface.

So, no, he had refused the urge to go to the kitchen, to sit at the table and to watch Angel move about in a cloud of domesticity. It was hardly likely that Princess Mila would be the kind of woman who would do such a thing, and Thierry had no wish to deepen his desire for something he could never have. He was not a normal man living a normal life, even though he craved such an indulgence.

Now it was evening and he was seated here in the great hall, staring at the fireplace and trying to rein in his temper, which felt even more out of sorts than it had been this morning. He rolled his shoulders and groaned as the tightness in his muscles made a protest. He heard Angel walk from the kitchen toward the hall.

"Hawk, are you ready for dinner? I reheated a casserole that I found in the freezer and warmed some bread."

"Quite the domestic princess, aren't you," Thierry responded, then instantly wished the words unsaid as he saw hurt flicker briefly in Angel's tawny eyes. She had not deserved that and he was quick to apologize. "I'm sorry, that was uncalled for. I am grateful for your expertise in the kitchen. We may have starved if you were not so capable."

Angel laughed but it was a small and empty sound. "I had some experience while attending university in America. It gave me the opportunity to do many things I had never tried before."

He could well imagine. Was that where she had gained her experience in matters of the flesh? Had she worked her way through her degree by conducting the oldest known profession? A bitter taste invaded his mouth at the thought and he discovered he had come to hate the idea of Angel with another man. He wanted her to himself, for himself—but even that idea was impossible. He would not be his father. He would not promise himself in marriage to his princess while he sought fulfillment in another woman's arms.

Thierry shook the thoughts from his mind and followed Angel to the kitchen, where they'd been taking their evening meals—both agreeing that the formal dining room with its table large enough to seat twenty-four was less intimate than either of them liked. Even though they ate a simple meal, he noticed she continued to make the small arrangements of fresh spring flowers from the woods and the garden, and set the table with fine linen placemats and napkins and placed fresh candles in a three-branch silver candelabra.

Yet despite the pleasant atmosphere she'd worked hard to create, conversation was strained between them throughout the meal, the tension of the morning still hanging between them like a palpable barrier. After they'd finished eating, Angel began to clear the table.

"Leave that," Thierry commanded.

Angel stopped stacking their plates and looked at him with a question in her eyes. "And who will tidy up after us?" she asked, with one eyebrow cocked.

He looked at her, taking in the sultry ruby-red gown she wore this evening and noting the way it caressed her curves. From the front, it was cut to conceal, yet with every movement it teased and hinted at the feminine delights behind the silky weave of fabric. And when she turned around the tantalizing line of her back was exposed to him, making him ache to trace a line of kisses down her spine. Every evening Angel had made the effort to change for him, to entertain him by word and deed—to be the courtesan he'd contracted. And every night he looked his fill while his body clamored for more. She was strikingly beautiful, fiercely intelligent and exhibited a warm humor that touched him on an emotional level in ways he hadn't expected.

He *wanted* her—was entitled to her since he had bought her services—and yet he continued to deny himself the privilege. Some would say he was crazy—hell, sometimes even he thought he was mad as he twisted in his sheets at night, his body craving the indulgence of physical pleasure he knew would exceed his expectations. But he had kept his discipline all these years. He could not loosen the reins now, no matter how much he wanted to.

"Hawk?" Angel prompted him, making him realize he'd been staring at her and had yet to answer her question.

"I will, in the morning. Come with me now. I have something to show you."

He held out his hand and felt a surge of masculine protectiveness as, without question, she put her smaller hand in his. Thierry led Angel back through the ground floor of the lodge and across the great hall to a corridor on the other side.

"Where are you taking me?" she asked, looking around her at the ancient tapestries that lined the walls.

"To my sanctuary within my sanctuary," he said enigmatically.

"That sounds intriguing."

"Very few people ever set foot in there and never without my express permission. It is a place I go when I want to be completely alone."

"And yet, you're taking me?"

"It seems appropriate," he conceded.

He took a key chain from his pocket and, selecting the correct key, he unlocked a massive wooden door at the end of the corridor. The door opened inward onto a small landing and light from the hall filtered down a descending curved stone staircase.

"You're not leading me to your dungeon, are you?" Angel said, half jokingly.

"No, I like to think of it more as a hidden treasure."

He reached out to flip a switch on the wall and small discreet pockets of light illuminated the grotto beneath. Thierry led the way down the stairs and smiled as he heard Angel's gasp of delight when she saw the massive natural pool gleaming in the semidarkness. He lit a taper and moved about the cavern, lighting the many candles scattered here and there.

Angel moved closer to the edge of the pool and bent to dip her hand in the inky water.

"It's warm!" she exclaimed. "How on earth did you build a heated underground pool?"

"Nature's grand architect provided it," he answered simply. "The pool is fed by a thermal underground spring and has been here for centuries. At some time, centuries past, I believe it may have been used as an area of worship or congregation, perhaps even healing. I know I always feel better after I have been in the water here."

Angel looked around her at the shadows cast by the subdued lighting and the flickering of the candles. She closed her eyes and breathed in deeply before letting the breath go on a long sigh of relaxation. "I see what you mean. There's an—" She broke off and wrinkled her brow, searching for the right words. "I don't know, maybe an *energy* about it, isn't there? You can feel the longevity and peacefulness of the place simply hanging here in the air. Almost hear the echo of voices long gone."

She laughed as if embarrassed by the fancifulness of her thoughts, but he knew what she meant. He felt it himself.

He nodded. "I thought you might enjoy the pool. It's a great way to unwind, especially when it's been a demanding day."

"Demanding, yes, you could say that. And I would love to swim here. I'll just go upstairs to get a swimsuit—"

"No need, I will let you enjoy the pool in privacy."

Angel looked at him from under hooded eyes, her head

cocked slightly to one side. "But what about you? Hasn't today been equally demanding for you also?"

In the half light it was difficult to see whether she was serious or if, once again, she was teasing him as she had so often these past few days. He settled on the latter, choosing it by preference because in his memory no one had ever had the cheek to mock him to his face before. He found her boldness tantalizing and infuriating in equal measure. And, even more strangely, he found he really liked that.

"You would like me to swim with you?" he asked, seeking clarification.

She nodded. "I think it would be an interesting lesson, don't you?"

In torment, perhaps. "And what would this lesson achieve?"

In response, Angel reached up to unfasten the top button at the back of her gown.

"It would enhance your appreciation of sensual delights. Of the combination of visual stimulation paired with the physical sensation of the water caressing your body. We need not touch, Hawk. You set the boundaries. I will respect them."

Would she? Could *he*? Right now he hated those boundaries, every last one. He watched as she slid her zipper down and eased her dress off her shoulders, exposing a delicate filament of lace, strapless and backless, masquerading as a bra. He was hard in an instant. This had been a stupid idea. He should leave her to her swim, but it was as if his limbs had taken root in the ancient stone floor beneath his feet. And all he could do was watch as she let the dress slither over the rest of her body to drop in a crimson pool at her feet.

His mouth dried as he followed the curves of her body, the shape of her rib cage, the nip of her waist and the lush roundness of her hips and thighs. Hers was a body made for love, for pleasure. A safe haven in a world of harshness. And he dare not touch her because if he did he would be lost, well and truly and very possibly forever.

She reached up behind her and unfastened her bra, allowing her full breasts to fall free. He swallowed at the sight of deep pink nipples and watched as, under his heated gaze, they grew tight—their tips rigid points. Thierry's hands curled into tight balls, every muscle from his forearms to his biceps taut with restraint.

Heat poured through his body. He should leave now, but arousal urged him to move forward—to touch, to taste. He fought the compulsion with every ounce of strength he had, but even he could not hold back the sound of longing that escaped him as she hooked her thumbs in the sides of her lacy panties and slid them down her legs.

"Are you just going to stand there?" Angel asked.

Her voice was husky, sensual—but the soft tremor behind her words belied a nervousness that caught him by surprise. She was a woman no doubt well used to the lasciviousness of male eyes, and yet she blushed before him.

"For now," he said through a throat constricted with need.

"Suit yourself," she answered with a brief curl of her lips.

She turned and he found himself captivated by the length of her spine, the dimples at the small of her back and the shape of her buttocks. Was there any part of this woman that didn't peel away his long-established layers of protocol and decorum and expose, instead, raw hunger in its purest form? It seemed not.

He watched as Angel found the steps that led into the pool and, captivated, saw her sink deeper and deeper into its warmth. He knew all too well the sensation of the warm, silky water against bare skin. How it teased and caressed the parts of your body that were normally hidden from view. Did she enjoy it—the freedom, that soft caress as it licked centimeter by centimeter up the smooth muscled length of her legs and higher to the soft curve of her inner thighs?

This was beyond torment, he realized as the muscles holding him rigid with tension screamed for release. But it didn't stop him from imagining how she felt right now as the water lapped gently at her belly, then higher to stroke the curve of her breasts until she sank right down, obscuring all but the gentle sweep of her shoulders from his view.

"This is divine," Angel commented as she did a smooth breast stroke from one end of the pool to the other, leaving a ripple of wake on the water behind her.

The paleness of her skin shone with an almost iridescent glow beneath the surface of the pool, distorting her image and making her appear intriguingly otherworldly. She turned and dipped her head until she was completely submerged, then rose again and swam toward the edge furthest from him—her long dark hair a black river down her back.

Burning need battled with disciplined restraint, just as they had done since he'd opened the door of the lodge to see his Angel standing before him. But now, for the first time in his life, need won.

Somehow, sometime, he made a decision, but he was not consciously aware of it. His clothes had melted from his body. The distance between the edge of the pool and where he stood had disappeared. He entered the water in a smooth slide of muscle and movement, gliding toward Angel as she sat on the ledge on the side of the pool, her legs still dangling in the water like some earth-bound mermaid.

She was a goddess here in this grotto. Her skin shimmering with the moisture that clung to her skin and which refracted light from the candles around them as if each one was a jewel.

Thierry pulled himself up between her legs, reaching for her as if he had every right to take her, every right to draw her beautiful body to his and every right to take her lips in a kiss that spoke volumes as to his hunger for her.

He was lost in a maelstrom of impressions that chased through his mind—of her acquiescence as she flowed against him, of her mouth responding to his kiss, of the sounds of pleasure from her throat, of the gentle drift of her fingertips across the top of his shoulders.

He kissed her and probed the soft recesses of her mouth with his tongue, tasting her and knowing that one taste would never be enough. His hands went to her breasts, cupping the full warm flesh with his fingers, kneading them gently and teasing the hard points of her arousal. She moaned and strained against him, her body slick and wet and warm and driving him crazy in the best way imaginable.

He bent his head to take one nipple in his mouth, rolling his tongue around the distended tip before gently grazing it with his teeth. A shudder ran through her body and he felt an answering response in his own. How had he managed to deny himself these pleasures for so very long? And how was he to stop now he'd allowed the floodgates of desire to open? The question was fleeting and all thoughts of bringing this to a halt were swiftly quelled as her fingers raked through his hair—her hands holding him to her as he licked and nipped and suckled at her.

Her hips undulated against him, her heated core brushing against the hardened length of his shaft. He wouldn't have believed it possible but he swelled even more under her gentle assault on his body.

Thierry let his hands drift down over her rib cage, past the sweep of her waist and the curve of her hip and then around to the fullness of her buttocks. Gripping her he pulled her firmly against him and groaned at the sweet shaft of pleasure that pieced him. But he still didn't feel close enough.

"You are a torment to man, a seductress simply by your existence," he murmured against her throat before gently nipping at her skin.

"And you are everything I have ever wanted," Angel sighed in response.

Her words, so simple yet so disingenuous, struck him to his heart and he gave himself over to the joy they engendered. At this moment she was the foundation of his existence. Here, in this natural grotto, in the heated spring water that felt like silk and seduction against a man's skin, they were locked in a world apart from the reality that lingered outside.

"And you, my sweet Angel," he said, kissing her once again and drawing her lower lips gently between his teeth before releasing it again. "You are so much more than I could imagine wanting. Ever."

His hands were still at her buttocks and he edged her slightly farther forward until the tip of his penis brushed against her entrance. All Thierry could think about was the woman in his arms, the need that pulsed and demanded as if it was the most fundamental part of his existence. She tipped her pelvis and he slid just inside her. They both gasped at the contact and Thierry reveled in the sensation of her.

He couldn't stop himself. His entire body shook as demand overtook him, his senses filled with the feel of her in his arms, the soft sounds of her ragged breathing and the incredible heat that generated where their bodies joined together. He thrust forward, but instead of sliding fully into her body he met with resistance. It didn't immediately make sense to him, but then again, right now, nothing did but the driving need to push past that barrier and find the fulfillment his body craved.

Confusion clouded his mind, pushed past the roar of desire that had driven him to this point, until the confusion suddenly cleared and realization dawned.

His Angel was a virgin.

Fourteen

"Please, don't stop now," Mila urged him.

Her fingers curled into his shoulders, her nails biting into his skin as ripples of pleasure surpassed the burning fullness of his penetration and cascaded through her body. But instead he withdrew.

"What's wrong?" she asked.

"You...you're a virgin," he said as if he could scarcely believe the words.

"As are you, are you not?"

She searched his eyes for some response but all she could see was shock reflected back at her. Eventually he nodded.

"Does it not make this sweeter?" she asked, sliding her hands down his body and slipping them around his waist, pulling him back against her.

She felt her body ease to accommodate his length and fullness and she wanted to move against him, to welcome him deeper into her body. She lifted her face to Thierry's and kissed him, sliding her tongue between his lips in a simulation of what she wanted him to continue.

"Touch me," she whispered against his lips. "Touch me, there, with your fingers. Feel yourself inside me."

He did as she asked and she saw his pupils dilate even more as his fingers touched that special place where they joined. She gasped as his knuckles brushed her clitoris.

"Yes," she urged, "and there, too."

"Like this?" he asked, repeating the movement.

"Yes, oh yes."

The ripples that had begun with his possession of her intensified with each stroke and she moved her hips in tiny circles, urging him to follow her movements with his hand. He was a quick study and, as pleasure suffused her, her inner muscles began to clench and release, to encourage him to push deeper, to conquer the barrier between them.

And then that barrier was gone, and so was she—on a wave of passion so intense it took her breath completely away as paroxysms of pleasure coiled and released over and over, spreading from her core to her extremities and making her arch her throat and shout his name so that it echoed back to them from the cavernous ceiling.

Thierry's hips pumped with increasing speed, water lapping all around them, until he, too, reached his peak, the muscles on his back taut with tension and his entire body straining as he surged and surged yet again.

"Ah, my Angel, I love you!" he groaned against her throat as with one final push he came deep inside her.

It was sometime later when he moved again and Mila finally became aware of the pressure of the smooth stones at her back. She shifted to ease her weight off the uncomfortable surface and reached for Thierry as he began to pull away.

"In a hurry to leave me now?" she asked, trying to inject a note of playful banter into her voice.

It was, perhaps, an impossible goal to attempt to keep the atmosphere light between them. They'd just been passionately intimate with one another and, judging by the look on Thierry's face, he was already beginning to regret it.

"Hawk?" she asked, prompting him again. "Is everything all right?"

"No," he said fiercely pulling free of her touch and pushing back in the water to where she could not reach him. "Everything is not all right. We shouldn't have done this. I gave in to weakness even though I'm promised to another woman. I've destroyed forever the one thing I wished to hold sacred between her and myself."

There was a wealth of self-loathing in his voice and she couldn't bear to hear it. "But—" she started.

"There are no buts," he said firmly, cutting her off. The self-loathing was now tinged with a bitterness that brought tears to Mila's eyes. "Don't you understand? By making love to you, I have become the man I least wanted to be. How can I go ahead with my marriage to the woman I have been promised to for the past seven years when I love you? It would make everything I believe in, everything I am, a lie."

Mila remained where she was, stunned into total silence as his words, riddled with pain and torment, echoed into obscurity in the air around them. Thierry finished crossing the pool and rose from the water. Rivulets cascaded down his back and over his firm buttocks and even now, in this awful atmosphere of disillusion and self-loathing, her body responded with desire at the sight of him.

"Hawk! Stop. Wait, please?" she begged, moving to follow. She staggered up the steps that led to the edge and reached for him, but her fingers found nothing but air. "Hawk, please. Listen to me. I love you, too."

He shook his head. "That only makes it worse. I am a

king. I cannot love you or accept your love—the entire situation is impossible. Knowing how I felt about you I should have sent you away the moment you arrived, but I didn't. In another lifetime, another world, perhaps we could have been more to one another, but we live here and now."

Thierry made a sound of disgust and reached for a towel from inside a discreetly hidden cupboard. He threw one to her and grabbed another for himself.

"Tomorrow you will leave. I will not see you off."

Mila's mind whirled. This was going all wrong. She'd achieved what she'd set out to do—he loved her. Yet now everything was falling apart. But then, he didn't know who she really was.

"We need to talk," she started again, desperate to get him to listen to her.

"No, the time for talking is done. We have nothing further to say to one another. The blame for what has transpired between us falls directly on my shoulders. I recruited your services. I kept you here even though I knew it could lead to trouble."

"Trouble? You're calling our love for one another trouble? That's not right, Hawk. Love is a gift."

"A gift? I thought so, but now I realize it is a burden. Tell me, how am I to face my bride and pledge myself to her, knowing my heart belongs to you?"

"But I am—"

He cut her off again. "No more!" he bellowed. "I've made a liar of myself. A mockery of everything that I told myself was important. Now I have to live with what I've done. I've made my decision. Your car will be here first thing tomorrow."

He stalked away from her up the staircase and was gone before she could work out what to say. What did he mean—live with what he'd done? Did he plan to call off the wedding? She had to find him, to tell him who she really was. To explain to him why she'd tricked him.

Mila dried herself quickly and dragged her dress on over her head. Her wet hair clung to her back but she barely noticed as she gathered up her other things and moved quickly toward the stairs. It was as she reached the second floor that she began to slow down, her heart hammering in her chest, her thoughts a whirl.

Thierry had been angry. Not at her, but at himself. Was now the best time to confront him with her duplicity? Yes, he'd just admitted he loved her, and she knew—after getting to know him better this past week—that he could not have made love to her if he didn't. The thought filled her with hope for their future but at the same time he loved a woman who, technically, didn't exist. *His Angel*, he'd called her. And she wanted so much to be that woman for him. But would he still love her when she revealed her true identity?

She came to a halt in the hallway at the intersection of the corridor to Thierry's rooms. Her heart pounded as she considered what to do next. Was it too late to explain to him, to make him see the truth? Had she ruined everything?

Understanding his past and his family, as she did now, she could see why it was so important for him to keep himself only for her. In this day and age his idea would be considered by most people to be ridiculously outdated, but to her it showed exactly how seriously committed he was to their marriage. Far from being the distant man she'd met so long ago, she'd learned he was multifaceted. Sure, he was powerful and handsome and had a higher IQ than many—not to mention the wherewithal to use that power and IQ for the good of the people who looked to him for leadership. And he had a good store of arrogance hiding under that handsome exterior, as well. But beneath all that he was vulnerable and caring and he'd wedged himself into her heart in such a way she knew that no one else would ever be able to dislodge him.

She loved him because she knew him, appreciated and valued everything about him. That was how she knew his honor was everything to him—and that she'd abused it with her deceit. He wouldn't look upon her actions lightly. She made him cross a personal boundary with her behavior tonight. It had been selfish of her, knowing how he felt, to tempt him into breaking his self-imposed chastity.

But as guilty as she felt for the torment he was experiencing now, she still couldn't completely regret their lovemaking. Their joining had been everything she'd ever imagined it could be. The pleasure had been far more intense and the act of lovemaking so intimate that she felt as though she was joined to him forever already. Marriage would simply be a ceremony to appease the rest of the world as to their intentions toward one another, but in her soul Mila was married to Thierry, her Hawk, already.

But what would Thierry say when she stopped hiding behind the veil of another woman's identity?

Thierry paced the floor of the library. He had been unable to settle in his room. Even his own bed appeared to mock him in the gloom of night with the way he couldn't help but picture Angel's naked form spread across its broad expanse of white sheets. His body told him he was all kinds of fool. Instead of abandoning her in the grotto, he should have simply brought Angel to his bed, used the bounty her body so freely offered. Whispered sweet nothings into the night until they were both so exhausted they could do nothing but sleep—until they woke and reached for one another again. He could not bring back his lost chastity, so why waste time mourning it when he could be enjoying his new sexual freedom?

If he was any other kind of man that is exactly what he'd have done. Hell, he'd have probably bedded her on the very first night she'd arrived. But, he thought looking up to the portrait of his late parents where it hung above the fireplace, he wasn't his father. Nor was he yet his mother— a woman who'd entered into marriage with all good intentions and yet found herself adrift and alone and desperate for the attention and love of a man.

He turned away from the portrait and went to stand over by the window. The clock chimed the half hour. Soon the sun would begin to rise and a new day would dawn, and he was no closer to making his decision about what to do next.

At the forefront of his mind was the long standing betrothal to marry Princess Mila. He knew if he went through with it, he'd end up inflicting the same kind of pain upon her as his father had upon his mother. No, he wouldn't neglect her or disrespect her the way his father had his mother. But even as he took his marriage vows, he would know that he would never be able to love her the way she deserved. Not when another woman had already taken possession of his heart.

But how could there be peace between their countries if their marriage did not go ahead? And on the other hand, could he imagine being married to one woman while longing with every cell in his body for another?

In the endless night just gone, he'd even asked himself if he could be like his father—maintain the facade of a marriage while continuing to keep a mistress. But how could he even think about doing that to Angel, let alone his new bride? He'd always vowed he'd be different to the other men who had been in his family—be a better man, period.

Perhaps his family was forever cursed to be unhappy in marriage—to be forever disappointed in love.

Half an hour later he began to hear movement about the house. He'd sent word to Pasquale for a skeleton staff to return, even though he had no wish for company right now. A car swept into the turning bay of the drive and parked at the front door—Angel's ride out of here, away from him, forever. The thought struck a searing pain deep into his heart. Having to send her away was unarguably the hardest thing he'd ever had to do. But do it, he must.

A sound at the door behind him made him wheel around. Angel. His chest constricted on a new wave of pain, even as his body heated in response to her arrival. She looked as if she'd slept as little as he had. There were dark circles beneath her eyes and shadows lurked in the amber depths.

"The car is here," he said in lieu of a greeting.

"Hawk, I need to speak with you. There is something important I need to say before I go."

Even her voice was flat and weary. He wished he could ease the sorrow he saw reflected back at him in her gaze. Perhaps he could give her just this opportunity to say her piece. Goodness knew he could offer her little else. He inclined his head.

"Please speak freely," he said.

She drew in a short breath and began to step closer to him, but then appeared to think the better of it. He was glad. He was strung so tight right now it was all he could do to maintain a facade of calm. If she touched him he'd weaken. He'd once again become the man he despised.

"I know you are undergoing a major battle with yourself over what we did last night," she started. "But I want you to know that everything will be all right."

"All right?" he barked an incredulous laugh. "How can you say that? I have betrayed everything I stand for. Nothing will be all right again."

She clasped her hands together, squeezing them so tightly he saw her fingertips lose all color. "I love you, Hawk. You have to believe that."

A prickle of emotion burned at the back of his eyes but he furiously refused to allow it to take purchase. To allow the sentiment to swamp the rationality he so desperately needed right now. "It makes no difference," he said harshly. "You are a courtesan. I am a king. Worse, I am a king betrothed to another."

"I know that, and you must not let what we have done stop your marriage to your princess. You must go through with the wedding."

"I must? Who are you to tell me what to do?" he demanded, taking refuge in the anger that continued to grow inside him at the situation he'd created through his own weakness.

For a second he caught a glimpse of hurt in her eyes but then she seemed to change. Her expression became less vulnerable, as if she'd assumed a mask upon her exquisitely beautiful face. Her shoulders and neck straightened and she lifted her chin ever so slightly, almost regally.

"I am Princess Mila Angelina of Erminia."

Shock slammed into him with the force of an avalanche. "Be very careful, Angel. There are strict laws governing imposters," he growled when sense returned.

She licked her lips and, damn him, he couldn't help but remember what the tip of that tongue had felt like as it delved delicately inside his mouth. He willed his body not to respond but, as with this entire situation, it refused to submit to his control.

"I am not lying to you. Not anymore."

"You had better explain."

"I was at school in Boston when I saw the news report on your visit to New York. I hadn't seen you in seven years, and with our wedding only weeks away, I couldn't resist the chance to try to contact you. When I met you in New York I had gone to your hotel with the intention of visiting you in your suite. I had planned to introduce myself—to see, somehow, if I could get to know you a little before our wedding. But my courage failed me. I was just on the verge of giving up on seeing you when you bumped into me."

"But you don't look…" He let his voice trail off. How did you tell a woman she looked nothing like her unattractive teenaged self?

She was quick to hear the words he'd left unspoken.

"I don't look like I did at eighteen? No, I don't. When you didn't recognize me in New York, it hurt me at first. But then I thought it might be a bit of fun—a good opportunity to get to know the real you."

"When I dropped you off, why didn't you tell me who you were?"

"I—I don't know," she admitted with her eyes downcast. "I guess I was enjoying the way you looked at me when I was just Angel. I didn't want you to lose that look when you connected me with the girl you met when we got engaged."

Thierry felt a flush of shame. Yes, he'd been taken aback when he'd met the princess that first time. But even then he'd committed to her fully—right up until last night when he'd done the unthinkable with a woman who he'd believed was a courtesan. Which brought them straight back to where they were now. The realization flamed the fire of his fury.

"You took a terrible risk doing what you have done," he bit out.

"Not so much in New York, but here, yes."

"And what of Ottavia Romolo? Is she in on your scheme also? Am I to expect to be blackmailed by her for her part in all of this?"

"No! Not that."

"Then what?" he demanded.

"She, um. She has been detained in Erminia."

"Detained?" Thierry gripped his hands into fists. "What

exactly do you mean by that? Are you holding her somewhere against her will?"

The princess hung her head, not answering. But he
could see the truth in every line of her body.

"Why? Why would you risk so much—with your reputation, with mine? What made you go to such lengths and
lie to me like that? Don't you realize what will happen
when the truth comes out?"

"I felt great lengths were required when I overheard that
my betrothed had contracted a courtesan just a few weeks
before our wedding!" she snapped back, a flash of temper
sparking in her beautiful eyes. "All these years, I'd worked
so hard to try to become someone you could value and desire. And then to hear that you'd invited another woman to
be your lover..." She turned her face away, dropping her
gaze to the floor. "I couldn't bear the thought of it. I had
to take her place."

She lifted her head to face him again and he could see
tears swimming in her gaze. "I just wanted you to love
me."

Something twisted in his gut at the pain in her voice,
on her face, in her eyes. Love? She'd done all this for love?
He closed his eyes for a moment, took a steadying breath.
He knew love didn't last, not for people like him. Eventually he sighed.

"I am at a complete loss, Princess."

"Why? Shouldn't this make everything okay? You love
me, you said so yourself, and I love you, too. You can let
go of your guilt. I'm your princess, you haven't betrayed
me. We can move forward from this, knowing we were
meant for one another," she implored.

"Really?"

A part of him wished their lives could be as simple as
she'd just said. But he knew they couldn't. Theirs were not
normal lives. Instead they were a confluence of expecta-

tions and protocols over which they had no control. And there was still the matter of her duplicity.

He continued, "I have to ask myself, if you were prepared to undertake such a deception as you have perpetrated since our meeting in New York, why should I believe a single word you say? Don't you think it would be more appropriate for me to question everything you say and do? What else would you be prepared to lie about to me? Your profession of love? Your promise, at our wedding, to love and honor me as your husband? I have to ask myself—how can I trust you?" He steeled himself to say the next words. "And the answer is that I can't."

Her shoulders sagged and he could see hope fracture and disappear in her eyes as the tears she'd been holding back began to fall. He wanted to step forward, to take her in his arms and assure her that everything would be okay. But how could it be? He'd told her how he felt. Had said on more than one occasion how important honesty was to him. And still she'd continued to lie.

"Leave me now," he commanded.

"No! Hawk—!"

The princess stepped forward, thrusting out both hands, imploring him with her body, the expression on her face, the raw plea in her voice, not to send her away.

It was the most difficult and painful thing he had ever done, but he turned his back on her. He didn't move when he heard her footsteps drag across the library floor, not when he heard the door close behind her. Out the window he saw her move outside and onto the driveway, hesitating just a moment at the car door that had been opened for her. He watched, telling himself over and over that he had done the right thing. That her lies had been a betrayal of everything he stood for. But as the car disappeared from view he sank to his knees and closed his eyes against the burning tears that threatened to fall.

* * *

All through that day and the night that followed he fought with his conscience—battled with the urge to follow his Angel and to bring her back to his side where she belonged. He'd made the decision by morning that he would contact her brother, request an audience with both Rocco and Mila to postpone the wedding, but that contact never eventuated as he read the newspaper left so neatly folded beside his breakfast in the dining room the next morning. The newspaper with the headline that shrieked that the virgin Prince of Sylvain had pre-empted his wedding vows with another woman. Paragraph after paragraph followed with endless speculation about the new Sylvano King's honor, or lack of it.

He felt sick to his stomach. Despite every precaution he'd taken, and there had been many, the news had still somehow been leaked. This was his worst nightmare. A scandal of monumental proportions. Grainy photographs taken with a long-distance lens from somewhere in the woods showed pictures of him with Angel—no, Princess Mila—as they rode together, picnicked together and kissed together. Every photo had its own lurid caption. Thierry left the table and made to leave the lodge—his sanctuary no longer.

The moment his people found out exactly who it was who was responsible, that person would pay for this invasion of his privacy and pay dearly.

Just before he got into the car that would return him to the harsh reality of his world, and no doubt the censure of his people, Pasquale arrived at his side with another newspaper that had just been delivered. Thierry's skin crawled as he read the headline, "Princess Mila Revealed as the King's Courtesan!"

Had she engineered all of this since last night in some kind of attempt to force him to go through with the wedding even though it went against everything he'd spent his lifetime trying to avoid? Did she think his fear of public disgrace would override his anger over her deception? If that was what she thought, she was wrong.

The scandal surrounding his mother's death had been an ongoing assault for years after her death. How on earth could Thierry think about loving or trusting a woman who had brought this back upon him, who had brought his carefully constructed world down around his ears? Worse, how could he ask his subjects to love or trust her, either? No amount of damage control would make a speck of difference. There was only one thing left that he could do.

He turned and marched back into the lodge and to his office where, on his secure line, he placed a call.

"King Rocco," he said as he was put through. "I regret to inform you that I can no longer marry your sister. The wedding is off."

Fifteen

Mila paced the floor of her bedroom. Back and forth like a caged animal. She'd known the minute she crossed the border and a palace guard had stepped out of the customs building, followed by her brother's head of palace security, that her ruse had been discovered. From the moment she'd been returned to the castle yesterday she'd been a virtual prisoner in her own rooms.

Not permitted to make or receive calls, her computer confiscated, her television disconnected—she was adrift from the rest of the world. Worse, she was actually locked in. She began to have a new appreciation for how Ottavia Romolo must have felt during her captivity. Although, it seemed, that the courtesan's incarceration had lasted only a matter of days. Somehow, the woman had managed to escape and warn Mila's brother of what she'd been up to—hence the welcoming committee when Mila returned across the border.

Mila hated waiting. Worse, she hated not knowing what

she could expect when she was eventually brought before her brother to face the music. And through it all was the fear and the worry that what she'd done had destroyed any chance of her and Thierry having their happy ending after all. She'd been a fool, going off half cocked and driven by emotion.

Hadn't she been raised to know better than that? Emotion couldn't be the main driving force in the life of a royal. Duty came before everything else. If she'd ever thought she knew that lesson before it was nothing on how she'd come to understand it now. She should have waited until her wedding. Allowed their relationship to grow and blossom the way it could have done under normal circumstances.

She should have trusted Thierry, even when she'd heard that he'd hired a courtesan. Should have believed he would never do anything to dishonor his commitment to her.

And there lay the crux of the problem. She hadn't trusted him. And in her insecurity, she'd set out to willfully deceive him. Her behavior had reaped the result she should have been doing everything she could to avoid. Whatever came next, she deserved it.

The aching hollow that had developed in her chest from the moment Thierry had sent her away grew even deeper. She doubted the pain of it would ever leave her.

There was a perfunctory knock at the door to her room which then opened, revealing General Andrej Novak, Rocco's head of the armed forces—the man who had escorted her home from the border yesterday.

"Your Royal Highness, please come with me."

So, Rocco had sent his top guy rather than one of the usual palace guards or even a general staff member. Clearly he wasn't taking any of this lightly at all. Unease knotted in her stomach as, wordlessly, she did as she'd been asked.

"He's furious with me, isn't he?" she asked the tall, forbidding-looking man at her side.

"It's not my place to say, ma'am."

She continued through the palace corridors until they arrived at her brother's office. The head of security tapped on the door and then opened it for her, gesturing for her to go inside. The sun beat in through the office windows, throwing the man seated in the chair at his desk into relief and putting Mila at a distinct disadvantage. If only she could see her brother's face, gauge his mood. Who was she kidding? Seeing his face wouldn't change a thing—he was undoubtedly furious with her, again. She sank into a curtsy. Her legs began to burn as she waited for his command to rise.

"Good of you to return home," her brother said in icy tones from behind his desk. He made a sound that sounded like a growl. "Get up, Mila, your subservience is too little, too late."

She rose and faced him, her eyes raking his face—searching for any sign of compassion. There was none. Banked fury lit his sherry-colored eyes and deep lines bracketed the sides of his mouth.

"Do you have the slightest idea what you've done?" he bit out. When she remained silent he continued, his voice lethally level and controlled. "Your impetuosity has destroyed any chance of a union between Erminia and Sylvain. King Thierry has called off the wedding."

"No!" Mila gasped in pain and shock. Her legs wobbled and she reached for the chair beside her to steady herself.

"Peace between our nations will now be impossible." Rocco rose from his chair and turned to face the windows, presenting her with his broad back.

"Surely not impossible. This is the twenty-first century, after all," she argued, futilely reaching for some thought or idea to present to her brother. "There must be something we can do."

"Do?" He turned to face her and shook his head. "You have driven open chasms in the very fabric of our security. I had hoped to avoid having to tell you this. Had hoped that your marriage to King Thierry would bring with it enough stability that this problem would become irrelevant, and you would have had no need to know."

"No need to know what?" she demanded. "What have you been hiding from me, and why?"

"Before your engagement I became aware of rumors of a threat against me. One that endangered you, too. We took steps to weed out the danger and we believed it under control, but before your return home the threat became a clear and present danger."

Mila's throat dried in fear. "What kind of threat?"

"At first we thought it might be a direct attack on my person, but it seems my position on the throne is the actual target."

"But how? You are the firstborn and only son of our father. Our lines of succession are quite specific."

"Firstborn and only *legitimate* son of our father."

"He had another son?"

Shocked, Mila couldn't remain standing another moment. She sank into a chair in an inelegant slump.

"Apparently."

"Who?"

"That's the problem. I don't know yet. But I will," Rocco said with grim determination.

"But even so, if he isn't our father's legitimate issue he has no claim on the throne."

Rocco made a noise that was between a laugh and a growl. "So we believed. However, it seems that there is an ancient law, still in force, that says that if I am not married by my thirty-fifth birthday *and* the father of legally recognized issue, I cannot remain king."

"But that's easy, isn't it? Marry. Have a baby! Or revoke the law."

"A list of potential brides is being prepared for me. But time is of the essence, so in the meantime, we are working with our parliament to see the law revoked. However that has opened a whole new set of problems. Some of our members apparently support the idea of a new king. It appears the flames of subversion have been subtly coaxed for some time."

"Oh, Rocco. What are you going to do?"

"Keep working to uncover who is behind this and keep trying to unravel the mystery before it's too late and we have a civil war on our hands. In the meantime, we need all the allies we can get, which is why I was counting on your now-canceled nuptials."

Mila began to shake.

"I…I…" Her voice trailed away. An apology seemed ridiculously insubstantial given the weight of what Rocco had said. "Sorry" just didn't cut it. "What can I do?"

Her brother came around the front of his desk and gave her look that she would never forget. He squatted down before her and took both her hands in his.

"I know that following orders has never been your strong suit, but I have one command for you now, little sister. Go back to Sylvain and change King Thierry's mind. Your marriage could be the only thing that saves Erminia from total destruction."

From the helicopter window Mila watched through the darkness as the lights at the border of Erminia disappeared behind her. Ahead lay Sylvain and what would unarguably be the most difficult task of her life. How did you convince a man who loved you but who no longer trusted you to go ahead with your marriage?

Flying had never been her favorite pastime and she usually survived long-haul flights with antianxiety medication that helped her sleep through most of it. That wasn't an option now, when she needed to stay alert, but taking a short flight in a helicopter had her heart racing and her nerves strung so tight she thought she might throw up if they didn't land soon.

As if he could read her mind the pilot made an announcement through the headset clamped to Mila's ears.

"We'll be landing at the palace grounds shortly, Your Royal Highness."

"Thank you," she responded. *And not a moment too soon*, she added silently as her stomach lurched in response to the change in altitude as they began to make their descent.

"Are you all right, ma'am?" the uniformed escort beside her asked.

She cast a look at him. In his late thirties, General Andrej Novak cut a dashing figure in his uniform and, as head of her brother's military, wielded an immense amount of power. But Mila felt there was always a hint of dissatisfaction hidden in the set of his mouth and the expression in his dark brown eyes. It made her wary of him, and served to increase her discomfort. She didn't understand why it had been so necessary for her brother to send him. It was hardly a high-profile visit. In fact, it was meant to be private and would, hopefully, remain so with just her and Thierry in the same room together.

Still, she reminded herself, appearances were everything to Rocco and he wanted to make it patently obvious that this visit to Sylvain was done above board and without a hint of scandal or subterfuge. Mila closed her eyes a moment and gripped the armrests of her chair as the skids of the chopper settled on the helipad set in the Sylvano palace's widespread and parklike grounds. A car waited nearby. The general exited the helicopter and turned to assist Mila to the ground. She was grateful for his steadying hand as she alighted and put her feet down on solid ground again.

A man got out of the car and walked toward them. He gave Mila a deep bow as he drew near.

"Your Royal Highness, Pasquale De Luca, aide to His Majesty King Thierry, at your service. Please come with me."

"Thank you, Mr. De Luca."

General Novak moved with her as Mila fell in step with Thierry's aide. The aide stopped abruptly.

"I'm sorry, General. But my instructions are clear. Only the princess is to come in the vehicle."

"And my instructions are equally clear," Andrej rumbled at Mila's side. "The princess is in my charge."

"King Thierry will see the princess, and no one else."

"It's okay, Andrej," Mila said, putting a hand on the general's arm. "I will be fine."

The man gave her a cold stare before making a short nod and taking a step back. "As you wish, ma'am."

She could tell by the way he'd bristled at her touch that he was none too happy about the situation, but she was grateful he'd given in, even if only temporarily.

"Take me to your king," she instructed Pasquale with as much decorum as she could muster.

Inside, her stomach roiled. Would Thierry listen to her plea? Could he forgive her the deception she'd wrought and the resulting flurry of scandal in the papers? Would he believe that she was not responsible for the leak? She had to believe that he would. That her love for him, and his for her, would help her overcome this awful situation.

As they reached the car, Pasquale opened the back door

and held it for her. Mila gave him a smile of thanks and got inside, but it wasn't until the door closed beside her and the vehicle began to move that she realized she wasn't alone in the back of the luxurious limousine.

"Thierry!" she said, startled by the sight of him.

"You asked to see me. I am here."

His voice was devoid of so much as a speck of warmth or humor and his eyes were as cold as steel.

"I expected to see you at the palace," she said nervously, her fingers pleating the fabric of her dress.

"You have no right to expect anything of me."

"You're right, of course." She forced herself to let go of her dress. "I'm sorry, Hawk, so very sorry for what I did."

"Do not call me Hawk."

She heard the underscore of pain in his voice and bowed her head in acknowledgment of her role in causing that pain. It made her heart sore that she had hurt him. That had never been her intention. She'd only wanted him to love her, as she loved him. Instead, she'd started their relationship on a series of lies. She'd abused his trust. It was no wonder he was still angry with her and looked at her now the way he did. She met his gaze—it was chillingly clinical, devoid of the passion and interest she'd come to take for granted.

"I apologize again. Can you ever forgive me? Can you please give me, us, another chance?"

Thierry shifted in his seat and turned his gaze to the privacy screen that shielded them from the car's driver.

"Another chance, you say?" He shook his head. "No, I don't believe in second chances."

"But I love you and I know you love me, too. You told me as much. Did you lie?"

He was silent for so long that Mila thought she might shatter into a thousand painful jagged fragments, but when he spoke, she knew the agony of waiting was infinitely preferable to the torment of hearing what he had to say.

"I didn't lie. I loved my Angel deeply, it's true. But love alone is not enough. I have seen what people do in the name of love, what they allow themselves to think is acceptable or permissible. You know from the confidences we shared what is important to me, don't you?"

Mila cleared her throat and tried to speak. The words came out rough and strained.

"Honesty and trust."

"Yes, honesty and trust. I trusted you, but were you honest with me?" He faced her again. "We both know you weren't, despite ample opportunity to be—both in New York and at my lodge."

She struggled with how to reply. Finally, she said, "Neither of us had an easy upbringing—in our positions, with our families, it was virtually impossible for us to learn about love. And yet we still prize love above all other things. I would do anything for true love, and I did. Right from when I first met you seven years ago I knew I could love you—but how could I have ever believed that you would love someone like me? I spent the next seven years trying to be the woman worthy of being by your side, of holding your heart. Even when I met you in New York that night, I knew I was more than half in love with you already. But then I heard that you had acquired Ms. Romolo's services, and I felt heartbroken. I had done so much, had worked so hard to make myself everything I thought you would need in a wife and partner, and yet you had chosen to turn to another woman instead. I know my actions were foolish. Reckless. Even dangerous. But I would have risked anything to find the intimacy and connection that we built together at the lodge."

She reached for his hand and held it firmly within her own.

"I wanted a real marriage—of hearts and minds and

bodies—not merely a facade to present to the people of our countries or to the world at large. I wanted a husband who would love me and stand by me as much as I want to love and stand by him. I came to the lodge in Ms. Romolo's place hoping we could build that together. I hate that I deceived you, but I'd be lying if I said I regretted those days we spent together. We can still have that relationship, that partnership based on love, if you'll just forgive me. I was wrong, I was stupid. I abused your trust, but I believed I was doing all of that for all the right reasons. I love you so much. You have my heart, my soul. You are my everything. Please…believe me."

For a moment she thought she might have broken through the shell of cold indifference that encased him, but then he pulled his hand free.

"I don't believe you. I can't. I can only regret that I misguidedly placed my trust in a woman who will do whatever it takes for whatever *she* wants and to hell with the consequences—just like my mother did."

Each word fell like a blow upon her soul and Mila felt paralyzed, unable to speak or move as her body suffused with the pain that filled her mind.

Thierry continued, "For the past seven years there was only one woman in my life. You. I didn't know you, but I planned to get to know you once we were married. I wanted to learn about what made you happy, what made you sad. What filled you with hope, what made you angry. What piqued your interest, what bored you rigid. I wanted to share your life, but I don't see how I can do that now. You destroyed our future with your lies. I simply can't marry a woman I can't trust."

He leaned forward and flicked a switch—to the intercom to the driver, Mila realized through the fog of grief that slowly engulfed her.

"Take us back to the helipad. The princess is ready to return to Erminia."

Her voice shook and she felt as if her heart had been absorbed by a gaping black hole of despair as she spoke once more. "Please, I beg of you—reconsider. We can delay the wedding—take as long as you need until you feel you can trust me again. Please give me another chance. I love you, Thierry. With all my heart. I will do everything in my power to make up to you for my foolishness."

"And what if *everything* is not enough?" he retorted as the car drew to a halt near the helipad. "There's nothing you can do to change my mind."

The car rolled to a halt.

Mila tried one more time to probe the seemingly impenetrable wall Thierry had erected between them. "Was it so very bad, loving me?"

Before he could respond, the door beside her opened. She barely acknowledged Pasquale as he offered her his hand to help her from the car. She waited for Thierry to respond to her question but he remained silent, his eyes forward. Her heart broke.

She had failed in her attempt to secure her happiness. Worse, she'd failed in her attempt to see to the security of her family, her people, her country. Even now, she didn't want to give up. Couldn't bring herself to accept that Thierry would never forgive her. Maybe it was too soon, perhaps she should have given him more time before making her approach. But time was a luxury they didn't have, not with the news Rocco had shared with her.

And even as she climbed back on board the helicopter and attempted to rationalize her thoughts, she knew that her mission would have failed, no matter what she'd said or how long she'd waited. Thierry was a guarded man. One who had shielded his love and emotions behind his duty and determination to live honorably. She had dishonored him, and herself, with her actions, and that was something he could not forgive.

Now she had to face her brother, the leader of her people, and tell him she had failed both him and them.

Flying in the dark was preferable to flying by daylight, Mila reasoned. At least this way you couldn't see how high you were or, conversely, how close to the ground that you were covering at unnatural speed. Even so, it seemed to her that they were descending far sooner than she'd expected. She looked across to the general who was again seated beside her.

"It feels like we are coming into land. Surely we're not in Erminia yet. Is there something wrong?"

"Perhaps it is a mechanical issue with the chopper," the general replied, looking unconcerned.

Mila looked out the window. Yes, they were very definitely being brought down to land, but where were they? In the dark it was impossible to make out any landmarks of distinction. The second they were down the pilot exited the chopper, and the general was quick to follow. Mila remained in her seat, wondering what on earth was going on. Through her window she watched as the two men began to talk.

Then, to her horror, she saw the pilot pull out a handgun and point it at the general.

A loud report followed and Mila screamed as the general fell to the ground in a crumpled heap. The pilot came to her door and yanked it open. "Come with me now," he demanded, waving the pistol toward her.

Horrified, she did as he told her. "What are you doing? Why—?"

"Silence!" the man shouted and grabbed her roughly by the shoulder, shoving her ahead of him. "Walk!"

Mila staggered but was pulled upright by the pilot.

"Don't try anything stupid, Your Royal Highness." He sneered as he used her title, as if it was an insult. "I will not hesitate to give you the same treatment I gave the general."

A large, black, all-terrain vehicle roared up out of the darkness and a group of men piled out before it was fully stationary. They all carried guns. She'd been frightened before, but now she was absolutely terrified. What on earth was going to happen to her?

Sixteen

"What do you mean the princess never returned to Erminia? We saw her helicopter take off with our own eyes."

Pasquale's features reflected his concern. "I know, sire, but it seems her transport was diverted before she reached the palace, and the princess was abducted. No one knows where she is."

"And the pilot and her escort? Where are they?"

"Her escort was the king's own general. He was shot but managed to escape, apparently. The report I received from inside the Erminian palace said he regained consciousness to find the princess gone and the helicopter abandoned. He flew it back to the palace himself."

Thierry shoved a hand through his hair and began to pace. This was his fault. He'd sent her away. If he'd only been more willing to listen, to give her that second chance she'd begged for—the chance they both deserved—then this would never have happened.

"What is Rocco doing?" he demanded.

"The king has dispatched troops to search for the princess. The general was vague about his whereabouts when he came to and it appears that the tracking on the helicopter had been disabled when it left here. He was battling to remain conscious during the flight, apparently, and has little recollection of the journey."

"And yet he made it to the palace?"

"It would appear so, sire."

Thierry sat back down at his desk and stared at the papers upon it as if they could shed some light on where the missing princess could be found. Something didn't feel right, but he couldn't put his finger on it.

"The general's injury, what was it?"

"A bullet wound, sire," Pasquale informed him. "He was shot at close range. He lost a considerable amount of blood and required transfusions and surgery to remove the bullet."

So the general couldn't have been party to the kidnapping, Thierry rationalized. No doubt Mila's brother would ensure the man was thoroughly questioned about the incident, but in the meantime Thierry wished there was something he could do. He'd been so full of fury since returning from the lodge he'd barely been able to see straight, let alone think or react rationally.

When Mila had requested an audience with him he'd agreed, but he hadn't been prepared to listen. He was so consumed with his anger all he'd wanted to do was make it clear to her that they stood no chance together. And yet, now, all he wanted to do was ensure her safety. The very idea that she was in danger sent an icy shaft of fear through him. But he couldn't show fear—he daren't. His focus now had to be on finding her, whatever it took.

Yes, that was what he needed to do. Find her, hold her and tell her he'd been a colossal fool to let her go. If he ever had the opportunity again he'd pull her in his arms and tell her he forgave her and he'd never let her go again. Certainly, he had been beyond angry when she'd revealed her identity. No man liked being taken for a fool. But he couldn't help but be moved by the way she had fought for their love. And when he considered the idea of his life without Mila in it, it stretched ahead of him like a barren desert.

He'd let his fury buoy him along these past days. Let it feed his outrage and disappointment in what she'd done. But how bad had it been, really? He'd opened his heart to her, shared his deepest fears and secrets with her— believing her to be a courtesan, rather than the woman he intended to spend the rest of his life with. How stupid could he have been? Those were the things he should have shared only with his wife, rather than a stranger.

What if Ms. Romolo really had come to the lodge— would he have come to regret sharing intimacies with her that should only be given to his princess? Instead, through Mila's machinations, he'd been sharing his thoughts and feelings with the right woman all along. He'd fallen in love with that woman. Shared the most intimate act of love with that woman.

And he'd reacted to her confession with an icy rage that far outweighed what she'd done. He'd been a fool. He didn't deserve her love. What she'd done, she'd done for them. For love. And he'd thrown that love away. He had to get her back.

"I must find her, Pasquale. Bring the tactical leader of our special forces team to me immediately."

A look of paternal approval wreathed Pasquale's face. "Certainly, sire. In fact, I believe the captain is already on his way here to your office."

Thierry looked at Pasquale in surprise. "Already?"

"I thought it best, sire, given how you feel about the princess."

"How is it that you know me better than I appear to know myself?"

The question went without answer when a sharp rap at the office door announced the arrival of the man Thierry needed most right now. As his aide let the captain in and made to leave, Thierry called out.

"Pasquale?"

"Yes, sire?"

"Thank you. From the bottom of my heart."

"Tell me thank you when you have her back, sire. Then we can all be grateful."

She'd been here five days already and the incarceration was driving her crazy. The room into which she'd been shown was austere and had the bare minimum of furnishings—just a bed and a straight-back wooden chair. The bed had nothing more than a mattress and a scratchy woolen blanket. She decided she should be grateful for small mercies. At least the rickety bed frame kept her off the cold stone floor.

From the familiar carved stone heraldic arms above the slit in the wall which served as a window, she realized that she was being held in an old abandoned fortress somewhere, probably inside the Erminian border. The border was peppered with these crumbling buildings that harked back to older, more dangerous and volatile times. Most of the structures were in a state of complete and utter disrepair. But judging by the hinges and locks on her door this one had been at least partially refurbished.

The irony of being kidnapped not long after she had done the very same to Ottavia Romolo was not lost on her, but at least she'd ensured the woman could enjoy some comfort, even luxury. This cell—it could be called nothing more than that—didn't even boast running water. It had galled her to be forced to use a chamber pot for a toilet and to have to hand it to a taciturn mercenary on guard outside her room when she was done. Once, she'd been tempted to simply throw it at the man and run for it when he opened the door, but where would she run? And who to? She had no idea where she was and her guards were no doubt well trained in how to use the guns they carried. She was certain they wouldn't hesitate to use them if it was necessary. No, she had to trust that Rocco would send his men to find her. And soon.

She'd had the briefest of audiences with one of her captors when she'd first been put in this room. He'd explained her purpose for being here, which had shocked her. He was a member of the movement that was determined to increase tensions between Erminia and Sylvain. Apparently the threat of potential war was big business and there were several players involved in this action—including the nameless and faceless pretender to Rocco's throne who had added his own demands. Mila was to be held until Rocco abdicated the throne voluntarily in favor of the illegitimate older brother. If Rocco refused, her captors would have no further use for her, which made it clear that her life was very much in danger.

She didn't want her brother to abdicate. Despite their differences she knew he was a good leader and a great man. It gave her no end of worry to know that she was now the cause of further unnecessary stress and trouble to her brother when he already had enough to deal with. And she didn't want to die, either.

Mila tried to distract herself by walking the perimeter of her room again, but she could already recite the number of blocks on each wall without even looking now and, besides, she felt as though she needed to conserve her depleting energy. It seemed that while a small portion of water was provided to her each day, her captors didn't think food was as important. The last time she'd eaten had been three days ago. Just thinking about the miserable serving of cold stew she'd been given made her stomach cramp on itself, but she tried to ignore the discomfort as she paused in front of the narrow opening to the world outside.

It was night and the cold dank air blowing through carried on it the promise of a coming storm. She hoped the thickness of the fortress walls would prevent any rain from entering her cell. It was bad enough to be tired and cold and hungry, but add wet to the equation and she had no doubt things would become infinitely worse.

Her thoughts turned to Thierry, to their last meeting together. She didn't want to die before seeing him again. She shook her head. She didn't want to die, period. Mila returned to the narrow bed and curled up beneath the thin blanket.

If she just closed her eyes she could turn her thoughts back to the idyllic week she'd shared with Thierry. To the long rides they'd taken most mornings, to the first time they'd properly kissed, to the night they'd made love before everything had imploded and she'd been sent home in disgrace.

Mila felt herself begin to drift off to sleep, her thoughts still firmly latched onto the man who held her heart in his hands whether he wanted it or not.

She was yanked from her dreams by the swoosh of her door being opened, followed by the murmur of a male voice.

"She's here."

"Mila! Are you all right? Wake up, my Angel," a familiar voice whispered fiercely in her ear.

Hawk? It couldn't be, she told herself as she shrank back under the covers. She had to be dreaming. Or maybe the days of little to eat and miserly rations of water had driven her over the edge into madness.

"Mila! Wake up!"

There it was again. That voice, this time accompanied by a strong hand on her shoulder giving her a solid shake. She opened her eyes. In the gloom it was almost impossible to see who it was. She could only make out the looming shape of a man, all in black, with his head and face covered by a dark balaclava. She drew in a breath to scream. Was this it? Was she going to be killed now?

The man put one hand over her mouth, muffling the cry that threatened to fill the air, and tore the mask from his head. Thierry! It was Thierry, he was here. He couldn't be real. She blinked her eyes as if doing so would clear her vision.

"Are you hurt?" the apparition demanded softly.

She shook her head and he took his hand from over her mouth before bending closer to take her lips in a kiss. If she'd doubted it was him before, the touch and taste of his lips on hers removed any lingering remnants of disbelief. His kiss was short and fierce, but exactly what she needed.

"Can you walk?" he asked in an undertone.

She nodded, wide awake now and fully aware of the need for silence.

"That's my girl." He smiled approvingly. "C'mon, let's get you out of here. Are you wearing shoes?"

"They took them off me."

He cursed softly and left her for a moment to speak to one of the men hovering in the doorway. One of them unslung a pack from his shoulders and pulled out several thick wads of dressing and rolls of bandages.

"These aren't ideal, but they'll protect your feet for a while," the man said as he bent to position the dressing on the soles of her feet before swiftly winding the bandages around her feet and ankles.

What happened next passed in a blur. All she was aware of was being flanked by a team of men carrying automatic weapons and wearing dark clothing, and the strength of

Thierry's arm around her waist as he silently hauled her along the passageway and finally, thankfully, outside.

The whole operation, from the fortress to the surrounding forest, couldn't have taken more than five minutes, and Mila was shaking with both fear and relief by the time they stopped running once they were deep in the forest. She couldn't understand it. No one had tried to stop them at any stage. There'd been no gunfire, no explosions. It had been nothing like what she'd seen in the movies that Sally had so loved watching back in America. Everything had been accomplished under a veil of stealth that had lent an even more surreal atmosphere to everything.

"Here," Thierry said, sliding out of the jacket he wore and helping her to put it on. "You're frozen."

"What now?" she asked through chattering teeth.

"Now I'm taking you home."

The call of a nocturnal bird bounced off the trees around them.

"That's our signal. Our transport is waiting a kilometer away. Can you make it just that bit further?" Thierry asked.

"Will you be with me?"

"Always."

"Then I can do anything," she said simply.

He looked as if he wanted to say something else, but one of the other men gestured to him that they needed to keep moving.

"We need to talk, but it will have to wait. First we get you to safety," he said grimly before wrapping his arm around her again.

It seemed to take forever, but eventually they broke out of the woods and piled into a pair of large armored vehicles. She was beyond exhausted, incapable of speech as Thierry lifted her into a seat.

"Radio ahead to the palace. Make sure a medical team is on standby and inform King Rocco we have her and we're bringing her home," Thierry informed the man standing nearest to him.

"N-no," Mila tried to protest.

She didn't want to go home. She wanted to be with Thierry. But, as Thierry climbed into the vehicle and pulled her onto his lap, the darkness fluttering around the periphery of her vision consumed her.

Seventeen

Thierry watched Mila as she slept in the castle infirmary. The grime of captivity still clung to her, but according to the doctor that had checked her over she was in good health considering what she'd been through. His eyes traced the tilt of her nose, the outline of her lips, the stubbornness of her jaw, and he felt his heart break a little as he realized he had almost sent her to her death. If he'd only been willing to forgive, none of this would have happened.

There was one thing that he knew without any doubt. He loved Princess Mila Angelina of Erminia with every breath in his body. He didn't want to face another minute, let alone another day, without knowing she'd be in his future.

"She's still sleeping?" Rocco's voice interrupted him.

"As you can see," Thierry answered, not taking his eyes off her for a minute.

"But she will be all right?"

"Yes."

Rocco settled on a chair on the other side of Mila's bed. "I can't begin to thank you—"

"Then don't. I did what was necessary. What you would have done yourself if you had reached her first." There had been several teams searching possible locations. It was just Rocco's bad luck that he hadn't been on the team that had been sent to the correct spot.

Rocco inclined his head. "I'm informed that the fortress was empty by the time my troops stormed the building. They must have left when they realized she'd been taken. Apparently there was an underground escape tunnel that wasn't on any plans."

"You're disappointed my men didn't detain Mila's kidnappers?"

"How can I be when an attempt to do so might have resulted in her being hurt...or worse? You did the right thing insisting on a stealth operation. We will catch the perpetrators eventually. They will be brought to justice."

Thierry nodded in agreement and the two men sat in silence, watching the woman they both loved as she rested. Eventually Rocco took his leave, pausing a moment to put his hand on Thierry's shoulder.

"Her heart is yours, my friend. Take care of it," he said carefully.

"For the rest of my life, if she'll let me," Thierry answered grimly.

Rocco made a sound of assent and then left, closing the door behind him quietly. On the bed, Mila began to stir and her eyes slowly opened. Her gaze searched for and found him. For a moment myriad emotions flashed across her open features—fear, relief, joy...and then they were hidden behind a schooled emptiness that scored Thierry's heart like a blade.

"You're awake," he said unnecessarily, and poured a

fresh glass of water for her. "Here, drink this. Doctor's orders."

She struggled to an upright position and took the glass from him. A wild flow of protectiveness shot through him when he saw her hand shake as she tipped the glass and drank deeply. He took the empty glass from her and re-filled it.

"No, no more." She looked around, confusion evident on her face. "I'm back at home?" she asked, her voice husky and her eyes avoiding contact with his.

"Your brother felt it best."

Slowly, she looked up. "It wasn't a dream, was it? It was you at the fortress?"

"Together with my elite special forces team."

The explanation of how they came to be there, how his men had used every legal source available to them—and several that weren't—to track the helicopter to where it had landed, and then create a list of possible targets where she might have been held, could wait until another time.

She sank back against the pillows and closed her eyes again.

"Th-thank you," she said weakly.

"You don't owe me any thanks. I hold myself respon-sible for your capture. If I had been more of a man and less of an unreasonable, spoiled and angry child, it would never have happened."

Again that wave of fear and self-loathing coursed through him.

"No, don't blame yourself. You could have done noth-ing to stop them."

"If I hadn't let you go—"

Her eyes opened again. "Why are you here?"

"I'm here to ask your forgiveness."

"*My* forgiveness? For what?"

"For treating you so damnably. For not listening. For

not accepting your love when it was so freely given with such a pure heart. For painting you with the same brush that I had painted my mother and believing you were no different than her—that you were the kind of woman who cared for nothing but her own pleasure."

"Wow, that's quite a list," Mila answered. "But I still believe there is nothing for me to forgive. I'm the one who lied to you and cheated to get to you—I even arranged the detention of an innocent woman so I could achieve my goals. I am hardly a paragon of virtue. I wouldn't have blamed you if you'd left me to rot in that vile fortress."

"But your actions came from a place of love—from a determination to give the two of us the best possible chance to know and learn to love each other," he said calmly, earning a look of surprise from her.

"That doesn't excuse my choices."

"No, only I can do that."

"Will you? Will you forgive me?"

"I have already done so. When I heard you were missing I realized how stupid and proud I had been. How empty my life would be without you in it. How foolish I was, to spurn the one thing that I have craved all my life. Unquestionable, unconditional love." He took her hands with both of his and lifted them to his lips, pressing a dozen kisses to her knuckles. "I love you, my Angel. I hope you will give me another chance. I promise I will do my best by you, in all ways."

Tears filled her eyes and began to spill down her cheeks, leaving tracks on her skin. "You still love me?"

"I never stopped. And that made my anger all the harder to bear. I hated every second without you, but my pride was still wounded, and it kept me from trusting you—from trusting in *us*."

"I just wanted you to love me. To enter into our marriage together with the knowledge that ours would be a blessed union. That we wouldn't repeat the mistakes of my parents, or—" she hesitated and drew in a breath "—yours."

"We hardly had the best of examples, did we? Which is why it is going to be all the more important that we work hard together to make sure our children, and their children, know exactly what it is like to love and to be loved, don't you think?"

"Our children?"

"If you'll have me."

"Say it again, first. Say you forgive me."

"I forgive you without blame or conditions or recrimination. I love you, Princess Mila Angelina, and I want you to be my wife—to rule the kingdom of Sylvain at my side as my queen. Will you marry me, my Angel?"

"Thinking of a future without you was torture—an endless black hole of loneliness and despair. So, yes, I will marry you, my Hawk. Nothing would make me happier. I love you with every breath in my body, every thought in my mind and every beat of my heart. I promise I will always love you and I will raise our children with you with much joy and pride. They will always know they are loved and important each in their own right, but always you will be the most important thing in the world to me."

Mila alighted from the carriage, allowing her brother to assist her from the ornately gilded old-fashioned contraption and bestowing on him a smile that came straight from her heart.

"You look beautiful today, little sister."

"I feel beautiful. How could I not when I'm the happiest woman in the world today."

"As you should be," he murmured. He tucked her hand in the crook of his elbow and they traveled up the red carpet that lined the stairs leading to the massive Sylvano cathedral. All around them they heard the cheers and well wishes of the thousands of people that lined the roads on either side of the church. Flags from both Erminia and Sylvain dotted through the crowds. "You deserve to be," he added.

"As do you, brother." Mila gave him a look of concern.

"One day, maybe," he conceded.

There was more going on with him than he was prepared to admit, Mila thought. And hadn't that been the story of their lives since he'd become king? She wished with all her heart that he could know the same love that she and Thierry shared. Rocco needed to know that there would always be someone there for him, standing by his side.

Her brother cocked an eyebrow at her. "Having second thoughts?"

"Not at all, why?"

"Because we're dillydallying here on the carpet while your future husband awaits you inside."

"Well, we had better not keep him waiting a second longer," Mila answered with a swell of joy in her heart.

From the second they entered the doors to the cathedral her eyes were locked on Thierry. She felt a burst of pride that the tall and handsome man in his ceremonial garb was hers. Music billowed from the organ to fill the air to the rafters as she and her brother began their path down the carpet that led to what Mila knew would be the best of futures. All around her, people turned to stare and comments flew amongst them as she moved by in her gown, her long train sweeping along behind her.

She'd chosen not to have any attendants. She wanted to show Thierry she needed no one other than him for the rest of her life. As the ceremony began and Rocco gave her in marriage to the man standing by her side, Mila felt nothing but exhilaration in the moment. This man before her was her future. Her everything. And, reflected in his eyes, she could see he felt exactly the same way.

Sally stepped forward from the front pew to take Mila's bouquet and whispered, "I told you—a fairy tale!"

"Every day for the rest of my life," Mila answered before turning back to Thierry and solemnly making the vows that would tie her to him for the rest of her life.

The rest of the day passed in a blur of pomp and ceremony, but despite her happiness at the celebrations, Mila wanted nothing more than to have Thierry to herself again. After the sumptuous formal reception and dancing she was only too happy when Sally drew her away so she could change for her departure. In the palace apartment that had been set aside for her, Mila hastened to disrobe from her gown.

"Slow down, you'll tear something if you're not careful," Sally chided playfully. "Besides, it won't hurt to make him wait just a little longer."

"It might not hurt him, but it's killing me!" Mila laughed as she shed the last petticoat and stepped free.

"I'm so happy for you, you know," Sally said as she helped Mila into a form-fitting gown designed by one of Erminia's newest up-and-coming designers. "You deserve your happy ever after."

"Thank you. I wish everyone could be as happy as I am right now."

And she was happy, incredibly so. The only potential fly in the ointment was the threat that still hung over Rocco's right to the throne, but she forced herself to put that from her mind. There was nothing she could do about it now.

A knock at the door sent the women scurrying to find Mila's shoes and bag.

"Just a minute," Sally called out when Mila was finally ready. "I'd wish you all the best but I can see you have it already," she said, giving Mila a warm hug.

"I do. I never thanked you enough for being my friend, or for suggesting that we take that trip to New York. Without that, I don't know if I'd be where I am right now."

Sally stepped back and gave her a smile. "Oh, I don't know. I like to think that fate has a hand in the very important things in life."

"Fate, friends—whatever it was. I'm grateful to you. Friends forever, right?"

"Forever."

Mila opened the door to discover Thierry waiting on the other side. He offered her his arm.

"Ready to come with me, my Angel?"

"Always," she answered.

* * * * *

LET'S TALK
Romance

For exclusive extracts, competitions
and special offers, find us online:

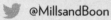 facebook.com/millsandboon

🐦 @MillsandBoon

📷 @MillsandBoonUK

Get in touch on 01413 063232

For all the latest titles coming soon, visit
millsandboon.co.uk/nextmonth

MILLS & BOON

THE HEART OF ROMANCE

A ROMANCE FOR EVERY KIND OF READER

MODERN

Prepare to be swept off your feet by sophisticated, sexy and seductive heroes, in some of the world's most glamourous and romantic locations, where power and passion collide.
8 stories per month.

HISTORICAL

Escape with historical heroes from time gone by. Whether your passion is for wicked Regency Rakes, muscled Vikings or rugged Highlanders, awaken the romance of the past.
6 stories per month.

MEDICAL

Set your pulse racing with dedicated, delectable doctors in the high-pressure world of medicine, where emotions run high and passion, comfort and love are the best medicine.
6 stories per month.

True Love

Celebrate true love with tender stories of heartfelt romance, from the rush of falling in love to the joy a new baby can bring, and a focus on the emotional heart of a relationship.
8 stories per month.

Desire

Indulge in secrets and scandal, intense drama and plenty of sizzling hot action with powerful and passionate heroes who have it all: wealth, status, good looks...everything but the right woman.
6 stories per month.

HEROES

Experience all the excitement of a gripping thriller, with an intense romance at its heart. Resourceful, true-to-life women and strong, fearless men face danger and desire - a killer combination!
8 stories per month.

DARE

Sensual love stories featuring smart, sassy heroines you'd want as a best friend, and compelling intense heroes who are worthy of them.
4 stories per month.

To see which titles are coming soon, please visit

millsandboon.co.uk/nextmonth